'Sophie Devine!' he whispered and thought he had never heard such a beautiful name. But men of his age did not fall helplessly in love with strangers. 'In love?' Astonished, he spoke the words aloud.

The phrase shocked him. Was it love? Maybe infatuation and the feeling would pass leaving him sane once more. But that idea depressed him. He did not want that to happen.

'I think I do love you!' he whispered and suddenly he no longer cared if he was making a fool of himself. He felt years younger, full of hope and brimming with confidence. Tomorrow he would go out into the troubled city and work miracles! Because Sophie Devine had come into his life and he loved her and nothing would ever be the same again.

JAR

Pamela Oldfield

LONG
DARK
SUMMER

WARNER BOOKS

For Joseph,
with love

A *Warner* Book

First published in Great Britain
by Michael Joseph Ltd in 1992

This edition published by Warner Books in 1993
Reprinted 1998

Copyright © Pamela Oldfield 1992

The moral right of the author has been asserted.

A CIP catalogue record for this book
is available from the British Library.

ISBN 0 7515 0137 9

Printed in England by Clays Ltd, St Ives plc
Typeset by Datix International Limited, Bungay

Warner Books
A Division of
Little, Brown and Company (UK)
Brettenham House
Lancaster Place
London WC2E 7EN

Chapter One

'HOW GOES THE CITY this morning?'

'It seems well enough.'

The apparently innocent question and its indifferent answer deceived neither mistress nor maid-servant. The health of the crowded city was of the utmost concern to them both.

'At least the sun has had the grace to appear,' said Sophie with a smile which hid her anxiety. She tied the strings of her young daughter's cap and bent to kiss her.

''Tis out, but there's no warmth in it,' Fanny replied as she dumped the well-filled baskets on the kitchen floor and flexed her aching shoulders. 'A nasty, biting wind, and cold as death – Oh! sorry, mistress.'

Sophie pretended not to have noticed the slip and bent her head to hide her face as the familiar frisson of fear touched her once again. Lifting the little girl from her lap she set her on her feet and watched with pleasure as Lizbeth ran into Fanny's out-stretched arms with a giggle of excitement.

Forgetting her painful shoulders, Fanny snatched her up and smothered her little face with kisses before holding her up at arm's length for the ritual morning inspection. 'And how's my Lizbeth today?' she asked. 'Saucy little blue eyes! Looking as bonny as a princess in her new silk cap!' With one finger she gently pulled one of the child's pale curls and watched with satisfaction as it sprang back into place. Fanny's own hair was mouse-brown and as straight as a pikestaff and the children's curls never ceased to fascinate her.

'It does look well on her, doesn't it?' said Sophie. 'Her grandmother will be well pleased. She has struggled so with her poor eyes, determined to finish it by today. Her candle was burning well into the night.'

'Shall I take this young lady up to see her?' Fanny asked, hopefully, but Sophie shook her head.

'She won't be awake yet. You'd best make us some breakfast and I'll take both children up later.'

She turned her attention to the boy who sat silent beside her, playing with a carved wooden horse which he galloped to and fro across his lap with immense concentration. Oliver Devine was six years old and very like his mother with brown eyes and dark curls.

'Time for your wash, young man,' Sophie told

him. She dabbled her fingers in the water, grimaced and added a little more hot water from the big jug.

As always her son preferred to undress himself and she waited impatiently as his podgy fingers struggled clumsily with the buttons of his nightshirt.

Fanny set down the little girl, took up the baskets once more and made her way towards the scullery with Lizbeth at her heels.

Sophie called after her. 'Did you catch the coalseller?'

'I did. He'll be here before noon.'

'He said the same yesterday and then didn't come.' Sophie shook her head, exasperated. 'The man's a dawdler. We may be halfway through March, but spring is still a way off yet. How does the old wretch expect us to keep the house warm? He knows we have two young children. I shall have something to say to him when he *does* arrive.'

Pausing in the doorway, Fanny glanced back and said carefully, ''T'wasn't the same man, mistress. I couldn't find Old Jerrold. This man was younger and more agreeable and swore blue that he'd come and I reckon he will.' She grinned suddenly. 'I think he took a fancy to me, if the truth be known. You should have seen the wink he gave me. He won't miss the chance to see me again!'

Sophie hid a smile at the girl's unquenchable optimism for she was far from a beauty, with eyes like currants in a round, pasty face. As far as Sophie knew the girl had never had an admirer. Suddenly a thought struck her and she raised her head sharply and asked, 'What news of Old Jerrold?'

Fanny shrugged. 'The milk girl said he was taken with a fit . . .' she admitted reluctantly.

'A fit?'

'A fit of sorts, anyway. He dropped his scuttle and fell down in a swoon and all his coals spilled on to the cobbles. 'Oh!' She clapped a hand to her mouth and for a moment the two women stared at each other fearfully.

Sophie swallowed hard. 'In a swoon, you say?'

'Yes, mistress, but I'm sure he's recovered.' Fanny searched her mind desperately for reasons with which to justify this conviction. 'Quite certain sure, because the milk girl said he got to his feet again and gathered up his coal and, well, he must be recovered then, mustn't he, to stand on his feet again so speedily?'

'Certainly.' Recovering quickly, Sophie forced a smile. 'Overwork, I dare say. He must be forty if he's a day and puny as a kitten. If he stood up again, why then, he came to no real harm. A momentary weakness and nothing for us to fret about. Matthew says there is nothing to fear; that the cold winter has been a blessing in disguise. The frost has cleansed the air of all malevolent odours and infections. We spoke of it only yesterday and he was most insistent.'

'The master would know a thing like that.' Fanny nodded earnestly. 'I would stake my life on the master's judgement.'

'We all must.' Momentarily distracted by her son's efforts, Sophie reached down to pull the nightshirt over his tousled head and then remembered the groceries the girl had been sent to fetch. 'Did you find any oranges?'

'None but some poor, bruised specimens and I would not buy them. "You can keep them," I told him. I bought lemons instead from the dumb woman at the corner.'

'And the eggs?'

Fanny held one up in triumph. 'New-laid. I bought all she had. I know how the master do love a new-laid egg lightly boiled. He shall have one tomorrow.' Her eyes glowed and Sophie thought how lucky they were to have found so loyal a servant. Fanny adored them all but the master was her favourite and in her eyes he could do no wrong.

'Nine eggs, she had,' Fanny went on, 'and still warm from the nest.' She laid the egg against her cheek and added, 'Barely cold even now.'

'Then later I shall make a cheesecake. And perhaps . . .' Briefly Sophie considered their supper. 'A piece of gammon would go well with the parsnips Henrietta sent up.' Seeing the hopeful look on Fanny's face she added, 'But I shall fetch the gammon myself later. You have plenty to do in the house today and no time for gallivanting the streets a second time!'

As Fanny disappeared into the kitchen to unpack her baskets and prepare breakfast, Sophie turned her attention towards her son. She supervised the washing of his face and hands, the cleaning of teeth and the combing of hair. Throughout these preparations he said very little but when at last he was warmly dressed he gave an exaggerated sigh.

Amused, Sophie asked, 'What ails my little man?'

'I do wish we were not going to die, Mama,' he said wistfully. Unaware of the effect of his words he went on, 'I don't think I shall care for it much, although Grandmother says we shall all surely be in a state of grace and for that we must thank God.'

Sophie stifled an exclamation of anger directed towards her mother-in-law. 'You must not believe all Grandmother tells you,' she told him. 'She teases you, Ollie. She teases us all with her gloomy prattle but it means nothing. Poor Grandmother is beset with morbid thoughts and likes to talk of calamities but we mustn't take them to heart.'

Oliver regarded her earnestly. 'But I dreamed last night that Death came into my room –'

'Stop it!' Sophie cried, more sharply than she intended. 'You mustn't speak of such things. 'Twas a foolish dream, nothing more, Ollie. A nightmare. You mustn't dwell on such sorrowful things.' She pulled him close and wrapped him protectively in her arms. 'We are not going to die. You know Papa would never let anything bad happen to us. We will take good care of ourselves. You know that, don't you? Eh?' She gave him a little shake but his expression did not change.

'But how will Papa cheat The Grim Reaper?' he

asked. 'Grandmother says that The Grim Reaper is tired of the world and all its wicked ways and will send the plague to punish it. She says . . .'

Sophie put a finger to his lips to silence him. 'I won't listen to such nonsense,' she said firmly. 'I shall be very cross with Grandmother for frightening you like this. I shall slap her hand!'

At last the ghost of a smile lit his face. 'Slap Grandmother's hand? Oh no, Mama! You mustn't. You wouldn't dare!'

'Oh, but I do dare and I shall!' she told him. 'Even grandmothers are naughty sometimes, you know.'

'Are they?' He sounded doubtful.

'Oh yes! They most certainly are. I shall slap her hand and say, "Don't be such a bad grandmother!" Then she will stop telling you such stories and you will stop having foolish dreams and we will all be happy again.'

For a moment he appeared reassured but then he frowned again. 'Am I wicked beyond redemption, Mama?'

'Wicked beyond redemption?' Sophie tutted irritably. 'What big words for such a small boy! You are not wicked at all, Ollie. You are my dearest, good little man.'

'And Lizbeth? Is she wicked?'

'Most certainly not! Lizbeth is my dearest, good little girl.'

'And Papa?' he persisted.

'Papa is not wicked and neither am I. And no one is wicked beyond redemption, Ollie. Even a bad man can repent and be sorry for his wickedness and then God will forgive him.' She stood up and ruffled his hair playfully. 'So, little man, I want to hear no more gloomy talk. Let me see a smile – Ah, that's better! Now, what are you going to do for your lesson this morning? Copy your letters?'

He nodded and together they went into the kitchen where Fanny was poaching fish for the kedgeree and Lizbeth was laying the table with bowls and spoons.

Sophie said, 'The master might be a little late this evening so we shall wait supper until he returns.'

'Again? The master works too hard,' said Fanny, tucking back a wisp of hair and coughing as a gust of wind from the chimney sent eddies of smoke into her face.

'We must get the sweep in again,' said Sophie quickly before she could complain. 'I'll just slip upstairs and see if Mistress Devine is awake but I'll be back directly.' She gathered up her skirts and hurried back up the narrow stairs towards the small room at the rear of the house where her mother-in-law lay bedridden.

*

As soon as Ruth Devine's sharp ears caught the sound of her daughter-in-law's footsteps on the stairs she reached for her bookmark. Slipping it between the pages she hurriedly closed the book she had been reading and put it on the bedside table. She was lying back on the pillows with her eyes closed when Sophie tip-toed into the room but then opened them with a show of reluctance.

'You can pull back the bed curtains. I'm wide awake,' Ruth told her pettishly. 'I've been awake for hours. As you know, I am never blessed with sound sleep. It's one of the many crosses I have to bear. But there – the Lord is merciful and has given me the nature to bear it without complaint.'

Ruth wondered for the hundredth time why her son had insisted on marrying this particular girl. She had intended that he should marry Eleanor, the daughter of a close family friend. Eleanor, demure to the point of dullness, was hardly a beauty but she came from wealthy, God-fearing stock and would have proved malleable. On the other hand, many people would consider Sophie Benworthy a beauty but her parents were, in Ruth's opinion, highly unsuitable. The father had been a military man who had married beneath him and who had then had the temerity to die soon after the birth of their second child – a boy. Less than a year later, the mother had been knocked down and killed by a grain waggon, an accident which Ruth attributed to carelessness on the mother's part. A feckless couple altogether, and demonstrably so, but Matthew had refused to hear a word against them. An aunt and uncle had reared the two motherless children and the boy, Giles, had later been taken into their uncle's household, a substantial farm. Admittedly Giles had inherited it on the uncle's death and was now doing well enough. He had married and had five children but that was no reflection on his sister, now Sophie Devine. Ruth was fond of telling herself that she would never be reconciled to the alliance.

It was true that Sophie had proved herself a good wife and had borne her son two handsome, healthy children but she had lost two more in childbirth; she was not strong. Ruth had told Matthew time and again that looks are not everything and that a wife must be stout-hearted and her body resilient. Sophie was slightly built; scarcely robust. Eleanor had had more *substance*.

Ruth held Sophie responsible for the fact that Matthew, her only child, had flouted his mother's wishes on the subject of marriage. It was the first time in his life that Matthew had rejected her advice; the very first time, in fact, that he had dared to cross her at all, and Ruth had been shocked and mortified.

Sophie opened the curtains and stood at the end of the bed. Ruth, seeing her expression, waited uneasily. This young woman had a mind of her own and would speak it. There was a gleam in the girl's eyes now that Ruth recognized.

'Well, what is it?' she demanded, never one to avoid a confrontation.

'I came to thank you for the cap you stitched for Lizbeth. It looks very well on her and will keep her head wonderfully warm. And . . .' She hesitated.

'And?'

''Tis the children,' Sophie began. 'I wanted to ask you, Ruth – to beseech you – to be more guarded when you speak to them. I know you intend no harm but you have frightened them with your tales of death and destruction.'

'Frightened them? Fiddlesticks!' Ruth cried defensively. 'Young children should know the power of the Lord to punish all those who do not keep his commandments. They should –'

But Sophie went on as though her mother-in-law had not spoken. 'Poor Ollie had a nightmare. He is only six, and I hardly think God will punish an innocent child.'

'Innocent? Huh!' Ruth snorted. 'Children today are far from innocent. They shirk their prayers. They no longer respect those God has put over them. They –'

Incredibly the girl interrupted her again. 'But God is love,' said Sophie loudly.

Astonished by Sophie's persistence, Ruth glared at her angrily. Really, she thought, the girl was becoming too outspoken for her own good and a sight too sure of herself. A little humility would be more becoming in one of her age. Twenty-four, was she, or twenty-five? Matthew should check her wilful spirit. A word in his ear might not go amiss, she thought crossly.

'Sophie Devine!' she said. 'I hardly expect my son's wife to bandy words with me like a fishwife. I have lived a great deal longer than you and have, I hope, acquired a little wisdom along the way.'

'I do not mean to bandy words. I simply ask that you stop frightening the children,' Sophie said firmly.

Ruth sat up a little straighter in the bed and fussed with the counterpane. ''Tis hardly a matter of frightening them,' she said severely. 'They must be brought up in the ways of righteousness. Matthew was never in any doubt as to the wages of sin. Even as a small boy he felt God's eye upon him. He understood that God's wrath is terrible. Oliver and Lizbeth must be made to understand what a sinful city London is and that its punishment is nigh.' She pointed an accusing finger at her daughter-in-law as though holding her personally responsible for the wickedness around them. 'You cannot hide from Ollie and Lizbeth the evil that men do. London is depraved. Every kind of vice flourishes within its walls. God has looked down in horror upon England's capital. He had seen lewdness, gluttony, popery. There is licentiousness on every stage and vile oaths on every lip. Murder and mayhem . . .'

Sophie interrupted for a third time, a stubborn look on her face. 'But the children know nought of this. They are as blameless as the birds. Why terrify them with talk of death?'

'Because the pestilence is coming and we must all prepare for it.' With satisfaction Ruth saw a flicker of fear in Sophie's brown eyes. and went on triumphantly. 'Oh yes! Make no mistake! The plague is coming! I have seen it all before. I still recall the horrors of the last visitation. This city will be stricken again. I know it *here*.' She placed a hand on her heart. 'The *plague* is coming. All the signs point to it.'

Now alarm had driven away all the girl's confidence, Ruth noted. As she watched Sophie's agitated fingers play with the silver locket Matthew had given her for her birthday. And that was another thing, thought Ruth irritably. Just recently Matthew was becoming far too generous towards his wife. The locket had been unnecessarily expensive but he had also taken to buying her flowers for no good reason that Ruth could see. She had remonstrated with her son but Matthew had been unrepentant, surprising her by his vehemence. 'Sophie is my wife and I love her above all women!' he had insisted but there had been something in his eyes that still puzzled her.

With an effort Ruth returned to the present.

'But Matthew says otherwise,' Sophie was saying. Her tone was defiant but a tell-tale tremor revealed her fear. 'He says the authorities would have told us if a plague was coming. They would be making plans – emergency plans. He says there is nothing to fear. Just a few isolated cases and too many rumours.'

Ruth shook her head. 'He tells you what you want to hear, Sophie,' she said contemptuously. 'My son is no fool. He sees the signs as well as the next man. Did he not tell you of the comet which appeared two nights since over this very city?'

'He said nothing.'

'Nor that the south and west winds have been blowing at the same time?'

Sophie shook her head unhappily.

'He wishes to protect you,' Ruth told her. 'All the portents are ominous. Mistress Velvay told me only last week that in the year sixty-three, Saturn was in conjunction with Jupiter and last year it was in conjunction with Mars! And as late as November! She says the meaning is perfectly clear to anyone who understands the mysteries of the heavens.'

Sophie said, 'Mistress Velvay? She is scarcely a scholar. What does she know of such things?'

'She heard it from her father who was schooled in Padua and is very learned. You may scoff but the signs are there. If Matthew spares you this information 'tis for your own sake, because he knows what a child you are and how easily you take fright. You mark my words! God's patience is at an end. Sixteen-sixty-five will be a dangerous year for all of us, may God preserve us. The sins of the fathers –'

Sophie, thoroughly unnerved, put her hands over her ears.

'I won't listen to any more! You shan't frighten me, Ruth, the way you frighten the children. And if you won't promise to watch your words I shall speak to Matthew on the subject.'

Ruth's eyes narrowed and she hesitated. She had no wish for the wretched girl to go tittle-tattling to Matthew. Not only was he becoming over-generous towards his wife but Ruth had noticed an increasing leniency towards her, deferring to her wishes on many occasions when Ruth considered it quite unnecessary. Matthew might well take his wife's side on this issue and Ruth did not relish that idea at all.

'I shall choose my words a little more carefully if that will satisfy you,' she conceded. 'But molly-coddling the children will not be to their advantage in the end. You will live to regret your weakness when you see how little mettle they show in later life. But there!' She shrugged her thin shoulders expressively. 'I shall not be alive to reproach you. My days are numbered.'

She waited for Sophie to protest but the girl merely drew a deep breath and nodded.

'Thank you, Ruth,' she said. 'I'm glad we are agreed. Now I shall go downstairs before my kedgeree grows cold. Shall I send up your hot water?'

'Yes. I shall be ready. But tell Fanny to keep her distance from me. She had been out and about in the city, mingling with Lord knows who, and may well harbour contagions of one sort or another.'

Sophie hesitated, opened her mouth as though to speak but apparently thought better of it. With a last look that lacked all warmth she left the room, closing the door carefully behind her.

'Young minx!' muttered Ruth balefully. 'You are

a sight too forward for my liking and always have been. Oh Matthew! Matthew!' She sighed deeply and shook her head. 'You would not heed my warnings and now I fear you will live to rue the day you married against my wishes.'

*

The following day Fanny made her way through the narrow streets of overhanging houses which effectively kept back what remained of the daylight. Because the winter frost had persisted, the street smell was less obnoxious than it might have been. The rotting refuse at every corner had frozen during the night and had only partially been thawed by the day's weak sunshine. Foul water still trickled along the central gutter, however, and Fanny stepped carefully. The usual assortment of mongrel dogs ran loose, snapping and snarling and circling each other, a permanent hazard to the unwary who occasionally tripped over them and sprawled in the mire, cursing. Here and there, from high places, cats spied on the dogs, smugly aware of the safety of their position but growling in their throats to show their disrespect. A large black hog with a tattered ear wandered through the crowd and paused from time to time to root hopefully among the thawing rubbish. The occasional dark shape of a rat could be seen scurrying among the shadows and pigeons swooped overhead between the close-built houses in search of food.

At four o'clock the light was fading but people

still thronged the noisy thoroughfares, dawdling at every shop counter that thrust itself out into the roadway, tempting the many thieves with a display of cloth, candles or pewter. A medley of street cries echoed ceaselessly in the narrow alleys, coal carriers staggered under their long scuttles and milkmaids clattered along on wooden pattens, shouting their wares. Newly deposited horse dung steamed in the cold air, while wealthy ladies, warmly dressed against the cold, descended reluctantly from sedan chairs and picked their way distastefully over the cobbles. Wherever possible, they avoided contact with their less fortunate sisters who hurried from one purchase to the next with nothing but a frayed shawl thrown carelessly over their shoulders. From time to time, fine gentlemen on horseback leaned down to exchange angry words with old men who blocked their passage as they strained their backs to push barrows laden with old clothes; or shouted at younger men who, trying to negotiate the street corners, held up the traffic with their hay carts.

Fanny paused to buy a few pennies' worth of sheep's trotters, a treat for her brother Jem, but resisted the temptation to spend more. Her meagre earnings did not allow her to be as generous as she would have wished so she contented herself with buying alternately for her brother and his wife, Maggie. Last time she visited them she had taken Maggie a bunch of violets. Today it was Jem's turn. Soon, God willing, she would have a third person on whom to spend her money for Maggie was going to have a baby and Fanny would be an aunt for the first time. She was looking forward to that.

As the youngest of three children, Fanny was disappointed with her other surviving brother, Charlie, who at twenty-two still had not found himself a wife. Fanny knew well enough that his mind was on other things – and none of them honest! She sighed as she thought of him. Charlie, the best looking of the family with his bright blue eyes and golden hair, had no lack of charm but no liking for hard work. He stole whenever and from wherever he could and despised his father and brother for what he considered their lack of enterprise, for both worked on the river as wherry men like his grandfather before them.

But Fanny adored Charlie in spite of his bad ways; she even felt a sneaking admiration for what he called his 'dash and daring' and his reckless disregard for his own safety. She lived, however, in a state of permanent terror that he would one day be caught and thrown into the prison alongside the Fleet river, there to spend the rest of his days among the dregs of society with little chance of eventual release.

Her father, Alfred Rice, pretended to know nothing of Charlie's activities for his wife's sake. Ellen's health was becoming a problem as her frail body was constantly racked by a persistent and painful cough. The extra milk and occasional herrings that Charlie's thieving brought were probably all that kept her alive.

Another worry for Fanny was that rumours of Charlie's wickedness would somehow come to the ears of her employers and she dreaded the shame this would bring upon herself. The Devines would hardly appreciate the fact that their maid-servant came from 'criminal stock'! Still, she must look on the bright side, she reminded herself, and that was that she had been working for the Devines for three and a half years now and, so far, Charlie's misdeeds had passed unnoticed.

Jem and Maggie lived in an upstairs room above a rundown court off Bow Street, not too far from the Thames where Jem earned his living. They shared the building with another hundred or so souls and it was a wonder that the dilapidated wooden-framed dwelling remained standing but Jem and Maggie considered themselves lucky to have a roof over their heads. They were a great deal better off than some of Maggie's friends who lodged in doorways and under arches, one of whom had frozen to death in her sleep during the severe winter weather.

Fanny made her way down Ludgate Hill, over the bridge across the Fleet and up the other side into Fleet Street. She was humming cheerfully as she hurried along Wich Street and turned left. Maggie was her closest friend, for the two families had grown up together less than a stone's throw apart in a squalid back street to the west of Drury Lane. For Fanny's parents it was still home but Maggie's family was long since dead.

Five minutes brought Fanny to the door of Jem's room and Maggie opened it with a smile of welcome.

'Oh Fan! You've come! I wondered if you would,' she cried and she hugged Fanny as closely as she could.

Fanny stepped back and stared in disbelief at her sister-in-law's large abdomen.

'Sweet Jesus, Maggie!' she exclaimed in mock horror. 'How many children are you expecting? Looks like a dozen or more in there!'

Maggie laughed as she put both hands protectively over her swollen body. 'You may well ask,' she said. 'Jem will have it that I'm expecting twins and the truth is it wouldn't surprise me. Come on in and sit yourself down.'

Maggie's bright red hair was her saving grace for she had little else to boast of in the way of looks. Her face was scarred from an early attack of smallpox which she had somehow survived and her teeth, though sound, were uneven and slightly discoloured. These faults, however, were invisible to Fanny who loved her like a sister. They soon made themselves comfortable on the mattress which doubled as seating and with a mock flourish Fanny handed over Jem's present.

'Sheep's trotters,' she announced.

'Oh Fan, you shouldn't,' Maggie protested half-heartedly. 'You've little enough money for your own needs.'

Fanny pulled a twist of paper from her pocket. 'Tea!' she told Maggie. 'No, don't use it now. I'm not thirsty. They'll never miss a couple of spoonfuls and from all accounts 'tis wondrously refreshing.'

'Tea! What a treat! You're too good, Fan, really you are.'

Fan glanced round the room and repressed a familiar shudder. The dingy walls depressed her and the window allowed in very little light. The furniture was minimal and only a few knobs of coal burned half-heartedly in the grate.

Seeing her look, Maggie said quickly, 'I don't feel the cold during the day but I make up the fire a bit when Jem comes home.'

Fanny said, 'I wanted to bring you a few parsnips – the mistress's sister sent some up from the farm – but they were large and easy counted so I didn't dare.'

'I should hope not!' Maggie told her. 'You mustn't take risks on our account, Fan. Jem would never forgive himself if you lost your place. He's real proud of you, Jem is.'

They talked for a while of the coming baby. Less than a month, by Maggie's reckoning, although she couldn't be sure.

'Jem a father!' Fanny giggled. 'I can't imagine it at all! But dandling a baby on his knee! Mind you,' she went on quickly, 'he'll make a good father, Jem will. 'Tis just that he scarce seems old enough to be married.' She laughed. 'My big brother. That's all he'll ever be to me.'

The talk turned eventually to the rest of the family. Fanny's parents were 'well enough considering' and Charlie was 'same as ever'. There was something in Maggie's voice, however, which made Fanny uneasy.

'You sure now?' she asked. 'He's not in any trouble, is he?'

Maggie shrugged. 'He's still a free man if that's what you mean but –'

'But what?' Her unease became anxiety.

Maggie frowned. 'Well, if you must know, Jem saw him being chased by some Revenue men the other day, down by Puddle Wharf. He got away thanks to Jem confusing them but Jem reckons he was dead lucky.'

'The Revenue men!' Fanny's heart skipped a beat as fear gripped her. 'Oh, the fool! The stupid fool!'

They stared at each other in dismay. The Revenue men were authority with a capital A. They were greatly feared and had long arms and longer memories.

Maggie went on reluctantly. 'Jem says Charlie had three of them after him but he ran to the river and jumped in.'

Fanny's mouth fell open with shock. 'Into the water? Charlie? But he can't swim!'

Maggie nodded. 'He held his breath under water while Jem persuaded the three men that he'd run right past and jumped into a passing hay cart. By the time they moved away Charlie was blue in the face and half drowned! But the Revenue will be looking out for him, Fan, and they've got eyes in the backs of their heads! Jem says they'll get him if it takes a month of Sundays!'

'Jesus O'Riley!' Fanny was trembling. 'Why couldn't he be content with the odd purse, like everyone else, or a yard or two of cloth? Does he want to dance at the end of a rope with one of us tugging at his feet to finish him off quickly?'

Maggie shuddered at this frightful thought. 'Don't talk like that, Fan,' she begged. 'It mustn't happen.'

'But it *will* if the Revenue catch him. Oh Charlie! Charlie! What on earth was he up to, do you know?'

Maggie lowered her voice as though, even in the privacy of her own room, she might be overheard. 'Tobacco, Fan. Charlie came here while Jem was out, asking for help. Had it on him! The nerve of the man! And begging me, if I loved him at all, to hide it for him! Strewth Fan, I could have brained him and that's the truth. After all that's happened!' She glanced away, unwilling to meet Fanny's eyes. 'I said "No", Fan. I wanted to help him but somehow I hardened my heart. Don't ask me how for I couldn't say but I've got the baby to think about as well as Jem. If they found tobacco here they'd run Jem in as quick as look at him! So I said "No".' She swallowed. 'But I daren't tell Jem, Fan. He'd half murder me if he knew. You know how he dotes on Charlie.'

'We all dote on Charlie but Lord knows why.'

Fanny sighed with exasperation. Once, she had thought that Charlie, and not Jem, would marry Maggie. She had adored him but Charlie, selfish then as now, had broken her heart, leaving good-natured Jem to pick up the pieces.

'I wouldn't do nothing to harm him – not a hair on his lovely blond head,' Maggie went on earnestly, 'but I won't have Jem put on the wrong side of the law. Brother or no brother.'

Fanny nodded. 'You did right, Maggie. You mustn't take any risks. Charlie had no right to ask it.'

It was Maggie's turn to sigh. 'I've told Jem to keep clear away from him. I daren't let him get mixed up in Charlie's doings. I just hope he has enough sense to pay me some heed. Poor old Jem. He looks so tired these days, so peaky. The winter's been hard for him. It's been perishing out on that water and he's no flesh on his bones to speak of.'

A brief silence fell and Fanny conjured up a vision of Jem's thin face, his poor nose, broken years ago in a fight and never straightened. He was round-shouldered and small-boned but his puny looks were deceptive. He lacked Charlie's easy charm but his heart was kind and loving and Fanny knew that he would fight like a tiger for those he loved.

To change the subject she said, 'The mistress was in a fine pother this morning. The old lady's been frightening the children half to death with words of the plague, so up the stairs goes the mistress to take her to task. I do admire her spirit, the mistress I mean. That old lady would frighten *me* if I let her. Always hinting about how we're all going to die for our sins. 'Tis morbid, if you ask me. 'Tis wishing it on us!'

'I hope to God she's wrong,' said Maggie. 'I'll have enough trouble to raise this little one as it is without plague setting in.'

Fanny tossed her head dismissively. 'She's just a foolish old woman with nothing better to think about. There'll be no plague. The master says so.'

Maggie's eyes widened suddenly at the mention of Matthew Devine. 'That reminds me,' she said. 'Jem bumped into your master a day or two back. Stepping out of a boat at Temple Stairs he was, with a little dog in his arms.'

'But we don't have a dog,' Fanny objected.

'But it was him. Jem recognized him straight away. A little spaniel. Jem smiled at him but your master looked a bit confused and didn't seem to recognize him.'

Fanny shook her head. 'The children have wanted a dog for as long as I've known them and the master's said "No" a dozen times.'

'Perhaps 'tis going to be a surprise.'

'I don't think so. He'd have brought it home by now.'

Maggie shrugged. 'Must have been the lady's dog, then.'

'What lady?'

'He was talking to a lady.'

Fanny shook her head. ''Twas some other man, Maggie, who looks like the master, I'll bet my life on it.' The clock on St Giles church struck the half hour and she looked up, startled. 'Is that the time? Oh Maggie, I must fly!' She jumped to her feet and they embraced quickly and Fanny made her sister-in-law promise to take care of herself and to send word when the baby arrived. Fanny was allowed a few hours off once a fortnight and she spent them with Maggie whenever possible.

As she made her way down the rickety stairs and out into the dark street, her cheerful mood deserted her. Snippets of Maggie's news troubled her mind and she was uneasily aware of a vague premonition of disaster but from which direction it would come she had no idea. With an effort she reminded herself that worry was a useless pastime. It could never change anything so she might as well try to recapture her earlier mood. By the time she reached Watling Street she had largely succeeded, all the gloomy thoughts effectively banished from her mind.

*

The following morning dawned calm and clear. High above the city the sun was bright but the smoke of thousands of fires hung in the still air, casting over the rooftops a pall which would only be dispersed if a wind sprang up. Soot from countless chimneys floated upwards and then drifted down again, adding yet another fine, dark layer to the already grimy streets and buildings. Those Londoners fortunate to have an indoor space for drying were thankful for the luxury of clean clothes and bed-linen but others, forced to thrust poles full of washing out of the windows, would take it in later covered with an inevitable sprinkling of smuts and almost dirtier than when it went out.

At seven-thirty-five the market-place at Smithfield was still comparatively clean although it was filling up fast with men and beasts. Already sheep huddled in some of the pens, jostling each other, their breath visible, bleating loudly at the change of routine that had brought them here. Along the outer rail a dozen or so cows had been tethered but these, for the most part, accepted their fate with apparent equanimity, chewing interminably with vacant expressions in their large eyes. A farmer drove five pigs ahead of him while a young lad, possibly his son, swung open a section of the wattle fencing to allow the animals access to their temporary quarters. A show of reluctance on the cows' parts gave the bad-tempered owner an excuse to prod them viciously with his stick and this sent them hurrying in, squealing resentfully. Farmers wandered about, inspecting the animals and shaking their heads doubtfully.

Charlie leaned on the outer rail and watched the scene with a jaundiced eye. The animals held no interest for him; it was the farmers, drovers and butchers who caught his attention. Animals did not smoke tobacco but their owners did and Charlie had plenty to sell. Smithfield market seemed the obvious place to dispose of some of his ill-gotten gains but he was alert for the first sign of trouble. This would come in the shape of Revenue men who knew, as well as Charlie did, that plenty of stolen property changed hands here, amidst the frenzied hustle and bustle of legitimate dealing.

At the far end of the market he could see a horse being run up and down under the critical eye of a prospective buyer. Charlie's eyes narrowed thoughtfully. A man who could afford a horse could afford tobacco! Slowly he stood up and began to stroll along in the direction of the horse. A toothless old woman sat on an upturned basket, her lap full of black and white puppies.

'Lovely Sheepdogs!' she called to him hopefully. 'Father's a champion!'

'So's mine!' Charlie told her, grinning. He picked up one of the puppies and held it at arm's length. 'Sheepdogs, you call them? That's wishful thinking. And much too young to leave their ma.' He gave her a dazzling smile. 'Take 'em home, old biddy. You'll not sell them today.'

Ignoring her mumbles he returned the animal to her lap and moved on, whistling, his hands thrust into the pockets of his breeches. Despite his harsh words, the old woman watched him go with a faint answering smile on her face, for she could still appreciate a young man with golden hair and eyes like cornflowers.

A flock of sheep suddenly materialized as though from nowhere and Charlie was surrounded, forced to stand his ground as they bumped and jostled their way round him. They were driven by a comely young woman with bright auburn hair and at the sight of her Charlie's eyes brightened and he snatched off his hat and made her a pretty bow.

'Good morrow, pretty maid,' he began but at that moment a large, red-faced man appeared from behind him. He carried a knobbly stave in his hand and looked tempted to use it.

'She's mine!' he grunted.

'Such a pretty daughter!' said Charlie, though he knew well enough what the man meant. 'I hope mine will do me as much credit when the time comes.'

The girl blushed, trying to keep a straight face, but her husband was in no mood for banter.

'She's my wife,' he told Charlie. 'And you'd best mind your manners.'

Charlie replaced his hat with a flourish and leaned confidingly towards the man. 'I see a clay pipe sticking out of your pocket,' he said in a low voice. 'Would I be right in thinking that a discerning man like yourself would only smoke the best baccy?'

'What's it to you?' the man asked grudgingly. Before Charlie could answer warning shouts were up suddenly from further down the walkway alerting them to the presence of a runaway ox that was thundering towards them. The furious animal's head was well down and its mood was obviously ugly. Charlie immediately flung his arms around the woman's waist and, swinging her sideways, lifted her clear just in time. Her husband, slower to react, was knocked to the ground as the animal rushed past with three breathless men in hot pursuit.

Charlie managed to give the wife an appreciative squeeze before offering a solicitous hand to the husband.

Once on his feet again the man grumbled, 'Poxy animal!' and Charlie made a great show of brushing him down. Never one to miss an opportunity he then repeated his offer about the cheap tobacco.

Feeling indebted to Charlie for his wife's escape the farmer hesitated. 'How cheap is cheap?' he asked.

'A third off the price. Finest Virginian.'

'And how did you come by it?'

Charlie's gaze did not waver. 'To tell the truth I found it,' he confided. 'The way I see it someone was being chased by the Revenue and was forced to hide it. I was lucky enough to find it. 'Twas thrown into my doorway.'

'Your *doorway*?'

Charlie shrugged and laughed. 'Well, 'twas my master's doorway if you must have it. But what matter? 'Tis finest tobacco and well worth the price.'

Seeing that her husband hesitated, the wife said, 'Do buy some, Luke. You are always griping at the price of baccy. The young man seems honest enough and has done us a service.'

Charlie drew a small bag from his pocket. After a quick look round to see that they were unobserved he tipped a little into the farmer's large red hand. While he was examining it, Charlie winked at the wife who blushed furiously and turned away in confusion.

To Charlie's satisfaction, after a further reduction in price, the farmer made a sizeable purchase before bidding him farewell.

Grinning broadly, Charlie watched them go. The woman was comely enough and had signalled her interest in him but, for Charlie, willing women were ten a penny and he had never yet met a woman who could reach his heart. Maybe he would find himself a wife one day but not yet. Oh no! Charlie had other ideas. Money was what made the world go round and Charlie wanted his share – and more than his share if that were possible. He needed money because he wanted to *be* somebody. With money he could drag himself up from the gutter towards the light of respectability. Charlie had made plans and an early marriage was not part of them. He did not intend to tie himself to a wife and rear a brood of children like his brother Jem. Charlie had to make his way up in the world, unencumbered and answerable to no one. Only then he would consider marriage. In the meantime, if he had to take a few risks then so be it. He would chance his arm.

This morning had started well and he felt intuitively that fate was with him. He mustn't allow himself to be distracted by pretty women when there was money to be made. He must find another purchaser and, as he looked round the market, he felt his confidence deepen. It was filling up rapidly with animals and men. Butchers poked and pried, drovers hallooed, dogs ran wild barking ecstatically and cattle added to the din. There was, as always, an exciting air of urgency at Smithfield market which suited Charlie's mood.

''Tis going to be a good day!' he told himself as he imagined his pockets bulging with money. Yes, it would be the first of many good days and Charlie felt sure that the realization of his dream was not too far distant.

Chapter Two

MATTHEW SETTLED HIMSELF on the chair beside his mother's bed. He did not relish the coming interview but Sophie had insisted that he speak to Ruth on the vexed subject of her influence on the children. Lately, he had tried to avoid unnecessary visits to his mother because he had come to dread her suspicious looks and probing questions. As her only child he was uncomfortably aware of the intensity of her love for him which showed itself in high expectations.

He leaned forward with his arms resting on his knees so that he need not meet her gaze.

'Sit up straight!' she snapped. 'How many times have I told you? Your spine will be permanently damaged if you do not maintain an upright posture.'

'My spine is well enough,' he said, his tone sullen.

'You may think so. I see otherwise. I see the

beginnings of a stoop.' She waited for him to reply but he said nothing. 'Do you hear me, Matthew?'

'I hear you, Mother.'

'Well, what have you to say to me?' she demanded. 'No doubt that wife of yours has told you some cock and bull story. All this fuss over a nightmare!'

Carefully Matthew launched into the little speech he had rehearsed, explaining that the children were at a very sensitive and impressionable age. He ended by asking her to moderate her language when speaking to them.

'Most certainly. I am always most careful.'

'I know you are, Mother.'

'Then why the homily?'

'To please Sophie,' he answered, thankful that Sophie was not present to witness his cowardice. He knew that Sophie was right but he dared not risk antagonizing his mother. He stretched out his fingers, examining them with apparent interest, a nervous habit. Too late he remembered that this infuriated her.

Her mouth tightened. 'Matthew! Stop twiddling your fingers. You know what your father used to say – 'tis a sign of a guilty conscience.'

'My conscience is my own affair,' he said. He regretted the words immediately, cursing his stupidity. He should have declared that his conscience was clear. Now he had suggested that, clear or not, his conscience was his own problem. His mother swooped, hawk-like, on his slip.

'I hardly think so,' she told him. 'If your conscience is not clear then we are all the poorer. Your family rely on you to –'

Matthew stood up suddenly, afraid of her change of direction. 'I must go,' he said hurriedly, backing away.

'You will do no such thing!' she retorted. 'I am speaking to you and the Lord knows how little opportunity I get to speak to my only child. Your wife, your children and your work all take precedence over the person who gave birth to you. Oh yes! Don't bother to deny it. I am fully aware of your priorities, Matthew. But today you have chosen to spend a little time with me, have been persuaded by your wife to do so, and you must bear with me. Sit down, Matthew.' He hesitated, halfway to the door. 'Sit down, I say!' she repeated.

'I have things to do.'

'More important than speaking to your elderly, bedridden mother?' Her tone was icy.

'Some papers I have brought home with me from my office . . .' he began.

She pounced again. 'When a man cannot finish his work at his place of work then he is not properly organized! A man at home should put family concerns above all others. He should leave – Matthew!'

He had taken a further few steps towards the door, eager to be gone. All his senses warned him that he was suddenly on very dangerous ground.

Ruth said, 'You have come home late five times

in the past fortnight. Five times. I've counted. If you stay late at your office then you should not need to bring work home. Are you finding your new duties beyond your capabilities?'

For a moment he felt real fear. His mother knew him better than anyone and her wrath could reduce him to the child he still was in her eyes.

He searched desperately for a way out before she could worm the secret from him. He needed a convincing lie.

'Henry Bolsover is sick,' he told her with a flash of inspiration. 'I am trying to do his work as well as my own.'

Her gimlet eyes were on him, unfaltering. 'I don't believe you. You never did lie with conviction,' she told him. 'Are you out of your depth, is that it? Tell me truly, Matthew. Was your recent promotion a mistake?'

He wanted to run from the room but that would merely compound his original error. Frantically he considered the choices open to him. He could deny the charge of incompetence and risk further questions about Henry Bolsover or he could allow her to believe that his own work was the problem. Neither choice was an attractive proposition. If he admitted to failure in his work his mother might well alert Sophie and her peace of mind would be shattered for no good reason. He supposed he loved Sophie as well as any man loved his wife after so many years of marriage and he had no wish to cause her unnecessary anxiety. She was a good woman and managed his household with reasonable success. He knew he should consider himself a fortunate man for Sophie adored him and tolerated his shrewish mother most of the time.

'Matthew!'

Slowly he returned to sit beside her, thinking frantically, playing for time.

'Well, Matthew? Are you going to honour me with a reply? Is that too much to expect?'

He decided on a further lie. 'My promotion was not a mistake, Mother. But poor Henry does have problems with his work,' he said. 'He is sadly out of his depth and I am trying to help him. Obviously no one must know.'

He saw with relief that she was willing to be convinced.

'He has been unwell these past few months. Head pains and – and a griping in the guts. He is scarcely fit enough to attend to his work but insists that he will take no rest from it. Where I can, I spare him a little time.'

'Hmm!'

He dared not look at his mother directly. Even to his own ears his story rang false but he hoped that the hint of his own altruism would persuade her to accept the excuse.

'Poor man,' she said without conviction.

Matthew looked up slowly, forcing himself to meet her gaze, feeling that his guilt must surely be blazoned across his forehead in large letters.

Her eyes narrowed as she regarded him more closely. 'Poor Henry Bolsover,' she repeated but her voice held not a shred of compassion.

Matthew felt hot with anxiety. Did she know? No, that was impossible. But had she guessed? The silence lengthened as he fought off a growing panic under her relentless scrutiny and he felt a cold sweat break out on his skin. Somehow he managed a slight shrug and stood up clumsily. He must get out of the room! He dare not allow her further questions.

From the doorway he said, 'You must sleep now, Mother. You know how talking tires you.'

'I know no such thing!'

' 'Tis gone ten o'clock. You should rest.' He tried to smile but his face felt stiff and his muscles unwilling. He added, 'I will tell Sophie of your promise, Mother,' and, ignoring her indignant protests, he fled ignominiously from the room.

*

The following afternoon Anne Redditch waited by the river stairs clutching the little spaniel to her chest for warmth. Several wherries pulled in alongside the steps but she shook her head when a waterman asked her destination.

'I'm waiting for someone,' she explained tersely. She had been waiting for the best part of an hour and her temper was fraying dangerously. When he *did* come, she told herself, she would tell him exactly what she thought of him. She would turn her face away when he tried to kiss her and she would refuse even to hold his hand. With a trembling hand she brushed away a tear and swallowed hard.

To the dog she whispered, 'Let him come! Oh, please let him come!' It was the first time in three and a half months that he had failed to meet her as promised and, mingled with her anger, was a growing fear that an accident had befallen him. He would come if he could because he loved her. She knew that as certainly as she knew her own name. He would be as eager to see her as she was to see him; he would be suffering the same anguish of longing. He had not stayed away from choice, she was certain, but what could have detained him?

Certainly not his wife, Sophie, for Matthew had told her many times that that particular passion had cooled long ago.

'Mistress! Do you want a boat?'

Anne hesitated. If he did not come soon she would have to return home and then she *would* need the services of a waterman but she could not bear to give up hope just yet. She shook her head and once more whispered, 'Please, *please* come! I want you so much!'

The dog wriggled but she tightened her grip on him. Seven-year-old Banner, named after his proudly waving tail, had not taken kindly to the long wintry walks and now wished himself back home, curled up on the hearth. He shivered and turned beseeching eyes upon his hard-hearted mistress.

'Soon,' she told him. 'We will go home. Just five more minutes.'

She knew he hated the cold but giving the dog a walk was her only excuse if she met any of her friends, since it was well known that she herself did not relish exercise. So far, this had not happened, but if it did she would say that at the ripe old age of seven Banner was getting overweight and she thought he needed more walks. This was rather clever of her, she thought, for not only would the pretence allay their suspicions, it would also establish her as a kindly person. She turned her face from the cool wind and tried to think generously of the man for whose sake she and Banner were suffering such discomfort. Five minutes passed and then ten.

'Oh, damn your eyes, Matthew!' she whispered at last. 'Where are you?' She shivered as she stared morosely across the river. A stout woman made her way down the steps and was helped into a boat. She was followed by a man and two small boys who argued over where they should sit until cuffed half-heartedly by their father. She watched them dispassionately for she had never wanted children and had been secretly relieved when she had failed each month to conceive. She had successfully hidden her delight from her disappointed husband and now she was a widow and almost past the age when pregnancy was a consideration.

The wherry pushed off, only half full, and another pulled in and tied up beside the steps. Two elderly men climbed stiffly out of the boat while a third paid their fares. Before the waterman could ask the inevitable question she called out irritably, 'I'm waiting for someone.'

The waiting was usually a delicious agony, knowing that every second brought her beloved a step nearer, but today it seemed he might not come at all and she felt sick with disappointment. He has been delayed at his office, she told herself, or he has been delayed in the street or has met a friend, perhaps, and can think of no excuse to hurry away. She imagined him making small conversation while he yearned to see her. If only he would come. Sighing, she closed her eyes and was startled when a voice asked, 'Are you well, mistress?'

She turned quickly at the unfamiliar voice and saw a young clergyman looking at her with concern. He had a kind face, she thought.

'Oh yes,' she assured him.

'Your eyes were closed. I thought you were taken sick.'

'No. I am –' She felt ashamed suddenly in front of this man of God. 'I'm waiting for my uncle,' she said.

'Ah. Then I'll be on my way.'

Impulsively she sought to detain him. Anything to pass a few moments. 'Are you waiting for a boat?'

He shook his head. 'Not today. My parish is that way.' He pointed towards the spire of a church. 'St Giles in the Fields. My first parish!' he confessed with a smile. 'One of my flock is taken ill, a lady of ample years, and I am waiting here for her son to return. He's a waterman.'

Something in his voice, a studied carelessness, caught Anne's attention.

'What ails the mother?' she asked.

'A fever,' he said after a moment's hesitation. 'Just a fever. The physician is quite adamant and yet –'

She read doubt in his eyes. 'And yet?' she prompted fearfully.

'And yet 'tis like no fever I have ever seen,' he said in a low voice. 'True she sweats but her eyes roll so. And her fingers are never still. She insists she is cold and must have a blanket yet her fingers pluck the fluff from it 'til 'tis almost bare! She speaks wildly and her –'

'Stop! Oh stop!' cried Anne in a sudden panic. 'It cannot be what you think!'

'I can only pray. We must put our trust in the Lord.' He shook his head. 'My poor little flock!'

He looked so young and defenceless that, for a moment, Anne was tempted to lay a comforting hand on his arm. But if it *was* the plague! They said it was highly contagious and this man had been ministering to the woman! She shivered and took an involuntary step backwards and Banner, sensing his mistress's momentary distraction, renewed his struggle to free himself and almost fell out of her arms.

'Banner! Keep still! Oh! You foolish animal!'

Seeing Anna's distress the young man was at once full of apologies.

'Forgive me. I've frightened you unnecessarily. I shouldn't have spoken as I did,' he told her. 'Most certainly 'tis no more than a fever.'

But his words had unsettled her and she came to an abrupt decision. Matthew had no right to expose her to such dangers, she told herself angrily; nor could he expect her to wait any longer. If he arrived and found her gone, it was no more than he deserved.

With a muttered courtesy she left the clergyman and went down the steps. As she climbed into the waiting boat three more fares arrived and climbed in beside her. The rope was untied and they were quickly carried into mid-stream.

As they pushed off from the steps she saw the young clergyman lean down towards an incoming boat.

She heard his words but they meant nothing to her.

'James Rice? I thought I recognized you. 'Tis bad news, I fear. Your mother is taken very sick and I'm sent to fetch you.'

*

'Charlie? Is that you, Charlie?'

'No, Ma. 'Tis me, Jem.' Jem went quickly into the room.

'The clergyman came to the steps to fetch me. He's going to pray for you.' He knelt beside her, his good-natured face wrinkled in anxiety. To his relief she did not look quite as ill as he had expected and her eyes seemed normal enough. 'I've a cure for you, Ma,' he told her. 'Fresh from the apothecary. 'Tis a certain cure for the – for most ailments. See!' He held up a walnut on a length of string. But she shook her head fretfully.

'You've no money to waste on such nonsense,' she told him.

''Tis no nonsense, Ma. The walnut is filled with mercury, a most potent and powerful counter to all contagions. Those were the apothecary's very words. He recommended it most heartily. Here, let me tie it round your neck.' Clumsily he leaned over and raised her head from the skimpily filled mattress which lay directly on the bare floor-boards. He saw that one of her hands was clenched; the other pulled nervously at the threadbare blanket. She shivered as though she was cold and yet her forehead was beaded with perspiration and her skin was flushed. Instinctively his eyes searched for blisters or blains but none were visible. That fool of a clergyman!

'Mercury, you say?' his mother whispered.

He detected a note of hope and nodded. 'He was full of advice and insisted you will recover within the week. What else did he say? Ah yes! You must say your prayers vigorously and sleep sound at night. Oh, and avoid excessive passions.'

His mother's mouth twitched in a faint smile. 'Excessive passions? I have little energy to spare for passions, Jem. Have no fear of that.'

'You'll soon be well again.'

She nodded and a thin hand strayed from the blanket and moved up towards her neck. She fingered the walnut and then she closed her eyes wearily.

'Charlie –' she began.

''Tis Jem,' he said gruffly.

'This mercury –'

'Does it help?' he asked, eager for reassurance.

'Aye, it does. I believe I feel calmer in my spirit.'

He brightened at once. 'Then 'tis surely nothing more than a common fever.'

For a moment he stared round the familiar room. There was no fire in the grate, no kindling wood, paper or coal. No food on the table. He remembered the apothecary's earnest words. 'Persuade her to eat well. A void in the stomach allows in pestilential humours.' Jem almost groaned as the wise words mocked him. 'Maintain great cleanliness.' He gritted his teeth. How was anyone to be clean in this place when the nearest conduit was on the far side of the Fleet river!

'I'll fetch you some more water,' he told her in a rush of tenderness.

'Your Pa fetched some before he went to work,' she protested. 'He'll fetch more when he gets home but he's gone for the day now. Hired by a gentleman with business at the docks at Chatham.'

'Chatham!' Jem was torn between envy at such a lucrative fare and dismay at the distance involved.

'He'll be worn to a shadow! I'll fetch some now, before I go back to work.' How could she eat well, he thought desperately? They were as poor as church mice. On reflection he wished that he had spent his precious money on food instead of the walnut but it was too late now. He patted her hand. 'And tomorrow I'll buy you some milk.'

She did not answer.

'Ma?' With dismay he saw that her eyes were beginning to roll in the way the clergyman had described. 'Ma!' he cried sharply. She whispered something and he leaned closer.

'Where's Charlie?' she repeated. 'I'd like to see Charlie.'

With a rush of resentment Jem sat back on his heels. At the first hint of trouble he had rushed here to his mother's side and at no small expense had bought her a walnut filled with mercury. He was going to fetch water and had promised her milk. But she must see Charlie! It was always Charlie. He was the blue-eyed boy who could do no wrong – at least in her eyes. She made allowances for Charlie, ignoring the worst of his scrapes, turning a blind eye to his faults. Damn Charlie!

'I'll find him,' he said at last. 'I'll send him to see you.' Perhaps Charlie would spend some of his ill-gotten gains on further medicaments. Without another word, Jem stood up and crossed the room to take up the two buckets.

As cheerfully as he could he said, 'I'll be back

before you know I've gone,' and went out, closing the door gently behind him.

*

He took a short cut through Lincolns Inn Fields but then had to turn left and make his way along Holborn as best he could, elbowing his way through the crowds, buffeting people with the empty buckets when necessary. The roadway was choked with horse-drawn traffic so that the unfortunate pedestrians were forced to edge their way along below the houses and shops with little or no protection from the flailing hooves of passing horses or the heavy wheels of carts and wagons. He paused on Holborn Bridge to stare down into the muddy water of the Fleet which, like the Thames into which it flowed, had fascinated him all his life. As a boy he had once traced it upstream, past Chicken Lane and Clerkenwell on the way to its source somewhere beyond St Pancras. Compared with the Thames it was little more than a wide stream, but a stream which held a thousand secrets in its murky depths.

While Jem watched, a small tree floated beneath him with a dead dog lodged incongruously in its branches. A string of oranges bobbed along behind the tree like a discarded necklace, jettisoned, no doubt, by a disgruntled orange seller who could no longer find buyers for his rotten fruit. Among the flotsam that passed, Jem saw a coconut husk, an old boot and a broken cart wheel. With apparent indifference a seagull alighted gracefully on the wheel and settled its wings. Once Jem had seen a dead body being pulled from the water and he shuddered anew at the memory of the grey, bloated face with its staring eyes. One side of the skull had been crushed as though by a heavy blow but to Jem's knowledge, the body had never been identified and no one had ever been convicted of the crime. Although Jem loved the unsavoury river he had no illusions about it. For criminals, the Fleet river had always been a convenient place in which to dispose of embarrassing bodies. From there, with any luck and a favourable tide, they would be carried into the Thames and out to sea.

Downstream the Fleet ran parallel to Shoe Lane until it went beneath the Fleet Bridge and on past the prison to join the Thames beside Blackfriars Stairs. There, at low tide, the ragged beachcombers would wade through the stinking mud, heads down, oblivious to everything but their pitiful search for anything that might be converted into currency. Jem wrinkled his nose at the rotten river smell, grinned and moved on reluctantly.

As always, there was a noisy crowd round the conduit; a shivering group that stamped their feet and blew on their hands while they waited impatiently to fill their jugs and buckets and be gone. Jem studied the faces, hopefully, to see if he knew anyone. A little conversation would lighten his day but he found no familiar faces and was forced to confront once more the fact of his mother's sickness. He would have to alert Fanny and he would mention it to Maggie but he would try not to alarm them. An idea came to him suddenly; an unkind idea. Suppose he frightened Charlie with exaggerated stories of his mother's sickness so that he would be afraid of the contagion and stay away. Would his mother hold that against Charlie, he wondered. Would Charlie's absence make her appreciate his own presence more? He sighed. He knew he couldn't do it because if Charlie didn't call on his mother she would grieve. The thought of her possible death filled Jem with sorrow. He had always nursed the belief that one day her eyes would be opened to Charlie's failings. Now, perhaps, time was running out for that particular miracle. As his thoughts whirled he watched that no one took his turn at the pump. He mustn't be too late back or his employer would think he was holding back the money. It would never do to lose his job.

Two men were squabbling over the pump handle while a third staggered away with a barrel of water on his back. Ahead of Jem, a young red-haired woman waited, two pails on a wooden yoke round her neck. She was talking animatedly to a younger girl who carried a bucket on her arm and Jem tried not to notice how pretty they were. He was a married man and would soon be a father. His thoughts lifted as he thought about his enviable position. He hoped for a daughter. They would call her Ellen. At least Jem would provide his mother with the first grandchild. Charlie could not better that, he reminded himself, and at once felt some of his bitterness fade. *Of course* he must find Charlie and send him to his mother.

Behind him several watersellers waited impatiently, one of them muttering that he had work to do. His language was as coarse as his appearance but Jem tried to ignore him. Unlike Charlie, he had no liking for a scrap and, anyway, had heard much worse for he carried all manner of men up and down the river and even so-called 'gentlemen' would swear like troopers when they were out of temper. The red-haired girl, however, grew tired of the ill-natured oaths and turned on the waterseller indignantly.

'Watch your filthy tongue!' she told him loudly. 'There's young ladies present.'

Her friend grinned at this euphemism and even Jem smiled.

'Call yourselves ladies? Huh!' The waterseller snarled. 'Bartholomew's babies, more like!'

As the girl had intended, an argument broke out between the various men in the group, some supporting the girls, others the waterseller. Jem saw his chance and took it. He quickly filled both buckets and was a hundred yards up the street before anyone missed him.

*

Sophie looked at the pigeon with irritation. It was not as young as she had expected and hardly suitable for roasting. It was her own fault, she reflected. She should have known better than to trust a servant with the choice of a bird. Fanny hated the pigeon loft and was apt to take up the first bird that came to hand instead of making a considered judgement. She *had* managed to wring its neck, however, which was a step in the right direction. For the first year of her employment Fanny had steadfastly refused to kill the birds, insisting that to do so 'turned her stomach something cruel'.

'I said a *young* bird,' Sophie now told Fanny reproachfully. 'This is in its dotage! I've told you before how to choose a young bird and 'tis so simple – look for pink legs and feet.'

''Tis dark up there. I could scarce see,' Fanny protested.

'Not *so* dark, Fanny. Remember, I have been up there many times and *I* see well enough to examine the birds. We shall have to boil this one.'

'They flutter so,' Fanny protested.

'Of course they flutter, you foolish girl. They're birds. What else should they do?'

'The master do like a roasted pigeon,' Fanny conceded guiltily. 'He's said so time and again.'

Sophie shrugged. 'Well, he'll be unlucky tonight.' She laid the small warm body in Fanny's hands and said, 'You pluck it while I took out that recipe that Mistress Devine boasts of so frequently. And try not to make a mess. Last time it looked as though it had snowed feathers!'

Ignoring the look of distaste on the girl's face she crossed to the dresser and took a slim leather-bound volume from the drawer. Her mother-in-law's book had proved invaluable over the years, filled as it was with a haphazard collection of well-tried recipes and tips on household management. It had been passed on to Ruth by her own mother on her wedding day and later expanded by Ruth herself. Eventually it would go to Lizbeth.

As Fanny settled to her plucking Sophie turned the pages . . . *Cod in black butter . . . On ridding a room of fleas . . . Neats' tongues – the drying of them . . . To sweep a chimney free of soot . . . On choosing lace . . . On fumigating clothes . . .*

Fanny sneezed loudly and Sophie said, 'Bless you!'

''Tis the dust from that dratted loft. 'Tis horrible up there. And the smell!'

'Perhaps you should clean it out then,' Sophie suggested innocently without looking up from her book.

'Oh! 'Twasn't that bad,' Fanny said hastily.' That is to say, I dare say the pigeons like it that way.'

Sophie found the page at last and read aloud, 'Wash the pigeon both inside and out and stuff with sweet butter to which you have mixed parsley and thyme. Let it boil in a pot uncommon slow with a large handful of spinach and when nearly tender strain the yolk of an egg with verjuice.'

There was a knock at the back door and Fanny leaped to her feet, scattering feathers in a cloud about her. While Sophie was scolding and Fanny was apologizing the door opened and Jem's face appeared. His face was pinched with cold and Sophie told Fanny to mull a little ale. While the hot poker sizzled in the liquid Jem gave them his unwelcome news.

'But she'll not die,' he said defiantly. 'The mercury will soon see her fit and well.'

'Did she ask for me?' asked Fanny, scraping a little nutmeg into the ale and handing the tankard to her brother.

Jem shook his head and sipped the hot drink thankfully, his hands clasped round the tankard to warm them. 'She asked for Charlie but he's nowhere to be found. But Pa will be home before long and I shall buy her milk tomorrow.'

Sophie said, 'She's fortunate to have such a good son, Jem.' And he fell silent, abashed by her praise.

Fanny said, 'Give her my love, Jem. I'll be over to St Giles as soon as I may.'

Sophie smiled at Jem. 'You must take her a few eggs – a gift from me. They'll strengthen her.'

As she spoke her fingers continued to turn the pages of Ruth's book. One of the headings caught her attention with a sickening jolt. '*In time of plague . . .*' There followed a list of directions in Ruth's neatly rounded script.

'(1) *Keep the dogs tied close by the house so that they shall not wander abroad.*

'(2) *Keep yards free of noisome matter; wash free daily*

of slops and dung . . .' She closed the book with a snap, forcing the unwelcome thoughts from her mind. With an effort she tried to concentrate on what Jem was saying.

'– so I'll be off. Maggie will wonder at my lateness and I must break the news to her also.'

Without speaking, Sophie put three eggs into a small basket and handed them to Jem who thanked her profusely. As he was halfway out of the door she called to him, her voice tense. 'Jem! If she should worsen – that is, if the fever be other than you think –'

Both Jem and Fanny were staring at her fearfully but she forced herself to continue.

'If 'tis so then I pray you keep your distance. Send word by another. For the children's sake,' she faltered. 'Lizbeth and Ollie, I must think what's best for them. Jem, you do understand, don't you?'

He nodded but added stubbornly, ' 'Tis a common fever. I swear it.'

'I'll pray for her,' said Sophie and turned away. If Fanny's mother had the plague then Jem must not come near them again; nor should Fanny be allowed to visit her mother. Matthew must be consulted. In the meantime, she re-opened the little book and searched for the directions for plague prevention. There was no harm in taking precautions, she told herself. Tomorrow morning Fanny must be sent out into the yard to clean it up. A good shower of rain would help but the sky remained treacherously free of clouds. As for dogs, well, they had none. She read on.

(3) *In a chafing dish or iron pan, burn charcoal with frankincense, juniper, rosemary and bay.* She had no frankincense but would buy some tomorrow. Also charcoal. Not that she expected to need it but there was no harm in laying in a few items. Matthew must give her some money. She would speak to him as soon as the children were in bed. At the thought of her husband her panic lessened. She thanked God nightly for her good fortune. She had a wonderful husband; he had told her many times that he lived for her and the children. He would move heaven and earth to protect them, she had faith in his goodness and was grateful for his wisdom. Feeling slightly comforted, she waved a farewell to Jem and hurried to the pantry in search of sweet butter and parsley. Matthew might have been denied his roast but in its place the boiled pigeon would be as tasty as she could make it.

*

My sweet Anne, [Matthew wrote the next morning]
  I beg you to forgive me. It was impossible to meet you yesterday as we had planned —

He had not wanted to confess that his mother's homily had frightened him, nor that he had considered inventing an excuse for his failure to keep their assignation. Eventually, he had decided against it; if she truly loved him as she insisted then she must trust him. He continued.

> *– and there was no way to notify you since you told me you would be with your aunt all day. I dared not send word there for fear of discovery. The thought of you waiting by the river in that cold wind tore at my heart. I trust you did not wait too long. Oh my dear, you can hardly believe how much I have missed you. I shall wait at Temple Stairs at the same time this evening and if you do not come I shall walk to and fro past your house for a brief glimpse of you.*
>
> *If you have visitors and cannot speak with me, I beg you be at your window around seven-thirty. A single smile will tell me I am forgiven and send me home with a happy heart.*

A knock at the door disturbed him and he quickly drew a ledger towards him so that it covered the notepaper. He called, 'Enter!' and looked up as Henry Bolsover entered the room, his round face beaming.

'Matthew, I have some interesting news for you,' he began, settling himself on a nearby chair.

Matthew hid his irritation at the interruption. Henry was an able man but a dull one. Short and comfortably built, he reminded Matthew of a friendly dog. His slightly bulbous blue eyes regarded the whole world with trust and there was an eagerness about him that some people found appealing, although Matthew found it mildly ridiculous in a man of his age. Henry was in his forties and his wife was nearer fifty. Matthew and Henry had worked together for the best part of seven years and occasionally came together with their wives for a little supper party or a visit to the theatre in Drury Lane.

Henry went on, 'A friend of mine has discovered a truly talented singing teacher and he is coming to the house this evening to give my wife a trial lesson to see whether or not he might prove suitable. I know you have spoken of a new teacher for Sophie and thought –'

'Tonight, you say?' Matthew shook his head, genuinely disappointed that he could not accept the invitation for Sophie had a sweet voice and deserved a better teacher. He himself had no voice to speak of but was accomplished on the viol. The offer to hear a new teacher was tempting, but the letter to Anne must be sent. He could not bear to pass another day without seeing her.

'I fear I have some business to attend to,' he began.

'Then perhaps Sophie might care to attend?' Henry looked at him hopefully.

Matthew hesitated. Sophie was a very pretty woman and wherever possible he tried to make sure that she did not spend time in the company of other men, no matter how innocent the occasion might be. True, Henry's wife would be there also but the teacher! What of the teacher? Was he young or old? Married or single?

'Sophie has been indisposed these last few days,' he said at last. 'I'm sorry, Henry, but another time perhaps.'

Henry's eyes narrowed almost imperceptibly. 'Indisposed? What ails her?'

Matthew cursed his rash words. Now he must invent more lies.

'A slight fever. 'Tis nothing,' he said.

Henry's cheerfulness deserted him and he leaned forward. 'They are saying at the Exchange that the contagion is more than a possibility this summer. I hear that the authorities are laying in stores of medicaments for the poor and considering what measures might be taken against the contagion. I overheard two men talking together and one insisted that the plague has already broken out west of the city.'

'What nonsense! The Bills of Mortality show no sign of the plague,' Matthew retorted.

Henry shrugged. 'They say the physicians are reluctant to reveal it. The authorities want to avoid panic.'

They looked at each other with growing apprehension.

Matthew said, 'The same rumours abounded six months ago but came to nothing. 'Tis scare-mongering at its worst and I refuse to be thrown into a panic by rumours.' He waited for Henry to agree but was disappointed.

'I shall send my wife to Hampstead,' Henry confided, 'to stay with her mother. I thank Heaven at such times that we have no children. If it does come, I dare say I shall join her there for the duration. You should think on these things, Matthew. You should make provision. My wife's mother recalls the last outbreak and talks of nothing else. I grow weary of her doleful chatter but she has lived through it and insists that we heed her warnings. Do think on it, Matthew.'

'Indeed I will.' He thought on it immediately but not in the way Henry had intended. It came to him suddenly that if he sent Sophie, the children and his mother into the country he would be able to visit Anne with complete freedom. There would be no need for lies and prevarication. A great longing arose in him to be unencumbered, followed by another exciting thought. Sending his family away would seem a totally reasonable thing to do; he might even be applauded as generous and unselfish. 'I could send them to Sophie's brother Giles,' he said.

Henry nodded earnestly. 'As long as they are out of London,' he stipulated.

'They live a few miles beyond Woolwich. They have five children of their own but their farmhouse is spacious enough.' His mind was racing. He would broach the subject this very evening. First, he would mention it to his mother and ensure her support for the plan; he must word the proposal very carefully, emphasizing that his main concern was the well-being of those he loved. Which was true. The affair with Anne was a separate matter altogether. But would Giles and Henrietta be willing to take them in? Sophie and her brother were not overly fond of one another but in times of plague they would surely not refuse.

Henry stood up. ''Tis a pity about the singing lesson but we will arrange something another time.'

Matthew nodded. 'You must tell me your opinion of him.'

'I will. And give my regards to your wife. I hope she is soon recovered.'

'Recovered?'

'From her indisposition.'

'Oh! Yes!' Matthew was not a good liar but practice would make him better. 'My thanks, Henry. You have given me much food for thought.' Much more than poor Henry would ever imagine.

As soon as the door closed Matthew allowed himself a broad smile. Perhaps, after all, Fate was going to be kind to him. He pushed the ledger aside and took up his pen. He would confide his new plan to Anne and hope that any resentment she had felt towards him would be swept away. He would tell her he was doing it so that they could spend more time together. It would be music to her pretty ears! Still smiling, he bent his head and continued his writing.

*

On the second of April, Luke Meridith, the physician, was approached by a handsome young man with blond curls and asked to attend his elderly mother who was sick.

'My father's with her. He'll be looking out for you.' The young man thrust money into Luke's hand and gave directions before hurrying off in the opposite direction 'on urgent business'. Luke made his way with a heavy heart into the sprawling maze of courts and alleys behind Drury Lane.

The patient appeared to be already dead. Her eyes had rolled upward and appeared fixed; her arms, like two thin sticks, lay palms upwards and motionless. The husband hovered uncertainly as Luke knelt at the woman's side and began to examine her. The pulse in the thin wrist was faint but still detectable.

'She's not dead, is she?' asked the old man in a voice that trembled with shock. 'She can't be dead.'

'She's not dead,' Luke agreed. He peered into her eyes and looked carefully into her mouth. She was barely conscious, and he thought it doubtful she would survive the night. He laid a hand on her forehead which was cold and damp to the touch. To himself, he acknowledged that he was playing for time; putting off the moment when he would have to look at the woman's body. Not that he was squeamish, he had been a physician too long for that, but for some weeks now he had gone about his work expecting daily to discover on one of his patients the purple marks which he so feared.

Pulling back the blanket, he looked at the scrawny neck and breathed a sigh of relief. There was no sign of a swelling and the rest of her frail body was also free of anything worse than liver spots. She was, however, badly undernourished and Luke hesitated. Was there any point in suggesting that lack of food had probably contributed to her condition? Whose fault was that? The husband had no doubt provided what he could. To reproach him would make him feel guilty to no purpose since he obviously could not provide more.

'She hasn't spoken since yesterday morning,' said the old man. 'Not since Jem was here. Not the one who sent you here. That's Charlie. Jem's our other boy. He brought her the mercury. It's in that walnut.' With a sudden display of bitterness he added, 'I dare say the apothecary lied. Swore it was a certain charm.' He sighed. 'Not a word since yesterday when all she said was "Charlie". One word, clear as a bell. She doted on that boy and yet he hasn't set foot in the door. Keeping well away if you ask me. Mind you, he put his hand in his pocket and we're grateful for that but she wanted to *see* him.'

With compassion Luke noted that already he spoke about his wife in the past tense, tacitly accepting that she would not survive. He tried to concentrate on his diagnosis. There were no distinctive signs and yet his intuition told him that it was plague. The first but not the last case that he would have to deal with in the coming months. Well, he hoped he would have the courage to face it when it came. He had chosen a career in medicine with a clear understanding of the risks entailed and, please God, he would not shirk his responsibilities.

He replaced the covers gently and stood up knowing that there was little he could do for the woman. If he suggested further medicines the old man would waste what little money he had; money that he might need if he too succumbed.

'There is little you can do,' he said quietly, 'except pray. A little milk if she regains consciousness but don't force it between her lips. You might choke her.'

'You mean her time's come?'

'I fear so. I'm sorry.'

The old man's lips quivered. 'My neighbour spoke of strong vinegar,' he said. "Rosemary steeped in strong vinegar." He said, "Cast hot stones into it so that the vapours rise into the room. Any stones will do, but flints be best."' He faltered and stopped.

Luke looked at him carefully, 'And you – how do you feel?' he asked. 'Any pains? Any sweating?'

'Nothing. I'm fit as a fiddle.'

'No swellings?' Luke did not meet his eyes. This old man would remember the last outbreak and would know where these questions were leading.

'Swellings?' The voice was suspicious now with a hint of panic.

'I told you, nothing. A fever, that's all.'

Luke nodded reassuringly but the damage was done.

The man stared at him, wide eyed. 'You don't think it's –'

'No, no.' What point was there, Luke asked himself, in spreading alarm since he could not be certain. 'I was just asking. We have to be on the look-out for –'

'I'm not going to die too, am I?'

The old man stared at Luke with horror. 'Don't let me die! Oh, God, don't let me die!'

With an effort Luke patted his arm. He knew that the man might well die but he would try to save him. He pulled a purse from his pocket and pressed a sixpence into the old man's calloused hand.

'Buy yourself some oranges and a lemon,' he instructed. 'Avoid raw vegetables and salt meat. Strong pickles can be beneficial and an egg will build up your strength.' He brushed aside the old man's thanks and made haste to leave. He was halfway down the stairs when a terrible scream sounded from the room he had just left. With a rapidly beating heart he raced back upstairs to find the old woman sitting bolt upright, staring at the ceiling, her rigid arms outstretched as though in supplication.

He knew at once that she was dead.

*

That evening Luke sat at supper with his son, Antony, and sister, Lois, and told them what had happened.

'And was it the plague?' Lois asked.

'No recognizable sign of it. No dark tokens below the skin. No swelling. So why did I *know* in my heart 'twas the plague.' He sighed heavily.

'How did you notify it?' asked Antony eagerly.

After a slight pause Luke said, 'Spotted fever.'

'But there were no spots! You said so.' His son looked at him accusingly.

Lois said slowly, 'But Luke, 'tis the same thing. Spotted fever and plague.'

'I know. A euphemism. But I couldn't call it plague without any recognizable symptoms, yet I believe the authorities need to know what is happening, that these isolated cases are occurring. At the moment it seems they choose to minimize the danger. I suspect they want to draw up emergency plans before they make it known to the public. My fear is that they will leave it all too late.'

Antony said, 'They hide the truth, you mean!'

Luke nodded unhappily, returning to his own dilemma. 'There were no tokens on the body, no swellings, nothing. I could not name it.' After a silence he went on. 'I have done a great deal of research into the question of epidemics and to me a pattern is discernible. Frequently, when an outbreak begins, the disease itself is weak and more people recover from it. Later, as it spreads, the disease seems to grow in intensity so that those who catch it later have less chance of survival. At present the symptoms are less obvious or even non-existent and the tokens may be slow to appear. They may not even show up until *after* death. If only the authorities would act quickly in the early stages, but no. They argue and procrastinate because no one is willing to take responsibility. It is always the way.'

There was another long silence and then Lois laid down her knife and stared at her half-eaten meal. 'I have lost my appetite,' she said defensively, seeing her brother's raised eyebrows.

Luke covered her hand briefly with his own. 'Forgive me,' he said. 'I did not intend to frighten you though God knows *I* am frightened!'

But Antony, undeterred, pressed on with his questions. 'And the husband of this woman? Will *he* die?'

'I fear so.' Luke looked at him. 'There are bad times ahead, Antony. You should go away. To Italy, perhaps. You are twenty-one and have never seen Rome. Go to Rome, Antony.'

He looked hopefully at his son; at the fresh young face under the bright red hair. Antony, the self-professed artist who had refused to follow in his father's footsteps and had earned himself a reputation as a wayward, free-thinking spirit at odds with the rest of society. Fearlessly outspoken, Antony was only truly happy when he was fighting for a cause, real or imagined. He was so unlike his father in every way. All that Luke had passed on to his son was his halo of red hair while his wife, long since dead, had passed on her restless nature. Luke thought briefly of his wife. She had disconcerted him at times but he had admired her confidence. If she had lived longer he would no doubt have understood her better; might even have loved her. As it was, they had married after a lengthy courtship and she had died thirteen months later. Luke had not looked at another woman since.

Now, he thought wearily, his own outspoken comments had probably provided fuel for his son's fire. As soon as the emergency *was* declared, Antony would no doubt seize the opportunity to confront the authorities over their handling of the situation. If only he could be persuaded to leave England, but that particular battle had been fought more than once and Antony had always won.

'Or Venice?' Lois suggested quickly, seeing Luke's line of thinking. 'Go to Venice, Antony, while you are still young. Take your easel and paints. Venice would suit you wonderfully. 'Tis a young man's city!'

Antony laughed aloud. 'How would you know that, aunt?' he teased her. 'You have never left London – nor wanted to! You simply want to be rid of me!'

She had the grace to blush a little at her own transparency but she took no offence at his words for there was a strong bond of affection between them.

'Verona,' said Luke. 'Or the Alps. Climb the Alps. Go to Switzerland.'

But Antony was laughing, his wide grey eyes bright at the prospect of yet another battle. 'Father, I'm staying!' he said with a grin and Luke knew that yet again, he had been defeated. His troubles were only just beginning.

Chapter Three

'Rumph! Rumph!' Oliver moved the elephant along the ramp which led to the ark. A few days had passed and he and Lizbeth were in their grandmother's room, playing with a wooden ark and the animals which went with it. The ark and its inhabitants, which had been carved by Ruth's father, was never allowed to leave the room but was kept as a special treat for the children when they visited her. As Lizbeth watched, Oliver marched the second elephant towards the ark, making what he imagined to be elephant noises.

'Rumph! Rumph! Rumph!' He turned towards his grandmother. 'The elephants don't like the ark,' he told her firmly.

'They don't?' She peered at him short-sightedly over her crochet work. 'How do you know that, dear?'

'They told me so. They whispered in my ear.'

Lizbeth said, 'I didn't see them whisper.'

'They did!'

'And elephants don't whisper, Ollie.'

'They do.'

'They *don't*! Do they, Grandmother?'

Ruth smiled. 'I don't think I know,' she admitted.

Lizbeth frowned. 'They're too big to whisper,' she explained. 'Only mice can whisper. Mice and rats and little birds. They whisper because they're so small and they have whispery voices. Elephants . . .'

'*You* whisper,' said Ollie, 'and you're not a mouse or a rat or a baby bird.'

'But I can whisper because I'm not an elephant,' she said. 'I shall ask Papa when he comes home.'

'*When* he comes home!' said Ruth, half to herself but her words did not escape Ollie.

He nodded. 'Papa is always late these days. Mama says he works too hard.' He led the two elephants down the gangway again. 'Here they go!' he said. 'They said it smells on the ark and there is no elephant food.'

Ruth looked over her spectacles. 'They'll drown!' she warned, 'if they are left behind. The waters rose and . . .'

'They won't drown, Grandmother. They can swim.'

Once more Lizbeth appealed to the old lady. 'Can they, Grandmother? Can they swim?'

'I don't think I know that either.'

Oliver turned large brown eyes towards her. 'If I

were as old as you I should know everything. Don't laugh, Grandmother! I *should*!'

'So should I!' said Lizbeth, not to be outdone. 'I will when *I'm* old.'

'We won't grow old if plague comes,' said Oliver, 'because we shall die. Everyone will die.' He picked up the two tigers and began to march them towards the ark, growling ferociously.

Uncomfortably aware that her own dire predictions had indeed coloured her grandson's opinion Ruth said hastily, 'Perhaps some of us will be spared. Yes, almost certainly some of us will.' With her son's words still fresh in her mind, she reminded herself that she had not intended to alarm the children, only to give them pause for thought. Now she searched for a way to undo the harm she had done. 'The good people may be spared, Ollie.'

'Am I good?' asked Lizbeth hopefully.

Ruth answered the familiar question from habit, her good intentions momentarily forgotten. 'Only the Lord sees into our hearts. Only the Lord in his infinite wisdom can separate the wheat from the chaff.' She stopped abruptly, annoyed with herself.

'I'm the wheat,' said Lizbeth. 'The wheat are the good people. Mama says so.'

Ruth laid down her crochet work. 'Mama this! Mama that!' she snorted. 'Your mother doesn't know everything! And don't look so smug, Lizbeth. It doesn't become you.'

'Papa knows everything.' Oliver kept his face

carefully averted in case he too was looking smug. Instinct suggested a change of subject. 'The tigers like the ark,' he said. 'They like the funny smells and Noah has some special tiger food for them. Stripey food.'

'Stripey food?' Lizbeth's eyes widened in disbelief. 'There's no such thing!'

'There is!'

'What is it then?'

Silently Oliver considered his answer and Ruth plied her crochet hook once more.

'Bacon,' said Oliver at last. 'That's stripey, Lizbeth.'

'Oh yes. So 'tis.' Disappointed by her brother's success, Lizbeth searched for a new challenge. 'Where are the rats and mice?' she asked, pointing to the collection of animals still awaiting embarkation.

Ruth smiled. 'I dare say my father ran short of time,' she told her. 'He made tigers and bears, elephants and monkeys.'

Lizbeth seized her chance. 'Then all the rats and mice were drowned.'

Ollie looked at her scornfully. 'How could they all be drowned? There are rats everywhere. There are some in our kitchen. Fanny has seen them. Big rats with long whiskers. Mice too. Fanny hit one of the rats with the rolling pin the other day and killed it. She threw it out into the yard and a cat came over the wall and carried it away. It was all squashed.'

'Oh, poor cat!' said Lizbeth.

'Not the cat, you ninny! The rat!'

'Children! Please!' Ruth put a hand to her head which was beginning to ache. 'And you must not call your sister a ninny, Ollie.' She did not care for the turn the conversation was taking and decided she had had enough of the children's company for one day. Much as she loved them, their constant demands for information or confirmation exhausted her. 'I think 'tis time you went downstairs,' she told them.

Lizbeth cried, 'Shall I ring the bell for you, Grandmother, to fetch Fanny?'

Before Ruth could answer, Oliver jumped to his feet, his face red with righteous indignation. ''Tis my turn to ring it!' he shouted. 'You know it, Grandmother! Lizbeth rang it yesterday.'

'Hush, child! Tut! Children are so loud these days. Does your mother never teach you –'

But ignoring her, both children made a dash for the small bell which stood on their grandmother's bedside table. Ruth held up a warning finger. 'Neither of you shall ring it,' she told them sternly and rang it herself.

They were still complaining shrilly when Fanny appeared in the doorway. Not the cheerful Fanny they knew, but a stricken Fanny whose eyes were red from weeping. At this dreadful sight the two children fell silent, staring at her in dismay, and even Ruth felt a prickle of alarm.

To Fanny, Ruth said, 'What ails you, Fanny? What has happened?'

Fanny's face crumpled and fresh tears ran down her cheeks. Oliver rushed forward and threw his arms around her legs in a bear-like hug.

'Don't!' he begged. 'Don't cry, Fanny! Please don't cry!'

''Tis my Ma,' Fanny gasped. 'Passed away, very sudden. Ohh!' She threw her apron over her head and sobbed uncontrollably.

Ruth said, 'The Lord giveth and the Lord taketh away!' Then, struck by a terrible thought, she asked, 'What was it? What took her?'

With a loud sniff Fanny lowered the apron a little so that her reddened eyes were visible. 'Not that!' she said defiantly. 'Not plague. The physician said 'twas a spotted fever.'

Ruth drew in her breath sharply. 'Spotted fever!'

All faces turned towards her and with an effort she checked her words. Instead she said, 'Does your mistress know of this? Fanny? Answer me!'

'She knows.'

'Then send her to me at once – and take the children downstairs. Give them something to eat.'

'But 'tis only just after three,' Fanny protested.

'I don't wish to know the time, Fanny. I want you to do as I say and at once!'

Alarmed by this exchange, Oliver released Fanny's legs and took Lizbeth's hand. 'Don't cry, Lizbeth,' he whispered. 'We're the wheat, not the chaff. God won't punish us.'

'Are we, Ollie?' She rubbed her eyes. 'Won't he?'

As Fanny left the room Ruth urged, 'Go along, you two. I wish to speak with your mother. Just for today you may take the ark with you but see that it comes back to me tonight.' She waited impatiently as Oliver bundled all the animals inside the ark and, awed by this special dispensation, he and Lizbeth followed Fanny downstairs.

As soon as Sophie appeared Ruth said, 'That girl must go, Sophie. Her mother has died of the plague and the Lord knows how many others in her family are infected. You must speak to Matthew.'

Sophie's mouth tightened. 'I shall not get rid of her, Ruth. She has nowhere to go. And how would she live without employment? And 'twas not the plague. 'Twas the spotted fever.'

'Spotted fever *is* the plague, you foolish girl!' cried Ruth. 'Or as near as makes no difference. Haven't I lived through it? Don't I know? For pity's sake, Sophie, be guided by me. Get rid of the girl before 'tis too late.'

The old lady's face was grim. 'Listen, Sophie. When plague breaks out families that have the infection are shut up by the authorities so that they cannot infect others. 'Tis for the good of the city. They are locked into their homes until the disease has run its course. Forty days. That's what it was last time.' She shook her head at the memory. 'To avoid the whole family being shut up the physicians sometimes pretended it was another disease. Spotted fever. 'Tis virtually the same thing.'

'I don't believe it!' cried Sophie. 'Her father is well enough *and* her brothers. I cannot turn her out. It would be too cruel. Oh, what's to be done for the best? She wants to go to the burying.'

'You cannot allow her to go,' Ruth told her. 'She will mingle with the rest of her family at the graveside and take the contagion upon herself and carry it back here!'

Sophie sat down slowly on the bedside chair. 'I shall talk to Matthew.'

'Huh!' Ruth snorted. 'Matthew knows a great deal less than I do. I have lived through plague. He hasn't. I have seen the terror of those afflicted – and the callousness of others. You have no idea what such a calamity does to people. Believe me, Sophie, London in the grip of plague is . . . Sophie? Are you listening?'

'I beg your pardon?' Sophie looked at her with sudden hope. 'If 'twas the plague then why are Fanny's family not shut up? It was as the physician says – a fever. Nothing more.'

The old lady shook her head impatiently. 'They haven't shut them up because regulations are not in force yet. 'Tis early days, Sophie, and people still hope against hope. But the Lord has looked down upon this sinful city and has laid his hand upon them that the wicked shall be punished and they that be innocent as a newborn lamb shall suffer with them!' She clasped her hands and closed her eyes.

Sophie sprang to her feet. ' 'Tis no time for

prayers!' she cried. 'Oh! What must I do? I wish Matthew would come home.'

'I have told you what you must do,' said Ruth. 'You must send the girl away.'

'She has done no wrong!'

'Would you endanger the lives of your little ones?'

'No!' Sophie covered her face with her hands, then suddenly glanced up. 'I shall seek out the physician concerned and ask him direct. Was it the plague or not?'

'And you think he will tell you? You are more gullible than I thought, Sophie.'

'There is no word of plague in the *Newes*.'

'There are no cases of plague recorded in the weekly Bills but that means nothing. I'll warrant there has been more than one body buried these last few weeks that have the tokens upon them.'

'Stop it! Please stop!' Sophie begged. 'I can't bear to think on it.'

Ruth said, 'Matthew will say as I do. Fanny must go. Certainly I shall not allow her near *me* again. I have a proper respect for the disease. You may take chances if you will. I will take all precautions.'

She folded her crochet work and set it on the table. 'Bring me my book of household management. There are some precautions in it which you must put into effect.'

Sophie stood up slowly. 'I will bring you the book but I will not turn Fanny away. If you will not allow her in your room that is your decision but I will not be at your beck and call. My hands are full already. If she goes who will we employ in her place? A stranger? How would we know how *her* family fares? She may also have sickness in the family and choose to keep it from us.'

Ruth had not considered this problem and now she hesitated. Fragments of a recent conversation with Matthew came to her mind. He had told her to say nothing yet about his plans but the temptation to put Sophie in her place was too strong. 'It may be that we shall have to go away,' she told her. 'If plague takes a hold, you and I and the children could go to your brother's house in Woolwich.'

Sophie stared at her. 'Go to Woolwich? Without Matthew?'

'He has his work to do. He will stay in London.'

'With all of us gone?' Sophie was horrified. 'But who would take care of Matthew?'

Ruth shrugged. 'Fanny might still be here. He would make out as best he could. At least he would rest easy in his mind to know that his loved ones were safe.'

'I would never, never leave him at such a time!' cried Sophie. 'What wife would leave her husband to take his chance alone? Suppose he fell ill? Fanny could never nurse him as I would! Oh no, Ruth. Put the idea to him if you must but he would never consider such a thing.'

Ruth smiled, her eyes glittering with triumph. 'I

think you will learn otherwise, Sophie,' she said. ''Tis already arranged – and 'twas Matthew's own idea!'

*

Later that night, Sophie gave up the pretence of sleep and, wrapping herself warmly in her robe, lit a candle and crept downstairs to the parlour. Setting the candlestick down on the table, she crossed to the window and opened the shutters. The moon cast dark shadows across the quiet street and she thought how sinister it looked by night. Few people ventured out after dark unless they had a very good reason because the lonely thoroughfares were haunted by thieves and cut-throats. Law-abiding citizens who needed to leave the safety of their own homes would take a sedan chair, if one were to be found, or they would pay a few pence to a link man who would light their way through the streets and, by his very presence, provide a sense of security.

She watched as a solitary rider made his way past the window, the collar of his cloak turned up against the cold air. The hooves of his grey mare clattered on the cobbles and a small dog ran out from nowhere to bark and snap at the horse's legs until a flick of the man's whip sent it howling back into the shadows.

Sophie shivered but not with cold, for the embers of the fire still warmed the little room. She shivered instead with apprehension, unhappily aware of the subtle changes that were taking place around her; changes which threatened her and those she loved. Until now, her life had been laid out for her like a well-planned garden. Her husband's love had thrived there; her children had sprung up, small but healthy plants. She had felt secure within its hedges. Now it seemed all that was changing. Weeds had appeared in the garden; vague threats and uncertainties had raised their heads, threatening disorder. The pathway she trod was taking her into the unknown. 'Oh Matthew!' she whispered.

A drunken man reeled suddenly into view and, roaring noisily, lurched against the window startling her. Instinctively she drew back but for a moment longer he clung to the sill and faced her, his mouth wide, his eyes vacant, the personification, it seemed to Sophie, of all that she most dreaded. Yet even as the thought crystallized in her mind, her conscience pricked her. Her natural compassion surfaced and with it the thought that he might not be evil but merely unfortunate. A product of the city's low life who had never had a chance to be anything better. Suppose he was feeble-minded through an accident of birth and could not be held responsible. More to be pitied than blamed. Poor wretch, she thought. I have misjudged him. He might not be drunk at all but ill . . . An unwelcome thought struck her.

'Oh no!' she whispered.

At that precise moment the man's face disappeared from sight leaving his fingers still clutching the sill.

A few seconds later they relinquished their hold and Sophie heard a grunt as the man fell to the ground. Fearfully she opened the window a little and looked down at him. He lay spread-eagled across the cobbles and was snoring loudly. She studied him fearfully in the light of the moon but could see no sign of any distressing symptoms. His face was unmarked and he did not appear to be in any pain. He was doubtless drunk, as she had first imagined. With a sigh of relief, Sophie closed the window and, as an afterthought, fastened the shutters. A few deep breaths steadied her but she decided she had seen enough of the city at night. Retrieving her candle, she carried it to the small desk where they kept their writing paper. She sat for some time, gathering courage for what she must do and then, taking a sheet from the pile, she began a letter to Giles's wife.

Dearest Henrietta,
I beg you not to show this letter to your husband for fear he finds it necessary to pass on its contents to Matthew . . .

In her haste the lines were uneven and the writing clumsily formed but she told herself this was no time to worry over the niceties of good script. She must contact Henrietta immediately and enlist her support.

It seems there is a chance the city may be visited by

plague and if that happens Matthew is determined that I shall leave London and come to live with you, bringing the children and his mother with me. Can you imagine how I feel? Would you be able to leave Giles in such circumstances? I am determined not to leave London without him and have suggested that we should all move out, renting another property somewhere down river, near you, perhaps. From there he could travel up river to attend his work.

Matthew insists we cannot afford it but I disagree. There is always money, it seems, for the things Matthew wants but none when my needs are mentioned! I mean him no disrespect, Henrietta, I love him more than life itself, but you know how men are.

What I ask is this. If the worst happens and Matthew writes suggesting that we come to you will you try to dissuade Giles? Say there is not enough room for all of us or that you do not like Mathew's mother or that you know we would all grate upon each other. Or say all of it! (It may all be true!) Be angry that Matthew has the temerity to make such a suggestion. Say anything that occurs to you that will make Giles refuse us shelter.

I could never rest easy if I knew Matthew was living alone in such dangerous times and unattended by his usual creature comforts. I know he would have Fanny but without my supervision she would become lazy or might even leave to help her own family. Left to his own devices Matthew would starve himself and would never change the bed-linen or wash his small-clothes. The house would be cold – need I go on? I cannot bear to think on it. As a wife you must surely understand my apprehension and help me. PLEASE, Henrietta.

Love to the children.

Your affectionate Sophie.

She sealed the letter and hid it at the back of the desk. She would despatch it the next day. Finally she crept back to bed with a lighter heart.

*

A pale sun lit up the churchyard and shone on the small group of people who stood beside a newly dug grave. Alfred Rice, miraculously untouched by the disease, stood bare-headed, his eyes closed, his hands clasped. Next to him Jem stared fixedly at the cheap coffin in which his mother's body lay awaiting interment. He held Maggie's hand, drawing a little comfort from her nearness. Almost too late for the simple service, Charlie had just joined them and had enjoyed a brief moment of glory as all eyes turned towards him. He sported a coat of blue silk (stolen, no doubt, thought Jem sourly) and floppy black bows adorned his satin shoes. The vicar had cast one astonished glance in his direction and then finished the prayer he was reading. Maggie and Jem had exchanged rueful looks and Alfred had scowled at his handsome son.

They all said, 'Amen' and, at a sign from the vicar, the sexton moved to the temporary coffin and carefully raised the side nearest the grave. It fell open and the body, wrapped in a cheap shroud and tied each end with cord, tumbled into the grave with a dull thump.

Alfred's face twitched. Jem whispered, 'Oh Ma!' Charlie fiddled with one of his curls and moved his lips as though in silent prayer. Maggie began to cry and Jem, fighting back his own tears, put his arm round her.

The vicar closed his book and bowed his head. Raising it again after a brief interval, he shook hands with each of them, murmuring final condolences. To Alfred he said, 'Forgive my haste but I have two more burials to administer.'

'Three in one day!'

'Four, to be precise, for one went before yours. Another case of . . . fever.' Seeing Alfred's expression change he added quickly, 'But the next two are not. One is a mere infant, found dead among the tombstones. Born out of wedlock, no doubt, and left to die.' He shook his head and Alfred tutted obligingly. 'The other was a young woman set upon by thieves. Died of a cracked skull, poor soul.'

'These are troubled times,' said Alfred, 'and will worsen before too long.'

'I fear so.' The vicar patted the old man on the shoulder and hurried away towards the church, his crow-like vestments fluttering in the breeze.

'Like an omen!' whispered Alfred.

'What's that, Pa?' asked Jem.

'Nothing.' He turned to Charlie. 'And what d'you

think you look like?' he demanded. 'Coming to your Ma's funeral done up like a dog's dinner! Not so much as a black ribbon. Where's your respect, you heartless wretch?'

Charlie grinned. 'I thought Ma would like it,' he told him. 'She liked to see me make a bit of a show. She always said I should have been born a gentleman.' Unperturbed by the rebuke he spun round to show himself off to better effect. 'What do you think? You must admit I do cut rather a dash.'

Maggie said, ''Tis unsuitable.'

Jem said, 'And where did the coat come from?'

'Bought it from a friend.'

'And where did *he* get it?'

'Ask no questions, hear no lies! But why pick on me? I'm here, but Fanny isn't. Missed her mother's burying!'

'You were late,' Alfred reminded him.

'But she's not just *late*,' he said, 'she's missing entirely!'

Maggie said, 'She couldn't come. She sent word. There's been trouble at her place. Her master wanted to send her packing but the mistress argued for her to stay.'

'Send her packing? What's she done?' Charlie asked.

Jem said bitterly, 'She's had a mother who died of the spotted fever. That's what she done! Plague, he said it was, and was unwilling to keep her on.'

'Plague!' Charlie's face paled. 'But you said – you told me –'

Alfred muttered, '''Twas a fever, nothing more!'

Charlie looked at Jem who went on, 'He finally said she could stay on as long as she didn't mix with her family. That's us!'

Maggie said, 'Poor Fanny. She'd want to be here, you know that well enough. Broke her poor heart, I shouldn't wonder, not being here, but what would she do without a job? She's got to live somehow.'

Jem nodded. 'Some of us have to earn an honest crust,' he said pointedly.

To show how little this jibe affected him, Charlie bent down to adjust the bow on one of his shoes and straightened up again to admire it. At that moment, the grave-digger appeared and asked if he should get on with his work. For a moment they all stared at him and from him into the grave where the body lay. Maggie covered her mouth with her hand and once more tears filled her eyes.

Alfred nodded. 'Fill it in,' he said. 'We can't do no more for her now, poor old girl!'

They watched as the first few spadefuls of earth pattered down but then turned away. Wordlessly they made their way towards the churchyard gate and as though in sympathy for their bereavement, the church bell began to toll.

*

Anne sat alone at the table, toying with the cold hashed mutton which Prue had served and deep in thought. After three mouthfuls she laid down the fork with a grunt of indifference and turned her head to stare into the flames of the fire, aware of an overwhelming sense of loss. This time yesterday she had been with Matthew; she had walked with him the best part of an hour. But it was never long enough. Their meetings were so infrequent and necessarily short; their partings were an agony to her, as they were, she hoped, to him also. The future seemed to hold nothing better and she could not imagine how she would endure it.

Anne wanted another husband; she was comfortably off financially but tired of living alone. She was by nature gregarious and found enforced solitude depressing. She had married at eighteen, imagining that she was exchanging the company of her parents for that of a husband. Almost immediately, however, she had realized her mistake because her husband was a middle-aged ship's captain who spent most of the year on the high seas. In the first flush of enthusiasm for married life, she had tried with some success to reconcile herself to his long absences, filling her days with home-making – polishing and dusting the furniture, and waxing the floors. She took a fierce delight in sewing sheets and pillows, making shirts, spinning a little when the mood took her, and weaving. She had taught herself lace-making and had looked forward to her husband's visits home in anticipation of the children he would give her.

They were married for many years and she loved

him for his genial humour but she was never with child. When he died, abroad of a foreign disease, she could not even bury his body for that was consigned to the depths of the sea. She found herself alone and, after her initial grief had subsided, began to look around for another husband. She had not intended to become involved with a married man but Matthew's good looks and romantic declarations had swept her off her feet while she had still believed him to be single. Her disappointment at discovering that he had a wife had been acute but by that time she was hopelessly infatuated and could not bring herself to put an end to the association. Now she told herself that being with him was all she lived for; life without him would be meaningless. If she allowed herself to consider his wife and children she was consumed by jealousy which she could not control and she had begged him never to speak of them to her.

''Tis so unfair!' she cried, with sudden vehemence. 'She cannot love him as I do yet she shares his bed!'

Anne longed for Matthew's body and was not ashamed to admit it (not to him but to herself) but, so far, she had had to be satisfied with a few stolen kisses. Matthew insisted that since the birth of their youngest child he was not his wife's lover and hinted that this restraint was on the orders of her physician. Anne wanted to believe him – she pretended that she did – but in fact she found it impossible and spent many anguished hours imagining them together.

She was still wallowing in this morass of self-pity when the door opened and her servant entered the room with a dish of cream. Prudence, at forty-five, was a few years older than her mistress who had inherited her with her marriage. Prue was small and round and now her shortsighted blue eyes widened in surprise as she saw the uneaten food on her mistress's plate.

'Don't gape like that, Prue,' Anne told her irritably. 'I didn't care for it. 'Twas stone cold.'

'But ma'am, you wouldn't let me heat it up!' Prue protested indignantly. 'And you could have had the fish pie. I asked you –'

'Oh, don't chatter so and take the wretched stuff away. And don't eat it yourself. You are too fat already. Give it to Banner. He will love it.'

'And the sweet cream?'

'I'm not hungry. I can't eat anything. Clear the table quickly and be gone. I can't think while you fuss round me.'

It was true, she reflected. She had lost her appetite; She had lost all interest in food and drink unless she could share it with Matthew and that seemed unlikely to happen very often for he was terrified to be seen with her in a public place. They had known each other for four months and had dined together only once. The inn at Whitechapel had proved a disaster. The food was unremarkable and the company too rough for her liking. Unfortunately she had drunk a little too much wine and her incautious asides to

Matthew about their fellow diners had caused offence. She has become the butt of ribald jokes and they were glad to settle the bill and leave. Anne thought it would be some time before she could persuade Matthew to entertain her again but for that she knew she had only herself to blame.

Miserably she stared round the small room which had once been the source of considerable pride and satisfaction to her. Regretfully, since meeting Matthew Devine, she had lost not only her appetite for food but also her interest in her surroundings. Her waking moments were now filled with a longing to see Matthew and she read his letters again and again until she knew them by heart. Matthew wrote beautiful letters in which he swore his undying love for her. 'You are my sun and moon . . .' She particularly liked that phrase. 'I yearn for a sight of you, my sweet, sweet Anne . . .'

With such assurances she could not doubt his sincerity. He obviously loved her with a passion which matched her own but what future was there for them while his wife and children claimed him. In moments of deepest despair she railed against him in her heart for having burdened himself with a wife and offspring. If only he had bided his time. It was not as though he loved his wife; he had constantly assured Anne that he had been an impetuous young man and had been hustled into the match with Sophie by his father who was eager to see him settled.

'Oh, 'tis hopeless!' she exclaimed and with a sigh she pushed back her chair and moved closer to the fire. As she knelt to add a few coals to the fire the door, which was slightly ajar, opened a little wider and Banner hurried into the room. Anne called the little dog to her so that she could feel his stomach and satisfy herself that the girl had obeyed her instructions. In Anne's opinion Prue was a greedy slut and would eat anything. The dog felt round enough and Anne sat down and patted her lap. He sprang up and within minutes was fast asleep and snoring gently. About ten minutes passed and then she heard a knocking at the street door and a moment later Prue came into the room.

'There's a gentleman to see you –' she began but Anne had leaped to her feet, throwing the dog to the floor.

'A gentleman? Which gentleman? Don't you yet know how to announce a guest?'

'His name's –' Taken aback by her mistress's reaction the man's name eluded her. 'It – it started with "D",' she said.

'Devine? Oh, it can't be!' Matthew had never dared to visit her at the house before. But Prue was nodding excitedly.

'Devine? Yes, mistress! That was the very name!'

Anne rushed to the mirror and tugged and pulled at her hair. It was too late now to change into a more becoming gown or add a few decorative spots to her face. She gazed at her ringless hands but her jewellery was upstairs. In an agony of indecision she stared at her reflection. Prominent blue eyes stared back; her face was a little too plump but her complexion was smooth enough and her dark hair curled naturally. She began to pinch a little colour into her cheeks but stopped abruptly. Perhaps it was better that Matthew should find her looking pale and wan, pining for love. Yet he had never seen her looking anything but perfect! Damnation! She threw up her hands in despair. He must take her as he found her. It did not matter. Nothing mattered except that he was here. Her lover had taken a bold step.

To Prue she cried, 'How do I look?' and then, without waiting for an answer, she ran out of the room and into the tiny hallway.

'Matthew! Oh my love!'

His face registered immediate alarm at this rash outburst in front of the servant but she threw her arms around his neck and kissed him. She went on kissing him in spite of his mumbled protests until he, too, abandoned all caution and returned her kisses. When they finally drew apart from their passionate embrace they became aware that Prue, open-mouthed with shock, was observing them unashamedly. Anne found her voice first.

'Don't stand there gawping, you useless creature,' she said and, with a flash of inspiration, added, 'Have you never seen a woman greet her brother? This is Matthew, home from abroad.' As Prue had apparently been struck dumb by the exhibition of affection Anne turned to Matthew. 'I sometimes think the poor woman is slow-witted.'

Prue gasped, 'Your brother?' and something in her tone implied disbelief.

Anne said airily, 'Oh, you've found your tongue, have you! Thank the Lord for that. Then fetch some ale at once. Enough for two and look quick about it.'

When she had gone Matthew let out a whistle of relief but asked, 'Was that wise, Anne?'

She pouted prettily.'Let me be the judge of that, *brother*!' and, linking her arm through his, she led the way into the parlour. The dog, remembering Anne's cavalier treatment of him earlier, regarded them sulkily from a corner of the room to which he had retreated but Anne was unaware of his resentment. Exhilarated by Matthew's unexpected arrival she positively glowed with excitement. Matthew had come to her house! He had been introduced to Prue as her brother so there was now no reason for him to refuse to make further visits. Happiness flooded through her as she imagined the possibilities ahead. She would send Prue out on an errand and they would be entirely alone.

She took his coat, offered him the seat she had just vacated and pulled up another so that they faced each other.

She reached out her hands and he took them in his own and held them tightly.

'Say that you love me!' she cried. 'Say it!'

'I do, but your servant –' he protested.

'Say the words, Matthew! I need to hear them.'

He lowered his voice. 'I love you. Indeed I do but –' He glanced anxiously towards the door.

'And I love you, Matthew, with all my heart.' She felt a surge of recklessness. What did it matter if Prue *did* know the truth? She knew better than to tittle-tattle. What matter if the whole world knew! Or if his wife knew. As long as they loved each other nothing else mattered.

'I've been so wretched without you,' she confessed. 'So lonely. I haven't eaten but we could dine together now. We have a fish pie, freshly made, and a cauliflower – and a dish of sweet cream –'

'But Anne, I cannot stay,' he protested. 'I intended to write to you but had no time so thought I would risk a brief visit –' He smiled, relaxing a little. 'I had an urge to see you in your own home so that I could imagine you here.'

She pulled down the corners of her mouth. 'And I would like to see where *you* live!' But that was not true and they both knew it. Anne could not bear to see the house where he lived with his family. The sight would depress her utterly and she had told him so on many occasions.

'But you will stay awhile?' she begged. 'I couldn't bear it if you left too soon.'

'I have come to tell you that I cannot meet you tomorrow as planned –' he began but she gave a cry of dismay and snatched her hands away.

'Oh Matthew! Not again! You are too cruel!'

'But I am with you now, my darling!' he protested. 'Rather than disappoint you again I have come in person. How is that cruel?' She did not answer but stared at him piteously. He went on, 'And wait until you hear my reason. You will not call me cruel then. You remember what we spoke about last time we met?'

Her gloom was dispelled instantly. 'You mean – oh Matthew!'

He nodded. 'I shall visit Sophie's brother tomorrow evening and see what arrangements can be made. Then all we have to do is wait for the right moment and – Voilà! We shall be rid of them. Your lover will be a free man! I have written to Giles but, so far, somewhat to my surprise, I have had no reply. But I am confident he will agree and then, my sweet Anne, we will have all the time in the world together!'

'Oh Matthew! My dear, dear Matthew!' She sprang to her feet but at that moment Prue's footsteps could be heard and she sat down again.

'I've brought the ale, mistress,' said Prue. 'Will your brother be wanting anything else?'

She laid a faint emphasis on the word 'brother' but Anne ignored it. She was searching for an excuse to send her out. 'Yes, he will,' she told her. 'I want you to fetch some oysters.' To Matthew she said, 'Your favourite food! You see I haven't forgotten!'

'Oysters? Oh, oysters! Yes! I adore them.' He smiled at Prue who regarded him stonily.

Anne said, 'Take some money from the jar.'

Prue said, 'Shall I hurry back, same as always?'

Anne hesitated. Normally she was always at great pains to make the woman hurry. She suspected that on many occasions Prue took her time in the markets or loitered at the conduit chatting with her feckless friends but today Anne wanted as much time as possible alone with Matthew. Prue was obviously unconvinced that Matthew was a brother and the wretch was trying to make capital out of the situation. Prue stared at her with a challenging expression as Anne struggled to overcome her reluctance to allow her this small triumph.

At last she said, 'On this occasion you may take your time – within reason. Matthew and I have so much to talk about.'

'Thank you, mistress.'

When she had gone Matthew laughed, 'I cannot abide oysters!'

'Then I shall eat them for you.'

The street door slammed and Anne smiled. 'She wasted no time. Went before I could change my mind – as if I would! Oh Matthew, when your family is gone we will be free. We can spend our nights together! Oh kiss me, Matthew. Say that you love me. I cannot hear it enough.'

They sat beside the fire and drank ale together, revelling in the novelty of the situation. Anne gave a lot of thought to how far she would allow Matthew to go if he wanted to make love to her. She must not allow too many liberties on this first occasion and yet she must not discourage him. She must not appear too forward. Matthew must make the first move. Then, little by little over the coming weeks, she would give him his heart's desire. Her own passionate nature must not betray her into anything precipitous.

She was still waiting for him to take the initiative when Prue came back and the chance was lost. He jumped to his feet at once, insisting that he had stayed too long, but Anne reminded him about the oysters and he was forced to sit down again. Unseen by Prue, Anne ate most of them and threw the rest on to the fire. Then reluctantly she helped Matthew into his coat and bade him farewell, standing at the street door to see him go.

For Prue's benefit she called after him, 'If your lodgings are not to your taste I can recommend others in the Strand.'

When she returned to the kitchen Prue was already busy, attending to a basketful of ironing. Trying to make amends for her earlier behaviour, thought Anne, but she let the moment pass.

'Did he like the oysters?' Prue asked with a nod towards the empty plates.

'Very much.'

'I wish I had a brother half as handsome as yours.'

Anne gave her a sharp look but Prue returned the look with one of exaggerated innocence.

'And *I* wish you would concentrate on your work,' said Anne, 'and chatter less.' This small snub effectively ended the conversation.

Anne retired to the parlour to reflect at leisure on the implications of Matthew's unexpected visit and the news he had brought. If his wife was sent away to the country with the children and Matthew's mother . . .

Her musings were interrupted by a most unpleasant thought which, by some strange oversight, had only just occurred to her. She sat up abruptly, frowning. If plague came to London, Matthew intended to ensure the safety of his family but he expected Anne to remain in town! Presumably he had been so bemused by the prospect of the unlimited time they could spend together that he, too, had failed to realize the risks to which she would undoubtedly be exposed. For a while she was cast down by this unkind twist of fate but, by the time she was ready for bed, she had come to terms with the problem. She would make it clear to Matthew that it was only her love for him which kept her in such a dangerous city when lesser women were fleeing for their lives. Under so great an obligation, he could then be made aware of the only way in which he could repay her devotion.

Chapter Four

HE SECOND DAY OF May found Fanny on her knees, scrubbing the kitchen floor, using more energy than she had used for many months past and muttering vindictively to herself as she worked. Her hands were raw from the soapy water (left over after the washing had been done); her knees were sore from contact with the hard flagstones and her back ached. Again and again she plunged the brush fiercely into the bucket and attacked the floor as though it were an enemy, then seized the cloth with which to wipe off the excess water. She then wrung this out vigorously, twisting it with all her might, almost strangling it, before applying it once more to the flagstones.

A small part of her resentment came from the fact that washing the floor was not her job. Mistress Quilley was employed on Mondays and Thursdays to do the heavy work but her daughter's husband had been badly injured in a fall from a ladder. This meant that the daughter was caring for her injured husband and four of their children while Mistress Quilley was having to care for the remaining three of her grandchildren until their mother could resume responsibility for all of them. Fanny was in no mood to suffer fools gladly and in her opinion a thatcher who could not stay on his ladder was in the wrong business. It was her suspicion, based on certain information that had come her way, that the fall had been the result of too much alcohol and in her present state of mind she had no sympathy for any of them.

The greater part of her resentment, however, dated back nearly two weeks and centred on her mother's burial and the fact that Matthew Devine had refused permission for her to attend. Her mother's death had come as a great shock but her sorrow had been compounded by dismay and then anger when she was told that she must stay away from the church and from the rest of her grieving family. Failure to attend was to Fanny a most serious dereliction of duty and one that her mother would never have understood or condoned. She imagined her mother's ghost hovering over the menfolk gathered at the graveside, looking in vain for her only daughter. Denied the natural opportunity to express her feelings, Fanny had channelled her emotions into a feverish hostility focused on the man she had once so much admired – Matthew Devine. She had sworn never to forgive him for what she considered his unnecessary cruelty. In a short space of time her high opinion of her master had been replaced by hatred. She made no attempt to hide her feelings, in fact she went out of her way to reveal them, although Sophie had hinted several times that she might well be looking for alternative employment if she did not watch her tongue.

Now Fanny gave vent to a little of her repressed anger.

'I'd like to scrub your face!' she told her absent employer as she raked the coarsely bristled brush over the floor for the last time and reached for the cloth. 'How would you like it if 'twas *your* mother that died and I refused *you* leave to pay your last respects? I hate you, Matthew Devine! D'you hear me? I hate you!'

The task finished at last, she struggled to her feet and staggered towards the back door with the bucket of dirty water. Outside in the yard, with a wild swing of the bucket, she threw its contents over the ground crying, 'Take that, damn you!' and wished she were throwing it into her master's face. 'I'll pay you out, you'll see!' she vowed. 'I'll make you sorry!' She thought of her mother's frail body being lowered into the dark grave and tears sprang into her eyes. Furiously she brushed them away. 'He'll suffer, Ma!' she promised. 'He'll live to rue the day he kept me from you. I wanted to come. I did! Oh Ma! Ma! Forgive me!'

In an agony of remorse she sent the leather bucket flying against the wall. It bounced back, fell to the ground and rolled once. Running forward, she kicked it as hard as she could, willing it to split. She snatched it up and wrenched at the handle then, with all her remaining strength, hurled it once more to the ground and burst into a torrent of weeping.

'Fanny! Oh, you foolish girl!' She glanced up to see her mistress at the back door, a look of exasperation on her face. Picking up the bucket, Fanny walked as slowly as she dared into the kitchen where Sophie waited, stern-faced.

'This won't do, Fanny,' Sophie told her. 'You must come to your senses before 'tis too late. Here, blow your nose and heed what I say.' She handed Fanny a handkerchief which she accepted reluctantly. Sophie went on, 'I know exactly why you are behaving this way. 'Tis hard on you, I know, but I did argue with my husband. He insisted.'

'He had no right!' muttered Fanny, scowling.

'He thought it for the best –'

'Best for who? For him, I dare say, but not for me.'

'For all of us,' Sophie insisted calmly. 'Even best for you. But whether you liked the decision or not, you must put it behind you and stop behaving like a sullen child.'

'The old lady hates me, too!' Fanny told her. 'Won't have me in the room. I might as well be a leper!'

'Nobody hates you. You do exaggerate so.'

'The master does.'

'And I tell you he does not. He did what he did –'

'For his own good! And because he hates me. Well, I hate him!' She glared defiantly at her mistress. 'If he wants to send me packing –'

'I fear he will if you go on this way. I don't want to lose you, Fanny, but you must see that your behaviour is making everything worse?'

Fanny felt a twinge of conscience. She had no quarrel with her mistress. What she said was true – she *had* tried to reason with Matthew on Fanny's behalf and for that Fanny was grateful.

Sophie continued, her expression anxious, 'These are troubled times, Fanny. It does seem that the plague will come – there are one or two cases this last week or so – and God knows what will become of us if it does.' Her tone changed slightly and she sat down on a stool. 'Matthew is determined to send us away to the country. He will listen to no arguments and I am torn in half between staying with him and going with the children.'

Fanny's eyes narrowed. 'Who's "us"?' she demanded. She was aware of her mistress's reluctance as she hesitated before answering.

'Myself, the children and the master's mother. We would have to stay with my brother in Woolwich and the house will be full to overflowing. There wouldn't be room for you, Fanny, but anyway, someone must stay here to look after the master.'

Hiding her dismay at this bleak prospect, Fanny tossed her head. 'Then I'll be off, mistress, as soon as you've gone! I'll not care for the master. Not after what he did to me. Never!' She was pleased to see that these words had the desired effect on her mistress.

'But Fanny,' she cried, 'where will you go if you leave? Other families will leave London also. Like rats leaving a sinking ship, so Mistress Devine says! A few have already gone. They have closed up their homes, leaving their servants to fend for themselves. Even if I have to go you will still have a home here and will be well cared for. Oh, please, do be sensible. Think it over. Try to forgive Matthew for my sake.'

'I'll try,' Fanny conceded, 'but I know I never will. And if you go to the country I'll run away.' Despite her brave words she felt her lips tremble. 'I'll take my chance.'

'Fanny!' cried Sophie. 'Can't you see that I want to help you? Please don't take everything so personally.' To Fanny's surprise she held out her hand but Fanny quickly withrew her own.

'I mean it!' she cried shakily. 'If you abandon me I'll do whatsoever I please!'

Before Sophie could remonstrate further Fanny darted past her and raced upstairs to her room in the attic. There she threw herself on the bed and surrendered once more to the relief of tears.

*

Charlie took the proffered broadsheet and glanced at it carelessly.

'. . . A main of cocks to be fought at the Cockpit at Whitehall this same afternoon . . .' He wavered as he read on. He had just left the gaming house in Bell Yard with a pocketful of coins and, flushed with success, was loath to risk losing them again. But a cockfight! It was his favourite sport. '. . . None to weigh less than three pounds six ounces nor more than four pounds eight ounces . . .'

Unconsciously he half turned in the direction of Whitehall and began to walk along the Strand. He had intended to call in on Fanny and tell her about the funeral. Jem had said she was 'mighty put out' at missing it and it seemed excuse enough. If the mistress was out, he was usually fed on cakes and ale and made much of, although things were not so easy since the plague rumours had started. If either of the Devines were at home it was doubtful he would get so much as a toe in the door and his journey would have been in vain. He read on, undecided. '. . . to fight in silver spurs and with fair hackles and to be subject to all the rules as practised in London this fourteenth day of April, 1665 . . .'

He came to a stop outside Bedford House and hesitated again. If he did not go to the cockfight or to Fanny's, there was time for a quick trip to Clare Market where he might buy himself a new sash or a second-hand cravat with some of his newly acquired wealth. He had seen the young farmer's wife at the market again and had noted the admiration in her eyes. Charlie knew he was handsome and that a man was judged by the clothes he wore. He had made a few inquiries and knew where the young wife lived. It seemed more than likely he would pay her a visit in the near future and he wanted to impress her.

Clare Market, however, was in the opposite direction to Whitehall and he tapped his foot indecisively. 'Damn it! I'll go for the cravat!' he decided and turned abruptly on his heel before he could change his mind. He could take in a cockfight some other day, he reflected cheerfully. He was taking a short cut through to Wich Street when the door of a house opened suddenly just as he passed and a young woman darted out and collided heavily with him. As he offered a hand to pull her to her feet he noticed with pleasure that she had a smooth complexion, unmarked by the ravages of smallpox. He did so appreciate a good complexion; that and white teeth. He could forgive a lot for good teeth and skin.

'More haste, less speed!' he told her with a marked lack of originality but gave her the benefit of one of his brightest smiles by way of compensation.

She said brusquely, 'You've come to no harm, seemingly,' and for the first time he became aware that her expression was grim.

Without receiving any encouragement, Charlie turned on his heels and fell into step beside her even though she was walking away from the market.

'He won't see me there again!' she told him firmly. 'Wash me, he says. The impudence of the man. I'm not washing that scrawny body. He's no kin of mine. I'm off home to my Ma and I told him so. Ugh!' She shuddered and strode on, her head in the air, her mouth fixed in a tight line.

'What ails him?' Charlie asked. 'This old man of yours.'

'We shall never know,' she said. 'Moan, moan, moan, that's him. First he's too hot and then he's too cold. Won't eat. Can't sleep. Won't call in a physician. Stubborn as a mule! Well, he can rot for all I care. I've done all I'm doing for the old fool.'

Charlie was thinking fast. Had a kind fate given him another chance to earn a few coins? 'All alone then, is he?'

'He is now!'

As they turned the next corner Charlie put a restraining hand on her arm. 'Dying, is he?' he asked.

She gave him a long, hard stare. 'What's it to you?' she asked suspiciously.

Charlie shrugged. Then, seeing that she regarded him in a way that was less than friendly, he made her a mock bow and, leaving her in the middle of the street, he hurried back the way they had come.

When he reached the house he went up the steps as boldly as though he lived there and with a fast beating heart, turned the handle. He was right. In her haste she had not bothered to lock the door behind her. Inside he quickly saw that the furniture was not cheap, the large mirror over the fireplace was gilded and several good rugs covered the floor. Before his courage could desert him he went to the foot of the stairs and called, 'Hullo there!'

A weak voice answered him and he ran up the narrow stairs in search of the bedroom. An elderly man with a white beard lay in a huge four-poster bed. Beside him on the floor was an unemptied chamber pot, and uneaten food was congealing on a tray on the bedside table. Only a candle stub remained in the candlestick and, as well as these signs of neglect, a smell of sickness was in the air. Charlie swallowed uncomfortably.

'Your maid sent me,' he lied and searched for a false name for himself. There was no point in taking any chances in case the old man survived. 'Samuel Bennett at your service. Your maid tells me you are sick and like to die. Would you have me fetch a physician before 'tis too late?'

'Like to die?' cried the old man. 'She said that? Oh the wicked girl!'

Charlie forced a smile as his eyes examined the room for anything of value. 'So you are not sick? I am sent here on a fool's errand. Then I'll say "Good day" to you, sir, and be on my way.'

He made as though to leave the room but the man held up a bony hand imploringly. 'Wait! Wait!' he cried. 'You young people are so impetuous!' He drew a long breath. 'It may be I do need the services of a physician.'

'What is it?' Charlie asked, his tone brisk and businesslike. 'Sciatica? Stone? Gangrene? Gout?' He recited them in a sing-song way, like a chant. 'Palsy? Pleurisy? – Plague?'

All the remaining colour fled from the old man's face at this last word. Clutching the bed sheets convulsively he began to shake his head. 'No, no!' he murmured. Faster and faster went his head as Charlie watched in amazement as the denials grew louder and the movement of his head more wild.

'Steady, old man!' cried Charlie but suddenly, without warning, the old man stopped. He closed his eyes, lay back on the pillow and let out a long sigh.

'Hullo?' Charlie ventured. There was no reply. Disconcerted he waited but the figure on the bed did not move.

'Hullo there?' Charlie repeated. He stepped forward and laid his hand gently on the man's thin shoulder. 'Has he snuffed it?' Taken aback by the speed of events Charlie stood beside the still figure. Eventually he bent down to peer into his face. The eyes were staring, the mouth was open.

'God's truth!'

First his mother; now this stranger. Death seemed to be following him around! It occurred to him that perhaps he should not linger. Whatever had killed the old man just might kill him too. Was it plague? He had a vague idea about the disease although the idea did not trouble him unduly. His philosophy was that he would go when his time came and not before. Death did not frighten him; he looked upon it more as an inconvenience. He was enjoying life and he wanted it to continue and certainly would not spoil what time he had with useless apprehensions.

Peering at the dead man, he looked for tokens upon the transparent skin but saw nothing to alarm him.

He straightened up, losing interest. 'Frightened himself to death, most likely, silly old goat!'

It took him a moment or two to come to his senses. The valuable objects in the house now lacked an owner and were his for the taking. He had intended to earn a shilling or so running errands for the old man and had not expected such a windfall but he accepted it gratefully nonetheless. From the bedside table he took a small snuff-box which he slipped into his waistcoat pocket. There was no time to lose for the old man might have relatives and Charlie had no intention of being discovered here with his pockets bulging. Downstairs he found a pair of silver buckles which would fetch a good price and, in a gold frame, a miniature of a woman in a green gown. Regretfully he rejected one or two larger items in case he was seen leaving the house. If he was intercepted on the way out he would say he was passing and heard groans and was now on his way to fetch a physician. Charlie understood the word discretion and would take only those items which could be hidden conveniently about his person, for he had no wish to be chased down the street by a constable.

This planned deception proved unnecessary, however, for when he left the house no one outside evinced the slightest interest in him. Beaming at his good fortune, he was soon on his way to find Will Wardle, his 'fence' who would convert his stolen goods into hard cash. Wardle would ask no questions and Charlie would tell no lies!

*

Luke laid down his book and said quietly, 'The plague is gaining ground. The death toll for May is up on April's total and we are not yet into June. The weather is going to be decisive. A hot summer will prove disastrous.' He shrugged.

His sister said nothing. She kept her head bent over her sewing and the needle flashed in and out through the soft creamy cambric of the new bodice. She was setting in the sleeve, trying to keep her mind occupied.

'They are openly reporting plague cases now,' he went on. 'I spoke with Doctor Marcham this afternoon and he says it is spreading into St Clement Danes in the Strand and another case is reported in Holborn near St Andrews.'

She glanced across at him, startled. 'Why then, 'tis creeping slowly across the city from the west to the east, for all the world like a live thing! Like a giant slug. An evil, poisonous slug!' She shuddered.

''Tis a disgusting thought,' he agreed. 'But the Privy Council has been in session and is beginning to consider what measures it can take.'

At last Lois laid down her work and Luke thought how drawn she looked. The uncertainty was affecting people in different ways. She was not eating as well as she should and had lost a little weight. Lois had never married and was devoted to her nephew, Antony, and Luke guessed that her main anxiety stemmed from Antony's refusal to leave London.

'Can they take *any* precautions?' she asked. 'The Privy Council inspire very little confidence in *this* breast!' She placed a hand across her chest by way of emphasis. 'What do they know about the plague that they didn't know last time it devastated the city?' Her voice held a trace of bitterness which Luke understood, for the young man she had hoped to wed had died in the previous outbreak.

Luke considered her question seriously before answering. The situation was hardly reassuring. Many years before a pesthouse had existed for the inhabitants of St Giles but it had since been taken over for use as a workhouse. Now, urgently, it seemed a new one had been authorized, to be built on a site in Marylebone. It was to be a solid affair on a brick foundation and work was already going ahead as a matter of priority. They would soon be advertising for a master to run it and Luke had secretly considered applying. Upon reflection he had decided against it. If, as he suspected, nothing halted the spread of the infection, the pest-house would soon be filled to overflowing and the plight of those unfortunates who could not be admitted would be even more desperate.

'They are building a new pesthouse at a place called Mutton Fields,' he told her. 'Very modern and it will have its own well. And there's talk of another at Soho Fields for the people around St Martins.'

'*Two* pesthouses!' Her tone expressed disapproval. 'It sounds ominous. They're obviously expecting the worst.'

He laughed. 'Now be fair, Lois. If they *failed* to provide them you would accuse them of negligence!'

He suddenly remembered another snippet of news passed on to him by Doctor Marcham who had it first hand from the friend of a member of the Privy Council. A Frenchman named Angier had been claiming amazing successes in various parts of France when the plague had taken a hold there. It was claimed he had stopped the spread of infection by fumigating the houses with a 'secret, new and most efficacious remedy' of his own invention. It was said to be a mixture of amber, saltpetre and brimstone which, when heated, gave off powerful fumes.

By way of reassurance, Luke described it all in some detail but his sister remained unimpressed.

'Just like the French!' she exclaimed. 'Just the sort of nonsense they would dream up. Well, I shan't be burning it in this house, I can tell you. We'd never get rid of the smell.'

Luke hid a wry smile, well aware that if the need arose she would try any method, however bizarre, that might save their lives. 'The King has invited him to England,' he told her, 'to demonstrate his remedy. So we shall know before too long.'

'I can tell you now!' Lois declared. 'He's a charlatan.'

He laughed. 'You can't be certain.'

'He's French, isn't he? Nothing good ever came out of that benighted country. They don't like us and we don't like them.' She re-threaded her needle and then glanced irritably towards the window. 'I just want to finish this sleeve and I do so hate working in the half light. Candle light is even worse. My eyes aren't as good as they once were.'

Reverting to her earlier comments, Luke asked, 'What have the French ever done to you?'

'Nothing. And they'd better not try!'

'*We* burnt Joan of Arc at the stake,' he reminded her. 'They'll never forgive us for that and can you blame them?'

Instead of answering, she glanced up and said, 'Antony's late. He spends too much time in the Golden Horn with those wild friends of his.'

'He deserves a little pleasure. He insisted on coming with me on my rounds this morning.' He sighed. 'I think it depresses him but I cannot dissuade him from coming.' Luke stood up and stretched his arms above his head. 'Well, this won't do. I must be off.'

Lois said, 'Where are you off to now? It's nigh on supper-time and I've made some sugar cakes. The ones you like.'

He grinned suddenly and his face was at once transformed. 'The ones *Antony* likes, you mean! That boy can twist you round his little finger.'

She returned the smile but only briefly. 'I do wish he'd go to Italy as you suggested,' she said. 'He might regain his interest in painting. He might be inspired to use that talent of his instead of frittering his life away ... I had a dream last night – a bad dream.'

'Don't tell me!' he begged. 'I have enough of my own!'

'I must,' she said, 'or else it will come true.'

'That's superstitious nonsense.'

She went on as though he had not spoken, 'I dreamed Antony fell sick and he was lying in the middle of a dense wood and I was looking for him, in and out of the trees, and you were nowhere to be found and – and I went round and round in circles and then I found him dead. . . Oh Luke!'

Neither of them spoke as the dreadful image burned itself into their minds.

She said shakily, 'If anything happens to that boy –'

'It won't!' He put his hands on her shoulders and looked into her eyes. 'Would I let my own son die? Now would I?'

She shook her head but the doubt in her eyes remained. 'It was so vivid. So real!'

Clumsily Luke put his arms round her and gave her a brief hug. 'Put it out of your mind,' he told her. 'What sort of physician would I be if I couldn't save my own son?' Releasing her, he moved to fetch his coat before she could speak further. 'I have promised to look in on one or two of my patients.'

Her fear returned with a rush. 'Plague patients?' she asked.

'Too early to say,' he answered with an attempt at cheerfulness.

She rushed after him and clung to his arm. 'But the infection, Luke. The risk!'

Gently he disentangled himself. ''Tis all in hand. The College are designing a suit of protective clothing for us to wear when attending plague patients.'

'Protective? But how can anything –'

'Made of leather. A lightweight suede. Full-length with some kind of head covering. We'll be safe as houses. Now stop worrying and –' He broke off as footsteps sounded in the street outside. 'Here comes Antony now.'

The door opened and Antony came in. As soon as he saw that his father was wearing his coat he said, 'I'll come!' but Luke shook his head.

'A woman due to give birth any day!' he lied cheerfully. 'She won't welcome onlookers!'

Lois hid her surprise but Antony asked, 'But why a physician? Why not a midwife?'

'The mother had problems with the last birth. Now I'm on my way. You stay and eat some of your

aunt's sugar cakes. I'll be back in less than an hour.'
And he hurried out of the house to prevent further
argument.

*

Sophie woke up panic-stricken, sensing disaster. As
her thoughts cleared, fragments of nightmare slipped
from her mind, resisting her efforts to retain them.
What was happening? What was going to happen?
Her heart raced as she stared up into the darkness,
trying to convince herself that the nightmare was to
blame for her fear but the terror persisted. Slowly
she sat up in the bed, conscious of her pounding
heart. What am I frightened of, she asked herself.
Matthew slept soundly beside her with the bedclothes tucked around his neck. She had teased him
about that many times, describing him as a dormouse
in a nest but now, as she turned towards him in the
gloom, the reason for her panic struck her with a
terrible clarity. Her husband Matthew no longer
loved her.

She had to clamp a hand over her mouth to
muffle an involuntary gasp of fear and a wave of
faintness seized her. For a moment the familiar room
seemed to spin.

'Oh Matt!' she whispered.

The back of his head was so familiar and yet, if he
no longer loved her, she was sleeping with a stranger.
She put a trembling hand to her chest in a vain
attempt to slow down her rapidly beating heart. But

was it true? *Had* Matthew stopped loving her? He had never so much as hinted at such a thing and yet her awareness of change had been growing within her for weeks. Tonight, it seemed, her subconscious suspicions had crystallized into certainty. During her sleep, the certainty had surfaced with devastating effect.

'Matt!' she said again. She longed to wake him and beg for reassurance but suppose he could not give it? Suppose he confirmed her fears? She dared not risk it.

Suddenly she felt unable to stay in the same bed with him and slid out carefully. Pulling on her wrap, she moved across to the window and stared unseeingly into the street below. The terrible question hammered at her brain. Was it true? Had Matthew stopped loving her and if so, how had it happened? Below her, the street was lit by a pale dawn light and the sweepers were still busy with their rakes and brooms, removing the worst of the previous day's rubbish and piling it into their carts. Carefully she pushed open the window and leaned out. The air was warm, promising a fine day. It appeared that spring was giving way to the hot summer everyone dreaded. She thought fleetingly of the threat of plague but now her horror of the disease had been overshadowed by her fears for her marriage.

How could Matt have stopped loving her, she wondered despairingly. What had she done – or left undone? How had she changed? She put a hand to her head and then, forsaking the street scene, sank down on to a nearby chair and willed herself to think clearly and honestly. Had she been less loving towards her husband since she had had the children or had she been less careful about her own appearance? She did not think she was guilty of either but the children did take up a large amount of her time. She searched for other possibilities. Had Ruth turned Matt against her? It seemed unlikely for the old lady had little to gain from a disunited family. Nor did Sophie think that Ruth would deliberately do anything that might adversely affect the children. True Ruth had not wanted Sophie as a wife for Matt but she now seemed resigned to the situation.

Was Matt regretting the fact that he had married beneath him? Sophie's heart skipped a beat as this unwelcome idea struck her. Perhaps he no longer considered her suitable to mix socially with his colleagues and their wives.

For a moment she stared longingly at the huddled shape in the bed. It was nearly three weeks since they had made love and that was a long time for Matthew. He was an eager lover; she could never fault him on that score, she thought with a faint smile. Of course, he was working long hours now that Henry Bolsover was having difficulties. She had assumed he was simply overtired, weighed down with all the extra responsibilities – and the worry about the plague was certainly not making his life any easier. She began almost imperceptibly to feel better, to recover a little of her composure and tried to convince herself that perhaps, after all, she was imagining dragons where none existed. She herself was tired. Running a home and coping with two lively youngsters was not easy and Ruth could be difficult at times. Perhaps the marriage was as stable as any marriage could be in such anxious times.

'Of course he loves me!' she whispered with as much conviction as she could manage.

She must not allow herself to become hysterical. That would serve no useful purpose. She must stay calm and in control of her emotions. She took a deep breath and let it out slowly. She would wait until Matt woke and then ask him if there was anything wrong; anything that she ought to know about.

He moved in the bed, grunting as he turned over. Stretching, he opened his eyes sleepily and caught sight of her on the chair.

In spite of her good resolutions Sophie found herself watching, hawk-like, for any tell-tale sign that his love for her had faded. Was it her imagination or did he avert his gaze guiltily? Surely he looked at her differently. Dear God! Throwing caution to the wind, she had actually begun to frame her question when his voice cut across hers.

'We have to talk, Sophie,' he told her.

Sophie uttered a strangled cry and almost fell from the chair. She felt as though she was suffocating and it was all she could do to recover her balance. He sat up in bed, alarmed.

'Sophie? Are you sick?'

'No, no! Talk about what, Matt?' Her voice sounded as though it came from someone else.

He stared at her.

'Matt! We have to talk about *what*?' She looked at him desperately, steeling herself for the worst.

'Come back to bed, Sophie. I'll –'

'Matt!' She almost screamed at him. 'You said we must talk.'

'Oh yes. About you going to the country, to Giles's place. You and the children and my mother. Giles is quite willing that you should go. At first I thought he was somewhat reluctant – I was quite shocked that he could refuse shelter to kinfolk at times like these –'

'Going to stay with Giles?'

'In Woolwich. It might be necessary.'

She stared at him. 'Is that what you wanted to talk about? Is that all?'

'Isn't that enough?' He stared at her in surprise. 'You have fought me every inch of the way on this and now you ask, "Is that all?" Sometimes, Sophie, I don't understand you at all.'

Her relief was overwhelming.

'Oh Matt!' she cried and ran across the room to throw herself on to the bed beside him. 'I've been so afraid. I thought – Oh no! 'Tis of no account. Matt, you do love me, don't you? You do love all of us – me, Ollie and Lizbeth? Please say you do!'

'But certainly I do!' He looked at her suspiciously.

'What has brought on such a question, Sophie? Are you sure you are not sick? Not feverish?'

She shook her head, smiling broadly. Being sent away to stay with Giles had paled into insignificance beside her earlier fears.

He said suddenly, 'You are not – Sophie! Are you with child?'

'No!'

'Heavens be praised!'

She felt hurt by his heartfelt rejoinder; wounded by the thought that if she had been pregnant he would not have welcomed the child. A little of her joy faded. In a cold, quiet voice she said, 'Have no fear, Matthew. I am not going to give you another child.'

She waited for him to realize his mistake and apologize but he appeared distracted.

'The situation is getting worse daily,' he told her. 'I think if we leave it too long you may have difficulty getting out of London. Henry thinks they are going to reintroduce health certificates. If you don't have one you won't be allowed to enter any of the surrounding towns and villages. I would be much happier if you were to leave London. Henrietta will make you very welcome.'

Sophie felt slightly betrayed by Henrietta although she knew she was being unfair. Henrietta *had* tried to dissuade Giles and had almost succeeded but Matthew had gone down to Woolwich to discuss it and obviously Giles had agreed. After that there was no reason for Henrietta to pretend unwillingness and she had obviously told Matthew that she would welcome them.

'You and the children will have to share a room,' Matt was saying, 'but 'tis large enough. You must take some bedding – we will hire a cart – and I have agreed a sum of money to be paid to them weekly. My mother will be accommodated in Sarah's room and Sarah will move in with her sisters. 'Tis only for a few weeks.'

'Weeks?' said Sophie. 'Months, surely!' It occurred to her that perhaps this was what had made Matthew appear so distant of late. He had been preparing to insist on their departure and had expected arguments. Sophie had intended to argue. She had however given in without a fight and she now saw with fresh panic that she was going to be separated from the man she loved.

'I will go, Matt, but not just yet,' she told him. 'Let's wait a while. And only if 'tis truly necessary. I cannot bear to leave you here alone.'

'I shall have Fanny –' he began.

Sophie hesitated. 'Fanny says she will not stay with you, Matt. Not since her mother's death. She has never forgiven you.'

'She'll stay,' said Matt grimly. 'Or if she leaves she'll come back. Where else can she go at such a time? She talks wildly but she has her wits about her. But what if she does leave me? I shall fare well enough on my own. I shall eat out, if needs be, and

Mistress Quilley is back with us. She will come in to wash and clean.'

Sophie said, 'We'll wait a few weeks, and then maybe, if matters are no better –'

'They'll be much worse, Sophie, and you know it!' His voice was harsh. 'I think you should pack and go as soon as may be.'

'No!' She stared at him defiantly. 'I'll go when I'm ready, Matt, so please don't try to browbeat me. I'll go when I must but not before.'

There was an uncomfortable silence while she tried to read the expression in his eyes. Something troubled her but it was so elusive. Suddenly she knew what it was. Matt was eager for her to be gone. He had not said he would miss her or that the house would be empty without the children. He had given not the slightest hint that he was reluctant to be separated from his wife and children.

Watching him closely she asked, 'Will you miss us, Matt?'

Again that strange expression in his eyes. 'Naturally. What man would not miss his family?'

She tried to meet his eyes but saw with dismay that he quickly lowered his gaze and all her earlier fears came flooding back. 'We shall see then,' she said, deliberately non-committal.

After a moment he said, 'Are you determined to stay and catch the plague? Eh? Are you going to put Ollie and Lizbeth at risk simply because you would prefer to stay in London with me?' He shook his head. 'I can't believe that of you, Sophie. You have always been such a good mother –'

'I still am a good mother!' she cried. 'Don't you dare suggest otherwise!' She felt her temper rising and tears pricked at her eyelids. This then was Matt's final weapon. He was going to challenge her love for the children. He was forcing her hand. As she looked at him she saw that he did not look at her with love but with what she could only interpret as veiled animosity.

'You want to get rid of me!' she whispered.

'That's arrant nonsense,' he retorted angrily. 'And you know it. I think I've heard quite enough for one morning. I shall be late for work if I sit here arguing.'

''Tis Saturday,' she reminded him dully.

He hesitated. 'I have some papers to discuss with Henry,' he said and reached under the bed for his slippers. Automatically Sophie rang for the hot water. As she sat in miserable silence she heard Ruth calling querulously from the back bedroom.

'I'm coming!' she answered but made no move to go to her. She sat on the bed as Matt washed and dressed. She passed comment on the fact that he put on his new suit with the lace neckcloth and braid trimming.

'I'll wear what I choose,' he snapped.

She heard him go downstairs and straight out of the house and she ran to the window and watched him leave. His back was stiff and he walked quickly.

From the back bedroom Ruth's voice rose irritably. 'Sophie! I'm calling you!'

Sophie muttered, 'Damn you! And damn your son!' and longed for the relief of tears but at that moment Ollie came into the room to tell her that Grandmother was calling for her.

She knelt down and kissed him. 'I know. I'm just coming.' Somehow she managed a cheerful smile but as she followed him out of the room she wondered with a heavy heart how she could possibly get through the day.

Chapter Five

THE TWO SMALL FACES, turned up to Sophie's, puckered in disappointment as she shook her head.

'Oh Mama! Why can't we?' wailed Oliver. 'We haven't been to see them for ages and ages!'

'And ages!' added Lizbeth dutifully. 'They'll be hungry.'

'They'll starve!' said Oliver mournfully. 'They'll get thinner and thinner and then they'll flutter down and die.'

'They'll do nothing of the kind,' Sophie told them, 'because the bird lady will feed them. She has plenty of seeds for them.'

'But why, Mama?' Oliver persisted. 'Why can't we feed them? Fanny says we can't go out! Why can't we?'

Lizbeth pouted. 'Is it because of the wrath of God? Grandmother says –'

Sophie came to a sudden decision and sat down, drawing the two children to her. She had avoided telling them of the extent of the threat to the city for fear of alarming them but now she decided that perhaps the plain truth was the best course.

'I don't know anything about the wrath of God,' she began carefully, 'but there is a great deal of trouble in London. There is a sickness – a very serious sickness – which is getting worse.'

As she searched for the right way to continue, Oliver said, 'Poor old London!'

She smiled at him. 'Poor old London, indeed,' she agreed. 'The sickness is flying about in the air, at least we think it is, and if people breathe in too much of the bad air they get sick.'

'I was sick once,' Lizbeth cried eagerly. 'I was sick on my nightgown and Fanny had to wash it.' She turned to her brother and added triumphantly, 'I was sick. You weren't!'

Sophie said, '''Tis a different kind of sickness, children. This bad kind of sickness makes people die.' She hesitated. 'At least it does sometimes. You remember when Grandfather died?'

They nodded earnestly although Lizbeth had been too young to recall much of the events.

Oliver said, 'Is that why we have to keep the windows shut? Fanny said 'twas to keep out the street smell.'

Lizbeth gave an exaggerated gasp. 'Fanny told a *lie*!'

They both looked at Sophie for an explanation of this wickedness. She said quickly, 'Fanny was quite right. We close them to keep out the street smell *and* to keep out the bad air.'

Oliver wrinkled his nose and then said excitedly, 'I can smell something horrible! I can! Mama, I think the bad air is getting in through the keyhole!'

''Tis so!' cried Lizbeth, not to be outdone. 'Ugh! 'Tis quite horrid!' She held her nose between finger and thumb, opened her eyes wide and pulled down her mouth in a grimace of disgust.

Sophie resisted the urge to laugh and said patiently, 'There is no bad air in the house, children. Only outside. And not everywhere, just in certain places. There is no bad air outside our house.'

'Where then, Mama?' they cried as one.

'St Giles, for example. The people around St Giles are very sick.'

'When I die, will I see Grandfather?' asked Oliver.

The innocent question tore at Sophie's heart. 'My dear little man, you are not going to die. Nor my dear little lady Lizbeth. Because we will look after you.' She paused and then plunged on, 'We might have to go away for a holiday so that all the bad air can blow away. We'll go to stay with Aunt Henrietta and Uncle Giles.'

'All of us? Hurrah!' cried Oliver. 'Then I can play with boys.'

Lizbeth retaliated. 'And I can play with *girls*!

Hurrah! Hurrah!' She poked out her tongue and Sophie fought back her exasperation.

'Stop being foolish,' she told them sharply. 'I said we *might* go. 'Tis far from certain. We must wait and see. Today I am going to church to say a special prayer to God to ask for his guidance. Perhaps he will tell me whether we should go away or not. But you do see now, don't you, why I must go to St Paul's alone and why you cannot come with me to feed the birds?'

Oliver said, 'Will we all go to Woolwich, Mama? You and Papa and Grandmother and Fanny – and the pigeons?'

'Pigeons?' Sophie laughed. 'Pigeons are fortunate. They don't catch plague.'

'Don't they breathe the bad air?' he demanded.

'No. That is – maybe they do. Yes, they do breathe it in but it doesn't make them sick because inside a pigeon is different to inside a person.'

'How is it?' asked Lizbeth but Sophie had had enough. She gave them each a kiss and stood up. 'You can help Fanny in the kitchen. She is making a marmalade and you may help her.'

Oliver gave a whoop of delight and Lizbeth beamed and as they made a concerted rush towards the kitchen Sophie suspected that her carefully monitored information about the plague had already been forgotten.

*

As Sophie hurried towards St Paul's, she held a small bunch of herbs to her nose, partly to keep the rank smell of the hot streets at bay but also in an attempt to keep away any contagion that might linger. She was not the only person to take this precaution, however, and the herb sellers at every street corner were doing good business.

To Sophie's surprise the steps leading to St Paul's were crowded with people and the plump old lady who sold bird seed was still in her place, reminding Sophie as always of a bulbous plant that had somehow taken root there. From habit and from a desire to help her, Sophie bought a bag of seed and, holding her nosegay of herbs to her face with one hand, she scattered the seeds awkwardly with the other. As they fell, dozens of watchful birds swooped on her from the high recesses of the church, sparrows, starlings, a few thrushes and the inevitable pigeons. She recalled Oliver's question. Would they die from the contagion, she wondered, imagining the streets littered with small feathered bodies and wishing she could warn them of their possible fate. They could fly from the plague – but so could she! The thought pricked at her conscience as she went thoughtfully up the steps and made her way into the gloomy interior of the church. Already hundreds of people were on their knees, hands clasped, eyes closed in fervent entreaty to God.

Sophie moved towards the rear of the church and knelt down. It occurred to her that, since her marriage, she had never been in church without Matthew and she felt very alone. A surreptitious glance to her left revealed a middle-aged woman weeping silently, her eyes fixed on the figure of Christ above the altar. To Sophie's right, across the aisle, an elderly man was slumped awkwardly against the wall. He was snoring heavily – or was he groaning? Was he sick? Her natural instinct was to inquire further but fear held her back. No one else showed any concern. Why should she take such a risk, she asked herself? She had two children to consider. Hastily she averted her eyes, ashamed that even in God's house she could harden her heart so easily. With an effort she returned to her own dilemma and tried to formulate a prayer. For a long moment she could think of nothing to say but slowly, stumbling for words, she whispered her plea for help.

'Dear Father Almighty, Look down upon this city and take pity on us. I beg you to spare my little ones, they have not sinned; they don't deserve to die. Protect them from the ravages of this foul sickness and show me what I must do. Oh Lord . . .' Her voice faltered. Didn't she already know what she must do? Didn't she know that she must take the children to a place of safety while there was still time? She almost groaned aloud with the weight of her guilt. She ought to heed her husband's warning; she should listen to Ruth's advice and take them all away to Woolwich. So why didn't she?

'Oh God, help me!' she whispered.

Deep inside her, alarm bells sounded at the prospect of abandoning Matthew. In spite of his insistence that he would care for himself, she was full of apprehension. He would eat out and the food would be contaminated, or else he would sit next to a man infected with plague. He would fall sick and Fanny would run away in fear and leave him to die. There would be a sudden end to his letters and she would have no way of knowing what had happened. In her mind's eye she saw him being carried off to the pesthouse in a sedan chair; saw him dying among harassed over-worked doctors. He might be dead and buried before she learned of his death. Life without Matthew was unthinkable.

'I love him!'

His love for her might have cooled but hers was as strong as ever.

'What shall I do?' In her anxiety she cried the words aloud.

Unable to resist, she stole another quick look at the man who lay against the wall. It seemed to her that he had changed his position, had slipped down a little further. His breathing had changed too and was less stertorous. As she watched, he slipped suddenly until he lay flat on the ground, staring upwards. She heard the thud as his head struck the stone floor, staring upwards. He was not asleep, he was sick! Dying, perhaps.

Somebody, surely, must notice him, she thought, unwilling to become involved, but it appeared that people were totally absorbed with their own troubles or else deliberately ignoring his plight. Trembling slightly, she stood up and moved slowly towards him, her gaze never leaving the crumpled figure on the floor. She took a deep breath when she reached him, then leaned over. Holding the nosegay closer to her face, she studied him fearfully and suddenly saw a large purple swelling just below his jaw and almost level with his right ear. 'A bubo!' she gasped. One of the surest signs of plague.

Her strength seemed to desert her and the posy of herbs fell from her nerveless fingers. She felt vulnerable without it but it lay on the dead man's chest and she dared not retrieve it. She stumbled clumsily backwards, disturbing several worshippers nearby who turned towards her in alarm. Trembling violently, she tried to speak but no sound came from her stiff lips. Instead she pointed to the fallen figure and then, desperate to escape the dreadful sight, forced her trembling legs to carry her towards the church door.

Once outside, she almost fell down the steps in her hurry to get away, but gradually, as she walked, she recovered her nerve and slowed to a reasonable pace. Halfway along Watling Street a familiar voice halted her in her tracks.

'Sophie! Is it you? Wait!'

Breathlessly she turned and saw the dumpy figure of Norah Bolsover waving and she waited for her friend to reach her.

Norah did not mince her words. 'Sophie Devine!' she cried as she embraced her friend. 'You're as white as a sheet!'

'Norah! 'Tis so good to see you. I've had such a fright.' The sight of a familiar face put new heart into Sophie. 'I was in St Paul's and –'

'But are you truly recovered? We were so sorry when we heard. You still don't look too well.'

Robbed of her dramatic story Sophie looked at her blankly. 'Recovered from what? Heard what?'

'Why your fever, of course. Matthew has been so worried about you.' Norah's kindly features were creased into a look of concern. 'To tell you the truth Henry is rather worried about Matthew, too. He has been so withdrawn lately. Can't seem to concentrate on anything, so Henry says.' She laid a comforting hand on Sophie's arm. 'Not that Henry minds. What are friends for, he told me, but he *is* growing a little anxious.'

Sophie stared at her. 'Henry has been worried about Matt?' she repeated. 'But there's nothing wrong with him. Or me for that matter. I've had no fever, Norah, I swear it. In fact –' She broke off, confused, frowning and drew her friend aside so that they would no longer be buffeted by passers-by. 'Matt says he has been worried about Henry.'

'Henry?' Norah laughed at the absurdity of such an idea. 'But 'tis quite impossible! Henry is blooming like the proverbial rose! Since his promotion he's been walking on air. He waited so long for it, he's determined to enjoy it.' As she stared into Sophie's face her smile disappeared. 'Matthew claims he is worried about Henry and Henry is worried about Matthew because he's worried about you. Now what are those two up to?'

Aware of Sophie's dismay, she said, 'Some time we must talk but today I have very little time. I was on my way to church to –.'

'Stay away from St Paul's!' Sophie told her and explained in graphic detail the reason for her own flight from London's premier place of worship.

Sobered by the significance of the account, the two women talked for a while longer before going their separate ways. Sophie walked home thoughtfully, her mind whirling with unanswered questions. Norah had told her that she had refused to leave London without Henry and it had now been agreed that either they would both go or they would stay on in London together and take their chances. Sophie's own determination to stay with Matthew was growing but she also had a duty to her children. As she neared home she also made up her mind that she would not tell Matthew about her meeting with Norah. A vague instinct of self-preservation warned her to keep her newly acquired information to herself, at least for a few days. She was curious to know how far Matt would develop the lies he had told and her fear was giving way to the beginnings of anger which was far easier to deal with. If her husband no longer loved her then she must somehow find the courage to stand on her own two feet and begin the struggle for her own and the children's survival. For the first time the idea entered her head that Matthew might have fallen in love with another woman. To her surprise the thought did not at once reduce her to hysterics nor did she feel like fainting. After a long moment's introspection she discovered to her astonishment that, for the first time in her life, she felt like fighting.

*

Her new-found courage, however, was quickly undermined by a letter from Henrietta which arrived the following day and effectively removed her choice of options, at least for the foreseeable future. It was dated June 5th, 1665.

My dear Sophie,

You will know by now that, despite my efforts, Matthew and Giles have decided that you, the children and Ruth shall stay with us. Since it must be, I urge you to come quickly. Giles is fearful that the plague will be outside the city walls any day now and he is wary of the contagion you might bring unknowingly to us. I trust you will not misunderstand my motives when I point out that if you wait too long it may prove disastrous. I am told on good authority that the disease can lie dormant within a living body for as many as ten days during which time the person may be unaware that he is stricken. He or she may suffer headaches or chill or rapid breathing which they may attribute to other causes and so be taken by surprise when the fateful swelling occurs.

We will do nothing to put our own dear children at risk so, if you are coming, I beg you come sooner rather than later. It would break my heart to refuse you sanctuary but we might be forced to do so. At present we feel comparatively safe here to the east of the city but if the plague should engulf the whole town, we too will have cause for anxiety. If necessary, we could move to Canterbury to my aunt's house but she could not take us all. We will cross that bridge when needs be. Pray God the authorities can halt the disease while 'tis still in the western out-parishes.

Believe me, dearest Sophie, I understand your reluctance to leave your home and husband but Matthew has chosen to remain in London and we must hope he does not live to regret his decision. A hot summer will do great mischief.

We no longer welcome letters from London for fear of contagion so do not write again but pack your bags and come post haste to Woolwich, for the love of God.

Your most true friend, Henrietta.

With a heavy heart Sophie folded the letter. The moment had come to face the unpalatable truth; she must accept the inevitability of their removal to Woolwich. For the sake of the children she must leave London but as she prepared to disrupt the family she could not throw off a growing sense of defeat. Over the next few days as she organized the packing and made the necessary travel arrangements she became aware of a certainty growing within her that by the time they all returned to the house their lives would be changed beyond recognition.

*

On June the eleventh at precisely six o'clock in the morning, the hired coach came for them and Matthew carried his mother into it. The children followed, their expressions guarded, conscious of their mother's ill-concealed anxiety but unaware of their father's impatience. A large leather trunk and two carpet bags were tied securely to the roof as Fanny watched tearfully from the doorway. The horses clattered their hooves restlessly and the driver was eager to set off before the streets filled with people. The 'farewells' were hasty and unsatisfactory and as Sophie leaned out of the window for a final wave her last glimpse of Matthew was blurred with tears.

*

In the event, Fanny's insistence that she would leave the Devines' employ was undermined by the realization that her master had been right. She soon discovered that there were already dozens of servants searching for new positions and without a reference Fanny knew she would be unlikely to find other employment. She decided to stay on but made up her mind that she would make her displeasure known whenever possible. If Matthew Devine thought he had won, she vowed he would soon find out his mistake.

She would make his life as uncomfortable as possible and she started that very morning by burning the porridge.

'Fanny!' he exclaimed, contorting his face in disgust. 'This is burnt!'

'Is it, sir?' She forced her features into a look of surprise. She dared not push him too far or he might sack her. Better to box clever, she told herself.

'I can't eat it.' He pushed the dish away.

Fanny stood with a look of patient inquiry on her face.

'Take it away, girl!'

'Shall I make you some more, sir?' If she did she felt certain it would have a little too much salt in it.

'Certainly not. I've no time to wait for it. You'd better eat it yourself. I don't want it wasted.'

'Certainly, sir,' she said with just a touch too much humility so that he glanced at her suspiciously. She took the dish from the table and carried it out into the scullery and then returned to clear the rest of the table.

'Will you be eating in tonight, sir?' she asked.

'Er – no. I am invited to Master Bolsover's house for supper. I dare say I shall eat out quite frequently now that I am alone.'

She gave him a long, cool stare. 'Shall you, sir?'

'I've just said so, haven't I?'

'Am I to do any shopping, sir?'

He paused. 'I suppose you must buy a few provisions. You can make yourself an omelette for your supper tonight.'

'Oh, thank you sir!' She returned his look with one of great innocence.

'And you had better find some work to do,' he told her. 'You know what they say about idle hands. Clean out the cupboards or something. Don't sit about doing nothing just because the family is away.' He reached for his coat and she helped him on with it, deliberately confusing him when he tried to put his left arm into the sleeve, making it seem accidental.

He paused at the street door. 'And keep away from your own people. The plague has taken a strong hold on St Giles and thereabouts. And don't let any strangers into the house.' As he lingered on the front step, searching for final instructions, a commotion broke out further along the street and they both went out to see what was happening. A shabbily dressed man with a noose on the end of a stick was trying to catch a mongrel dog and a well dressed but portly man was trying to hinder him. The dog was long-legged and of an indeterminate brown and was treating the tussle as a huge game, barking and leaping about, obviously enjoying itself.

'The animal has done you no harm!' shouted the portly dog-lover, dodging between dog and dog-catcher. 'Let the poor creature be. You can see 'tis in good health and no danger to anyone.'

The dog-catcher paused in his work and wagged a finger at him furiously. 'What's it to you, you interfering old baskit! I've got my job to do and I mean to do it. I've got mouths to feed, same as anyone and money to earn.' With a sense of the dramatic he appealed to the gathering crowd. 'What I say is — Rules is rules. No stray dogs on the street. That's what the magistrate says. NO DOGS! Got it? Come here, damn you!'

He darted to one side and made a grab for the dog which leaped sideways, barking joyfully. More passers-by were joining in the argument and voices were raised and a few fists waved threateningly.

'Poor thing!' said Fanny. 'They'll kill it if they catch it. Cats and dogs. They've all got to be killed now.'

'Only the strays,' Matthew reminded her. 'They might well be carrying the infection. How would you like to be bitten by an infected dog? You'd be the first to complain if they were left to roam the streets at will. The poor man is only doing his job. He doesn't make the rules.'

'But 'tis hardly fair,' Fanny argued. 'How do the dogs know about the plague? Or the cats. They're not doing anything wrong. They don't know why someone wants to kill them!'

At that moment the dog bounded straight between the dog-catcher's legs, bringing him heavily to the ground, and those who had sided with the dog laughed delightedly at his discomfiture. The dog seized its chance and fled along the street towards Matthew and Fanny followed by shouts of 'Catch it!' from those who had sided with the dog-catcher.

Inspired by his own eloquence Matthew lunged towards the dog as it passed but it sprang sideways at the last moment and escaped round the corner.

'Oh dear!' said Fanny. 'You missed it!'

Matthew looked as though he would like to continue the argument but at that moment the church clock struck the half hour and he tutted angrily. 'I shall be late,' he told her, as though she were in some way responsible. 'Now remember all I have told you. There is still plenty of work for you to do and when I come home I shall want to know how you have filled your day.'

As he turned away she put out her tongue before going inside. As she slammed the door behind her she smiled grimly. 'I haven't started with you yet, Master Devine!' she muttered. 'You'll be more than sorry you tangled with Fanny Rice!'

She went into the kitchen and opened the larder door. There was no way she was going to eat the burnt porridge; that would be thrown out into the yard, an unexpected treat for the birds. From the crock she chose a large brown egg and then reached above the fire for the frying pan. 'While the cat's away,' she murmured and for the first time for days she began to laugh.

*

That same afternoon Matthew sat in his office surrounded by papers and wondered why he felt no exhilaration now that Sophie had left London. He had looked forward to the heady freedom he would experience and to the knowledge that he could, within reason, go when and where he pleased without having to account to anyone for his actions. He was also free to spend as much time as he liked with Anne. Now, however, faced with the reality, he found himself feeling curiously bereft and the thought of his empty home appalled him. In three hours from now he would be in the arms of his beloved and yet his heart did not jump for joy at the prospect of their reunion.

He shuffled the papers which lay on the desk before him and tried to focus his attention on the most urgent matter but almost immediately his thoughts veered off in another direction and he found himself wondering exactly how far he dare go in his affair with Anne Redditch. Much as he loved her (and he did love her most passionately, he assured himself), they could never be man and wife. They both knew it. He had a wife and two children and suddenly he felt tremendously grateful for that. Anne was adorable, exciting and different but he did not want to marry her. So would she be content to be his mistress and if so, for how long would the affair last? And cost was another consideration which was beginning to trouble him. Anne could not expect him to lavish money on her; he was neither rich nor single. Yet undoubtedly she would expect gifts and outings, a birthday present perhaps and other generous tokens of his affection.

He sat back in his chair and rubbed a hand over his forehead. If only he could confide in someone but there was only Henry and that was a risk he dare not take. He doubted that Henry had ever fallen in love with another woman. He was a dull old stick and would never understand how Matthew had allowed his affair with Anne to reach its present intensity. Matthew remembered the first time he had seen Anne when she had been elbowed roughly aside by the men carrying the sedan chair in which he was travelling. She had slipped on the cobbles and fallen to the ground and he had felt obliged to get out and make reparation for her muddied gown and ruined shoes. He had been entranced within minutes by her round, sweetly dimpled face, blue eyes and soft husky voice. She was rounder than Sophie and her dark hair was straight and smooth while Sophie's curled. She had accepted his apology so prettily that without a word being exchanged on the subject of love, they had both known that they could not simply walk away from the encounter. Matthew liked to remind Anne that that moment had been the most exciting in his whole life.

He had paid off the sedan and insisted on taking her to her destination (the shoemaker) and on the way he had bought her a basket full of violets, an extravagant gesture which had thrilled them both. It had been a romantic start to an equally romantic relationship and the sense of danger inspired by their secret meetings had added spice to an otherwise mundane life. They had met on many occasions since that date and until this day Matthew had lived for the moments they shared. Now, perversely, when he need no longer deceive his wife about his whereabouts, the magic had mysteriously gone from the affair and he suddenly found himself wishing he could turn back the clock and erase Anne from his affections.

As his fingers played idly with the sheaf of papers before him he wondered, for a few wild moments, if he dare miss their appointment later in the day – but what excuse did he have? Anne knew that this was the day he was ridding himself of what she had laughingly called 'all his encumbrances'. She had often complained that he would never persuade Sophie to leave London and had once accused him of not trying hard enough. He swallowed miserably as he remembered the way he and Anne had plotted together.

A timid knock on the door admitted one of the junior clerks but without waiting to hear what he had to say Matthew snapped, 'Get out, man!'

He sighed heavily and leaned his elbows on the desk, putting his head in his hands. He would feel better, he assured himself, when he held Anne in his arms. She would inspire him. But that thought raised another problem. Anne had hinted more than once that she wanted more than romance. She wanted what she coyly referred to as 'more than just words' and that involved certain risks which sent cold shivers down Matthew's spine. Suppose she became with child! The idea terrified him for she had told him more than once that she longed for a child. Still, he reminded himself, she had been married for many years and had produced no children. So, possibly she was barren. He could only hope and pray so — if matters went that far between them. Not anticipating the ramifications of the plague, Matthew had never expected to be in a position to meet her for more than the occasional hour and this new and unexpected freedom was confusing.

With a cry of exasperation he gave up all pretence of working, stood up and wandered to the window where he stared down gloomily into the street. Guiltily he allowed himself to recall the expressions on his children's faces as they climbed into the coach. Woken from their slumber at such an early hour they had been sleepy and uneasy. Had he imagined reproach in their eyes as he waved them off? His mother, too, had given him a strange farewell.

'Be very careful, Matthew,' she had whispered. 'Don't take *any* risks.' In the present climate she could have been referring to his health and yet he did not think so for she had lowered her voice. She suspected him! Remembering the expression in her eyes, he felt a sweat break out on his skin.

'Oh Sophie! Sophie!' he whispered and thought with desperation that if she were suddenly to materialize before him he would confess all and beg her forgiveness. And her help, too, if that were possible.

Sophie would know what he should do; she would put Anne in her place, if that was what he wanted. He sighed heavily. What he wanted was to enjoy his relationship with Anne, free of any doubts or anxieties. Was that so much to ask? All he needed, he told himself, was a little time to sort out his feelings and he wished most earnestly that he could wriggle out of today's meeting.

There was another tap at the door.

'Enter!'

The same clerk put his head round the door and held out a letter. 'This came for you by hand and Master Wainwright says I *must* give it to you.' Dropping it on the small table just inside the door, he withdrew hastily before Matthew could shout at him again.

With a heavy heart, Matthew picked up the letter, broke the seal and unrolled it. Two words only had been scrawled across it.

'Congratulations! Anne.'

The page was decorated with kisses and it smelt of the lavender water she always wore. He stared at it in dismay, astonished by her perception. She had *known* his courage would fail him and she had acted promptly to bolster his resolve. There was to be no way out. He would have to go.

*

The following morning Fanny woke in the very early hours. She sat bolt upright and listened to the silence. As she sat there her eyes grew rounder and her mouth tighter. The wooden floors had shrunk over the years and the planks had parted sufficiently to allow sound to travel from room to room. Her master snored but she had grown used to it and it no longer kept her awake. Now its absence disturbed her. If no one was snoring then Matthew had not come home which meant she was in the house alone and that thought caused her a ripple of unease. Alone in the house she was at the mercy of thieves or cut-throats!

She lowered herself quietly to the floor and crept downstairs avoiding the fourth step which creaked. Outside the bedroom door she hesitated a moment then gently turned the handle. The bed was empty. She stared at it, then crossed to the bed and sat down. So where was he? Her mistress had been gone less than twenty-four hours and he was staying out all night. After a moment, however, she smiled. She threw herself on to the bed and stared up into the darkness. It was a feather mattress with pure wool blankets and for a few moments she luxuriated in the unfamiliar comfort. So this was how it felt to sleep in a real bed. Her own truckle bed boasted nothing so grand, just a straw mattress on a webbing base with two thin covers. She slept in her stockings and undervest to keep herself warm in the coldest part of winter.

She rolled over and buried her face in the downy pillow, then curled up small, mouse-like. She stretched out her arms and legs like a starfish and wriggled her toes in delight. Finally, greatly daring, she crawled between the sheets and lay on her back, her arms folded across her chest, her eyes closed. It occurred to her that, if her master was going to make a habit of staying out all night, she might as well sleep in the bed in his stead. It would be a shame to waste it. As she lay straight and still she thought that it would be a good bed to die in and she tried to imagine that she was dead and already laid out.

'At least you'd be comfortably dead,' she said.

Eventually tiring of the novelty, she abandoned the bed, smoothed it out again and quickly made her way back to her own room. She was intrigued by her discovery that her master was still out and keen to explore the possibilities which this knowledge offered her. Suppose he did not admit to staying out all night. Should she let him know that she knew? It might be wiser to say nothing and await developments. To the best of her knowledge, he had never stayed out all night before but presumably Master Bolsover had offered him a bed. Her eyes narrowed as she snuggled down into her own but there was no question of further sleep. She was wide awake and her mind was buzzing with ideas.

A new thought occurred. Had he really spent the evening with the Bolsovers? Maggie's words came back to her about Jem seeing him with a small dog down by the Temple Stairs. That still puzzled her and she could not make sense of it but it might be fun to *follow* her master one evening.

The church clock struck four and at the same moment she heard footsteps in the road outside and the sound of drunken singing. Throwing back the covers she rushed to the window, leaned out as far as she dared and could just make out two shadowy figures stumbling towards the house. One, obviously a linkman, carried a burning torch and was supporting the second. After a short altercation, one slipped away and Fanny guessed that the one who remained was her master. She thought it strange that if Master Bolsover had plied him with wine he had then sent him home with only a linkman for company!

Fanny was strongly tempted to leave her master on the doorstep until morning. That would serve the wretch right. Perhaps she should go down and push home the bolt on the inside so that if he did try to get in he would be unable to do so. Let him stay on the doorstep until dawn! On the other hand it might be to her advantage to let him know she knew of his shameful behaviour. He might pay her to keep quiet! The thought of the money she might earn finally sent her scurrying down the stairs, candle in hand. Wiping the smile from her face, she replaced it with a frown of disapproval.

As she opened the street door her master fell in. He stared up at her blearily and began to sing.

'Come all you bonny cockers

In the merry month of May!

And wager all your money
On the –'

'That'll do!' Hands on hips, Fanny glared down at him, keeping her face straight with an effort. 'A fine way to come home! Just look at the state of you. You should be ashamed!'

He smiled weakly and said, 'Oh, I am, Fanny! I am!' He tried to get up but fell back and Fanny was forced to pull him to his feet.

'And where have you been?' she asked, hoping that in his inebriate condition he would prove indiscreet.

'Out!' he said, leaning heavily on her shoulder and belching loudly. 'I've been out.'

'A blind man could see that much!' She did not fancy her chances of getting him up the stairs so she led him into the parlour and eased him into the rocking-chair. He sprawled back, smiling idiotically.

'You're a good girl, Fanny. I've always said so. We've always been friends.'

'You might think so!'

She was not going to try and undress him, she decided; let him stay in his finery for what remained of the night. It would be beautifully creased by morning. She ran upstairs and brought down a blanket from his bed. He reached out an unsteady hand and touched her face as she leant forward to tuck it round him.

'That's enough of that!' She slapped his hand and fleetingly wished that she still admired him the way she once had. Regretfully he had never tried to take advantage of her, the way some masters did. Servant girls at the conduit were full of stories of their lascivious masters and had held Fanny entranced more than once by their adventures. It seemed that amorous employers were numerous and Fanny had been forced to invent a few imaginary misdemeanours to attribute to Matthew, in case anyone thought that she was not sufficiently attractive to tempt him into wrong-doing.

Quickly she hardened her heart, reminding herself of his treachery on the occasion of the funeral. She had vowed on her mother's name never to forgive him and she meant to keep the vow. Her mother's ghost might be looking down on them at this very minute! Guiltily she glanced upwards. Before she could weaken further, she turned abruptly and went back upstairs. She lay wide awake until dawn, considering how interesting her life had become and feeling, for the first time since her mother's death, a distinct lightening of the gloom.

Chapter Six

MATTHEW WOKE UP THE next morning with a severe headache and an alarmingly hazy idea of what had happened the previous night. He had obviously reached home safely but he had no clear recollection of getting into the rocking-chair in which he now found himself when he awoke. Had Anne sent him home or had he insisted on it himself? And had he braved the city streets alone? He felt hastily for his purse and was relieved to discover that he had not been robbed. His mouth was dry and his stomach rolled. He glanced around him and saw with relief that he had not vomited. Thank Heaven for small mercies!

He turned his attention to his clothes and was shocked to see that his new coat was crumpled and would need very careful valeting if it was ever to recover. His feet, still in his best shoes, felt swollen to twice their usual size and his cravat was choking him. With an effort he straightened himself in the chair and ran a finger round his collar to loosen it. His eyes ached and they were probably bloodshot. He decided that he would be unable to attend to his work at his office so would stay at home; Fanny must take them a message to explain that he was taken with a sudden chill.

As he thought of Fanny he wondered whether or not she had witnessed his arrival home. If she had slept through it he might, just *might*, crawl upstairs and get himself to bed and . . .

Too late! He heard her footsteps on the stairs and when she appeared in the doorway he could see by her expression that she knew. She had undoubtedly witnessed his fall from grace. Hell and damnation!

Fanny regarded him scornfully. 'So you lived through the night!' she said.

'This is not quite what it seems,' he began. 'I think I have a chill.'

'That's come on mighty fast then, for you were right as rain this morning at four o'clock. Singing away, fit to wake the dead.'

'Oh!' He could think of nothing else to say and his head was throbbing.

She nodded. 'Spoilt your new suit, too.'

He nodded silently. Sophie always pressed his clothes. She had a sure way with fabrics. Matthew wondered if he dare risk asking Fanny to do it but in her present mood she might well scorch it on purpose. Maybe Anne would do it? No. He rejected that idea at once. He did not want to explain to her how it came to be so badly creased – but then, she must already know that he was drunk when he left her. He frowned unhappily. Just what *had* happened? He had drunk too deeply, he knew that much, and he vaguely recalled opening Anne's bodice. But did he – did they –?

'Oh God!' he exclaimed, panic-stricken.

Fanny was looking at him severely. 'You had quite a skinful, Master Devine. Not like you at all. Really naughty you were – or would have been if I'd let you.'

He closed his eyes despairingly. Now he was truly in a mess. Fanny would tell Sophie unless –. He fumbled for his purse and wondered how much it would take to keep Fanny's tongue from wagging.

She said, 'You're not trying to bribe me, are you?'

He started to shake his head but it hurt too much so instead he protested weakly, 'Not a bribe, Fanny. No, no. Not at all. But I do apologize if I did anything to offend you. I don't recall drinking that much.'

That was true. He had thought he was being very temperate. He had never been a drinking man because he did not enjoy the ensuing loss of control. He was always aware of the effect he was having on other people and he had seen too many men stupid with drink to wish to emulate them. It was extremely odd that he should have lapsed so whole-heartedly and the more he thought about it, the more incomprehensible it appeared. Unless Anne had encouraged him.

Fanny accepted the coin he offered with a nice show of reluctance and slipped it into her apron pocket. 'Thank you kindly,' she said. 'I'll do my best to forget all about it.'

Matthew thought her mouth twitched a little and half hoped she was going to smile. Then they could laugh about it and perhaps he could suggest that it could be their secret. She did not smile, however, and his hopes in that direction faded.

But when she said, 'Shall we get you up to bed, sir,' he fancied her tone was a few degrees warmer. As they negotiated the narrow stairs, his mind returned to the previous night's dalliance and he remembered Anne's breasts and the salty taste of her creamy skin and, in spite of his regrets, he smiled.

Mind you, no one could say that Anne Redditch came cheap; he had bought her a small locket on a chain that had cost him the best part of a day's wages, not to mention the jar of crystallized cherries he had given her. And next time he visited he would have to take further gifts. But she was warm-hearted and generous with her favours. But exactly how generous had she been? How far had she allowed him to go? His short-lived moment of satisfaction was replaced by one of apprehension as the unwelcome thought recurred that perhaps, already, he had gone too far.

*

Luke hesitated at the street door and tried once more to persuade his son not to accompany him further.

'This child's not going to survive,' he said. 'Born early and hopelessly underweight and there's no chance of feeding it up. Poor as church mice. The mother also troubles me. Why don't you go on to that broken leg in St Martin's Lane? The buxom lady who fed you on comfits.'

'Because I'm coming with you!'

'Please yourself.' Realizing the futility of his argument Luke went inside, treading carefully on the rotten stairs, avoiding contact with the dirty banister rail. A black cat with one eye missing sidled past them on the first landing; on the second, behind closed doors, a fierce argument was raging.

Antony said, 'Nice neighbours!' and raised his eyebrows humorously. Luke envied his ability to remain detached from the squalor which he himself found so depressing. His own feelings were of helplessness in the face of so much neglect and apathy on the part of the authorities, not to mention an illogical guilt that his own life was so much richer. He knocked on the door and, to his surprise, it was opened with exaggerated caution by a young woman he did not recognize. She looked at them suspiciously and said, 'There's no one here. Leastways, just me and Maggie.'

'I'm Doctor Meridith,' he told her, 'I believe I attended to your mother.' Her face fell and he went on hurriedly, 'I've come to see the new baby.' Indicating Antony he said, 'I've brought my assistant.'

Her face lightened and, opening the door, she called, 'Don't fret, Maggie! 'Tis only the doctor.'

As they followed her into the room she said, 'We thought you might be the Revenue men. You can't be too careful these days. One of them came here last week looking for – someone, but Maggie sent 'em packing!' She looked from one to the other and then jerked her head towards the woman on the mattress in the corner who held a child in her arms. 'I'm the baby's Aunt Fanny! He's my first nephew!' A proud smile softened the lines of her plain face. 'Pity my Ma didn't live to see him. Little love, isn't he? He's going to be handsome like his Pa.'

Luke looked at the wizened child with its scurfy head and dribbling mouth. He saw no redeeming features and marvelled silently and not for the first time at the power of love.

Antony, however, flashed the mother a dazzling smile and said, 'You've got a son to be proud of there, mistress,' and earned himself a look of deep gratitude.

Luke's attention was also on the mother and he regarded her with growing disquiet. She lay back against the wall as though her neck could no longer support her head. Her thin face was flushed a bright pink which dulled the red of her frizzy hair and her eyes glittered unhealthily. Kneeling beside her, he took hold of her wrist to check the pulse and felt the heat of her flesh.

'How do you feel?' he asked.

'Well enough.'

Fanny said, 'I brought her some jellied eels but she can't get them down. Doesn't fancy them.'

'I'm just not hungry. Haven't got my appetite back yet.' Maggie looked proudly at the baby. 'He's a good little mite. So contented. No fuss. Not a sound out of him all night. Doesn't even wake up for a feed.'

Fanny said, 'They're calling him Alfred after his grandfather. We shall call him Alf or maybe Alfie. My Pa's cock-a-hoop about that, isn't he Maggie?'

Luke's pessimism grew. 'When did the babe last take some nourishment?' he asked.

'Yesterday, about three in the afternoon. He took a few mouthfuls and then –' Maggie shrugged. 'That was all he wanted. Went straight back to sleep. Contented. That's what his Pa says.'

She jiggled him in her arms but the child did not respond. Carefully Luke took it from her, trying to hide his dismay. A premature child that did not eat or cry probably lacked the strength to survive. In contrast to the mother the boy was quite cool. His head lolled, his arms and legs were limp and his eyes remained closed. Familiar despair gripped him. If it lacked the will to feed there was nothing he could do for it. Luke sighed. He was going to lose the child and possibly the mother also for she was running a high fever.

Almost fiercely he told her, 'You *must* eat! Buttermilk, eggs, a little cheese, perhaps; build up your strength. Do you have any other aches? In your back, perhaps? In your head? Any feeling of restlessness? Any feeling of – dread?'

He was aware that Antony's head swivelled sharply towards him.

'None of those,' she answered. 'I'll be fine. I'm just tired.'

'She had a rotten time giving birth,' Fanny protested. 'She's entitled to be tired. You'd be washed out if you was in labour for nearly two days! Here, give the little love to me for a bit.'

While Fanny fussed over the baby, Luke wrote out a prescription and handed it to Antony. 'Get these from my dispensary, please,' he said. 'Perhaps the baby's aunt could go with you to collect them.' Forestalling the mother's anxious query he said gruffly, 'There'll be no charge.'

He stood up, nodded briefly by way of 'Goodbye' and hurried out with their thanks ringing in his ears. He was annoyed with himself for the futile gesture. The medicaments were expensive and nothing would save the child. The mother had child-bed fever and would in all probability be delirious before morning with no hope of recovery. A weak constitution aggravated by malnutrition reduced the resistance to any infection. Like so many of London's poor, it was only a matter of time before Maggie Rice succumbed to the natural hazards of her lowly existence. At least if she and her child died now they would cheat the plague of two victims.

*

On the way back to the physician's house, Fanny learned that her companion's name was Antony and that he was, in fact, the doctor's son. He told her that he was probably going to become a doctor like his father. He was so courteous towards her that she began to suspect, with her usual optimism, that he had taken a fancy to her and in the space of five minutes had given him a potted version of her life story. She also told him about her master's little lapse the previous night and the money he had given her.

'That's how I came to buy the jellied eels,' she confided. 'I'd have bought the baby a rattle if I'd known he was born but I'll get one next time. Now that my mistress is away I can get over there more easily.' She smiled suddenly. 'Lovely little lad, isn't he? I love babies. Have you got any?'

He was astonished. 'Me? Lordy, no! I'm a bit young for a family but I dare say I shall risk it one day.' Grinning he added, 'I rather fancy an older woman; one with a bit of money.'

'I'm older than I look,' said Fanny with forlorn hope but he let the hint pass.

When they reached the house he led the way into the dispensary at the rear and Fanny's eyes opened in astonishment. ''Tis like an apothecary's shop!' she exclaimed.

The room was narrow and lit by a small window set high in the wall. One wall was shelved from top to bottom and these shelves were full of containers of all shapes and sizes. Green, brown and blue bottles were carefully labelled in spidery brown writing; stone jars were firmly corked and china jugs were stuffed with bunches of different herbs. There was a row of phials in wooden holders and a stack of unused pillboxes and canisters. A large wooden counter supported a further selection of sandalwood boxes and baskets, as well as an untidy pile of leather-bound books and papers. In the middle of the counter there was a large stone pestle and mortar, a block of salt and another of chalk. A single stool stood between the counter and the shelves.

The smell added to the mystery of the room, a subtle blend of aromatic oils and spices which made her close her eyes in delight. She inhaled deeply and then let her breath out again with a sigh of pleasure.

'Cloves,' she began, attempting to isolate individual smells from the complex fragrance. 'And aniseed . . . and is it, ginger?' She sniffed inquisitively, frowning with concentration. 'What else? Yes, I can smell sandalwood . . . vinegar, I think . . . and mint!' She gave up with a laugh. 'And hundreds more!'

Antony laughed at her obvious enjoyment. ''Tis a smell I grew up with,' he told her. 'As a child I used to come in here whenever I could. My grandfather was a physician as well as my father. I used to pretend to be like them. They'd give me a few things to grind up with that.' He indicated the pestle and mortar. 'I'd grind away, imagining myself a learned doctor.' He sighed. 'Then, suddenly, when I was old enough to enter the profession I no longer wanted to!'

'Did they mind?'

'My father did. He minded very much. My grandfather was dead by then.' As he talked he consulted the prescription and began to assemble the ingredients. 'My father was bitterly disappointed. Now though, suddenly, I feel the desire returning. I feel the need to save mankind!' His tone was deliberately light and self-mocking but Fanny had the feeling that he meant what he said and wished again that she was older and wealthy. She could imagine herself as a doctor's wife and felt sure it would suit her to be married to Antony.

She watched fascinated as he ground up the various herbs and then, adding a little gum, rolled the mixture into tiny pellets which he transferred to a round pillbox. His hands moved with such confidence that Fanny was moved to say, 'You *look* like a physician already!'

He shook his head. 'This part is easy. 'Tis knowing which herbs and in what proportions. That's what separates the doctor from his apprentice.'

As she prepared to leave, he touched her gently on the arm. 'Life is full of sorrows, Fanny,' he said awkwardly. ''Tis hard to lose loved ones but life goes on. It must. We must be brave. Do you see?'

Fanny thought she did. She thought he was referring to the death of her mother. Two days later she realized that he had meant little Alfie. He had known the boy would die.

Soon after Maggie died too, and Fanny thought her broken heart would never mend.

*

Three days later in the Whitehall cockpit the morning's programme was in full swing and Charlie was having an unusually good run of luck. He had bet successfully on three out of the first five contests and was about to wager a considerable sum on the sixth. On his left an elderly man was losing steadily and had now decided to follow Charlie's lead and bet on the same cock, a gingery bird weighing three pounds eight ounces, which was being held aloft by its proud owner.

'My brother!' shouted a young man on Charlie's right. He had a newly-healed scar down the left side of his face and a swollen lip and Charlie marked him down mentally as a bruiser. 'He's got five birds in today's mains,' he boasted, 'but that's his best.' He leaned towards Charlie with a show of confidentiality, breathing onions all over him. 'Feeds it on the spiciest food he can lay hands on! Reckons it makes him more bad-tempered in the pit!' He grinned and offered a guinea to the nearest bookmaker who, reaching across the intervening heads, snatched the coin adroitly and scribbled in his grimy ledger. The noise was tremendous and Charlie was forced to shout back in order to make himself heard.

'How many wins has it had?'

'This'll be its tenth!'

The second bird now appeared, a charcoal grey with a bright red comb and legs like black twigs. It was displayed briefly then tucked beneath its owner's arm.

'My brother's bird'll murder that!' The young man sniggered and rubbed his sleeve across the end of his nose. 'He'll make mincemeat of him! Mincemeat! You mark my words.'

Charlie paid him scant attention. He was wearing his new cravat and a silk jacket and had hoped to be seated among the more affluent members of the audience where his fine clothes might be appreciated. He found the bruiser next to him coarse and offensive but there seemed no suitable space into which he could move. As his eyes roved over the crowd he recognized the local rector deep in conversation with a warder from the Tower and behind them a member of Parliament was lighting up his pipe. He spotted Lubbett from the fish market and 'Jolly' Hollis from the Magistrate's Court, not to mention a few apprentices who should have been about their work. On the far side of the pit, he saw a face he vaguely recognized from somewhere – a thin face with protruding cheek-bones and sandy-coloured eyebrows. For a moment he stared at the man uneasily but he could not place him.

The fight would take place in the circular pit which was being sprinkled with a fresh layer of sawdust which would soak up the blood. A low wooden wall surrounded the ring and served to separate birds and onlookers. Behind this, the seating rose in three tiers so that even those in the back row could see what was happening. The front row was taken up by the owners of the birds and the bookmakers but behind them the crowd was packed closely together and there was an over-riding smell of stale sweat mingled with burning tobacco. The audience were a motley crew, a few with their wigs askew, some drunk, others arguing fiercely with much waving of clay pipes and stabbing of irate fingers. Large sums of money were being wagered, wins were being hotly disputed, a young man screeched into his companion's ear trumpet while another was apparently trying to brain his neighbour with hefty whacks from a walking stick. The victims' cries were largely ignored although a few by-standers cheered on the aggressor.

Charlie, sitting in the second row, loved the passionate hurly-burly of it all. He was trying to forget that his brother's wife and child were dead and, harder still, trying to forget that he could not mourn as his brother felt he should. Maggie was not family in the strictest sense of the word, he reminded himself, and he had hardly had time to get to know the new baby. Jem was half-crazed with grief and had stubbornly resisted all Charlie's attempts to cheer him up, but then poor Jem did not share Charlie's robust attitude towards life and death. In Charlie's opinion, he was determined to be devastated by his double loss. Finally, Charlie had been forced to leave him to it and had come here to find a bit of cheerful company to take his mind off the tragedy. Life, Charlie had explained to Jem, was a precarious business; by the time the month was out they might *all* be dead so they must take what pleasures they could while there was still time. If the plague increased the authorities would probably prohibit cockfights along with other public performances. Meantime, a little harmless gambling would pass the time. The sight of sparring cockerels could always distract Charlie from life's little sorrows and he saw no reason why it should not help his brother. Jem however, had chosen not to accompany him and made it clear that he despised Charlie for his insensitivity. At the memory of Jem's face Charlie felt a twinge of conscience, but at that moment a bell rang heralding the next contest and, with an excited roar, the crowd turned its attention to the pit.

As the two birds met in a flurry of feathers and shrill squawks all conversation died, heads swivelled eagerly and all eyes were on the two feathered combatants. To the accompaniment of shouts and jeers from the crowd, the cocks sprang apart then rushed together once again, raking each other murderously with their spurred feet and pecking furiously at each other's eyes. Their neck feathers stood out like Elizabethan ruffs and their clipped wings beat the air with desperation. The noise from the crowd swelled as people shouted encouragement to their favourite bird and Charlie yelled as loudly as any of them. This was life and he would live it to the full. There must be no time for remorse or regret.

Seeing that his chosen bird was getting the worst of the battle Charlie renewed his efforts. 'Get to it, you worthless creature!' he bellowed. 'You're not even trying! Rip his wings off!' A lot of money was riding on the outcome and he was reluctant to part with it so soon after its acquisition. 'Go for him! Oh, by all that's holy! Kill him! Go for it! Go! Dammit! I've seen a sparrow go at a worm with more energy! Go! Now's your chance!' But the unfortunate cock was faltering as blood spattered onto the sawdust from a badly torn comb, and a bare patch had appeared on its breast as feathers continued to fly. The owner yelled obscenities at it and some of the disappointed members of the audience threw small coins or stones at it in disgust, thus adding to its plight. It staggered and fell then tried to rise again but the other cock renewed its attack with frenzied wings and wickedly stabbing beak.

'God's teeth!' groaned Charlie but he was already resigned to the bird's failure and the loss of his stake money. Never at a loss, he promptly began to consider alternative ways of making money. Half a pound of best Virginia tobacco was hidden in the false lining of his coat and he had thought he might sell some to members of the audience. In the pit the gingery bird was almost dead and the audience rose to its feet, cheering and hooting as the charcoal-grey cock was held triumphantly aloft. Charlie found himself staring once more at the thin-faced man on the other side of the ring and suddenly his stomach churned ominously as recognition dawned. It was one of the Revenue men, out of uniform! At that precise moment the man caught sight of Charlie with an answering flash of recognition. For a couple of seconds neither man moved but then the Revenue man was on his feet. With a gasp of fear, Charlie also leaped up from his seat and began to clamber awkwardly over the closely-packed audience who complained shrilly of his behaviour. The Revenue man shouted, 'Stop him!' but public sympathies were not entirely on the side of authority and many of the men feigned sudden deafness. Others quickly abandoned the spectacle of the dying cockerel and welcomed the promise of a further diversion. The audience began to take sides, some trying to catch Charlie and as many again trying to help him escape. Charlie broke free and began to make a run for it, fumbling desperately in his pocket for the incriminating tobacco, wondering how best to dispose of it. If it was not found on his person he might escape the worst punishment; he could at least protest his innocence. But it seemed his luck had finally forsaken him. Before he could get rid of it a small, mongrel dog appeared and, snapping excitedly at his ankles, brought Charlie heavily and ignominiously to the ground. With a cry of pain he sat up dazedly, nursing a horribly painful right wrist, and before he could retrieve the situation, his pursuer arrived with a string of triumphant oaths and grabbed him securely by the shoulder of his coat. As the crowd gathered round them, the Revenue man hauled Charlie roughly to his feet, cuffed him round the ear and then shook him as a dog shakes a rat. When he tired of that he said grimly, 'I want to talk to you, my bonny lad!' and for the first time in Charlie's life his natural optimism deserted him.

*

20th June, 1665
My dearest Matt,

I am writing this letter in bed while the children sleep. I can scarce believe that we have only been down here a week. The time goes so slowly when my thoughts are elsewhere. The news of the plague terrifies us all. Henrietta's neighbour brought us a recent copy of the Intelligencer *and the figures from the weekly Bills are far from reassuring. I beg you to take all prudent precautions. If only the temperature would fall. Surely God could spare us a little rain to cool the air and wash away the contagion. Henrietta's physician recommends that at the first sign of any indisposition you should breakfast on bread dipped in sorrel sauce and fast until you are yourself again. He also suggests wearing a dried toad as an amulet against disaster but, in truth, I cannot put much faith in that idea and Giles is adamant that it cannot work.*

Do please write to me, Matt. We now purify all letters from London between two large flat stones which are heated in the fire. Giles says that the heat kills any possible contagion so there is no risk.

The children are behaving well enough but ask constantly for their beloved Papa. They miss you, Matt. Lizbeth did not sleep well at first but she now shares my bed and I do not sleep well! However, I am not complaining. We are safe and that is what matters. Henrietta and I find pleasure in each other's company and Giles is surprisingly tolerant. Your mother sends her good wishes. She is in good health and Giles is teaching her to play chess.

I trust Fanny is looking after you and performing her tasks dutifully.

Try not to be too lonely, dearest Matt. Be assured that I think of you and pray for your well-being. Please God this wretched plague will burn itself out shortly and we can be reunited as a family again.

Your devoted wife, Sophie.

She sighed as she re-read the letter. She had tried so hard not to upbraid him but she was deeply hurt by the fact that he had not written. Again and again, the suspicion that Matt no longer loved her returned to torment her but she could not bring herself to confide in Henrietta. In spite of her brave letter, life in her brother's house left much to be desired, for she hated their dependence on others. She missed the daily routine of household management, deciding what to eat and when to eat it. She worried constantly that Lizbeth and Oliver might be making too much noise and, when all the children squabbled and arbitration was needed, she tried so hard not to favour her own two that she went too far the other way and discriminated against them.

Unhappily aware that so many visitors were bound to be a source of disruption in her brother's house she made desperate efforts to compensate, taking all the children out for walks to give Henrietta a little freedom but managing in the process to have none herself. Ruth had been very difficult for the first three days, insisting that she would never settle in the country and demanding to be taken back to London to 'take my chances with the plague!' Even now she constantly criticized the food, Henrietta's clothes and Giles's management of the farm and Sophie, struggling to keep the peace between them all, went to bed each night in a state of mental exhaustion. She did not sleep well and was aware that there were dark shadows under her eyes and occasionally a tell-tale tremor in her voice. Nobody was unkind to the refugees, however, and she appreciated the fact that Henrietta and Giles were also finding the situation a strain. It was a stressful time for all of them but Sophie's secret worries about Matthew did nothing to make her life any easier.

She wanted to write, 'Do you love me?' at the end of the letter but at the last moment dared not commit the words to paper for fear of giving substance to her doubts. With tears pressing at her eyelids, she sealed the letter, blew out the candle and slid between the sheets, careful not to wake her sleeping children. She put her hands together and closed her eyes in prayer. Vulnerable and afraid she turned to God. If he could not help her she was lost.

*

When, a few days later, Anne opened the door to her lover, she saw at once that he was not in a very happy frame of mind. For one thing, he had brought her no flowers but somehow she stifled her disappointment, telling herself that some men were more romantically inclined than others. She would have to train him! Smiling brightly in spite of her reservations, Anne threw her arms around him and held him close, her face against his chest. Matthew said nothing, paid her no compliments and whispered no endearments.

'My sweet man!' Anne protested, as he drew back from their rather brief embrace. 'What sort of welcome is this? You are so late the meal is quite spoiled and now you kiss me as though you have other things on your mind! Poor little Anne! Do I deserve such cavalier treatment?' As she spoke she was helping him off with his coat.

'Forgive me!' Matthew sighed deeply and gave her a wan smile. 'My maid is behaving very badly and has put me out of humour. I would not burden you with my problems but . . .' He shrugged.

But you will! she thought resentfully, thinking of the hours she had spent making the rich pork sausages with which she had hoped to impress him. The cauliflower had cooked to a soggy mash and the damson tart would have to be re-heated which would spoil the pastry.

He sat down wearily and she hurried to provide him with a drink of raspberry sack. 'She has attended a funeral against my express wishes,' he began as Anne settled herself beside him with a drink of her own and an expression of sympathy. 'To make matters worse, she tried to deceive me. She failed to tell me that her brother's wife and new-born child had died, knowing that if I knew I would forbid her, as I did when her mother died. I only found out because I returned home unexpectedly and found her red-eyed and still wearing a black ribbon. When I taxed her with it she broke down and sobbed again.' He sighed deeply and shook his head.

'What did they die off?' Anne spoke as carelessly as she could.

'Child-bed fever, I'm told, and the child simply failed to survive.'

'And you believe her?'

'I do.'

Anne thought rapidly. 'Why don't you get rid of her?' she suggested. 'You could spend most of your time here with me. You wouldn't need her.'

Instead of jumping at the suggestion, he looked at her warily. Almost fearfully, she thought, exasperated. Why were men so lily-livered?

'Oh no!' he said. 'I couldn't do that.'

'Don't you want to be with me?' She pouted, blinking her large blue eyes reproachfully.

'Naturally I do but 'tis out of the question.' His tone was sharp and she decided not to press the point until his mood was sweeter. A good meal and plenty of wine should soften him up and make him more receptive. He had no head for wines as she had discovered not so long ago. This irked her a little for she rather admired a man who could hold his liquor but since she had discovered Matthew's weakness she might as well exploit it.

Sipping her drink daintily she said, 'My poor darling! You are unhappy but Anne will soon have you smiling again. I have made you some sausages.'

Paying her words no attention he went on, 'I have had a letter from Sophie. She has settled in well enough but I wonder if I should visit. I don't relish the idea but the children miss me.'

Anne swallowed a caustic remark. She did not wish to be reminded of Matthew's responsibilities and thought it tactless of him to speak of his wife. Anne had gone out of her way to suggest that

Matthew should *not* visit his family, pointing out that he might well be putting them at risk, although the real reason was that she hated the idea of Matthew sharing a bed with his wife, even for one night.

She stood up abruptly. 'Time to eat,' she smiled. 'I will tell Prudence to serve the food.'

*

Much later, Anne persuaded a sleepy Matthew to accompany her to the bedroom where, she assured him, they would be more comfortable. He had drunk more sparingly on this occasion, however, and was well aware that they were on the bed rather than in it.

'You lay with me the other night,' she teased when he resisted her attempts to take off some of his clothes, 'for comfort's sake. You were so beautiful! Such a wonderful lover, Matthew. My husband was never like that. I had to send you home eventually for the sake of appearances but I do believe, had I allowed it, you would have stayed 'til morning!'

She touched the lobe of his ear with the tip of her tongue and he moaned softly. If only she could seduce him, she thought, with growing excitement. If *only* she could bear him a child! He could never wed her but at least he would be forced to support her and the child, and he would have a reason to continue their association indefinitely. She slipped from the bed and began to unfasten her petticoats, enjoying the look in his eyes, well aware that he was beginning to desire her. This would in fact be the first time he had possessed her although he believed it had happened once already. She smiled at her own wickedness and realized that she, also, was becoming aroused. Tonight it would happen. Tonight she would steal from Sophie something every wife valued above all things – her husband's fidelity!

She was loosening his cravat and murmuring into his ear when something clattered noisily against the bedroom window, startling them both. Banner woke up and, barking furiously, ran out from beneath the bed towards the window.

Matthew sat up abruptly, staring at the window in alarm. 'What was that?' he demanded.

'It sounded like small stones or earth!' she said fearfully.

It happened again.

'Something is being thrown at the window!' Matthew cried and she thought how quickly fear could sober up a man.

'Then see who 'tis!' she cried.

'Show myself at *your* bedroom window?' cried Matthew. 'Are you mad?'

'Then I must see for myself!' First blowing out the candle, she hurried to the window and stared down into the apparently empty street. Matthew warned, 'Don't open the window, Anne! Don't show yourself! You are only half dressed!'

But she had already unfastened the catch and was

swinging it open, peering down into the darkened street.

'Who's there?' she cried. 'What do you want with us?'

'Not "us"!' cried Matthew. 'I'm not here!'

She gave him a withering look and then glanced again into the darkened street. She saw no sign of life but suddenly a third handful of soil spattered against the window and into her face and she drew back hastily, muttering a particularly coarse oath she had learned from her sailor husband. From the corner of her eye she saw a figure dart away into the shadows.

Matthew cried, 'Who is it? Can you see the wretch?'

To hide her confusion she bent to fondle the dog.

'My brave little Banner!' she murmured. 'You would save your mistress from the bad man, I know!'

Carefully avoiding the scattered soil she stepped back towards the bed and sat down, shivering a little with shock now that it was over.

Matthew put his arms around her. 'My poor sweet-heart!' he whispered. 'Are you hurt?'

'No, not hurt,' she said with a brave smile.

'Did you see anyone?'

She shook her head. 'Not a soul!' she lied.

Her fear had faded, leaving her angry and resentful that their unknown tormentor should have succeeded in shattering the romantic mood she had worked so hard to create. Now Matthew would see her as someone less than entirely lovable; as someone who had, perhaps, behaved so badly that she invited retaliation. She hoped he had not heard her swear.

'Who would play such a spiteful trick?' he asked. Mortified, she could think of several people who might wish to frighten her. She had argued with the milkseller about the quality of the last quart of milk and had haggled with the fishwife over the price of yesterday's herrings. Still, she doubted if either of them would feel it necessary to revenge such slight provocations. Only her own servant remained. Anne had been forced to box the woman's ears earlier in the day but it could not be Prudence because she was now in her attic room, with orders to stay there until daybreak.

'Someone meant to frighten you,' said Matthew. 'If I ever get my hands on him –'

But now Anne's mind was working feverishly as she saw new possibilities opening up. Was there a way she could turn the incident to her advantage? Perhaps she could persuade Matthew that she was too nervous to be left alone. Suppressing her anger she said, 'Oh Matthew, please don't leave me. Not tonight. Suppose he comes back? He might break in and murder me! Oh, tell me you'll stay.' She stared at him with wide frightened eyes. 'My husband may have made enemies. He had no respect for the men under his command. He was a ruthless man, that much I do know. He always said that sailors were the scum of the earth.'

'But all that was years ago,' Matthew protested.

'But men bear grudges!' she countered. 'Oh Matthew! Do you think one of them has come for revenge? It must be so for *I* have no enemies in the world!'

He hesitated. ''Tis possible, I dare say, but –'

'Then do stay with me, Matthew. Just for tonight. You cannot leave me here with only Banner to protect me.'

At the sound of his name the dog thumped his tail softly against the floor and Anne laughed shakily. 'You see how he adores me? *He* would die for me, I'm certain, but the wretch might kill us both!' She said the last few words with a catch in her voice and at last Matthew nodded slowly.

'I'll stay, Anne,' he told her and she clung to him helplessly as hope flared within her.

'And you didn't get a glimpse of his face?' Matthew asked as he stroked her hair.

She shook her head, trembling convincingly. 'But he was tall,' she told him, 'and heavily built.'

She must never let him know it was a woman.

*

Luke was reading when the knock came and he laid down the *Newes* with a sigh. It was the first time he had sat down since early morning and he was looking forward to the meal they would all share when Antony returned. With a sigh of resignation, he made his way to the door. No doubt another call for his expertise but what else could be expect. Doctor Syddon had left London and so, to his certain knowledge, had two other physicians. It was inevitable that those doctors who remained would be hopelessly over-worked at times like these.

He went to the door and opened it. A young woman stood outside wearing the familiar expression of anxiety.

'What is it?' he asked although he thought he knew the answer.

To his surprise she asked, 'Is your son in?'

'My son?' He stared at her. 'Do we know you?'

'I'm Fanny Rice. Your son will remember me. I came here to fetch medicaments when –' Her eyes filled with tears and he suddenly made the connection.

'Ah yes! The mother and her new-born babe. That was very sad. I'm sorry we could do so little for them.'

'You knew they would die?'

'Sadly, yes.'

'Poor Maggie!' she burst out. 'She never did anyone any harm! Why should she die?'

'The ways of the Lord are –'

'And poor Jem. He's like a lost soul without them. Like a drowning man.' She swallowed her grief and straightened her back. 'But I haven't come about sickness. I've come to see your son. To ask him a favour. He seemed very kind.'

Luke hid his surprise. What kind of favour could

this young woman be asking for? 'He's out at the moment but should be home before long.' He spoke with some reluctance because he had hoped that the family might relax and enjoy their meal in peace. 'Is there anything I could do to help?'

She looked at him doubtfully. ''Tis a letter to my mistress. I have no schooling and 'tis my master, you see. He has taken up with another woman while my poor mistress is in the country with the children.' She tossed her head angrily. 'I'm determined she shall know but I can't write. I was hoping your son . . .'

As she fell silent he supplied the missing words. 'You hoped my son would write the letter for you?'

She nodded.

'But there are plenty of scribes who would do this for you,' he said.

She avoided his eyes. 'I've no money left! I thought he might do it out of friendship. He seemed quite taken with me.'

Luke smothered a smile. Antony 'taken' with this sad little scrap? 'I see,' he said.

'No, you don't!' she cried. 'The master's angry with me for going to the funeral. Poor Maggie! And poor little Alfie. I never did give him his rattle.' Her lips trembled. 'I had to go, sir, because of Jem. What with Maggie and Alf and my poor Ma already gone –' She drew a deep breath. 'I couldn't let him stand there with just my Pa and Charlie! I *had* to go!'

He nodded.

'The master was in a proper tantrum when he found out. Refused me my wages as a punishment.'

'And you want to punish him by telling your mistress of his liaison.'

'No sir! Well –' She looked a trifle discomfited. 'Maybe I do – but 'tis the children I fear for. They mustn't lose their father, must they, sir? And my poor mistress has been good to me. Never laid a finger on me and 'tis more than you can say for some. She deserves better and that's the truth.'

He held open the door. 'You'd best come in,' he said.

Once inside, the girl stared round at the small room he used as a surgery but although her eyes were busy her story continued. 'He came home in his cups a few days ago, the wretch! Then last night off he goes again! I – I followed him!' Her tone was defiant. 'I saw him go into the house and she kissed him, sir! I saw it with my own eyes. Then I saw them through the window. Then, later, I saw the candlelight upstairs.' She waited for his comment but when he failed to make one she said, 'In the bedroom! Well, I dare say you think badly of me . . .'

''Tis not my business.'

'But you do!'

He hesitated. 'I merely wonder whether you are doing the wrong thing for the right reason.'

'What's that, sir?' She looked at him doubtfully then continued. 'I was that mad and I threw some earth and stones at the window to frighten them and the dog barked. Jem said he'd seen the master holding a dog by Temple Stairs but –' She shrugged. 'Then I thought he was wrong. Now I know better. So you see I must tell the mistress. You would, too, if you knew my mistress.'

For a moment he looked at her flushed, anxious face and then he smiled. 'I'll write the letter for you,' he said simply and reached for a sheet of paper. He dipped the quill into the inkpot. 'Tell me what it is you want to say.'

Chapter Seven

THE PRISON STOOD ON the eastern side of the River Fleet from which it took its name. Charlie had often passed it, pitying the poor wretches who thrust their hands out of the grating to ask for food or the money with which to buy it. Now, after a brief appearance at the court of the Old Bailey, he found himself pushed unceremoniously through the main door and heard the dull clang as it closed to behind him. It had an ominous ring to it.

The court constable who had accompanied him now said, 'Smuggling. Twenty weeks,' and handed over a sheet of paper which concerned Charlie. His duty done, he prepared to leave. 'A free man!' thought Charlie enviously.

A jailer, unshaven and with few teeth, sat behind a huge desk which supported a number of large ledgers and dozens of papers, the latter separated into three piles, each of which was weighted down by a large stone. The man regarded Charlie with apparent indifference.

'Read that!' he said, jerking a stubby finger towards a list of rules that was nailed to the wall.

'Can't read!' said Charlie with a cheerfulness he did not feel.

The man began to gabble them at a rate that revealed long familiarity with them.

'General Rules of the Fleet Prison. One – No prisoner to bring weapons further than the lodge. Two – No prisoner to buy provisions from outside without permission. Three-Prisoners are only permitted to go outside the prison upon payment of eight pence a day. Four . . .'

Charlie tried not to listen, depressed by the constant repetition of the word prisoner. He, Charlie Rice, was a *prisoner*, denied his freedom, denied his dignity. He shivered with revulsion at the very idea and spoke sternly to himself. "This won't do at all, Charlie Rice. You must make plans for an early escape. You must get out and stay out."

'Got all that?' demanded the jailer.

Charlie nodded and began to whistle tunelessly to show how little he cared about his situation.

'And no whistling!'

'Where does it say that?'

'I say so! Name?'

'Charlie Rice.'

'Age?'

'How do I get out of here?' Charlie demanded.

'You don't!' The man wheezed with apparent amusement.

'Suppose I had money, what then?'

The man tapped the side of his nose meaningfully. 'Ah now, that'd be a different kettle of fish! A bit of money to the right person – But you *don't* have any, I'll wager. I have a nose for these things. Been here a long time, see. I can smell money the minute a man walks through the door – and I smelt nothing when you came in.'

Charlie made up his mind then and there to get some.

After the formalities, he was led roughly along a dank and gloomy passageway which sent his spirits plummeting. Somehow he must get out of the place but first he must let his family know where he was. He might have to bribe his way out and that would be costly; otherwise he must outwit his jailers and that would be a challenge. It might even be fun.

They stopped in front of a heavy wooden door and this was duly opened with a large key. As the door swung open he was at once struck by the stench of unwashed bodies mingled with pipe tobacco and the babble of raucous voices, male and female, which screeched and bellowed, presumably in an attempt to be heard above the general din. Charlie longed to turn and flee but the jailer stood beside him watching eagerly for signs of fear. Instead Charlie stepped forward boldly and at once became the object of everyone's attention. As all heads turned inquiringly towards the newcomer, the noise diminished and Charlie felt that something interesting was required of him.

'Charlie Rice at your service!' he declared with a self-mocking laugh which brought a mixed response from the unfortunate men and women who were to be his fellow prisoners. Some found it amusing and smiled, others stared dully, a few more muttered with disgust at this pathetic show of bravado. Charlie thought that at a rough guess the low-ceilinged cell with its rough stone walls must be home to nearly a hundred prisoners.

Again he heard the dread clang of a door and the sound of a key turning in the lock as the jailer left him to his fate. His stomach fluttered treacherously within him as he looked at the motley collection of individuals who would share his life for the next twenty weeks – if he didn't find a way out before then. At that moment they were no more than a blur of faces and a buzz of voices but Charlie knew that if he was ever to leave this dreadful place he would need all the help he could get. There was no point in antagonizing them. He must get to know those whom he could and could not trust; must learn to distinguish friend from foe. Squaring his shoulders, he adopted a confident smile. Might as well make a start now, he decided, and he began at once.

By the time the evening arrived he had put names to a few faces and had learned to his surprise that his fellow prisoners were not all from the dregs of society as he had imagined but came from very varied backgrounds. Stony-faced Jane Tooney was a clever street thief: John Blewett, better known as Rosynose, was a habitual drunkard; Billy Cox, tall and thin as a lamp post, had set fire to a farmer's barn: Lucy was a pick-pocket; Simple Sammy had sold brass rings as gold. All these he had expected, but there was also a parson imprisoned for writing lewd verses; a playwright who had somehow offended his audience and a woman of gentle birth who had tried to poison her unfaithful husband. Most of them, however, were debtors who might never be released and would probably die in the notorious Fleet.

For some habitual offenders, prison was a way of life and these men and women found the conditions in The Fleet no better and no worse than their existence outside the prison. With these people, Charlie could find no point of contact but many of the first offenders warmed to his cheery manner and found him good company. It was the parson, however, who finally caught and held his interest. The Reverend Sydney Carraway was forty years old and as round as a ball. His head was bald and his lips were thick but Charlie was impressed. He was even more impressed when, later that evening, Sydney suggested, over a shared lump of bread, that he knew a way Charlie might be able to earn enough money to buy himself out of The Fleet.

'Tell me more!' cried Charlie whose natural optimism was slowly reasserting itself.

'You could become a father, Charlie!' Sydney told him. He grinned at Charlie's sceptical expression. ''Tis true. One way for a young woman to escape this hell-hole is to find herself with child. Don't look like that, Charlie my boy, 'tis the truth. They can't hang a woman who's with child. They have to send 'em out when it's due. Then they have to try and get 'em back again after it's born but –!' He adopted an air of extreme astonishment. 'What do you know? They can't find 'em! Now, women'll pay well for a young man's services! Specially a man with your good looks.' He indicated the rest of the men and muttered, 'If you was a woman, would you find it easy with one of these wretches?' His gaze roamed disparagingly over them. 'Disease-ridden, covered in lice, pock-marked! Would you care for a bit of pokey with one of them?' He gave an exaggerated shudder. 'No, they'd go for a fresh young man. You! I've been waiting for a chance like this. We could coin it in, you and me. What do you think?' As Charlie still looked dubious he said, 'I suppose you do know how it's done! Or are you a –' he lowered his voice, '– a virgin?'

Charlie forced a broad grin. 'Oh, I know how 'tis done, Reverend! Sounds an easy way to make a shilling or two!' But his smile hid his distaste at the notion for most of the women looked as unsavoury as the men.

'There's another way, too, Charlie,' Sydney went on. 'Sometimes a high-born but *single* lady gets into debt and ends up amongst us. If she were married her husband gets lumbered with the debt and she can go free. Fancy marrying a high-born lady? She pays you, you give a false name and who's the wiser?'

'But who marries us in here?'

'Why, yours truly!' He dug Charlie in the ribs with a plump elbow. 'I'm a reverend, remember. Between us we'd make a nice little bit! You think it over, Charlie, my boy. You think it over.'

Charlie asked, 'But is it legal?'

'Legal? Course it's legal. The Fleet's well known for its marriages. I've married dozens of 'em.' He rolled his eyes. 'Not that they stay married, but that's not my problem. So what d'you say, Charlie, my boy? Are you with me?'

Charlie hesitated. He certainly did not wish to get himself into further trouble with the law but on the other hand he *did* want to get out and for that he needed money. Marrying under a false name sounded more bearable than Sydney's alternative. He drew a deep breath and impulsively held out his hand.

'I'm with you, Sydney!' he said.

*

After reading the first few lines of the letter Sophie's mind began to close to its true meaning and she had to force herself to read it all a second time before she could accept its significance. Then the shock set in. A terrifying blackness descended on her so that she could no longer see the other members of the household who sat round the breakfast table with her. As though from a great distance she heard Henrietta ask if she was ill and she thought she shook her head in denial. There was roaring in her ears and she felt dizzy. She tried to speak but could not utter a word. The letter slipped from her hand and she was aware that Oliver scrambled from his chair to retrieve it. She heard his piping voice but could make no sense of his words.

'Matthew!' she whispered and then a merciful oblivion seized her and she knew she was falling.

When she came to, she was lying on the sofa with the children grouped anxiously round her and Henrietta kneeling beside her with a small phial of *sal volatile* in her hand.

'Oh Sophie! Thank the Lord! You frightened us out of our wits!'

For a moment Sophie was tremendously grateful for a sight of Henrietta's friendly face, puckered into an expression of concern, but almost immediately the cause for her own weakness struck her a second time and she winced with the pain of it. 'Oh Henrietta!' she gasped. ''Tis Matthew! Oh Matt! Matt!' She began to cry long anguished sobs and Henrietta put her arms round her comfortingly.

Oliver said, 'Mama? What has happened to Papa? Is he dead?'

'No, no!' Sophie told him brokenly. 'Not dead, Ollie, but —'

'Sick then, Mama?' he persisted. She could not see him for tears but she heard the tremor in his voice.

'He's not sick, Ollie,' but then she broke down once more and sobbed hysterically.

Henrietta said, 'Is it the plague, Sophie?' and there was fear in her voice too, but Sophie could not answer. She thrust the letter into Henrietta's unwilling hand and the tears streamed down her face as though they could never be halted. She was overcome by a bewildering rush of emotions as fear and humiliation mingled with hate and despair. She felt Henrietta withdraw her arms and knew she was reading Fanny's letter. Briefly Sophie nursed a fierce hatred of Fanny for being the bearer of such terrible news but she knew that that was unfair and struggled to convince herself that the little servant had acted in her best interests. The wording of the letter was obviously Fanny's and every word was engraved on Sophie's heart.

> *Dear Mistress,*
> *I think you should know that the master has taken up with another woman, one Anne Redditch by name. He is away some nights. He does not know I am writing to you.*
> *Fanny.*

Henrietta cried, 'Anne Redditch? Do you know her?'

Sophie shook her head and, finding a handkerchief, tried to stem her tears. Already her eyes felt sore and her throat ached with grief.

Henrietta sent one of the children for a towel and Sophie took it gratefully and held it to her face.

'Forgive me,' she said, 'I have frightened you all.' She dabbed at her eyes and managed a very watery smile for the benefit of the children. 'Oliver, Lizbeth, don't look like that,' she urged. 'Mama has had a shock, that's all.'

Lizbeth said, 'Is Papa dead of the plague?'

'No, my lamb, he is safe and well.'

Her eyes met Henrietta's who, refolding Fanny's letter, mouthed something uncomplimentary about the absent Matthew.

Then Henrietta said, 'Poor Uncle Matthew is in a spot of trouble but 'twill blow over. There is nothing for Ollie and Lizbeth to fret about.' She smiled cheerfully. 'In fact I think you should all go out into the garden and feed the rabbits and chickens. They want their breakfast, poor things.' As the children began to demur, she wagged a finger sternly. 'Out I said and out I mean. The sun is shining and there is no reason why you should linger here.' She put an arm round Oliver and Lizbeth. 'Your mama will be better in no time. See, she has stopped crying. Give her a big kiss and then go and feed the animals.'

She finally shooed them all out, fetched brandy from the cupboard in the parlour and poured a generous measure for each of them.

As Sophie hesitated Henrietta said, 'Drink it. You have had a bad shock.'

Obediently Sophie sipped the fiery liquid and was at once aware of a small but welcome warmth, somewhere within her.

'Oh Henrietta!' she said. 'How could he do this to me? To Ollie and Lizbeth too! I can scarce believe it and yet I must. Fanny could not be mistaken about such a thing – could she?'

'She names the wretch,' Henrietta pointed out. 'Anne Redditch. Who in the name of God is Anne Redditch and how did they meet? You are sure you do not know her?'

Sophie shook her head which was beginning to ache abominably. It seemed so unreal to be sitting with Henrietta discussing Matthew's infidelity. She ran a feverish hand through her hair and discovered a large bump. Seeing her expression change Henrietta said, 'You hit your head on the fender when you fell. Poor Sophie! I can't tell you how sorry I am. Nor can I believe that Matthew could be such a fool – to risk so much for the charms of this stupid Anne Redditch, God rot her!'

Sophie said,' And what of Matthew's mother? Should I hide it from her? She has eyes like a hawk and will see that I am not myself.'

Henrietta pursed his lips, considering. 'I should tell her,' she advised. 'He is her son. Why should she continue to think him such a saint?'

'It seems cruel, though. She's so old and –'

'Fiddle faddle! She's as strong as a horse! Tell her at once. Invite her help! She can be very formidable and she won't want to see her son's family broken up.'

'But she never really liked me –'

'She'll like this other wretch a deal less! You mark my words. She'll force him to see reason.'

Sophie clutched at this straw for a moment but then doubts crept in again. 'But this Anne —' she murmured distractedly, 'she may be very beautiful or very rich. Oh Henrietta! I have this terrible feeling here —' She placed a hand over her heart. 'I think I am going to lose him.' She swallowed convulsively. 'How could he do this? Doesn't he love me? Doesn't he love the children? What have we done to deserve this?' The thought of her husband's betrayal again overwhelmed her; the effort of self-control proved too great a strain and again she sobbed unrestrainedly, the towel pressed to her face, grateful for Henrietta's arm round her shoulder. When at last the worst was over Henrietta stood up. Pouring another brandy she ignored Sophie's protests and thrust the glass into her hand.

Sophie stared at it dully.

'You're going to drink it!' Henrietta told her, refilling her own glass, 'because I'm proposing a toast. We'll drink to the damnation of Anne Redditch!' She raised her glass.

Sophie whispered, 'I'll drink to that!'

But by this time the alcohol was beginning to take effect and she felt drained of emotion and utterly exhausted. When Henrietta suggested that sleep was the greatest restorative she did not argue for long but allowed herself to be led up the stairs, undressed and tucked up in bed. Henrietta leaned over and kissed her. 'Giles will know what to do,' she promised. 'We'll deal with that wretched woman and bring your husband to his senses.' She placed a hand over her heart in a parody of Sophie's earlier gesture. '*I* have a feeling here that all will turn out well! Now go to sleep.'

Sophie was already feeling drowsy and a welcome numbness had descended on her mind. The last thing she heard was the sound of Henrietta closing the shutters.

*

Sophie slept for the best part of the day and was woken just as dusk was falling by a gentle but persistent tapping on her hand. As she opened her eyes the events of the morning flooded back but Oliver was standing beside her and she tried hard to keep her expression cheerful.

'Are you awake, Mama?' he asked hopefully. 'Aunt Henrietta said you were sleeping but I said you never sleep in the daytime, only at night and she said –' Sophie raised herself on one arm and reached over to kiss him.

'I am awake now,' she told him.

'Grandmother is very anxious. She wants you to talk to her as soon as you are awake.'

Sophie's thoughts whirled. Had her mother-in-law been told or was she guessing, she wondered.

'Is Uncle Giles home yet?' she asked.

Oliver shook his head. 'I asked Aunt Henrietta

about Papa's "trouble" and she said I mustn't bother my head. Is it bad trouble, Mama? Is it secret trouble?'

Sophie thought quickly. She did not want the children to know of Matthew's rejection; later they might have to know but at present she would rather they remained in ignorance. She decided she would have to lie.

'Papa has a lot of troubles at his work,' she told him.

'Will he go to prison?'

'Go to prison? Certainly not!' Sophie smiled at him. 'Nothing bad will happen to Papa.'

'Then why did you cry?'

'Because – because I know your Papa is worried and unhappy and that makes me unhappy, too.' She ruffled his hair. 'But there is nothing for you or Lizbeth to fret about. We will soon put everything to rights and then we will all be happy again.'

'And will you talk to Grandmother?'

'Yes, I will. As soon as I am dressed again.'

His face brightened. 'May I tell her that?'

'You may.'

He hurried away, bristling with importance, and Sophie lay back on the pillows. Her head still throbbed and there was an uneasy sensation in her stomach but she told herself firmly that matters could be worse. Matthew could have the plague; he could be dying. That would be worse. Yes, she must cling to that thought. She tried to imagine Matthew with another woman in his arms and was engulfed by a rage which startled her by its intensity. And yet she had half expected something like this; she had wondered about Matthew's lies about Henry and herself but had suppressed her doubts. If only she had confronted Matthew when she first discovered his deceit. Why had she kept the knowledge to herself, thus allowing him to believe he had fooled her?

'Because I didn't want to be told unpalatable truths!' she said aloud. 'Because I am such a coward!'

The admission did nothing for her self-esteem and yet she felt marginally better for having made it. She felt suddenly that an important truth had been revealed to her. There must be no sheltering behind evasions or relying on other people; no pretending that she did not know what was happening and no feeding herself false hopes that if she waited long enough Matthew would realize his mistake. Now truth was everything. They must all lay their cards on the table. She felt stronger now that she saw the way ahead and suddenly decided that she would not ask Giles for his advice. What did he know about affairs of the heart? What experience did he have on the subject of unfaithful husbands? How could she be sure that her brother's advice, no matter how well meant, would be sound? No, she told herself. If she was going to make mistakes they must be her own. She would tell Ruth what had happened but she would not beg for help. This was not an issue between mother and son but between husband and wife.

With an impatient gesture she pushed back the bed covers. She would go back to London and confront Matthew but she must refuse to say how she came by her information. She would demand to know if it was true.

'But what then?' she whispered. If he said he loved the Redditch woman how should she react? What could she say or do? For a moment her courage deserted her but as she brushed her hair she felt it slowly returning. After she had bathed her face she moved to the mirror and took a long, hard look at herself.

'You're a good person, Sophie,' she said, but, noting the lack of conviction in her voice, she repeated the words with a little more vehemence. Staring at her own reflection she tried to see herself through Matthew's eyes, to understand why she had suddenly become unlovable. She was older certainly but still attractive. Suppose he deserted her! How would she support the children? Suppose this hateful woman had a child by Matthew! Seeing the shock in her own eyes she turned quickly from the mirror. It was no good frightening herself with supposition. There would be time enough to deal with those problems if and when they arrived.

'Be calm, Sophie,' she whispered. 'One step at a time!' But she was now seized with curiosity about the other woman in her husband's life. What was she like? Was she young? Pretty? Fanny would know. Fanny obviously knew a great deal more than she had written in her short note. And who had written it for her? How had she paid for it? Sophie shook her head. So many unanswered questions. There was only one way to find out and that was to go back to London. No matter how much it hurt her she had to know everything. She would go back without warning Matthew and she would ask Fanny about the other woman. Maybe she would even confront Anne Redditch.

Sophie turned back to the mirror and confronted her reflection again with a challenging look. 'Do you dare?' she asked.

Before she could reply, Oliver appeared once more at the bedroom door, his large eyes full of reproach.

'You *said* you would come and Grandmother is getting crotchety,' he told her.

As she turned towards him Sophie's smile was a little crooked but it *was* a smile. 'I'm coming, little man. I'm coming.'

*

Three days later Sophie went into Ruth's room to make her farewells. The old lady was pretending to be asleep but when Sophie coughed she made a show of reluctantly opening her eyes.

'Oh, 'tis you, Sophie,' she said somewhat ungraciously. 'You startled me, creeping in·like that. I was dozing.'

'I'm sorry. I didn't want to leave without saying goodbye.'

Ruth tutted. 'Well, if you are determined to go on this wild-goose chase I dare say nothing will stop you.'

'Nothing, no.' Sophie thought how frail Ruth looked and yet, as Henrietta had said, appearances were deceptive. Ruth had refused to accept Fanny's version of Matthew's infidelity. She had steadfastly maintained that she knew Matthew better than anyone and she was quite certain he would never behave so dishonourably. Fanny, she had insisted, always had been a scatterbrain and was obviously putting two and two together to make five. Sophie was relieved that she had taken it all so well but Henrietta had been suspicious.

'She knows more than she allows!' she had insisted. 'She's as cunning as a cartload of monkeys!'

Now Ruth was giving Sophie a baleful glance. 'Such an unseemly way to go about things,' she said. 'Sneaking up to London without telling your husband. Spying on him! To stoop so low! I never would have believed –'

Sophie fought down a rising resentment as she interrupted the familiar homily. 'We have been over this ground before, Ruth. I have no time for further arguments. My bag is packed and I am about to leave. I came to ask whether you have any message for your son when I do make contact with him.'

'*If* I make contact,' she amended silently. The

prospect of what lay ahead appalled her and this morning, when she woke panic-stricken, she had almost cancelled her journey. Henrietta had talked very sensibly to her however, reminding her that Giles also agreed that a protracted series of letters would solve nothing and he, too, thought she must go. He had also said that if Sophie ran the risk of contagion she must not expect to return but must take her chance in London while he and Henrietta cared for the children in her absence. Sophie dreaded the possibility of a long separation from Oliver and Lizbeth but she had weighed all the risks and had decided to make this one effort to try and save her marriage.

Suddenly Ruth drew a crumpled letter from beneath her pillow and handed it to Sophie. 'Give him this,' she said.

Sophie eyed it nervously. Whatever had the old lady written to her son? Nothing to Sophie's advantage, she thought bitterly. With an attempt at indifference, she stuffed the letter into her pocket but said nothing. It was natural that a mother would side with her son, Sophie reflected, but the thought increased her feeling of isolation.

'I trust I shall be back before too long –' Sophie began.

'I most certainly hope so!' said Ruth. 'Henrietta means well but she is a muddly housekeeper and Ollie and Lizbeth need their mother.'

These thoughtless words caused Sophie a

moment's agony of mind but she blinked back the threat of tears. Somehow she had to tear herself away from this comparative haven and face the loneliness, heartache and danger that awaited her in London. For a moment she could not trust herself to speak at all.

She became aware that Ruth was looking at her with a strange expression on her face. 'I dare say you would like to know what is in the letter.'

Sophie shook her head.

'Of course you would!' Ruth insisted.

'Only if you wish to tell me,' said Sophie, managing a little shrug. She waited, bracing herself for unwelcome news.

For a long moment it looked as though Ruth was going to change her mind. Instead, she said gruffly, 'If you must know I have told my son he is a fool!' She cleared her throat as though the words were difficult for her. 'A bigger fool than ever I thought him!'

'Oh Ruth!' Sophie gazed at her in astonishment, completely taken aback by this change of heart. 'How very generous!' she added.

Ruth fiddled with the coverlet, avoiding Sophie's gaze. 'I have told him that if he has any sense at all he will send this wretched woman packing! Anne Redditch, indeed! If I were younger I'd come with you, just for the pleasure of boxing her ears. Not that she's entirely to blame.' Her voice shook a little at her treacherous words. 'Matthew cannot be considered blameless. I'd like to knock their foolish heads together.'

'I don't know what to say —' stammered Sophie, overwhelmed and immeasurably heartened by this unexpected demonstration of loyalty. To her surprise she suddenly saw tears in the old lady's eyes.

'Take care of yourself, Sophie!' said Ruth. 'If anything happens to you I shall hold that son of mine responsible!'

Sophie leaned forward to kiss her. 'I'll take all precautions,' she assured her. 'But pray for me, Ruth. Pray for all of us!' And then she ran from the room and made her way quickly down the stairs, aware of a growing sense of impending disaster.

*

Unaware that his wife was at that very moment travelling upriver, Matthew was walking to Anne's house in a state of great agitation. The day was unbearably hot and it was only the second of July. The streets were full of contagion. Everyone who could afford to travel by coach did so with the result that, on this occasion, Matthew had been unable to obtain one and had been forced to walk. This was making him sweat and his temper was growing shorter with every step. While he dodged passers-by, he tried to think rationally about the situation in which he found himself with regard to Anne Redditch.

He had become very frightened of late by the

speed with which things were happening and the dawning realization that Anne wanted the affair to become a permanent arrangement had taken the edge off his affection. It was not that he no longer desired her but he was beginning to feel trapped. She had become very possessive and, on his last visit, she had even asked him to take the dog for a walk! He had done so with a very bad grace and now felt that he was losing control of events and suspected that Anne was manipulating him. She had even hinted that she would like to bear him a child and although that flattered him immensely it also terrified him. A bastard child could not be kept hidden for ever and eventually, inevitably it would come to Sophie's attention with the most dire consequences.

Matthew could not begin to imagine the devastating effect such a disclosure would have on his marriage. An illegitimate child would also involve him in great expense because he would have to support the mother as well. He was coming to the conclusion that he must tell Anne that he was having second thoughts. He would break it to her gently and hope she was sufficiently sensible to see that he was right. He was still willing, he would tell her, to visit her occasionally, maybe once a week, but he would never again stay overnight. Nor, he promised himself, would he be persuaded to drink so heavily as he had done lately. Anne's insistence was embarrassing him. He knew he was unable to deal with too much alcohol but Anne believed that drink was the test of manhood. She frequently spoke with admiration of her first husband who had been 'a hard-drinking man' and Matthew had felt obliged to try and compete with his ghost. Now all that must come to an end.

'My dear Anne –' he would say. 'My dearest Anne, there is something I must tell you; something that is breaking my heart!' That was an exaggeration but it would soften the blow. And if she refused to accept his argument and they quarrelled? If she refused to see him again? That certainly *would* break his heart! He did not want to give her up entirely, but he had much preferred it when their meetings were rare, brief and exciting and the hours between an agony of longing. Now, with Sophie away, their meetings lacked the spice of danger and Anne was demanding a commitment and too much of his time.

Aloud he muttered, 'Much as I adore you, I have, to my eternal regret, a wife and two children –' He bit his lip, feeling treacherous, but went on, 'and can never be to you all that you deserve.'

He smiled suddenly; this next part was rather clever, he thought. 'You are too fine a person to spend your life alone and I must release you.' Yes, that was the way. If he suggested they should finish it *entirely*, then he could later relent and she would be grateful for a compromise. Less time together would be better than none! If she proved intractable he would have to be very firm. He would tell her that they could meet occasionally as they had done formerly or they would not meet at all. He would make the point that he did not want to hurt her, he *loved* her, but he must be strong for both of them.

'I have to be strong for both of us!'

A man who was passing looked at Matthew curiously and he realized that he had been speaking aloud. He was within sight of Anne's door when it opened and Prudence appeared, looking ill at ease. She was carrying a small basket and a bundle of what looked like clothing. 'Good day to you, Prue,' he said curiously, glad that she was going to be out on an errand. It would be easier for him to talk to Anne.

To his surprise, he saw that she was trembling. She cast a frightened glance over her shoulder before she answered.

'I can't stay, sir, and that's the truth!' she told him. 'I'm no hero and never said I was. 'Tis against human nature to ask it of me. If 'twas my own kin that would be different but she's nothing to me but a mistress and a bad-tempered one at that!' She tried to force her way past him but he took hold of her arm.

'Prue! Wait a minute! Tell me what's happened. Is your mistress sick?'

From upstairs he heard a weak voice call his name.

Prudence jerked her arm free and said, 'I'm going and you can't stop me. You're her *brother*!' Her tone was mocking. '*You* tend her!'

'You don't mean –' Matthew's voice was suddenly hoarse. 'Not the plague! Oh no, Prue, you don't mean –'

'That's exactly what I mean.' She looked at him with obvious malice. 'Leastways, so she says, and who am I to argue? She's such a coward! She has made up her mind 'tis the plague and reckons she's dying. *And* she has the sauce to try and blame me! Said 'twas caught from my aunt in Cripplegate. How come I haven't caught it then, I asked and she couldn't answer!'

A very real terror gripped Matthew. 'Your *aunt* has the plague? Are you sure?'

'Course she hasn't.' Prue moved the bundle to a more comfortable position on her hip. 'Leastways, no one said it was the plague.'

'The physician. What exactly did he say about your aunt?' Matthew was trying to still the fluttering in his stomach but his legs felt weak. To steady himself, he leaned against the door jamb, his heart racing.

'We don't have no money for physicians!' she said scornfully. 'They're for the likes of you. But we bought her some physic from the apothecary. She'll live.'

Matthew clutched at this straw. 'Then how could Anne – your mistress, I mean, catch the plague?'

'Don't ask me! Maybe she caught it off *you*!' She laughed as Matthew winced. 'All I know is she's got it – or says she has. And I'm off! You're welcome to her!'

'But hasn't the physician called?'

'She thinks I'm fetching him now but that's as may be. When I think how she's treated me, and now when I'm leaving she expects favours!' Her expression hardened. 'I asked her once for another blanket when there was ice on my window panes and she refused. Said two was enough but I met a girl at the conduit whose mistress gave her four! Four blankets! And another girl was given a few hot coals in the grate when the snow lay thick.'

Matthew cursed inwardly. If only the wretched girl could be persuaded to fetch a physician. Once he had discovered whether or not Anne had the plague he would know better what to do. He said, 'But surely 'tis too cruel to refuse a physician to a sick woman! 'Tis too heartless!'

' 'Tis heartless to refuse a woman an extra blanket when 'tis freezing!' Prue's eyes shone with spite at the memory. 'Selfish cow!'

Matthew drew out his purse and gave her a handful of coins.

'Send a physician,' he begged. 'That's all I ask.'

She hesitated but her fingers closed round the money possessively. 'I may and I may not!' she told him and, ducking round him, she hurried away, her back stiff with righteous indignation.

'Dear God!' whispered Matthew, his heart pounding. Anne might be mistaken – but suppose her diagnosis *was* correct? He remained on the doorstep, poised for flight, but even as he hesitated Anne's voice came again, querulously.

'Matthew! Is that you? Oh my love! Come quick and help me!'

'I'm coming!' he called but he did not move. Every instinct warned him to save himself while he still had the chance but his conscience urged him to offer help. He clung to the door jamb while his thoughts churned and frightful visions filled his mind. If only he had issued his ultimatum to Anne a few days earlier; then they might already have parted and he need not know of her frightful situation. If it was frightful . . .

'Matthew?' Anne cried again. 'Are you there?'

He longed to walk away and leave her to her fate but if he did he would lose his self-respect for ever. And suppose their roles were reversed – would she desert him? He thought not.

He took a deep breath and levered himself upright.

'I'm coming!' he called again but as he closed the door behind him he felt like an animal lured into a trap which had been well and truly sprung.

*

Anne lay in the rumpled bed and one glance at her feverish face told Matthew that she was indeed ill.

'My dearest Anne!' he said, pausing just inside the room, afraid to venture further. He saw that her clothes had been dropped in a crumpled heap on the floor (ominous evidence that she had taken to her bed in a hurry, he thought), and that Prue had presumably been unwilling to move them.

Anne held out her arms to him. 'Oh my love! I'm so pleased you are here. That wretched Prue, the ungrateful slut! Oh Matthew!' He saw that tears slipped down her cheeks as he moved slowly towards the bed. 'I'm dying, I know I am, and she has deserted me. Can you imagine such ingratitude?'

Seeing that Matthew did not take her hands in his, she dropped them to the coverlet. 'She would not even fetch a physician!'

He said, 'I think she might. I have paid her well enough.'

'And I feel so hot! Matthew, I am sure I have the plague. I am going to die! Oh, God forgive me! Take pity on me! My throat hurts and my head bangs like a drum.'

He said, 'My poor Anne,' and was immediately aware how lame it sounded. 'But what makes you so certain 'tis the plague?' he asked, sitting on a chair as far away from the bed as he dared. 'It could be anything. Do you have any other symptoms?'

'I have a soreness in my neck, here,' she told him and turned her head to reveal the site.

Matthew recoiled instantly. 'A swelling?' His voice was thin with fear.

'Hardly a swelling yet but it could become one. Oh Matthew, you must fetch me a physician at once. I think Prue was leaving me to die, the unfeeling wretch! And poor little Banner hasn't been fed.' She put a hand to her head and gave a small moan.

Anne's face wore a sheen of perspiration and her

eyes glittered unhealthily. Her once glossy hair clung damply around her shoulders, her lips were dry and cracked and her fingers fidgeted constantly.

Matthew was struggling with a feeling of revulsion. He had never liked sickness, in himself or in others, and now he felt, illogically, that the woman he had so adored had betrayed him. Not only was she sick, but she probably had the plague and might well die in which case she would most likely kill him also. He felt a wave of self-pity. Why was life so unfair? What had he done to deserve such an untimely end? He stood up uncertainly. He must have time to think, he told himself, and must on no account do anything hasty.

'I'll fetch you a drink,' he told her, 'and then I'll tidy the room.' He forced a smile. 'Has Prue washed you this morning?'

She began to say that Prue had done nothing but pack her own belongings but Matthew was now regretting the question. Anne might expect him to wash her and he preferred to keep his distance. A wave of pity for her swept over him, and with it a feeling of deep shame that he could feel so ungenerously towards her when she was in such trouble.

But even as he searched for something loving to say, he saw that she was fingering her neck, and as her face registered pain, all Matthew's kindly feelings were swept away on a sea of panic. With an effort, he resisted the impulse to run from the house. But she might well recover; might live to reproach him.

He must think very carefully and do nothing to jeopardize his own life. He had his family to think about. Of course! This thought came to him like a lifeline and he grasped it thankfully. Surely he was not being selfish in thinking to preserve his own life; he was simply acting to protect his wife and children! He thought of Sophie with a great rush of affection. If only he could be safely in Woolwich with them and be done with all deceit. He wanted to run to Sophie and reveal all his sins and beg her forgiveness. But he dare not. Her faith in him would be shattered for ever and their marriage would never recover.

He said, 'I'll bring you some water and you can wash your face and hands.'

Before she could answer, he slipped out of the room and closed the door quietly behind him.

'Dear God, help me!' he whispered. 'I swear I will be a better man if only you will give me another chance.' He would be more considerate, more generous, more hard working – and totally faithful until death. He realized suddenly that this was God's punishment for his infidelity. He had brought this disaster on himself. He groaned with vexation at his own stupidity as he hurried downstairs and into the kitchen. Filling a jug from the big kettle, he carried the water upstairs and then moved the wash bowl and soap dish so that it was all within Anne's reach.

'Sit up when you can,' he told her, filling the bowl with hot water. 'I'll find some food for the dog and maybe something light for you.'

'I can't eat, Matthew!' she told him. 'My throat is too painful. Oh, do please –'

But he hurried out of the room again and went back to the kitchen. There he found Banner scratching at the back door, wanting to be let out. As he opened it, he said, 'Your mistress will be the death of me!' but the little spaniel had urgent matters of his own to attend to and ran into the yard. Matthew sat down and tried to concentrate. What should he do? He covered his face with his hands and tried to think of all the plague symptoms he knew. A bubo or swelling was certainly one of them but Anne had only said 'a soreness' which might be a boil or a carbuncle. But if she *was* stricken, the house would be locked up. An idea came to him suddenly. If he could arrange to be away from the house on some errand when that happened he would not be allowed back in! He could pretend to argue unsuccessfully with the watchman. Surely that would exonerate him from any accusation of desertion. Eagerly he examined the idea for flaws but it seemed sound enough.

'I'll do it!'

He went to the bottom of the stairs and called up, 'Anne! I think Prue has betrayed us. I shall go for the physician myself.'

She made some reply but he could make no sense of it and, desperate to be gone, he did not ask her to repeat it. He had just reached the street door when somebody knocked on it and his spirits rose. Prue had had second thoughts! He opened it with a welcoming phrase on his lips but found himself staring into the cadaverous features of a tall man. Below sunken eyes, his mouth and nose were covered by a cloth which smelled strongly of vinegar. In a slightly muffled voice the stranger said, 'Ask me in then, man, I've other patients to attend to.'

Matthew stammered, 'But who – how –'

'Doctor Pumphrey! For God's sake, man, don't stand there gawping, let me in. You are the brother, aren't you? The servant said this was the place.'

Prue! Oh, that wretched girl! Suddenly Matthew hated her as he had never hated anyone in his life! She had done the decent thing and now he was well and truly ensnared.

Doctor Pumphrey snapped, 'Let me in and then close the door. If your sister *does* have the plague you'll have the whole street down with it! Have you no sense, man? Or –' He peered into Matthew's face. 'Are you, too, unwell?'

As the doctor pushed his way in, Matthew said, 'I'm well enough. The patient is upstairs.' He was wondering whether to deny that Anne was his sister but decided it was easier not to do so.

'Lead the way then.'

Matthew hesitated. He could follow the physician upstairs and so seal his fate or he could turn and run. His tired mind seemed unable to make the decision but the physician made it for him. He shook Matthew roughly by the arm and said, 'Lead the way, man! Are you deaf?'

Matthew opened his mouth and shut it again. With despair in his heart and a feeling of unutterable dread, she preceded the physician up the stairs.

Chapter Eight

THE MOMENT SOPHIE put the key in the lock she knew instinctively that the house was empty. Inside all was silent. The kitchen was neat enough, with no dirty pots and pans, but no fire burned in the grate, nor had it been laid with paper and kindling wood; the coal scuttle had not been replenished. There was bread on the table but the crock was empty; there was no milk and only one egg in the pantry. In the meat-safe she discovered a small joint of cooked venison but the ham which usually hung from a hook near the fire was missing and the tub of salted herrings was less than a quarter full.

Her heart beat a little faster. Where on earth was Fanny? The church clock had struck five long since. It was getting late. Sophie made her way into the little parlour with growing dismay. By now Matthew should be on his way home from work and Fanny should be preparing supper. So what had happened to them? Even if Matthew was with Anne Redditch, Fanny should be around.

Slowly she went upstairs and found their bed unruffled. Had Fanny made the bed or had Matthew slept elsewhere? The chamber pot was empty and there was no washing water in the slop bucket. It was the same in Fanny's room. Either the bed had been made that morning or the girl had not slept in it. Sophie was reassured to see that Fanny's few clothes still hung on the hook behind the door. The window was closed and the room had a stale smell but that was normal. She went back to their own bedroom. A glance in Matthew's half of the wardrobe revealed his new suit, badly crumpled, hanging crookedly as though tossed there in a hurry. She drew the watered silk towards her and sniffed it warily but to her relief it smelt of nothing except the lavender which hung in a bag in the corner of the wardrobe.

'Matt, where are you?' she whispered, as though afraid to disturb the silent house. Had he taken advantage of Fanny's absence to move in with the Redditch woman? Anger warmed her frozen heart. If he had abandoned her and the children then he was not the man she thought he was and if he no longer loved her she could, possibly, withdraw her own love. She could learn to hate him. Anything was possible. Absentmindedly she ran a finger along the mantelpiece. The room had been dusted fairly recently which was slightly reassuring. She sat down on the edge of the bed, considering the situation as calmly as she could. She had come to London with no real plan in mind and now, with Fanny missing, she had no idea where to start. Only Fanny knew Anne Redditch's address and Fanny could be anywhere. She might be with her family in St Giles but Sophie knew the plague was well established in that quarter and dared not go in search of her. There seemed nothing to do but wait. Perhaps she could find some kindling and light the fire and boil a kettle. She tried to imagine boiling the only egg and eating it in solitary splendour and then going to bed alone in the empty house. This held no appeal but what else could she do? Could she go to Henry Bolsover's? No, that would mean revealing the problem and Matthew would never forgive her. She could wait here for Fanny to return which presumably she must do, unless she were taken with the plague in some far-off corner of the city. Was she in the pesthouse, perhaps? If so, then she was beyond Sophie's reach.

Sophie fought back tears. She had promised herself that, for the children's sake, she would be strong. Her tears must wait. Perhaps she would boil the kettle and make some tea. Staring at the empty grate, however, she realized that she had never learned to light a fire because there had always been a servant to do it – but in any case, there was no coal. If she ventured out in search of a coalseller she might miss Fanny if she called back.

'Lordy, what a muddle!' she exclaimed. Jumping to her feet she went downstairs again. She must occupy herself. She must be patient. Surely Fanny would expect her to return to London after sending such a letter. She would do nothing until she had spoken to Fanny. Unable to face eating she began to do some dusting. Anything to pass the time.

When daylight gave way to dusk, Sophie was still waiting for Fanny or Matthew to return home and at nine o'clock she finally gave up hope. She ate a handful of currants and went to bed.

The following morning she scribbled a note to Henrietta.

The house is empty. No Matthew. No Fanny. I know not what to make of it but shall wait here as long as I dare. I have so much to lose that I cannot give up at the first hurdle but if no one comes I shall be forced to return to Woolwich. Be reassured, I have been in contact with no one so am certainly still free of the contagion but deal with this letter cautiously. Please kiss Ollie and Lizbeth and my love to all of you.

Your affectionate friend, Sophie.

*

Two days after Doctor Pumphrey's first visit, Anne was noticeably weaker and the disease, correctly diagnosed as plague, had taken a more severe turn. She was frequently delirious and vomited any food which Matthew was able to coax into her unwilling mouth. The swelling on her neck was very painful and the hot poultices ('to coax out the poisons') made her scream in agony. Leeches had been applied ('to draw out the infected blood before it entered the body's recesses') but without any apparent success. As Matthew had feared, the house was shut up – the back door barred on the outside, the front door padlocked. No one was allowed in or out, with the exception of the physician. Outside, a burly watchman, by the name of Will Stookey, had been stationed on the front step to see that these regulations were carried out and to fetch any food or medicaments that the unfortunate inmates might need. He was willing enough when sober but surly and uncooperative when he had been drinking. At night, he was relieved by another man but there was little to choose between them.

The obligatory cross had been painted on the door and Matthew was aware of the fearful glances this inspired from passers-by. He felt unclean, like a leper, although as yet he showed no symptoms of the disease and the physician had assured him that a third of those who caught it survived and his 'sister' might well be one of them.

However, Matthew had resigned himself to catching the disease and lived from one hour to the next in a state of despair, ministering to Anne half-heartedly. He gave her a token wash each morning, cleaned up after her when she vomited, helped her on and off the chamber pot and changed the sheets when they were soiled. If his distaste for these tasks showed in his face, then Anne was too ill to see it. Somehow he kept his patience in the face of her ravings when she sometimes mistook him for her dead husband or railed against her husband's death as though it had only just happened. She asked after Banner constantly but Matthew dared not admit that the dog had found a way out of the back yard and had last been seen fleeing from one of the many dog-catchers. He told her, instead, that the physician had warned that dogs could also die of the plague and that he had recommended that the little spaniel be kept downstairs.

In the middle of the afternoon of June 10th, the cadaverous physician was again admitted to the house. He had seemingly abandoned the vinegar-soaked cloth which had covered half his face on previous visits and now, instead, held a pomander to his nose. The temperature was in the high seventies and beads of sweat stood out on his forehead. He looked jaded but his manner was as professional as ever. After a few preliminary remarks to Matthew, he examined the patient carefully but with growing dismay.

'I believe she is a little better,' Matthew suggested hopefully but the physician dashed his hopes with a quick denial.

'She's weaker, if anything,' he said. 'If only the swelling would come to a head! Then I could open it up and release the poisons. 'Tis quite crucial if the disease is to wear itself out before it exhausts the patient. Timing is everything.' He sighed. 'I would cut it open but I fear 'tis still too hard. I may have to cauterize it but only as a last resort. The pain with cauterization is very great and in some cases it drives the patient to lunacy.'

Matthew paled. 'Dear God!'

'Has she taken *any* nourishment today?'

'A little buttermilk; all that remained. Doctor, I regret to say that the watchman is a lazy rascal –'

The physician waved a hand dismissively. 'They all are, believe me. A good watchman is as rare as a snowball in Hell! Poor Will is as good as any. Some are a lot worse. Pray that you never need a nurse-woman! They are the dregs of the earth! Disgusting old harridans and quite unscrupulous.' He glanced up at Matthew while he checked Anne's pulse. 'They don't do it for the money, these nursewomen, but for what they can steal from the victims. I heard of one only yesterday who had smothered the patient with a pillow! To end her agony, she said. Only her age saved the old wretch from a whipping!'

Matthew suppressed a shudder. If Anne died and he then contracted the disease – who would nurse him? He dared not think about it and hastily thrust the unwelcome thought from his mind.

The physician concluded his examination of Anne's restless body, tidied the coverlet and fumbled in his bag for the ingredients of the plaster Matthew must make up and apply to her neck. 'Apply this as before,' he told Matthew, 'as hot as she can bear it.'

'She struggles so,' Matthew said wearily. 'And when I *do* manage to get it on she tears at it and tries to snatch it off again.'

'Tie her hands if you must,' said the physician. 'We must be cruel to be kind. I know it must come hard to treat a sister so callously but if you save her life she will thank you for it later.' He closed his bag and rubbed his eyes tiredly. 'There are not enough hours in the day – or the night. It seems that no sooner does my head hit the pillow than I am awake again and another dismal day begins. Still, I mustn't grumble. We all have our problems.' He flexed his shoulders. 'They are saying that the Law Courts will soon be closed. The lawyers are a squeamish lot and some are gone already to friends in the country. Inner, Middle Temple and Lincoln's Inn are all in turmoil. I'll wager that in a week or two the Courts will be deserted.'

'Can you blame them?' Matthew asked enviously.

But the physician ignored his question. He gave the patient a final glance and hesitated. At last he said, 'There just might be tokens appearing. I cannot be certain. Time will tell.'

'Tokens? *Tokens*!' Matthew was jolted out of his apathy. 'The spots that – you mean she – that there is no hope?'

'Who can say? And I said "might be". I may be wrong and I hope I am. I was reluctant to speak of it because I am not sure but 'tis always wise to prepare for the worst. The plague is very fickle. Sometimes it takes the fittest and leaves the weak. If we do lose her, then 'tis no more than I expected. The wretched bubo has proved so stubborn.'

'Then she *is* going to die? God in Heaven!' Matthew's haggard face was chalky white as he followed the physician down the stairs.

'A great many good souls are going to die,' said the physician as they reached the street door. He paused momentarily. 'I heard a most interesting theory yesterday that the plague is caused by earthquakes. It seems the eruptions release fumes full of pestilential seeds which are carried on the winds. If there is plenty of rain the seeds are washed down harmlessly into the ground; if not –' He rolled his eyes expressively.

'Pestilential seeds?' Matthew repeated dully but already the physician was banging his fist on the door to alert the watchman.

As the door opened Matthew resisted the by now familiar urge to shoulder his way out and run for his life. If he did he would be chased and arrested and thrown into prison, and he preferred his present incarceration to the hell of Newgate or The Fleet.

Matthew cried, 'Will you call again tomorrow?' but the door was slammed to before the physician could answer and he could not resist a shudder as the key turned in the lock.

*

The following morning Fanny saw Jem and her father off to work and drew a deep sigh of relief. At least her father had not contracted the disease which had killed her mother, and both he and Jem were beginning to emerge from the shocked despair which the three deaths had induced. First her mother, then Maggie and little Alfie. Fanny was beginning to suspect that God had taken against the Rice family and intended to wipe them from the face of the earth. Whose turn would it be next, she wondered, as she quickly washed up the breakfast pots and wiped down the kitchen table. After Maggie's death, Jem had returned to live with his father and the two men, never particularly close, had been drawn together by their mutual grief. Fanny, finding that Matthew did not return, had moved in with them temporarily, in preference to the empty house where she could be of no use to anyone.

She had intended to return from time to time to see whether or not her mistress had come back to London but then Charlie had disappeared and she had spent her days searching the city and the teeming waterfront for news of him. At last someone had reported seeing a young man, who might fit his description, being hauled out of the Cockpit by a man twice his size. Who this man might be Fanny's informant could not say but he thought it likely Charlie had been arrested. Fanny, thoroughly alarmed, had decided to visit all the prisons in the city in an effort to find her brother.

Newgate was first on her list, a prison dreaded by Londoners. Built in the twelfth century, it was old, unsanitary and desperately overcrowded. Jail fever killed many of the prisoners; other inmates, fit and youthful enough, were 'recruited' into the Army or Navy to reduce the numbers. An acquaintance of Charlie's had been transported from Newgate to Jamaica for stealing a crate of live pigeons! As she hurried towards the prison, she wondered which crime Charlie had committed or, more accurately, for which of his many crimes he had been arrested. There had been some talk, she knew, about tobacco and earlier rumblings about cheating at cards at the Black Horse in Drury Lane. Much earlier, he had been involved with a horse thief at Smithfield market and Fanny knew he was not averse to stealing from those who could afford it. But never before had Charlie been caught and Fanny had taken his arrest very seriously. While he remained a free agent she had been able to ignore his failings but now, seemingly, she was about to face up to harsh reality. Her father and Jem had been inclined to ignore Charlie's plight, arguing quite reasonably that he had brought it on himself. They had warned him often enough and her father insisted that a few weeks in clink might do him the world of good. 'Teach the young fool a lesson,' he had said. Jem had agreed moodily that it was no more than Charlie deserved. Fanny, however, felt obliged to find her brother, discover the worst and help him if she could.

Newgate, situated near Pye Corner, was a forbidding building and Fanny looked up at it with a feeling akin to dread. The main gateway boasted a portcullis and there were two smaller doors flanking it. Halfway up, three statues did nothing to lighten its austerity but higher still, incongruously, wallflowers had taken root in the cracks of the stone work. All the windows were iron grilles and Fanny could see no way a man could escape from such a fortress. Timidly she approached the right-hand door and knocked three times. A burly, unshaven jailer looked out through the rusty iron grille and, when told Charlie's name, was adamant that he had not been admitted during the past week. Fanny breathed a sigh of relief.

'Nor been transported?' she asked. 'Nor recruited into the King's service?'

'Not to my knowledge.'

'And you would know?'

He looked indignant. 'I'd know if he was 'ere or if 'e'd been 'ere. I know all what goes on in Newgate. I wouldn't know if he was committed to Ludgate, the Marshalsea, The Fleet or one of the Bridewells. I wouldn't know and I wouldn't care, neither!' He spat to show his disrespect and added, 'Got the idea, 'ave you?'

'Yes, thank you' said Fanny humbly.

'Then 'op it!'

As Fanny turned to go, she heard him mutter

something that sounded like "Bloomin' scrambag!" and thought how unfair life was. If she had been what Charlie called a 'comely wench', the jailer would have been pleased to talk to her; he might even have tried to hold her in conversation as a means of brightening his day. Instead, he had been rude and unmannerly. She thrust the thought from her mind and squared her shoulders defiantly. Remembering Antony Meridith, however, she brightened. Antony had taken time to talk to her and to be pleasant. He had not called her names. In short, he had appreciated her and Antony was most certainly a better judge of women than the surly jailer.

Ludgate was next and she hurried down Warwick Lane and turned left into Ludgate Hill. Here the jailer was a little friendlier but his answer was the same. No one by the name of Charlie Rice was held there, nor ever had been.

Fanny knew that it was mainly pirates and debtors who were kept in the Marshalsea so she decided to leave that until last and made her way along Old Bailey towards The Fleet. Here she was allowed inside to speak with an official of some kind who was sitting at a desk and gave every appearance of being desperately busy. In answer to her query about Charlie, he said, 'Yep! He's here,' and continued to shuffle his papers.

Fanny's heart leapt with excitement. 'He's here!' Her pleasure at finding him was diluted by the realization that Charlie, her beloved brother, definitely *was* a felon.

'Your young man, is he?'

'He's my brother!' said Fanny with an attempt at dignity. 'Will he be here long?'

'That depends!' The man tapped the side of his nose meaningfully and, looking up, grinned to expose a row of broken teeth.

She hesitated. 'On money, you mean?'

'You learn fast!' he growled. He scribbled something on the paper in front of him and added it to a pile on his left.

'I don't have any,' Fanny told him.

'Then he might be in for a long stay!' He chuckled as though he found his remark very witty.

From the end of the passage two men appeared, a jailer leading a prisoner who shuffled along, hampered by a set of leg irons. Fanny watched, fascinated as the appropriate paperwork was handed over from one jailer to the other with a few whispered comments.

Seizing her chance, Fanny addressed the prisoner, 'Sir, do you know Charlie Rice? I'm his sister. Is he well?'

To her surprise he grinned at the question. 'He's doing very well!' he said and winked at her.

The man at the desk said, 'You! Hold your tongue! You're not out yet!' But his leg irons were duly removed and the man at the desk offered the ex-prisoner a paper on which he drew a large X by way of signature.

'Get going! – before I change my mind,' he was told.

'I'm going!' the man assured him. 'And pleased enough to be out of this hell-hole!'

To Fanny he whispered, 'Your brother's a married man now. Did you know that?' and lurched towards the doorway and freedom without a backward glance. Fanny stared after him in astonishment. Charlie married? There must be some mistake. Unless there was another Charlie Rice. It was just possible.

The two jailers stared after the departing prisoner derisively and the man at the desk said, 'He'll be back! We'll hang him yet. You'll see!'

Then to Fanny he said, 'You can speak to your brother through the grating,' and Fanny, following the direction in which he jerked his head, found herself back on the pavement. For a moment she wondered if she had misunderstood but suddenly from a grating further along the pavement an arm appeared accompanied by a voice calling for, 'Alms for the love of God!' Hastening towards it, she realized that she could look down through the grating to one of the prison dungeons. Kneeling down she peered into the confusion of heads below.

'Bread, mistress!' cried the owner of the arm, a woman who seemed about Fanny's age.

'I'm sorry. I have none,' Fanny told her. 'I'm looking for my brother, Charlie Rice. Is he down there? Could you tell him I'm here. I'm Fanny, his sister.'

'Charlie who?'

'Rice.'

'Oh! *That* Charlie!'

Fanny frowned slightly, wondering exactly what the remark meant. Did everyone know Charlie? The woman's face disappeared and another appeared, a wrinkled, bearded face with wild staring eyes. Fanny thought, with a shudder, that if she had to spend even an hour among such misbegotten company she would die of misery. Yet Charlie, her bright and beautiful Charlie, was locked away down there, among the unfortunates that society had for the most part forgotten.

Suddenly, miraculously, there he was, beaming up at her. He looked exactly the same but with a growth of golden hair on his chin. Instinctively she thrust her hand through the grating and he caught it in his own and put it to his lips with a gallant gesture which drew loud cat-calls and a roar of laughter from his fellow prisoners.

'Fanny, you angel!' he cried, releasing her hand. 'I knew you'd find me.'

'Oh Charlie!' The relief of seeing him again and in such good spirits cheered her enormously. 'I was so afraid. I've been looking everywhere for you. Are you well?'

'Never been better – except for this!' He fingered the light beard.

'It suits you, Charlie. Oh Charlie! They said you were married. Are you?'

'A dozen times over!' cried a voice from Charlie's right and she saw a parson in ragged black, grinning up at her.

Charlie introduced this scarecrow as the Very Reverend Sydney and there was yet more laughter. Charlie then explained in a low voice how he was earning the bribe money for his escape. He asked after Jem and their father and then Fanny told him about Matthew and his paramour and the letter she had written to her mistress.

Charlie frowned. 'You did wrong there,' he told her. ''Tis never wise to meddle betwixt a man and his wife. Neither one will thank you for it.'

'But should I turn a blind eye and let the wretch play fast and loose?' cried Fanny indignantly. 'If my *mistress* had been unfaithful you would sing a different song! But 'tis done now and I'm not sorry. I hope the letter brings her back to London.'

Charlie shrugged. ''Tis your funeral,' he told her.

Fanny said, 'But 'tis you I want to talk about. Is there any plague in there?'

'Hard to tell,' he replied cheerfully. 'There's so many dying of one thing and another. But don't look so gloomy. I'll survive! You know me. Would I die? Certainly not!'

'Are they feeding you?' she asked. 'I've no money since the master disappeared. Damn his eyes.'

'You could bring me a file for these bars!' he suggested, then seeing her alarm, added, 'No, no! 'Tis only a joke, Fanny. I wouldn't risk your pretty neck.'

She glowed with pride at the compliment. 'So you will be out as soon as you have earned enough at your marrying? You are sure? Pa will want to know.'

His cheerfulness deserted him momentarily. 'Ah! Pa! I dare say he is not well pleased!'

She had intended to spare him their father's opinion of Charlie's behaviour but his earlier criticism of her letter had annoyed her, so she said, 'He says you are a fool and deserve nothing better.'

'Dear, fond Pa! And Jem?'

'He is too busy grieving for Maggie and little Alfie.' She blinked rapidly. 'Oh Charlie, I did so want to be an aunt,' she told him. 'And I didn't even get to buy him a rattle!'

'Jem will marry again, you'll see. He's the marrying type.'

'So are you by the sound of it!'

He laughed at the disapproval in her voice. 'A means to an end,' he said airily. 'But you must understand it is never Charlie Rice who weds but another who looks like him. Once I was Derek Jacobson, another time it was Hans Frick because my "wife-to-be" was a Dutch woman. I am very adaptable. Oh yes! I was also Lionel de Courcey, to satisfy the whim of a French lady of high degree.'

Fanny's lip trembled suddenly. 'Do get out soon,' she urged. 'I hate to see you here.'

'I will, Fanny. I promise.'

'I wish I could bring you something but I have

nothing. I stole some food from the house for Jem and Pa; it was going to waste with that wretch gone.'

''Tis "that wretch" now, I see!' he teased. 'You used to speak so highly of him. You were quite devoted to the man.'

'We all make mistakes,' she said stiffly. She was going to say more but at that moment she was roughly pushed aside by a group of people who called through the grating for 'Ernie'. As Ernie pushed forward, Charlie was also elbowed aside. There was just time for her to call a farewell before he disappeared from view and there was nothing else to do but abandon him temporarily to his fate.

*

That same afternoon when Antony returned home, he found his father in the bedroom holding up a long leather coat.

'The protective clothing. 'Tis here at last,' Luke told his son. 'It was delivered by messenger less than an hour since. It looks very heavy but is in fact more suede than leather and weighs less than I expected.'

Antony gave a whistle of admiration and said, 'They don't do things by halves, do they!' He reached into the box and pulled out a pair of leather gloves. 'Gloves, too, with sturdy gauntlets.'

Luke held up another item. 'A headpiece! But what a strange shape! And all made of leather. If the hot weather continues we shall be boiled alive!'

'But if it protects you from the contagion –'

'Most certainly it will. I am not so much complaining as marvelling!'

They both laughed and Antony said, 'You must put it on. This I must see.'

He helped lower the long straight garment over Luke's head and stood back to admire the effect.

'You could pass as a woman in a leather nightgown!' he teased.

Luke tried to move his arms and found the unfamiliar garment rather constricting. 'But I dare say it will get easier with wear,' he said hopefully. He pulled on the gloves and Antony allowed himself a giggle of delight.

'The very height of fashion!' he mocked. 'But now the head-piece. The *pièce de résistance!*'

Together they regarded it wonderingly. It was designed to envelop the head totally and to cover the shoulders like a short cape. The eye-holes were of thin sheep horn and just transparent enough to see through. The nose-piece resembled a long, sharp beak.

In answer to his son's raised eyebrows Luke explained that the 'beak' allowed room for a selection of herbs so that any pestilential smells could be safely filtered out.

'They've thought of everything,' Antony conceded.

When Luke had donned the head-piece, the outfit was complete and he regarded himself in the full-length mirror with a groan of dismay.

'I shall terrify my patients,' he said in a muffled voice. 'If the plague doesn't kill them this will frighten them to death!'

Even Antony had to admit that the sight of such a macabre figure appearing in the doorway of a sick-room would strike a chill into the stoutest heart.

'But if it protects you, then it has my vote,' he added.

Luke nodded. The outfit felt cumbersome in the extreme but it was all-enveloping and must surely safeguard him. For a moment or two he walked up and down the room, trying to familiarize himself with the weight and shape of it, and then he carefully lifted off the head-piece.

'The Lord only knows how I shall manoeuvre stairs,' he marvelled, 'but no doubt I shall find a way. If I don't I shall fall and break my neck!'

Antony sat on the edge of the bed and watched him in silence. Luke, reading his thoughts, said quickly, 'And you shall no longer be allowed to accompany me into a sickroom since you will be unprotected.' As his son began to argue he held up one hand. 'Don't try to argue with me, Antony. I have been too lenient so far. This is going to get much worse. The disease itself is intensifying. Fewer and fewer people will recover from it. I spent an hour at the College of Physicians this morning and the meeting was a gloomy affair.'

Wordlessly Antony helped his father off with the rest of the costume but finally he blurted out, 'I have changed my mind, Father. When this is over I want to study medicine in Padua. I am sorry I did not heed your advice earlier. I've been a hot-headed fool and I confess it but now I am quite determined.'

Luke's face lit up with pleasure at his son's words but before he could speak Antony went on.

'But don't think to hurry me off just yet, Father. Oh, I know how your mind works! No, I will stay in London and do whatever I can to help you through this crisis. Then I will go – and not before!'

For some time they argued the point, without rancour, but in the end, Luke had to accept his son's decision. He was delighted that Antony was now prepared to follow in the family footsteps and that he could look forward to working with him at some time in the future. First, however, they must survive the plague and Luke did not overestimate their chances.

*

Sophie was almost on the point of returning to Woolwich when she heard footsteps outside and the welcome sound of a key turning in the front door. She dropped her book and rushed to the door. For a long moment she and Fanny stared at each other in delight.

'Oh Fanny! Where have you been?' cried Sophie, resisting the urge to throw her arms round the girl. Instead she kept a wary distance.

Fanny, obviously understanding her restraint, said,

'I'm fit as a fiddle, mistress! And so pleased to see you!' Her smile suddenly faded. 'But my letter. I do hope I did right. Charlie says —'

'Quite right, Fanny,' said Sophie, her own delight tempered as quickly. 'I have come to see what can be done.' Although she had been longing to learn more about Anne Redditch, Sophie now felt unable to speak her name. Suddenly she did not want to hear whatever Fanny had to tell her. To hide her reluctance she said, 'I have been here the best part of a week, Fanny. Where have you been?'

'Caring for Jem and my father. I daren't stay here on my own.' She looked round the kitchen and a smile lit up her face. 'Oh! You've lit the fire.'

'After a few disastrous attempts!' Sophie confessed. 'Now that you are here you can make some tea. I think we deserve a little pampering.'

'Tea!' said Fanny, suitably impressed.

'Henrietta, bless her, insisted that I bring some with me.'

Dutifully Fanny bustled about the kitchen, explaining about her own family's problems and talking in general about London and the changes brought by the plague. Sophie listened for some minutes before her courage returned. She interrupted Fanny suddenly.

'Who wrote that letter for you, Fanny? The one you sent to me.'

Fanny's face brightened visibly. 'A physician, mistress. His name's Luke Meridith.

'So no one else knows about the master and — and

this woman.' Still Sophie found it impossible to speak of her rival by name.

'Certainly not, mistress,' Fanny said righteously. 'I reckon 'tis your business and yours alone – and his, too.' She turned from the fire. 'How could he do such a thing? I won't ever forgive him. Not ever! To treat you so and those sweet children! His brain must be addled, mistress, and that's all there is to it.'

Embarrassed, Sophie stared down at her own hands which were tightly clenched in her lap. Never, in her wildest dreams, had she expected to be sitting in her own kitchen, discussing her husband's infidelity with a servant. She was lost for words but Fanny went on relentlessly.

'I followed them. The master didn't see me, I swear it. Right to the very house. Oh yes, I can take you there. I saw her with my own eyes! A great fat woman with bulging eyes.'

Sophie's head snapped up, startled. 'Fat? Bulging eyes? Are you certain, Fanny? I cannot imagine Matthew becoming enamoured of such a person.'

Fanny hesitated and it was her turn to look embarrassed. 'Plump, then,' she amended. 'Not near so neat a waist as yours. And her eyes – well, they did bulge a little. Like a pug-dog. Horrible!'

Sophie was touched by the girl's loyalty. 'But passing fair, none the less?' she prompted with a faint smile.

'If you like that type.' Fanny tossed her head. 'But I found her a vulgar sort of person.'

Sophie frowned. 'You *spoke* to her?'

'Not exactly, no. But I could see she was a vain sort of creature. And she greeted him with a kiss! The wicked minx! And she's a widow woman. I went back the next day and asked the neighbours, very casually.'

'And the master is —' Sophie swallowed and her voice was little more than a whisper. 'The master is still there?'

'As far as I can tell, mistress. I've popped in here a few times and the house was always empty and no sign of life.' She poured the tea, casting a troubled look in Sophie's direction. 'Do you think — I mean, would he move in with her? Would he dare?'

Sophie fumbled for a handkerchief and pressed it to her eyes, forcing back tears. She was going to be strong, she reminded herself. No matter how distasteful or distressing matters became, she would be strong for the sake of the children. She had done a lot of thinking over the past week and had decided that she would give the marriage a fresh start, if Matthew was prepared to give up his new love. If not, Giles would speak to a lawyer friend to decide what she must do next.

'Then it seems he *has* moved in with her,' she said at last and sipped gratefully at the hot, sweet tea. 'You must take me to the house — no, better still, you must take a letter from me and hand it in at the door.'

'But what if *she* comes to the door? She might

well tear the letter up!' Fanny pursed her lips. 'She's that sort of woman.'

'Then you must insist on handing it to the master. You must ask for him by name.'

Fanny grinned. 'He'll be that shaken, seeing me there with a letter from you.' Her eyes gleamed with mischief. 'And I'll say, "Here's a letter from your wife!" I'll say it very loud so Pugface shall hear every word – and the neighbours, too.'

Sophie looked at her anxiously. 'I wonder if she knows that Matthew is a married man? Suppose he hasn't told her? If she doesn't know . . .'

'I'll wager she knows,' said Fanny. 'I told you, she has that look about her. Just the type that would steal another woman's husband.'

Sophie shook her head. 'Oh Fanny!' she said helplessly. ''Tis all so unsavoury!'

They fell silent, sipping their tea and Fanny was the first to speak. 'I thought I would frighten them,' Fanny told Sophie. 'I waited to see if they went upstairs and they did.' Hearing Sophie's gasp of dismay, she went on hurriedly, 'I threw soil up at the window and she looked down into the street but I doubt she saw me for I dodged back into the shadows. Oh, how I hate her!'

There was another long silence. At last Sophie said somewhat belatedly, 'Ollie and Lizbeth sent you their love.'

'Ah! Bless them!' Fanny's expression softened.

'Do they like their cousins? Are they happy? Do they miss dear old London, stuck out in the wilds of Woolwich?'

'Yes to all three,' said Sophie who knew that to Fanny 'the country' was a desolate place where no right-minded person would choose to live. But Sophie's mind was on the letter she must write. She would tell Matthew she was here and ask him to come back to the house to talk matters over. She must be careful not to sound hysterical but calm and reasonable. After all, she had the benefit of surprise on her side for Matthew had no idea that she knew about the affair nor, for that matter, that she was back in London. Matthew and Anne would both have a very nasty shock, she thought with relish.

But what if Matthew would not come to her to discuss the matter? Suppose he wanted to bring the Redditch woman with him. If he insisted she would have to agree. Imagining them together, a wave of jealousy swept through her so that she closed her eyes in agony. How could she bear it?

Twenty minutes later, the letter was finished. After much deliberation she had written:

Dear Matthew,

I have learned of your association with Anne Redditch and am naturally distressed. I am presently in London, at home, and willing to discuss the matter. I shall stay here for twenty-four hours after the delivery of this letter

*and then I shall return to the children who were very
disturbed by my return to town.*

    Your wife, Sophie.

                    *

Filled with importance, Fanny set out for the house
of Anne Redditch, the letter tucked securely in her
pocket, her head held high. Now, Master, she
thought triumphantly, the avenging angel is on its
way! She could imagine his face when he read the
letter and he would never know that it was she,
Fanny Rice, who had undone all his schemes. Serve
him right! Not that she wanted him to remain in
ignorance of her part in the affair. She would like
him to know that she had paid him back for keeping
her from her mother's funeral but she knew she
dared not admit it. If he did return to his family, he
might well give her the sack on some pretext or
other and she could not allow that to happen. No,
she would remain in the household, but would
always be slightly aloof so that he would wonder
just how much she knew. *If* he came back. There
was always the possibility that he would choose to
stay with Pugface.

    She was thinking quite cheerfully along these lines
when she turned the corner and drew near to the
house. To her astonishment she saw that a red cross
had been painted on the door, with the words, 'Lord
have mercy upon us'. The door was padlocked and a
rough-looking man was camped on the doorstep.

Instinctively she drew back. 'Not plague!' she whispered. 'Oh no! Not that!'

Deeply shocked, she leaned for a moment against the wall and then, summoning her wits, cautiously approached the watchman. 'What's happening?' she asked, rather superfluously. 'I've a letter for someone in the house.'

He stared at her indifferently. 'A letter?'

'Yes!' Was he daft? 'A letter for Master Devine. How can I reach him?'

'Don't know the name! There's Redditch. That do?'

Fanny was furious. 'No, 'twill not do!' she told him. 'I must put this letter into the hand of Matthew Devine and no one else.'

'The house is shut up,' he told her. 'Don't you know what that means?'

'The plague?'

'Right first time. Her, not him. Dying, so they say.'

Dying! Anne Redditch was dying? She fought down an un-Christian impulse to cheer. 'Who says she's dying?'

'Why, the physician. Doctor Pumphrey.' He regarded her craftily. 'I could deliver the letter for a price,' he offered.

'I've no money,' Fanny told him. 'Is the gentleman stricken?' She hoped not for the sake of her mistress.

'Not yet.'

Fanny raised her voice. 'Sir! Master Devine! I've a letter for you!'

There was no immediate response but while she

stared up at the window a small brown spaniel with a well-fringed tail ran past her to the door and began to scratch at it, whimpering as he did so. The watchman aimed a hefty kick at the animal and sent it howling.

'You great bully!' cried Fanny. 'What's the poor thing done to you?'

'Pesky animal!' The dog had retreated about ten yards and was crouched against the wall, still watching the door.

'Why did you kick it?'

He glared at her. 'They carry the plague. Should be dead by rights. How he keeps dodging the dog-catcher I'll never know.'

While he was speaking, Fanny suddenly realized that a window was being opened above her head and she looked up. Matthew Devine was staring down at her as though at a ghost.

'Fanny? Oh Fanny! Is that you?'

'Sir?' For once Fanny was almost speechless. Her master was unkempt, his hair wild, his face thin and haggard. He looked so pathetic that a little of her hatred for him faded into pity. 'That *is* you, sir?' she asked in return.

'Certainly 'tis me! Am I so changed? But in God's name, what are you doing here? How did you find me? How did you know I –'

She recognized his confusion as the full implication of her presence at Anne's house dawned on him. 'This is hardly a safe place,' he warned her. 'You must go home at once.'

'Please sir, I have a letter from the mistress.' Remembering her earlier threat she added loudly, 'A letter from your wife!'

He seemed unable to understand. 'My wife? From Sophie?'

'Yes sir.' Fanny produced her trump card. 'I left her at home not half an hour ago.' She could not resist a smile as this fact also registered. That would teach him to keep her away from her mother's funeral. She hoped her mother was watching and would see how well the wretch had been punished.

'At home?' he faltered. 'But how –' His face crumpled. 'Oh Fanny! She doesn't know? Tell me she doesn't know!'

'She does know sir.' Fanny regarded him severely. 'Someone told her and she's here in London. 'Tis all in the letter.' She pulled it from her pocket and held it up.

'Dear God!' he cried. 'This all so terrible! A nightmare!' He suddenly caught sight of the dog which was once more creeping towards the door. 'Banner!' He shook his head dazedly and then apparently recalled what Fanny had said. 'The letter from Sophie? I must read it. Wait there!'

He disappeared from view and then reappeared at the window with a small basket on a rope which he began to lower. From his manner she could tell that he had done it many times before.

'Listen carefully, Fanny,' he told her earnestly. 'Do not touch the basket whatever you do! Do you understand? Do not touch it! Throw the letter into it without touching it.'

'I will, master.'

As soon as the basket was low enough she tossed in the letter and watched the basket rise again with a sense of growing excitement. Times might be hard but they were far from dull! She saw her master lift in the basket and then there was a long silence. The dog crept towards her and Fanny held out her hand to it. Banna, her master had called it, or some such name.

'Here, Banna!' she cried and the poor, neglected animal pushed a cold nose into her hand with a little whimper of pleasure.

The watchman cried, 'Serve you right if you get the plague! Don't say I didn't warn you! Dogs is the very devil!'

'He's healthy enough,' said Fanny. 'His nose is as cold as ice. Just half starved.'

Above her, Matthew's head reappeared and she saw with a shock that he was red-eyed. He had been crying!

'I dare not send a letter,' he stammered brokenly. 'Tell your mistress that I love her . . . above all people and that . . .' He brushed fresh tears from his eyes. 'Anne is most likely dying and I must stay and care for her. I may well die also. 'Twill be no more than I deserve . . .' He broke down suddenly and began to sob. Fanny stared at him speechlessly until, with an obvious effort, he regained a little of his self-control. 'Tell Sophie and the children, fare-well –'

'Farewell? Oh no, sir!' cried Fanny. 'I cannot say that! Farewell? 'Twill break her heart.'

But with a last anguished look at her he withdrew his head and closed the window. Shocked and confused, Fanny stared upward. 'Master!' she called. 'Give me a more hopeful message, I beg you!'

She waited but the window remained firmly closed. The watchman said, 'They'll both be dead 'fore long!'

She rounded on him fiercely. 'What do you know about such matters, you ignorant oaf! You know no better than to kick defenceless animals!' She stared past him to the clumsy message on the door. 'How long?' she demanded. 'How long before you unlock the house? You do know that much, I dare say!'

He shrugged insolently. 'Don't rightly know and wouldn't tell you if I did!' he said. 'If you can't keep a civil tongue in your head –'

'Oh, go to Hell!' shouted Fanny and, turning on her heel, she hurried away down the street, unaware that the dog trotted hopefully behind her.

Chapter Nine

❧

SOPHIE WAS IN THE loft feeding the pigeons when Fanny arrived home but she hurried downstairs and listened in growing dismay to Fanny's account of Matthew's plight. At the end of it she sank down on to a chair without a word and covered her face with her hands.

Fanny said, 'I want to think "Serves him right", but, to tell the truth, I don't. I wanted to punish him for – you know, mistress – but on the way back here I kept thinking of all the good things he'd done.'

Sophie listened half-heartedly, stunned by the news that Matthew was likely to die.

Fanny went on, 'Like the times he took us all to Bartholomew's Fair – and there was that little drummer who kept winking at me.' She smiled at the memory. 'And we tossed for gingerbread, and then you tried your luck at the skittles and won a tortoise-shell comb for your hair! Do you recall?'

She seemed to be waiting for an answer and Sophie said, 'Yes. Yes, I recall.'

Fanny gazed past her, unseeing, as ghosts of the past flitted into her mind. 'And one year we saw that fat lady – the fattest in the whole world and the master said they must have blown her up with bellows she was so big! And the children went on the roundabout and had toffee apples and there was a painted lady dancing with a veil over her face!' Her own face fell suddenly. 'I dare say the fair will be cancelled this year because of the plague – but we did have fun and the master – he laughed as much as any of us.' She sighed deeply. 'And once when the pedlar called on my birthday the master bought me that brooch in the shape of a butterfly. I keep it in my little box.'

Sophie lowered her hands and nodded dully. 'I remember.'

Slowly Fanny sat down opposite her mistress, her face troubled. 'Once I spilled the milk and thought he would be angry but all he said was, "Go quickly and find another cow!"' She smiled faintly at the memory. 'Oh mistress! He wasn't a bad man until now. A little tetchy at times, perhaps, and he did do me wrong but –'

Sophie drew a long, shuddering breath. She felt exhausted, crushed by the sheer weight of her misery. 'We all make mistakes,' she said. 'Nobody is without sin. It says so in the Bible. Perhaps he has regretted his mistakes.' She looked hopefully at Fanny.

Fanny hesitated. 'Maybe Pugface beguiled him,' she suggested, 'against his wishes. She could have powers – or maybe she used a love potion!' Her eyes widened. 'She might be a witch!'

'A witch? Really, Fanny! Your imagination is running away with you.' Sophie spoke more firmly but her eyes gave the lie to the words and, bizarre though Fanny's suggestion sounded, she wanted to believe it possible. She was willing to consider any notion that Matthew's feelings for Anne Redditch were less than genuine. 'There may be something in what you say,' she agreed cautiously. 'The wretched woman may have ensnared him by some devious means. But whether she did or not the question is, does he still love her? Oh Fanny!' A new thought struck her and her voice broke slightly. 'Do you think he has chosen to die with her rather than to live without her?'

Fanny snorted at this romantic idea. 'I doubt the master would love anyone that much!' she said.

'Fanny!'

Too late, Fanny saw that her mistress was not yet ready to accept so low an assessment of her husband's character. 'I mean, no man would be that foolish,' she amended hastily. 'Nor no woman, come to that.'

'The instinct for self-preservation, you mean?' Sophie looked at Fanny gratefully. 'Perhaps you are right. I do hope so. But whether he loves her or not we cannot leave him there to die. Did he look ill, Fanny? Oh, God in Heaven! My mind is going round in circles. We must get him out of there and bring him home.' She sat up a little straighter. 'No, don't shake your head at me, Fanny. Whatever his faults he is still the children's father and I will not abandon him.'

'But they won't let you take him anywhere, mistress,' Fanny told her. 'I told you he is truly a prisoner with a padlock on the door, 'Tis the law!'

Sophie jumped to her feet. 'Then we must bribe somebody!' she said.

'Bribe somebody?' Fanny's mouth fell open with shock. 'Oh no, we daren't!'

'I dare.' Sophie began to pace the room, her hands clasped in agitation. 'There is always a way. We must get him away from that wom–' She corrected herself hastily. 'From that *house* and bring him home. Then, if he is ill, *I* will care for him.'

'But the children! Suppose you should fall sick and die also?' Fanny had now risen to her feet and stared at her mistress greatly disturbed.

Sophie came to an abrupt halt, one hand clapped over her mouth. 'The children!' she gasped. 'My poor little lambs! How could I forget them? You are right to remind me of the dangers but – poor Matthew! What on earth am I to do?'

In the ensuing silence they both became aware of a desperate scratching sound at the front door and Fanny hurried through to the front of the house to investigate. 'Oh dear!' she murmured guiltily, turning to face Sophie. ''Tis the dog. The dog from –

from *her* house. Pugface's dog.' She opened the window and shouted, 'Go away, Banna! Shoo!'

Fascinated in spite of herself, Sophie followed Fanny to the front window and together they looked out at the sad little spaniel which looked up at them appealingly, wagging a feathery tail.

Fanny said, ''Tis my fault. I was kind to it. But the poor thing is starving. 'Tis said the King himself has dogs like this one. Three or four, so they say.'

Sophie looked down at it. 'The children have always wanted a dog,' she said.

'It wanted to go back into the house but her watchman kicked it down the street.'

Sophie considered this in silence and Fanny glanced at her surreptitiously. 'She's abandoned the poor little thing. That's the sort she is.'

'I expect 'tis hungry' said Sophie.

The spaniel, sensing their interest, began to whimper, its liquid eyes fixed first on Fanny and then Sophie. Its fiercely wagging tail drooped sadly.

Sophie said, 'Matthew has never cared much for pets.'

'No, mistress – but Jem saw him once with a dog in his arms and 'twas most likely this very one.'

Sophie listened as Fanny recounted the story Maggie had told her and was aware of a frisson of anger overlaid with jealousy. For a moment she struggled with her feelings. Then, she sighed heavily. 'I suppose if Anne had a dog he would have to pretend he liked it,' she said.

The little spaniel barked suddenly and sprang into the air.

Fanny said, 'He's a handsome little dog, as dogs go.'

'Mmm.' Sophie caught the wistfulness in Fanny's voice. She herself was strangely drawn to the animal because of its tenuous link with Matthew although her common sense warned her against such weakness.

Together they watched the animal's antics. Aware of its audience, the dog now retreated to the far side of the street and, taking a run, sprang up at the house, trying unsuccessfully to reach the window which was still closed. For a moment its large brown eyes were fixed on Fanny's face as its front paws scrabbled unsuccessfully for a foothold before it slid down out of sight.

Fanny said, 'Poor thing.' She looked at Sophie's face from the corner of her eye. 'Should we give it a little something to eat?' she suggested. 'Maybe it would go away then.'

Sophie said, 'Fanny Rice! You know it would do no such thing! Feeding it would be fatal! It would adopt us. We must ignore it and then –'

The dog had now returned to whimpering and scratching at the door. A man passing in the street paused to shout, 'Let your damned dog in and keep it in!' and stalked on.

Sophie hastily retreated from the window and said crossly, 'You should never have spoken kindly to it in the first place! 'Tis all your fault. Come away from the window.'

They returned in silence to the kitchen, where Fanny, chastened, hovered uncertainly. Sophie stared out into the back yard.

'She should have taken better care of it,' said Sophie.

Fanny nodded. 'She'd turn it out when it suited her. No heart, that one! Never mind. It won't starve much longer,' she said. 'One of the dog-catchers will get it before long and then —' She pulled a finger across her throat.

'Oh no!'

'No, they don't cut their throats. They hit them on the head with a heavy brick.'

'Fanny!'

'It takes only one blow, I was told, or maybe two or three so 'tis very merciful.'

'Merciful?' Sophie swallowed hard. 'I don't want to hear about it.'

'Sorry, mistress!' Fanny said and Sophie, seeing through her little strategy, was tempted to slap her.

Instead she said briskly, 'That's enough about dogs,' and began to pace the room once more. 'I have more to worry about than someone else's pet,' she said but in her mind's eye she saw the dog in Matthew's arms and unexpectedly she found tears on her cheeks. They fell faster and faster until at last she felt Fanny's arms round her in an awkward hug.

'Oh Fanny!' she wept. 'I can't bear it! I can't let

Matthew die like this. All our hopes . . . all our plans
. . . how will I tell the children that their dear Papa
is gone?'

''Tis very hard, mistress,' said Fanny. 'Sit yourself
down and have a good cry. My poor Ma used to say
it does you good. Lets the grief out, you see. I'll
heat you some milk and I dare say there's still some
brandy in the bottle in the parlour.'

As Fanny bustled around her, Sophie thought of
Matthew and his terrible predicament. How he hated
sickness. It frightened him, she knew. How was he
coping with a dying woman – even one he loved?
And Fanny had described how haggard and worn he
looked. Was he going to die in a strange bed in a
strange house while she did nothing to help him?
However much he had hurt her she could not wish
such a sad end for someone who had once meant all
the world to her. Wiping her eyes she sat up again
and reached dutifully for the mug of milk which
Fanny now offered.

'Wait, mistress, for the brandy!' Fanny told her
and went into the other room. Suddenly Sophie
heard her cry out.

'Oh mistress! 'Tis Banna. 'Tis the dog! The dog-
catcher has him!'

Sophie leaped to her feet and rushed to join
Fanny once more at the front window. Sure enough,
the brown dog, with its head in a noose, was now
struggling at the end of a long pole. The more it
struggled the tighter became the noose. Several

people had stopped to share the spectacle, some cheering for the dog, others for the dog-catcher.

Fanny covered her eyes and said, 'Oh! The *poor* thing!'

Sophie watched in silence, her hands clasped in front of her mouth. Taking in a stray dog was a foolish thing to do, yet amongst so much misery it seemed she had the chance to save just one life. Perhaps she could not save her husband but she could save the dog he had once held in his arms. It was quite illogical but without being aware that she had made a decision she found herself rushing to the front door. As she pulled it open she cried, 'Fanny, fetch my purse!' and without taking time to reconsider she was out in the street.

'That's my dog,' she told the dog-catcher peremptorily.

He was slowly working his hands along the pole towards the brown dog and ignored her remark.

'I let it out by mistake,' she told him. 'I'm sorry. I'll take it in now and I'll be more careful in future –'

'Too late now, mistress,' he replied. 'A quick blow to the back of the head and Bob's your uncle!'

'But you can't!' she insisted. 'I tell you the dog's mine. I know its name. 'Tis Banna.'

The man had reached the dog and now held it firmly between his knees. 'He can be called Jesus Christ for ought I care!' he told her. 'I get paid per dead dog. No dead dogs, no pay. Simple!' He looked at her craftily. His hands tightened threateningly round the dog's neck and frantically the little spaniel renewed his struggles.

Fanny appeared breathlessly beside them, the purse in her outstretched hand. Sophie gave the man a few coins.

But he looked at them dismissively. 'You don't care much for your dog, do you, mistress?' He slipped them into his pocket but made no move to release the dog.

'Damn you!' cried Sophie. 'I've a good mind to report you.'

'And I could report you, mistress,' he answered. ''Tis against the law nowadays to let a dog loose on the streets.'

Sophie bit back an angry rejoinder. He was right and she was wrong. Silently she offered him a shilling and without further words the man pocketed it and slipped the noose. Freed, the dog gave a howl of fright and bolted into Sophie's front room. She and Fanny hurried in after it and closed the door before the dog-catcher could change his mind or demand more money. The terrified animal was cowering in a corner but, after some encouragement, it crept out and followed them into the kitchen. For a moment they regarded it wordlessly.

''Tis a boy dog,' said Fanny.

Sophie gave it a crust of bread which it gobbled ravenously and the two women exchanged sheepish looks.

At last Fanny's grim expression relaxed into a grin and Sophie said wonderingly, 'We seem to have acquired a dog!'

*

Will was having a bad day. His head ached, his stomach rumbled and a passing horse had dropped steaming dung onto his out-thrust left foot while he had been dozing. He had no objection to the dung but he did mourn his lost opportunity. When he awoke, only minutes after the incident, a young urchin told him that the rider of the horse had been a fine gentleman and fine gentlemen could be persuaded to part with a few pence if the unlucky recipient of the dung hollered loud enough. Being asleep, Will hadn't hollered at all and the knowledge that he was poorer because of his innocent doze still rankled two and a half hours later.

He was also somewhat displeased by the commotion going on in the house he was so carelessly guarding. He had sat through three horrible screams soon after the arrival of the physician and had then had to endure the sound of hammering upon the upstairs window, as though all the fiends of Hell were loosed in there and trying to get out. It was enough to frighten the wits out of a weaker man and it was to his credit that he suffered it all so calmly – though it did his headache no good at all. Passers-by stared up at the house when they heard the screams and some passed comments while others averted their faces. A few crossed themselves and had the audacity to ask him what was going on up there, as though it was his business or he was in some way to blame! He knew better than to inquire into the process of dying, he told them. He was paid to guard shut-up houses and that was all. If they wanted him to give out daily bulletins on the occupants' health they should pay him more!

He was still pondering his lot when the physician came down the stairs and gave three raps on the inside of the door. Will struggled to his feet and fumbled blearily with the padlock. Doctor Pumphrey called impatiently, 'Get a move on, man!' and Will deliberately slowed down, just to show him who was in charge. At last the door swung open and the physician stepped thankfully out of the house, wiping sweat from his brow with his sleeve. He looked tired, his face was drawn and his eyes held a look Will was dimly beginning to recognize as defeat.

'Dead, is she?' Will asked, without much interest.

The physician nodded. 'I'll send a woman along to lay her out and a searcher to record the cause of death.'

Will sniffed disdainfully. Searchers were the poorest specimens of humanity in his reckoning, but there! Someone had to enter the shut-up houses and examine the bodies and as long as it wasn't him he couldn't give a tuppenny damn. The physician stood for a moment as though trying to collect his thoughts. 'Poor soul!' he muttered, half to himself. 'What a way to die.'

'Painful, was it?' Will asked eagerly. 'I heard her screaming. Went through me like a knife through butter! Horrible!' He shuddered realistically.

The physician looked at him and said almost defensively, 'I had to attempt it. I had to cauterize. 'Twas her only chance.'

'And it finished her off, like!'

The physician drew in a long breath, his eyes unseeing, and said again, 'Poor soul!'

'And the body? Who's collecting that?' Will demanded.

'I shall notify the proper authorities. They'll collect the body after dark. A cart, most likely.'

'I'll be off home by then,' Will told him. 'I'll tell Old Sammy to keep a look out for them.'

The physician said, 'The gentleman is also infected. He has taken to his bed. I shall call on him again tomorrow.'

He walked away, stumbling with tiredness, and Will watched his retreating figure with an expression of resentment. Just his luck to miss the plague cart, he thought morosely. He got all the screaming and hullabaloo and the nightshift got the excitement. Old Sammy had seen two bodies loaded into the cart so far and that could be a bit of a caper, by all accounts. All the relatives begging to go along with the body to the graveyard and being refused. They didn't like that at all! According to Old Sammy they kicked up Hell's delight, going on about their rights and last respects, sobbing and whatnot. Huh! Will snorted with exasperation at the nerve of some folk. Who has rights when the plague's taken over the city? If him upstairs wanted to follow his sister to the graveside he'd be unlucky because Old Sammy would have none of it. Not that the brother would be in any state to go anywhere, by the sound of it. Gone down with it himself, so Pumphrey said. Which was all to the good, in one way, because sick men did not expect the watchman to leave the premises and go chasing half round London in search of food and medicaments. Leaving the premises was always a bit risky. He'd heard of folk sending the watchman on a fool's errand and then climbing out of the window! And who got the blame? Why, the poor old watchman, that's who!

He settled himself more comfortably on the doorstep and prepared to doze again. Then, remembering his earlier loss of revenue, he slid further down into the roadway with his left leg thrust well out. With any luck another fine gentleman might ride by and if God saw fit to give the horse a bit of a hint Will didn't want to miss out on a second load of dung!

*

Matthew surfaced from an uneasy sleep and was dimly aware that his limbs ached and his skin burned. He tried to change his position but every muscle screamed in protest. He was sweating and the bedclothes seemed to weigh a ton. With an effort he pushed them back and for a moment revelled in the coolness but after a few moments he began to feel cold and started to shiver violently. He wondered dazedly what the time was; it was still light so it was daytime. It hardly mattered. If he was going to die nothing mattered very much. He was in Anne's house, in her bed, that much he knew, but when he attempted to make sense of the events leading to his predicament a certain confusion set in. Anne was dead, he knew that. Poor Anne. He wanted to remember her as she had once appeared to him, laughing and loving with a faint blush in her cheeks. Instead he recalled only her last agonizing hours when, half demented by the pain of the physician's ministrations, she had struggled free from Matthew's grasp and tried to throw herself from the window. That horror would stay in his mind until he too was dead.

But had he ever really loved her? Had she loved him? Her last words had been for the dog, not for him. As she fell to her knees she had summoned her failing reserves of strength to whisper his name in a final moment's lucidity. She had loved Bànner for longer than she had loved him and probably the dog's devotion had been stronger than his own. A chastening thought and one Matthew did not relish. Poor foolish Anne. She had given her heart to the wrong man. Still, he had not deserted her in her last desperate hours although he would have done so had it been possible and that knowledge depressed him. But at least Anne had believed him loyal and hopefully that belief had comforted her. She had thanked him again and again for staying with her and he had allowed her that small consolation. But he was not proud of himself. Her last hour had been terrible and he prayed that when his time came God would allow him a more merciful end.

He tried once more to move his aching body and wondered vaguely if he was hungry or ought to eat. The thought of food revolted him and swallowing was painful. He would like a drink but knew he could not manage the stairs. Pumphrey had offered him a nursewoman but Matthew had refused. He would rather die alone and in his own time than be hurried to his end by an impatient old harridan. He told himself he was in God's hands. He would live or die according to God's will but in his heart he thought he would die. Faintly, through the closed windows, he heard sounds of life going on in the street below – the clip-clop of horses' hooves, a burst of raucous laughter, the chant of a cheeseseller and the singsong voice of the pie man. He heard a mother scolding and a child crying and almost hated the uncaring people who passed by his window blithely unaware – but no! He corrected himself. They would not be unaware. There was a red cross on the door, and 'Lord have mercy upon us' and that stupid watchman earning his meagre pittance. They would know someone was stricken and would think themselves most fortunate by comparison.

When would the physician come again, he wondered. Had he called once today or was that yesterday? A glance at the bedside table revealed a bottle of elixir and a box of pills but they had been prescribed for Anne. Should he take some? Was there any point? Had he the strength? He gave up the idea and slid into another, restless doze.

Later he woke with a start and with great clarity remembered that Fanny had called by with a letter from Sophie; a letter that had become his most prized possession and was even now tucked safely under his pillow where he could touch it. Poor Sophie. He had ruined her life. And his two dear children . . .

He seemed to hear a voice calling his name.

'Matthew! Matthew Devine! Where are you?'

It sounded like Sophie, he thought incredulously. Perhaps he was dreaming.

'Matthew! Come to the window!'

Was she out of her mind, he wondered irritably. He was dying and she expected him to –

'Matthew! I must talk to you!'

It *was* Sophie! With a tremendous effort of will he pushed himself to the edge of the bed, wincing with pain. He tried to shout that he was coming but his voice was hoarse and very weak. Oh God, let her wait for him, he prayed in sudden desperation. Sophie was in the street outside and he would see her sweet face once again. If only he could reach the window. He fell to the floor and lay there, panting, then almost immediately began to crawl towards the window. Would he have the strength to open it when he got there? Oh God! He must!

'Matthew! Matthew Devine. 'Tis me, Sophie! I must talk to you. Please, Matthew!'

At last he reached the window and pulled himself up so that he could look down into the street. There he saw Sophie, Fanny and the watchman staring up at him.

'There he is!' cried Fanny, pointing.

The watchman said, 'I knew he was in there. Took his time, though.'

Sophie stared up, wide-eyed, shocked. Matthew was not surprised. He knew he must look like a scarecrow. His fingers scrabbled for the window-catch but it resisted his efforts. Exhausted, he stopped and looked down at his wife. To his surprise she appeared blurred and indistinct until he realized that he was seeing her through his tears. Impatiently he brushed them aside. This was no time for self-pity, he told himself angrily. He must speak to her; he must tell her how sorry he was for the whole sad mess. It might be his last chance. Once again his fingers closed over the window-catch and slowly he felt it move. The window swung open and, clinging desperately to the sill, he leaned out as far as he dared.

'Sophie!' he croaked.

'Matthew! My love!' Sophie's tone was anguished.

Grinning, the watchman said, 'Not a pretty sight,

eh, mistress?' and Matthew thought bitterly that if by some miracle he survived he would seek him out and strangle him with his bare hands.

Sophie said again, 'Oh Matthew!' and he could see that she was crying.

Fanny said, 'We've brought you some food. You must let down the basket.'

He shook his head wearily. 'I can't –' he began.

Sophie's head snapped up at his words. 'You *must* eat, Matthew. We've brought you a pot of buttered eggs and a jar of honey and Fanny has made you a rice pudding – all easy to swallow, Matthew. Oh dearest, you must eat! For all our sakes.'

He was beginning to feel very dizzy and knew he would not be able to remain at the window much longer. All the talk of food wearied him; he had so much that must be said. 'My dearest Sophie, I want to ask –'

The watchman said something to the women and Sophie cried, 'Oh, that's too terrible!' To Matthew she said, 'You must have someone to nurse you. I'll find a good nurse – if not I'll nurse you myself!'

His heart leaped with a confusion of hope and horror. Just to have her near would be heaven but she must not take such a risk. She must consider the children.

Fanny called, 'Master! Let down the basket and we shall put in the food.'

He ignored her. 'Sophie!' he called feebly, 'Tell me you forgive me! Just tell me you –' There was a wild trembling in his legs which spread upwards until he shook all over. His head swam and he felt his grip on the sill loosen. There was a blackness all around him like a dark fog. He heard her voice as though from a great distance.

'I do, Matthew! Don't speak of it! Matthew!'

Was that Sophie's voice, he wondered vaguely. He seemed to be lying on the floor now but through a haze of pain he heard the watchman. 'Oi! You up there! If you're done talking then shut that window!'

He could no longer decide if his eyes were open or shut. It was so dark. He drew a long, trembling breath. Was he still alive? Was this dying? Where was Sophie, his own dear wife?

*

Outside the two women conversed anxiously. There was no way to get the food to Matthew unless they could persuade the watchman to look after it and pass it on to him when the physician made his next visit but that, they agreed, seemed risky in the extreme. The wretched man would probably eat it himself! They could come back with it later and try again or they could try and discover the whereabouts of Doctor Pumphrey and enlist his aid. The watchman sulkily refused to give them an address, pretending that he did not know it. It was then that Fanny had her brainwave.

'Doctor Meridith!' she exclaimed, her face brightening with excitement. 'Why didn't I think of that before! He's a good, kindly man and he has a son, Antony!' She allowed herself a mysterious smile. 'He will know what we should do. Come with me.' And, glowing with triumph at her own cleverness, she led her mistress away in search of certain help.

*

Luke Meridith left his last patient at six o'clock and, hot and sweating beneath his protective leathers, he turned his feet homewards with mixed feelings. He was weary and depressed but he had seen one of his patients pass the crucial stage in the disease and he now considered him to be on the way to a complete recovery. His one success cheered him a little since many good, hard-working doctors could employ all their skills without the least certainty of the patient's recovery. The plague was an implacable enemy and frequent deaths affected the doctors' spirits and sapped their self-confidence.

Luke knew he was well skilled and experienced in his profession yet he would probably have only a few more cures than the average quack or devious charlatan. All his knowledge could do little more than the fake elixirs and dubious remedies of the growing band of cheats who preyed upon London's fearful, gullible inhabitants. The disease came in so many forms and, it seemed, different patients withstood them in different ways. The strongest constitution could collapse in a matter of days, sometimes hours, while a less hardy soul lingered for weeks and then suddenly recovered. With one man the fever would break with sweating pills, with another the pills would prove useless. The plague had already showed itself to be a cunning and capricious adversary, totally unpredictable, seeming always to be one card ahead in the game. Luke did not make the mistake of underestimating its power. He suspected it had further tricks up its evil sleeve and that it scorned his dedication and commitment.

As he made his way through the streets, he was aware of the impression he made on passers-by in his extraordinary outfit. Some looked twice as though unable to believe their eyes, while children either pointed excitedly or hid behind their mother's skirts, depending on their courage.

As always he used these last moments of the working day to review his progress and to work out a strategy for the next day. Poor Mistress Rippon would still not agree to have her two bad teeth pulled and until she did she would suffer from the poisonous roots. If the poison entered her blood she would very likely die. Master Crickett, the intemperate old fool, would never be rid of his gout. They were the failures. The Mellor child might be a success; she had finally stopped vomiting and had kept down a little bread and milk. The urchin boy knocked down by a horse was still not conscious but might surprise them all and recover his wits. But these everyday cases were the least of his worries. He sighed heavily as he considered the plague cases.

The meat-porter had died early this morning. Mistress Byrnne, a middle-aged widow, had reached a critical stage in the development of the disease but she was the owner of a sturdy constitution and might well survive. That would make two this week snatched from the jaws of death, he told himself with a wry smile as he opened his front door and called out a greeting to his sister and his son.

'Ah, there you are at last.' Antony appeared very promptly from the parlour. He looked excited, Luke thought curiously. 'I have two visitors for you who have waited patiently for nearly two hours now. But first let me help you off with those dreadful garments.'

Luke stepped back out of reach and shook his head emphatically. 'Don't touch them,' he warned. 'I told you yesterday to keep away from them. I'll take them upstairs to the fumigator myself.' He pulled off the gloves and dropped them to the floor and then began to remove the head-piece. Suddenly, he asked, 'Have you written the letter to Allynson as you promised?'

Allynson was a renowned medical man in Padua under whom Luke, many years before, had studied for twelve months. Then, Allynson had been highly regarded as a promising exponent and teacher of the medical sciences. Now, older but fulfilling everyone's expectations, he had written many learned theses on the practical application of medical theory and was, in Luke's opinion, the best man in his field. He wanted Antony to study under him and was eager to establish contact while Antony's enthusiasm was at its height. His son's change of heart with regard to his future in medicine was the only bright star in a sky heavy with clouds.

Antony smiled. 'I was on the point of sealing it when our visitors arrived. You know one of them already. 'Tis the little servant, Fanny Rice, and she has brought her mistress, Sophie Devine.'

As Luke tugged himself out of the main garment he repeated, 'Fanny Rice? Do I know her?'

'You wrote a letter for her, to her mistress.'

'Ah!' As the significance of his son's words dawned on him Luke raised his eyebrows humorously and lowered his voice. 'The unfaithful husband! I will be down again as soon as possible. Please apologize and explain the necessity for the slight delay.' He gathered up the leathers and stumbled upstairs to the attic where a wooden framework had been constructed above a long chafing dish. He draped the leathers over this framework and set fire to the layer of charcoal. At once the smoke spiralled upwards through the garments, carrying the smell of herbs and spices which had been liberally sprinkled on to the charcoal. When he was satisfied that it would continue safely without further supervision, he hurried to his bedroom and washed his hands and face, paying particular attention to his hands which he scrubbed with a small brush. When he felt clean and free from all infection, he made his way downstairs and into the parlour.

Fanny Rice he recognized at once and he gave her a polite nod before turning to her mistress. As he greeted her he wondered curiously what had inspired her husband to cheat on such a wife. Sophie Devine's unhappiness was obvious from the intensity of her brown eyes and the vulnerable curve of her mouth but her natural good looks remained undiminished. Her skin was good, her features small and regular and her dark hair curled around her face. Unaware that he did so, Luke stared at her with pleasure.

'Mistress Devine,' he murmured, releasing her hand. 'Forgive me for keeping you waiting. I hope my sister has offered you some refreshment.'

Lois began to say that indeed she had, but Sophie Devine was obviously in no mood for the niceties of etiquette for she ignored his words and burst at once into an account of her husband's incarceration and begged him to advise her. As she spoke she twisted her hands anxiously in her lap, her voice shook and there were unshed tears in her eyes. Luke watched the line of her throat as he listened in silence to her impassioned plea for help although he found it difficult to concentrate on the husband's problem. He was astonished that her husband had found a woman he preferred. He became aware that her words were making no sense and with an effort he tried to put his mind to the matter in hand. He nodded earnestly once or twice but almost at once his thoughts abandoned the husband in favour of the wife.

'Luke!'

He started guiltily as Lois spoke and he caught her warning look. It was too ridiculous, he told himself, and most unprofessional to be distracted by a woman's eyes at this time and in such sombre circumstances. It was also most uncharacteristic for he was a cautious man where women were concerned; not the type to lose his heart suddenly or unwisely.

She was not thin, he decided, nor overly plump. Comely, was that the word? No, that failed to do her justice. Handsome was more apt.

He realized suddenly that Antony was looking at him with ill-concealed amusement and was immediately annoyed with himself. Was he being so transparent? He said hurriedly, 'I shall do all I can,' and hoped the phrase was sufficiently unspecific to pass as a suitable comment.

It came to him suddenly with a painful jolt that Sophie Devine reminded him of his wife. The same dark colouring, the same eager, unsophisticated way of speaking, a similar quality in the voice. He sighed deeply and his conscience pricked him. Since the onset of the plague, he had had little time to think about his wife.

But Sophie Devine had asked him a question and now she waited for his answer. Playing for time, he said earnestly, ''Tis far from easy,' and pursed his lips as though in contemplation.

They were all regarding him with the same puzzled stare.

With an effort he gathered his wandering wits and said, 'Forgive me. I am so very weary –' and at once Sophie Devine looked chastened.

'No, no, 'tis my fault,' she said unhappily. 'You have had a long day and I have no right to make further demands on your time. Your son has told us how busy you are but Fanny thought – that is, I hoped –' She fumbled for a handkerchief. 'I was so desperate and you seemed the only person – do please forgive me!' Tears broke through and as she sobbed helplessly, Fanny moved to stand beside her. Tentatively she laid a hand on Sophie's arm and begged, 'Don't cry, mistress.'

Startled by Sophie's tears, Luke at once blamed himself for his lack of attention. Her impassioned words had scarcely registered and she had obviously noted his apparent lack of interest. His behaviour was little short of churlish. He made a stern resolve to keep his mind on the matter in hand.

'Please don't!' he begged 'I will help you, Mistress Devine, in any way I can. Most certainly I will!' He looked guiltily at Antony who offered to fetch the *sal volatile* and promptly disappeared in search of it. Luke went on hastily, 'You must not give up hope.' In spite of his resolution he found himself envying the servant's closeness to her mistress and the thought entered his head that, had he been alone with the distraught woman, he himself might have felt able to pat her arm by way of consolation – or take her hand in his own.

He stood up abruptly and moved to the window as Antony returned with a phial of *sal volatile*. After a few whiffs of this restorative Sophie Devine sat up, dried her eyes and handed it back.

'I am quite recovered,' she said, rather unconvincingly and, to Luke, 'I think I owe you an apology, Doctor Meridith. You deserve your rest. We must not take up any more of your time.'

She rose to her feet but Fanny made no effort to hide her disappointment. She gave Antony a reproachful glance and her jaw tightened.

'Wait!' said Lois, with a quick look at Luke. 'I am sure my brother has no intention of turning you away.'

Luke hurried to agree. 'Certainly not. I am not so tired that I cannot help you.' He waved a hand to indicate that they should resume their seats, then perched himself on the edge of the table and went on quickly, 'I am thinking about your husband's plight.'

Desperately he looked towards Antony who, aware that Luke had missed many of the details, said, 'Matthew Devine is alone in a shut-up house with no one to nurse him. A nursewoman is hardly the answer to the problem. Mistress Devine is at her wits' end.'

Sophie said, 'I would tend him myself in spite of everything but I have two children to consider.'

Within Luke the thought rankled that she still loved her undeserving husband. Aloud he said, 'I have a suggestion to make.' All eyes regarded him eagerly. 'Suppose I were able to have him transferred to the pesthouse in Old Street.' He held up a hand to prevent their anticipated protests. 'Indeed, I understand your reluctance but 'tis well equipped for its purpose none the less.'

'The pesthouse?' cried Fanny.

Sophie continued to regard him earnestly, however, and he went on, 'You would not be able to visit him there, Mistress Devine, for obvious reasons, but you could hand in food for him and he would receive proper medical care. Nathaniel Upton, Master of the pesthouse, is known to me. I would judge him to be a most capable and honourable man.' He forced himself to look straight into her eyes, praying that his feelings were not stamped across his forehead.

Lois said, 'My brother's idea has great merit, Mistress Devine. And what are the alternatives?'

But her powers of persuasion were not needed. Sophie was nodding her head, a glimmer of hope in the dark eyes. 'I agree, Doctor Meridith,' she said. 'If you could arrange that it would be most helpful. With careful nursing and – and nourishing food my husband would at least stand a chance.'

Fanny said triumphantly, 'I told you, mistress, that Doctor Meridith would help us!'

'So you did, Fanny. You are a very clever girl!'

To Luke's surprise Sophie Devine flung her arms round the girl and hugged her.

Cautiously Luke said, 'You should not raise your hopes too high. Mistress Devine. I cannot promise anything. There may not be a bed – and if there is, they may not be able to save him.'

Sophie Devine turned eager, bright eyes towards him. 'But there's hope! I cannot thank you enough!' She stepped forward impetuously and for a moment Luke thought she was going to hug him too. She recollected herself in time, however, and blushed with embarrassment and Luke had to be satisfied with a smile.

*

Much later that night, a very sick Matthew Devine was carried through the deserted streets by sedan chair and safely ensconced in the Old Street pest-house. Luke, meanwhile, lay awake in bed staring up at the moonlight which slanted across the ceiling overhead. He looked peaceful enough but in fact a heated argument raged within him. London was in the grip of a catastrophic epidemic with grief and misery on every side and he told himself he had no right to feel so happy. But he did. He felt truly happy for the first time since the death of his wife. He felt that life was quickening again and was astonished and absurdly grateful. Through all the lonely years he had functioned as a doctor, a father and a brother and had accepted the limitations of his existence. Now he knew that he had been only half alive, a puppet going through the motions of life – and very convincingly.

He thought of his wife and, for a moment, the grief he had felt at her passing struck him again. Whatever would she think, he wondered, if she could see him behaving so foolishly over a woman he scarcely knew? A married woman at that. He hoped she would not disapprove but in his heart he knew that even if she did he could not change the way he felt about Sophie Devine.

And was it only because she reminded him of his wife? Perhaps at first. But Sophie was older – and stronger, in spite of those tears she had shed. And wiser, perhaps? In exasperation he shook his head. He knew so little about her – except that the woman who had stolen her husband's heart was probably lying in a communal grave and Sophie had not uttered one word against her. That took restraint and he was full of admiration.

'Sophie Devine!' he whispered and thought he had never heard such a beautiful name. But men of his age did not fall helplessly in love with strangers. 'In love?' Astonished, he spoke the words aloud.

The phrase shocked him. Was it love? Maybe infatuation and the feeling would pass leaving him sane once more. But that idea depressed him. He did not want that to happen.

'I think I do love you!' he whispered and suddenly he no longer cared if he was making a fool of himself. He felt years younger, full of hope and brimming with confidence. Tomorrow he would go out into the troubled city and work miracles! Because Sophie Devine had come into his life and he loved her and nothing would ever be the same again.

Chapter Ten

THE TWO CHILDREN were in their grand-mother's room when Henrietta found them. Oliver was writing a letter to his mother, a frown of intense concentration on his face. Lizbeth was trying to pull off the clothes from a doll her grandmother had made for her.

'They don't come off!' Ruth told her irritably. 'Don't tug at them like that, child. You'll tear them.'

'Why don't they come off?'

'Because they're stitched on.'

'But why are they?' Lizbeth looked up, aggrieved. 'My clothes aren't stitched on so –'

'That will do, Lizbeth!' cried Ruth. She glanced up at Henrietta. 'I swear I've never met such a child for talking back to her elders! I shall have to speak to her mother when –'

She broke off, suddenly becoming aware of Henrietta's expression and the letter she held in her hand. 'Oh my dear,' she began.

With forced cheerfulness Henrietta said, 'Now you two children run down into the garden and help Lou and Eddie to pick strawberries. Your Mama is coming home tomorrow and I shall make a strawberry jelly.'

Ollie looked up from his letter. 'Tomorrow? You mean it? Then hurrah!' He thrust a podgy fist into the air and beamed at his sister. 'Tomorrow, Lizbeth! Mama is coming home. Did you hear? Aren't you pleased?

'I'm pleased, Ollie,' she said, still tugging disconsolately at the doll's clothes. 'But I do wish her clothes would come off!'

Ruth snapped, 'If you don't like her the way she is I shall take her back and give her to your cousin.'

Henrietta said quickly, 'She's a dear little doll, Lizbeth. You're a very lucky girl to have such a clever grandmother. Now downstairs, both of you and quick! Shoo, shoo, little chickens!' She clapped her hands and chased them out of the room. 'Come back to your grandmother later,' she said and closed the door firmly behind them.

Ruth said, '''Tis news from Sophie! 'Tis bad news, I know it.'

Henrietta sat herself on the edge of the bed and said, 'Yes, Mistress. She wrote to me and asked me to read it to you but first I'm to say that —' She faltered as Ruth's hands crept to her heart and her faded eyes widened fearfully.

'Matthew's left her! Oh dear God! The fool!'

'No, no!' Henrietta said hurriedly. 'He has not left her. At least, er — not exactly. Matthew is well enough. That is, not well exactly, but unwell but —'

Ruth saw that Henrietta was avoiding her eyes and suddenly gave a little scream. 'He's dead! My son's dead and you dare not tell me! Matthew's dead!'

'He's not dead!' cried Henrietta. 'In truth, he *is* ill but in good hands and —'

'Ill? Of the plague? Oh God! Then he's as good as dead!' Ruth threw up her hands despairingly and then covered her face with the bedcover. Henrietta remained silent, allowing her time to deal with the worst of the shock and regain a little of her composure.

At last she uncovered her face from which all colour had fled. 'You swear he is not dead? You swear it, Henrietta, on your father's grave? Matthew is — Oh tell me he will live!'

'He is alive,' Henrietta said carefully 'and may well survive!'

'Then I shall pray to God. He will intercede for me. He will save my son.'

Henrietta saw the relief in her eyes but it was brief. Apprehension followed.

'But what of *her*? What of this other woman Fanny spoke of? Was there such a woman? Tell me the truth, Henrietta! What of the marriage! Are they together again? Oh, you shake your head. I can't bear it! Where will it all end?'

'Sophie asks me to read you the letter. Would you like me to?'

Ruth nodded then burst out, 'Oh I could box his ears! If this woman –'

Henrietta gave a little cough and began to read.

Dear Henrietta,

Where to begin? I hardly know any more for Anne Redditch is dead of the plague and was buried . . .

'Dead?' Ruth's eyes gleamed. 'Dead, is she? Then 'tis no more than she deserved!' A little colour was returning slowly to her cheeks. 'I shall weep no tears on her behalf. This was her punishment. God sees the just and the unjust! He strikes down the ungodly and –'

'May I finish the letter?'

'I'm sorry. Please go on.'

Henrietta continued:

and was buried yesterday but no one attended the funeral as this is now the law to prevent people gathering together and thus spreading the contagion . . .

'Go to her funeral indeed?' Ruth snorted. 'Who'd want to see such a wanton buried? Wild horses wouldn't drag me to see such a woman laid in her grave!' A look from Henrietta silenced her once again.

It seems Matthew has been tending her and he too now

*has the sickness and has been carried to a pesthouse which
was recommended –*

'A pesthouse? My son is in a *pesthouse*!'
Henrietta went on quickly.

*which was recommended by a local physician who speaks
well of the Master there. So please assure Matthew's
mother that he is in good hands and that many people do
recover and are afterwards quite themselves again. I
know you will remember him in your prayers.*

   *Since I am not allowed to visit him, the physician
suggests that I return to the children for the time being. As
I have not been in any contact with the disease, tell Giles
that you may safely re-admit me to the house without
fear of disaster. The physician's sister will visit the
pesthouse to hand in extra food for Matthew, to aid his
recovery . . .*

Henrietta smiled at Ruth. 'So you see poor Matthew
is in good hands.'

'Good hands! Huh!' Ruth's fingers twitched the
coverlet nervously. 'At the mercy of strangers! I
should be with him,' she said. 'Or Sophie.'

'Sophie? Would you put her at risk also?'

'Fanny, then!'

'Fanny? Ah, allow me to read on.' Her finger
traced the words, searching for the place where she
had broken off.

Poor Fanny has troubles of her own for her brother

Charlie is arrested and locked in the Fleet Prison but I cannot solve everyone's problems so must harden my heart and leave him to his fate.

London is a sad place. Rich folk desert the city daily in their loaded carriages; the poor fall sick in the street; maids and prentices are out of work since their masters and mistresses have gone into the country. But more news when I see you. I shall come by water which I am told is safer than the roads. Hopefully I shall find a wherry and I should arrive about six or seven o'clock.

The evening before I leave London the Meridith family are coming to supper. They have been so kind 'tis the least I can do. I shall feel very strange entertaining without Matthew at my side but my life is changing so rapidly now that almost nothing surprises me. I am learning to take everything in my stride.

I long to see you all, especially my two little ones. Please kiss them for me.

Your affectionate Sophie.

For a moment neither woman spoke. Then, as Henrietta folded the letter, she said, 'Matthew will recover, Ruth. I know he will.'

'If 'tis God's will,' Ruth said shakily. The bad tidings had had time to register and the shock was taking its toll.

'She adds a post script for the children,' said Henrietta. 'She has found them a dog.'

'A dog?' Ruth stared at her. 'But Matthew can't abide them!'

Henrietta shrugged. 'That's what she says.' She

stood up. 'But I will leave it for you to re-read at your leisure and will fetch you a sip or two of brandy – for medicinal purposes!

'Hmm!' Ruth picked up the letter cautiously between thumb and forefinger and Henrietta, noticing her reluctance, said, 'It has been between two hot stones – and Sophie assures us she has been in no contact with the plague.'

Ruth eyed her scornfully. 'Can we say the same of the postman?' she asked.

Henrietta laughed. 'Perhaps we should put *him* between two hot stones!' she suggested and was pleased to see the faintest of smiles on the old lady's pale face.

*

Lois pinned her hair carefully, revealing a few discreet curls, and tucked the rest demurely beneath her best lace cap. She regarded herself in the long mirror with some satisfaction but puckered her lips a little at the severity of the brown dress. Designed some years earlier, it now looked out of date in the light of the new court fashions which King Charles encouraged but, since the Meridith family rarely dined out, it would be an extravagance to replace the dress. Turning to one side and then the other she saw that her figure, unspoilt by child-bearing, was still neat enough despite her forty-one years. The pearls that her grandmother had left her gleamed as softly as ever at her throat.

Abruptly she lost interest in her appearance and sat down on the chair beside the bed. Why did she feel so nervous, she wondered? Supping with friends was hardly a major event. Clasping her hands she stared at the floor, remembering her brother's face as he had prepared for his rounds that morning. Catching him in an unguarded moment she had seen the gleam in his eyes and had caught the snatch of melody that he hummed under his breath. Was he really falling in love with Mistress Devine, she wondered. It seemed hardly possible and yet she had sensed a change in him. There was an inner excitement which he could not hide — at least not from her.

In the early days after his bereavement, she had encouraged him to find a new mother for Antony but he had shown little interest and she had eventually given up. She knew only too well how easily he became set in his ways and how he hated change. He had courted his first wife for four long years, infuriating his mother with his doubts. Lois had never thought him capable of impetuosity, and certainly not where women were concerned. But now he appeared to be falling in love with another man's wife, a sure recipe for disaster in the normal course of events, but times were far from normal and only God knew what might happen. To covet another man's wife was most certainly a sin yet Lois could not find it in her heart to begrudge Luke his happiness. It was rare enough in time of plague and might prove all too fleeting.

This morning he had kissed her on the cheek. Kissed her! And what had he said? 'Enjoy the day!' How preposterous! How was she supposed to do that with plague raging, the Bills of Mortality rising so rapidly and everyone so fearful of his neighbour? How could Luke enjoy his day surrounded by so much misery unless he had a secret source of joy which no one else shared? Sighing, she closed her eyes and clasped her hands.

'Dear Lord, Forgive him and have mercy upon him. He is a good, dear man.'

From the room opposite he called, 'Lois! Are you ready?'

She started guiltily and turned once more to the mirror as the door opened and Luke looked in.

'You will do very well, my dear,' he said, trying to hide his impatience. 'You are not being presented to the King; only taking supper with a friend!'

He looked excited, she thought, with a slight pang of envy. She had never met a man who made her feel that way; had never been truly in love in her whole life.

'No one will outshine Mistress Devine,' she said slyly and, watching in the mirror, saw his face light up.

'She asked that we call her Sophie,' he reminded her and then, unable to resist the question, asked, 'How do I look?'

She laughed delightedly. 'You are not supping with the King!' she mocked. 'Only with a friend!'

'This suit hangs on me,' he protested, coming into the room to make use of her mirror.

She looked at him critically. 'You have lost a little weight,' she agreed, 'but it looks well enough. Better to lose a little than to put it on and be bursting at the seams!'

He went out again and called, 'Antony! Are you ready!' Lois joined him at the top of the stairs.

He called again, 'Antony! We are ready to leave!'

Antony appeared at the door of his room, astonished and only half dressed. 'So early?' he protested. 'There is still more than half the hour before we should arrive.' He regarded his father, agreeably surprised by his appearance. 'You are wearing the amber silk!' he exclaimed. 'I had almost forgotten it. 'Tis so long since you put it on. Now who is all this finery in aid of, I wonder?'

Luke glanced down at himself and said, ''Tis as old as the hills! All this fuss over a suit of clothes!' And he went quickly downstairs.

Lois looked at her nephew and he raised his eyebrows humorously. Leaning close he whispered, 'Wonders will never cease!'

'Whatever do you mean?'

'You know well enough!'

Lois, smiling, kept her voice low. 'What nonsense! Sophie Devine is a married woman with two children.'

'She might soon be a *widow* with two children!' he insisted.

They regarded each other like two plotters.

Lois said, 'Would you object? He has been alone too long.'

Antony smiled. 'And she is very beautiful and has been treated most unkindly. If her husband dies I think my father will woo her. How would *you* feel about that?'

'I'd wish them well with all my heart.'

His smile broadened into a grin. 'I could ask for no better stepmother. If the husband dies and my father woos her I shall cheer him on.' He leaned forward and whispered softly, 'But if he doesn't woo her, maybe *I* shall!'

And he followed Luke down the stairs leaving Lois to stare after him in astonishment.

*

At twenty minutes to seven, Sophie looked round the kitchen with one hand pressed to her forehead.

'The bread is baked,' she muttered, 'the oysters are – Oh Fanny! The oysters!'

Fanny, red-faced and rebellious, pushed back a stray lock of hair and said, 'What about the oysters, mistress?'

Her tone held a note of warning which Sophie ignored.

'We are having oysters in the pie!' cried Sophie. 'We should not be repeating them in the first course. Oh, how foolish of me. Why didn't you say something?'

Fanny said, 'Because I'm already run off my feet and I've no time for thinking! And don't ask me to fly out at this hour and find something new for there's no time as well you know.'

Sophie was not listening. 'If we must have them twice then we shall have to serve them in a new way. I wonder could we treat them like mussels, with buttered crumbs?' She tutted and sighed and Fanny rolled her eyes in exasperation. She was hoping to snatch a few moments to tidy herself before Antony arrived.

Sophie went on, 'I shall look in my mother-in-law's book . . . Oh! The sauce! The apricot sauce. Is that ready?'

'Ready an hour since, mistress,' Fanny told her. 'You said we should serve it cold.'

'Ah yes! So I did . . . And you are sure you removed all the bones from the pigeons?' She did not wait for an answer which was fortunate because Fanny was not giving one. She had set her mouth in a stubborn line and was mashing butter into the turnips with all her strength.

Sophie stared round the kitchen. 'The nutcrackers!' she exclaimed. 'Don't forget the nutcrackers.'

Fanny swung round from the fire. 'But we've no nuts, mistress.'

'What?' Sophie stared at her in dismay. 'Are you certain? Fanny! How could you forget the nuts?'

'I fetched home all that you asked for,' said Fanny belligerently, 'and the money was all spent.'

Sophie could not argue with that. She had pawned a leather-bound book and the money had been less than she had expected.

Fanny tossed the tongs on to the table, gathered up the vegetable peelings and dropped them into a small basket, aware that Sophie's eyes were upon her.

'Whatever are you up to now?' Sophie demanded irritably. 'Throw the peelings out, girl.'

Fanny took a deep breath and said, 'I save the scraps for the egg lady. For her chickens. She – she gives me a penny for them.'

She waited for her mistress's wrath to descend upon her but, already distracted, Sophie had begun to count the various dishes on her fingers. 'Oysters, gravy-soup, pigeon and oyster pie – Oh, I do wish I had decided on artichokes but 'tis too late now. Soused mackerel – did you decorate it with bayleaves as I told you? Oh, good girl! Now what else? Yes, the lemon snow and the barley cream.'

Fanny muttered, 'Enough there to feed an army and there's only to be the four of you!'

'What's that?' cried Sophie but, without waiting for an answer, ran upstairs and pulled off her apron. She rushed to the mirror but nothing she saw in her reflection pleased her. Surely the dress was too fancy for the occasion; the collar too pointed. Her face was flushed and her expression desperate and it was all Fanny's fault, she told herself. The wretched girl had been as awkward as possible all afternoon and –

'Oh! The pie!' she cried and rushed to the top of the stairs and screamed, 'Fanny! The pie! Look at the pie!'

If the pie was burnt, she thought, that would be the last straw. The very last straw. She would call it all off and Fanny should say she was taken sick. Oh no! That would bring Luke round faster than ever! Snatching up her apron again she hurried down the stairs, nearly falling in her haste. In the kitchen Fanny was peering into the oven.

''Tis caught the very slightest bit on one corner,' she reported but Sophie, vexed, pushed her aside to examine it for herself.

'A little! Oh, 'tis quite, quite ruined!' she exclaimed and she sank on to the nearest stool and burst into tears of disappointment.

Fanny ventured rashly, ''Tis only a pie, mistress.'

Sophie sobbed. 'It may be only a pie to you, you useless chit –'

'Shall I take it from the oven?'

'Do what you like with it!' cried Sophie wildly. 'Throw it in the yard. What do I care?'

Fanny withdrew the pie and set it on a corner of the table on a large trivet. 'It smells good' she said. 'Don't cry, mistress. You'll ruin your eyes and every-one –'

'My eyes?!' Sophie stared at her miserably. 'What do my eyes matter? What does anything matter? Who cares if the whole meal is burnt to a cinder? 'Tis only the Meridiths.'

Fanny, watching her warily, wiped down the table and began to refill the best cruet.

'My poor husband is sick of the plague,' cried Sophie, 'and my children are miles away, yearning for their mother and what am I doing? Fretting over a burnt pie! What a stupid, selfish woman I am! Oh Fanny! I think I have never been in such a state in my whole life!'

Fanny said kindly, ''Tis understandable, mistress. Don't blame yourself so. You've many worries and are bearing up bravely.'

Sophie looked at her eagerly. 'Do you think so? Do you truly understand my predicament? I just want it to be a good evening. I want to repay them for all their kindness. Where would we be without them?'

'I don't rightly know.'

Sophie sniffed hard and fumbled for her handkerchief. 'I do so want Lois to admire my cooking. I want them to enjoy themselves. In the midst of all this misery I want us to be happy – just for a few hours? Is that so wrong?' Hastily she dried her tears and turned to Fanny. 'Do my eyes look red?' she asked.

'A little, mistress,' Fanny conceded then added more honestly, 'Well, yes, they are red roundabout.' She traced a line below her own eye. 'What about a dusting of flour to lighten them?'

'Flour? Oh Fanny! That would be no good at all.' She stared round the kitchen. 'Chalk, perhaps,' she murmured. 'A little powdered chalk. No! I shall look like a clown! Oh! I can't think clearly. What is the matter with me? How long before they arrive?'

As she hurried from the room, Fanny stuck out her tongue at her retreating back. 'What a lemon you are, mistress,' she said crossly. '*I* know why you're in such a pother even if *you* don't! 'Tisn't the sister you want to impress, mistress. 'Tis the good Doctor Meridith who has taken *your* fancy!'

*

The visitors arrived promptly and Fanny, in a clean apron, was sent to let them in. As she opened the door she smiled beatifically at Antony who winked humorously in return. She led them into the parlour and Lois said, 'Something smells very good, Fanny.'

Fanny was on the point of revealing the menu when Sophie appeared, and greeted the Meridiths warmly.

''Tis so good to have people around,' she said, clasping Luke's hand. 'The house feels lived in again. With the household scattered, Fanny and I rattle around like two peas in the proverbial pod!'

Fanny took the cloaks upstairs and Lois said, 'What a charming room!'

She made no mention of the reddened eyes although Sophie knew she must have noticed them and her heart went out to her in gratitude.

Luke said, 'A most comfortable room. It does you credit, Sophie.'

It was the first time he had used her Christian name and Sophie could not meet his gaze. To hide the awkward moment Antony crossed the room to examine a small oil painting which Ruth's husband had painted many years before. Luke and Lois settled themselves on the sofa and Sophie said, 'We are hoping to buy a tapestry for the end wall but Matthew thinks we should wait –'

She stopped in mid sentence, shocked by the ease with which her husband's name had slipped out, as though everything was normal; as though Anne Redditch had never existed and Matthew was not lying at death's door. She wondered sadly if this is how it would be for the rest of their lives, if Matthew recovered. Would they simply pretend that nothing had happened, conveniently forgetting his love for Anne Redditch? Trying to shut out the unwelcome thought, Sophie became aware that they were all staring at her.

To break the silence Lois said quickly, 'I always think a tapestry gives a room warmth,' and they all agreed with unnatural heartiness. Sophie's smile was a trifle forced. Lois went on, 'Perhaps you noticed the tapestry on the wall in our parlour, the hunting scene. It belonged to my mother and I set great store by it.'

'I did notice it,' said Sophie, recovering her poise. 'I admired it very much.'

There was another silence while Sophie searched desperately for something else to say. Antony, however, was quick to fill the gap.

To his aunt, he said, 'I shall keep an eye open when I am in Padua. I might see a tapestry you would like. I'll send it to you for your birthday. Your twentieth!'

He rolled his eyes humorously and Luke said, 'Impudent puppy!' and as Lois punched Antony gently on the arm Sophie relaxed a little, telling herself that the first few minutes of any supper party were difficult. Not that she and Matthew had entertained frequently but Henry and his wife had visited from time to time. Then, of course, the two men were quite at ease with each other which made the first few moments easier. Would she ever have Matthew by her side again or was their life together over? Her stomach suddenly churned at this frightening prospect but, at that moment, she realized that Lois was speaking to her.

'Don't you wish you had such a gallant young nephew, Sophie?'

'I do indeed!' said Sophie but in fact she could not recall what Antony had said to prompt such a question.

Fortunately, at that moment Fanny came in and drinks were offered. Soon they were all seated with a glass of madeira and to Sophie's relief unselfconscious conversation began to flow. She found herself talking with great animation to Antony who made her laugh a lot and then to Lois who proved a very sympathetic listener on the subject of servants and their shortcomings. To Luke she said very little but he appeared completely at ease, saying little, sipping his wine appreciatively. When she did glance his way she noted with pleasure that he looked cheerful, his eyes shone and he appeared less tired than when she had last seen him.

Promptly at seven-thirty Fanny announced that the supper was ready and led them all into the dining room.

Luke said, 'I must confess to a certain hunger! Some days I am too tired to eat but today I am ravenous.'

''Tis scarcely a feast,' said Sophie disparagingly but then caught Fanny's eye and began to laugh. Fanny retreated, grinning, leaving Sophie to explain.

''Tis so long since I – since we have entertained,' she confessed. 'I have been at sixes and sevens all day and poor Fanny has suffered the sharp edge of my tongue more than once!'

As Luke and Antony commiserated with her, Lois said, ''Tis always the way with me that I can bake a cake perfectly when there are just the three of us but when visitors are expected the wretched thing sinks in the middle.'

Antony said, 'But it tastes the same. Why do women fret so about the look of their cakes?'

Sophie laughed. 'It may taste the same but it doesn't say much for the poor cook. The cake looks what it is – a failure!'

Antony shrugged. 'But why do we all dread failure, I wonder? 'Tis a most human trait. I might almost say an endearing one. How dull life would be if we were all perfect.'

Lois raised her eyebrows at this little homily. 'There speaks one who thinks himself quite perfect!' she teased. 'Oh, don't deny it, Antony!'

Antony laughed delightedly, quite unabashed by his aunt's criticism. 'I confess I did nurture the idea until recently,' he told them, 'but now that I see that I am as frail as the next man – why, I am as happy as ever I was!'

Sophie said, 'That sounds remarkably wise, Antony.'

'I *am* remarkably wise,' he told her.

'And modest!' said Luke.

Antony summed up cheerfully, 'A remarkably wise and modest failure!' he said and they all laughed good-naturedly.

In the ensuing pause Lois said, 'How did we find ourselves on the topic of Antony Devine? We were talking about cakes!'

Luke said, 'Lois has a clever way with sad cakes. She up-ends them and decorates the bottom!'

Amid laughter Lois protested, 'Don't tell everyone, Luke! Oh, men are so tactless!'

'*Guileless*!' said Antony. 'Not tactless! There's a world of difference.' He looked up and saw the oysters which Fanny was setting in front of them. 'Oh, this looks intriguing.'

'Cooked with fried butter and crumbs,' Fanny said proudly. ''Tis a French dish and no end finicky!'

'French!' said Luke and smiled at Sophie. She felt ridiculously pleased with his approval and, afraid she might blush, hastily lowered her eyes in case he read her expression.

Fanny hovered by the door as they began to eat and only returned to the kitchen when total approval of the oysters had been expressed. It seemed the 'farewell' supper party would be a success after all.

*

By the end of the evening, Sophie had completely forgotten her earlier anguish. The meal had been very well received and Sophie thought the Meridiths were impressed. The pie (the burnt corner removed by judicious scraping) had proved delicious; the turnips had been praised for the touch of nutmeg and even Sophie thought the lemon snow was fluffier than ever before. They had eaten well and had consumed plenty of Matthew's best wine. Sophie, flushed with success, had remembered to propose a toast to 'absent friends' and Antony had followed it with another to Matthew's recovery.

The conversation had been in turn merry and serious and they had touched on a number of the usual topics. The war with the Dutch had been thoroughly aired and the extravagance of King Charles's Court had been condemned. Lois had shown great interest in Sophie's children and Luke had spoken in warmest terms of his sister's devotion to Antony after his wife's death. The two women had touched on fashion and cooking and Antony had told Sophie of his plans to go to Padua to study medicine. The one subject that was not allowed, by mutual consent, was the progress of the plague. In all, Sophie thought the evening had been a success although an attack of hiccups around nine-thirty had warned her not to drink any more.

Antony, however, was less circumspect and drank rather too freely and Lois and Luke exchanged one or two wry glances. Just before ten o'clock, when Sophie was suggesting she might play for them on the dulcimer, Antony suddenly leaned forward on the table, put his head on his folded arms and fell into a deep sleep. Amid the laughter he began to snore and Luke started to apologize for him. In spite of Sophie's protests, Lois tried to rouse him.

'We must take him home,' she said, embarrassed, but Sophie would have none of it.

'Poor Antony! Let him be!' she said. 'There is no need to disturb him. He can sleep in my mother-in-law's room overnight and I will send him home in the morning.'

There was a little argument but, when they again tried to rouse him without success, Sophie's argument won the day and when, just after eleven, the guests left, Antony was fast asleep in Ruth's bed.

Fanny, dozing in the kitchen, was shaken awake by a jubilant Sophie. 'They have all gone home,' she told her, 'except Master Antony who is sleeping in Mistress Devine's room.'

Fanny stared at her, confused. 'Who's sleeping here?'

'Antony. He suddenly fell asleep and it seemed a shame to waken him.' She smiled happily. 'It has all been the greatest triumph!' she told Fanny, 'and you were spoken of most highly for your part. If only poor Matthew could have been with us.' She smiled. 'I don't feel at all tired but doubtless sleep will come. They did so enjoy themselves so our efforts were not wasted.'

Fanny smiled. 'And Master Antony is sleeping *here*!' she repeated and suddenly became much more alert. 'Should I wake him in the morning? Take him some breakfast, maybe?'

'Very likely,' said Sophie, 'but now 'tis bedtime. We'll wash up tomorrow and you shall take all the leftovers to share with Jem and your father since I shall be gone back to Woolwich.'

Fanny mumbled her thanks. 'And everything was to your liking, mistress?'

'Everything,' Sophie told her and gave her a hug. 'Lois complimented me on the lemon snow and I have given her the recipe.' She hesitated. 'I'm sorry I snapped at you earlier. 'Twas just my way and I meant no offence by it.'

'None taken, mistress,' said Fanny and added sincerely, 'I wish you weren't going back to Woolwich tomorrow – but there, poor Ollie and Lizbeth will be missing their mother.'

'I shall miss you, Fanny,' said Sophie and thought

with a flash of regret that Woolwich was a long way from the Meridiths.

*

While Sophie was preparing for the supper party, Jem Rice had been out on the Thames as usual. Business was very slow however, and at mid-day he waited at the Temple Stairs and had time to look about him and observe the river. The sloping bank was now exposed because the tide was out and the unpleasant smell from the exposed mud was intensified by the sunshine. Behind him Essex House rose abruptly and he could see Arundel House further upriver. Downriver he would have seen Dorset House if he had bothered to look but they were all as familiar to him as the palm of his hand and just as interesting. The river looked strangely empty and Jem's experienced eye knew which boats were *not* in evidence. Coal barges were reluctant to use the port now and pleasure boats were almost totally absent. Several of the foreign ships carrying timber were tying up further down the river, leaving their cargoes to be brought into the capital by waggon. Even a few of the ferrymen were missing, presumed sick or dead.

On the far side of the river there was little to see but some mud and the low-lying fields of Lambeth Marsh. Further east Southwark raised a few rooftops but it was mainly known for the Bear Garden at Bankside or St Thomas's Hospital. Jem reflected miserably on his lonely existence and uncertain future but he reminded himself that at least he was still a free man, whereas Charlie was not. That thought, however, gave him no comfort at all. A visit to his brother the previous night had left him astonished by his resilience. Charlie was locked away in a filthy cell with dozens of undesirable companions and yet he appeared to be enjoying himself! Jem envied him his adaptability but could not resist the feeling that life was unjust. While honest folk reeled under life's misfortunes, the dishonest ones flourished. He, Jem, had always done a fair day's work and had robbed no man, yet his wife and baby boy had been taken from him. Charlie had always cared for no one but himself, boasted of his dishonest tricks. He was cheerfully unrepentant yet God had not seen fit to punish him. Perhaps Charlie was right, thought Jem reluctantly. Perhaps it did not pay to be too honest in your dealings. He wondered half-heartedly whether to take a leaf out of Charlie's book and turn his hand to a little petty crime. It was becoming easier by the day with so many people fleeing the city, abandoning their homes to any thief willing to take the time to force a lock.

He was still wondering, while the boat rocked gently, when another wherry pulled in alongside and he recognized the screwed-up features of Hal Starke. Hal was a well-meaning but loquacious man and normally Jem avoided him if possible but today he was glad of any company to keep his own sombre thoughts at bay.

'Good morrow, Hal,' he said, achieving a passable smile.

Hal snorted. 'If one more person says "Good morrow!" to me I shall spit!' he grumbled. 'There's nothing good about today or yesterday. Nor will be tomorrow, neither. Seven fares I had yesterday. Seven! That's all.' He spat. 'A man can starve on that.'

'If he doesn't die of plague first!'

The man shook his head. 'This plague! 'Tis a most damnable thing. I had a fare yesterday who had read the weekly Bill. Nigh on two thousand deaths! In a week! Can you believe that? God's teeth! There'll be nobody left to take to the river if it goes on.'

'Two thousand?' Jem's mind boggled at the figure. 'And 'tis getting hotter every day. They say the hotter it gets the more 'twill kill. The plague likes hot weather.'

'Two thousand,' Hal repeated with a dismal shake of his head. 'And rising! Did I say that?'

'No, but I guessed as much.'

'Rising steepish! That's what he said. They were his exact words. How steep is steepish, I thought to myself, if you know what I mean.' He pulled in the oars and settled himself more comfortably. 'Did you hear about Smiler? Took on a fare, an elderly woman, quite cheerful, she was, the way he told it to me. Day before yesterday it was and she wants to go to way past Chatham. Clutching a fat purse and looks tidy enough so he thinks he'll chance it. You know how it is, Jem. Ask some of them for a glimpse of the money before you set out and they take the hump! You might lose the fare. Well, they're nearly at Chatham when all of a sudden she ups and faints! God Almighty! he thinks. She's croaked and hasn't paid a penny! So he looks into her face and she's still breathing so there's nothing amiss there. Just looks like she's sleeping, see. Her sleeves are so tight he can't see her arms so he hoists up her skirts and her legs is covered with plague tokens!'

Jem gasped.

'Aye! Plague tokens as big as shillings! Dozens of 'em! Great blacky spots. Her days are numbered right enough, thinks Smiler.' He chuckled. 'Poor chap! He's in a panic so what does he do? He finds her purse, for the money that's due but what to do with her? She's going to die anyway so why prolong the agony?'

Jem looked nervous as he saw the train of thought. 'But she wasn't dead?'

'Not yet. But she soon would be and Smiler reckoned he'd be doing her a favour to put her out of her misery while she was still in a faint. See, that way she wouldn't know anything about it! Nice way to die!'

He ignored Jem's expression and went on, 'He doesn't want to touch her so he uses his feet and finally manages to tip her over the side! Splash! Off she goes, floating downstream with her feet in the air, peaceful as a sleeping baby. So good riddance! Smiler, thinking he'd had a narrow escape, looks in her purse and 'tis full of buttons! Military buttons off a uniform. No money at all!' Hal threw back his head and roared with laughter. 'Not so much as a farthing! All the way to Chatham for nothing.' He slapped his thigh at this cruel twist of fate and his wheezing laughter set the wherry rocking crazily. At last he wiped his streaming eyes on his shirt sleeve and sighed deeply. 'Take me to Chatham, she says, and all the time she knows her purse is empty. But what can you expect? That's how people are, these days. Enough to break your heart! Can't trust no one.'

Jem shook his head. 'It makes you think.'

'Think? *Think*! It makes me want to *puke*!' He spat into the water. 'How's a man to earn a living with folks going down like flies. At least you lost your two more natural, Jem. I mean, 'twasn't the plague.'

'They're still dead,' Jem protested. 'Plague or not.'

'Yes, well –' Hal decided to change the subject and suddenly whipped open his leather jerkin and pulled up his shirt. Jem saw with surprise that three letters had been finely scratched on his skin and now glowed as thin red weals bright against the pallor of his hairless chest.

'That,' Hal told him, 'is a sure charm against the plague.'

'But what is it?'

As though explaining something elementary to a

child of five, Hal touched each letter gingerly with a grimy forefinger. ''Tis an I, an H and an S,' he recited. 'So what's it mean, you ask. So I'll tell you. 'Tis a genuine Jesuit mark! That's what 'tis. That'll keep me safe from the plague. Safe as houses. That cost me tuppence from a famous Dutch physician I came across in St Paul's churchyard. Lining up for it, folks was, him being so famous.'

'Dutch?' Jem queried. 'You'd trust a Dutchman when they are busy trying to sink our ships!'

Hal regarded him loftily. 'Don't you know about the oath?' he demanded. 'Doctors take an oath. Doesn't matter which country they're in they're still bound by it. Hippo-something.' He squinted downwards for a last glimpse of the charm before tucking his shirt in once more. 'One hundred per cent sure!'

'How does it work, then?' Jem asked, wondering whether or not he might spend tuppence himself.

'Don't ask!' cried Hal, tapping the side of his nose. 'Folk asked just such a question but the Dutchman was very stubborn that if the secret was revealed the power would be lost.' He wagged an emphatic finger. 'The power resides in the secret!'

Jem said, 'And 'tis a certain sure charm?'

'Most certainly 'tis!' Hal told him, 'but if it should fail, why then I have this!' With a flourish that would have done credit to a magician he produced a folded sheet of paper from his pocket and waved it aloft. 'Abracadabra!' he cried and began to run his fingers over the lines of writing.

Jem was curious. He held out his hand and Hal surrendered the paper with a show of reluctance. The word "abracadabra" was written at the top. Beneath it the word had been repeated eleven times and each time a final letter had been omitted. The resulting letters formed an up-ended triangle with the whole word at the top and a single 'A' at the bottom. Before Jem could comment Hal snatched it back, kissed it and refolded it. As he thrust it back into his pocket he said, 'I hear your Charlie's in The Fleet.'

Jem nodded.

'My uncle spent half his life there,' Hal said casually. 'Then he was transported. Sent him to Jamaica and we've never seen him since. Mind, he was a hardened offender. Your Charlie's a first offence. They'll let him out when he coughs up enough money.'

'Serves him damn well right!' said Jem with an uncharacteristic burst of spite.

At that moment a small, elderly man appeared at the top of the step and Jem said, 'He's mine!' in case Hal tried to steal his fare. The man stepped lightly into the wherry and sat down with the easy familiarity of one who has travelled by water frequently. He said, 'St Thomas's Hospital on the far side and hurry it up.'

He was well dressed in a suit of dark brown silk with embroidered sleeves; he was smoking an expensive looking pipe and appeared to be in good health but the mention of the hospital made Jem wary.

'Not sick, are you?' he asked.

'No, dammit, I'm a medical man. I have a consultation to attend and a ward full of patients before that!' He looked at Jem and said sharply, 'Don't you smoke, man?'

Jem, pulling towards midstream, shook his head. The tide was not helping him but nor did it flow against him. He settled into a regular rhythm, forward and back, moving the oars skilfully from years of habit.

'You should,' the medical man told him. 'Everyone should smoke. Keeps the plague at bay. I'd make it compulsory if I had my way.'

'I'll bear that in mind,' said Jem grimly. He thought there was little point in explaining to this obviously wealthy man that he needed all his earnings to feed and clothe himself. Smoking would be a luxury, unless Charlie gave him some of his ill-gotten baccy. He had done so once but Jem had made such a performance of it, choking and spluttering with streaming eyes, that Charlie had deemed it a waste of good tobacco and would not give him any more.

In the middle of the river where the current was strongest, the milky brown water flowed swift and deep. Jem increased his efforts until the muscles in his upper arms showed against the cloth of his flimsy sleeves. As he rowed he watched his passenger, trying to imagine himself in his shoes, a wealthy man, respected by his colleagues for his accumulated wisdom. No doubt he had a wife and children, he thought, who would welcome him home at the end of each busy day.

He thought of Maggie and her halo of bright hair and the tiny scrap of humanity that for such a short time was his beloved son. He had a sudden urge to tell this man that he, too, a common waterman, had once had a wife and child. He said, 'I was married once –' and then stopped abruptly.

The man said, 'Indeed?'

Immediately regretting the confidence, Jem shrugged his shoulders and went on rowing but he could see the man considering him.

'What's your name?' he asked Jem.

'James Rice.' He wished he had kept his mouth shut. His father had told him often enough – 'Save your breath for your work!'

He had almost reached the other side of the river, in sight of the steps below London Bridge, when his fare suddenly grunted in pain and clamped a hand to his chest.

'God in Heaven!' he grunted.

'Sir? What ails you?' cried Jem.

'A cramp. 'Tis nothing. 'Tis not the first time.' But with Hal Starke's grim story still ringing in his ears Jem's mind made the obvious connection and he froze. So this was how it happened. This was how those other watermen had lost their lives. One unfortunate passenger could spell disaster.

The man stared at him speechlessly. His eyes rolled upwards and then he doubled up in agony, leaning to one side so that the boat rocked violently, nearly tipping them both into the water. Jem put out a hand and caught hold of the man's coat to steady him.

'Hold on, sir!' he told him. 'We'll soon be there!'

With difficulty the man nodded. His face was ashen, his features distorted with pain. Jem thought he was dying. He had heard of such sudden deaths from plague, where a body was well one minute and at his last gasp the next – just like the old lady in Smiler's boat.

Jem smiled encouragement although his face was stiff with shock and fear. 'Soon have you ashore, sir. Don't you fret.'

'The hospital!' The words were barely audible.

'The hospital 'tis!' cried Jem. 'We'll get you there, safe and sound.'

It came to him suddenly as he tied up at the steps that this was perhaps God's way. He meant Jem to die of the plague so that he could be reunited with his sweet Maggie and little son. It was meant to be. God had not separated them for long. With this thought to sustain him, fear of his own death faded away and he decided to do all that was necessary for his passenger.

With an effort he dragged the man from the boat and sat him down while he went in search of help. It was not forthcoming. It seemed that no one was willing to take his unfortunate fare to the hospital and, on reflection, Jem couldn't blame them. No doubt they all had families to think of. All except him. Jem Rice was no longer a family man. In desperation he went back to his fare who was now doubled up on the ground, groaning pitifully.

'I'm going to have to carry you!' Jem told him. ''Tis either that or leave you here to die and we can't do that.'

Good job the man was so slightly built, thought Jem, as he bent down and, with some difficulty, hoisted him on to his back.

'Just you hang on tight, sir,' he said, steeling himself to ignore the man's groans, as he headed towards the road. 'We'll have you safely tucked up in hospital before you can say "Wink!"'

Fortunately the hospital buildings were not too far away but it took Jem the best part of half an hour to stagger with his patient to the main door. He dumped him unceremoniously on the step and hurried inside to summon help.

'You his son?' someone asked.

'Me – I'm nobody,' said Jem and made his escape before any more questions could be asked. He had a natural distrust of formality and authority and knew that the wrong answer could cost a man dear.

Ten minutes later he was back on the river feeling strangely calm now that he had accepted his fate. He wondered how long it would take before the first symptoms made themselves known.

*

Sophie woke early the next morning, before daylight had crept over the rooftops and, as she lay in bed, began to formulate plans for the coming weeks. She would persuade Fanny to spend a large part of each day in the house with the dog for company. Because Fanny was afraid to sleep in the house alone Sophie would allow her to sleep at her father's home as long as she returned first thing in the morning to let the dog out into the yard and generally busy herself around the place. This way she hoped that thieves would believe the house was occupied and pay it no unwelcome visits. During the night Banna must be locked in the kitchen so that he could bark and deter any potential intruders.

In spite of her feelings towards Anne Redditch, Sophie was becoming very fond of the little spaniel and did not for one moment regret the rescue. She was longing to see the children's faces when they saw the dog for the first time. If Matthew survived she would stand up to him on the matter of the dog. He had been seen carrying Banna; he had accepted the dog in Anne's house; he must accept it in their house too. Sophie was also aware that the animal would serve as a permanent reminder to Matthew of his infidelity. An ungenerous thought, perhaps, but the idea appealed to her. She was still unsure that she would ever be able to love her husband as she had loved him in the past. She had once considered herself so fortunate to be his chosen partner. Now, knowing that he had rejected her in favour of another, she would know for the rest of her life that in his eyes she was second best. Living with that knowledge would not be easy but she would tackle the problem as and when it arose. For the present too many other matters demanded her attention and she thrust the thought from her.

Lois had insisted that she would pay daily visits to the pesthouse and would write regularly to Sophie with news of Matthew's progress. Luke had given her a little hope that he might recover although he admitted that statistically Matthew's chances were not good. The intensity of the disease was now so great that seven out of ten people who contracted it died, most of them succumbing within four or five days of the first symptom. It was now the fourteenth of July and as Matthew's symptoms had appeared on the eleventh he might well be over the worst although no bubo had yet appeared and that was causing the physician some concern.

With an effort Sophie tried to look on the bright side. At least she would be seeing her children again and if her husband *did* survive there was no Anne Redditch to come between them. They could patch up their problems and somehow make a new start. Her thoughts had turned to Luke Meridith when Fanny knocked on the door. She came into the room carrying a jug of warm water and looking very anxious.

'What is it?' cried Sophie, all her resolutions to look on the bright side fading at the sight of Fanny's frown.

''Tis Master Antony, mistress. I peeped into his room and he was fast asleep so I coughed loudly to waken him, it being past seven o'clock and me with all the clearing up to do.'

'And what happened?'

'I didn't go right in,' she said. 'I coughed louder and said his name and then I knocked on the door. I knocked louder and louder but he *still* didn't wake.'

'I dare say he is sleeping heavily this morning. Out of sorts, maybe.'

Fanny seized her opportunity. 'Should I go right in and just shake him gently by the arm?'

Sophie saw the appeal in her eyes. 'Someone has to wake him,' she agreed. 'Wake him gently and ask him if he would like anything to drink or eat before he goes home. Explain that we do not wish to be unhospitable but we have a lot to do.'

Fanny was half out of the door when Sophie called, 'And what of your mistress, Fanny? Don't you want to know what *I* would like to eat or drink? I may not be as handsome as our guest but –'

Fanny had the grace to look embarrassed. 'I'm sorry, mistress,' she said. ''Tis just that I'm flummoxed this morning what with so much to be done.'

Sophie said, 'I would like a small omelette, please, Fanny. The same might comfort Antony's stomach if, as I suspect, the wine has unsettled it.'

Fanny smiled delightedly. 'Drank a mite too much, did he?'

'Let's just say he ate and supped very well and

thoroughly enjoyed himself. He's a charming young man with grace and wit.'

'Oh, he is that, mistress! And when he smiles! He makes me go all wobbly at the knees!' She beamed. 'Funny, but he seemed to take a shine to me from the first moment we met.'

'Did he now?' Sophie hid her amusement and slid out of bed. She glanced out at the weather, hoping as she did every morning that the sky would be full of clouds promising a downpour of rain to clean the streets. A lowering of the temperature would also be welcome to discourage the plague but she saw only clear blue sky and knew it would be hot again.

'I shall go to the pesthouse before I leave,' said Sophie, pouring warm water into the bowl. 'I must ask about Matthew. There may be no change in his condition but his mother will want to know that my news is up to date.'

''Tis a most fearful thing for her,' said Fanny. 'Losing her only son.'

'Matthew may well survive,' Sophie told her quickly. 'She hasn't lost her son yet. They say there has been no change in his condition for several days now and that may be a good sign.'

As Sophie began to wash Fanny took her chance and slipped out of the room.

She had been gone less than two minutes when Sophie heard a terrible scream. Snatching up a towel she dried her face and ran to the door of her bedroom. 'What is it?'

'Mistress! Oh, come quickly!'

Barefooted and still in her nightgown Sophie ran across the landing and into Ruth's room. Fanny was standing beside the bed, her hands clasped in front of her, staring in horror at the still figure in the bed.

'He won't wake up, mistress!' she cried. 'No matter how much I shake him. Is he dead, do you think? Oh, not poor Master Antony! I couldn't bear it!'

Frantically Sophie bent over Luke's son, her heart heavy with dread. Not Antony! she echoed.

'Antony!' She, too, shook him by the arm and the head with its bright flaming hair rolled against the pillow. Antony's face was red and flushed but Sophie saw with relief that his chest still rose and fell.

'He's still breathing,' she stammered. 'Antony! Can you hear me?' She touched his face. His skin was burning.

Fanny had moved round to the other side of the bed and together they stared at him helplessly. 'He can't die!' wailed Fanny, her lips trembling. 'His father wouldn't let him die. Not his own son!' She looked appealingly at Sophie. 'I can scarce believe it. He was so full of fun last night, winking at me and laughing . . .'

Sophie was slowly recovering from her fright. 'His father! You are right, Fanny. We must fetch his father,' she cried, annoyed that it had taken so long for her to think of the obvious. 'You must run round straight away.'

'Me tell him? Oh no!' cried Fanny, aghast. 'I couldn't!'

'You can and you will!' Sophie insisted. And quick! Every minute counts. Do you want us to stand idly by until 'tis too late?'

'I dare say I must go, but how will I find the words –' She shook her head despairingly. 'What shall I say? That 'tis the plague?'

'*No!*' shouted Sophie, catching her by the arm as she made her way reluctantly to the door. 'Say no such thing. We must hope 'tis something kinder. Just say – tell them – Oh! dear God!' She gazed at Fanny distractedly. 'Say we cannot wake him. That is the simple truth and 'twill suffice. Yes, Fanny, that's it exactly. Say he will not rouse up and I am anxious about him.'

'*Very* anxious?' suggested Fanny.

'Yes. And run all the way!'

Fanny darted from the room and clattered down the stairs and then shouted, 'And if they are not in? What then?'

'Why then –' Sophie's mind raced. 'Then go in search of any doctor you can find, Fanny. Any will do. Ask whoever you meet where there is a good physician. A *good* one, Fanny. We want no quacks.' She glanced fearfully at the still form on the bed and added, 'And for God's sake, hurry!'

Chapter Eleven

S FANNY HURRIED through the streets her
lips worked silently. 'Don't let him die, God!
Don't let him die!' It seemed to her that
God must surely notice such a direct appeal if it was
offered up with sufficient frequency. He might find
it irritating but at least he would take note of it. She
assumed that his Godly ears were in perfect working
order and would pick up the softest whisper. 'Don't
let him die, God!'

As she began to run, she heard the egg lady call a
greeting but ignored her. She dodged the pie man
and cannoned into the coalseller but merely ran on,
calling an apology. Let him pick up his own coals,
she thought impatiently. There were more important
things to do. She had to fetch Doctor Meridith and
so save Antony's life. She imagined a rather touching
scene in which he rose from his bed, whole, and
said, 'Tis Fanny I have to thank for my life!'

'And God, naturally.' Yes, that was what she would say with a modest shake of the head although everyone would know that it was her own speed which had made the miracle possible.

Turning a corner, she ploughed on, elbowing her way among the shoppers, darting between waggons and horses and pretending not to hear the uncouth comments which followed her erratic progress. 'My dearest Fanny,' Antony would say, taking her hands in his. 'Let me devote the rest of my life to you for without you I would lie in a cold, dark grave!' And she would try and dissuade him but he would insist that she was the only woman he would ever marry.

'Oh Antony!' she gasped breathlessly and, clutching her side, she stumbled on determined not to stop until she had reached the physician's house.

When she came in sight of it, she redoubled her efforts and finally fell to her knees on the step, almost on top of a large black cat which was washing itself fastidiously. Just in time, with a yowl of protest, the cat sprang sideways, arched its back and hissed angrily. At once Fanny's heart gave a little jump of fear. A black cat! She had offended a black cat and everyone knew what that meant! Mother Shipton's black cat was a demon in disguise and had only to glance at a person to bring about a stroke of ill-fortune – or worse. Tentatively she put out a conciliatory hand, calling, 'Forgive me, pusskins!' but the ruffled cat turned from her quite deliberately and walked away stiff-legged with disapproval.

Fanny was transfixed with a sense of looming disaster. Had she unwittingly ruined her beloved Antony's chances of recovery? Or would God's intervention swing the scales in his favour? Feeling distinctly unhappy she scrambled to her feet and reached for the knocker.

Knock! Knock! She gave it an extra one for luck – Knock! – and waited impatiently, keeping a wary eye on the cat. It was watching her inscrutably from a safe distance and only when it suddenly resumed its washing did she feel a little safer. Perhaps it had accepted her apology, or had decided to overlook the incident.

She lifted the knocker and gave it a much louder knock. What on earth was keeping them? Didn't they know Antony was ill? No, of course they didn't and she would have to break the news. She was thoroughly upset by Antony's condition but could not help enjoying the drama in which she was playing a starring role. She knocked again and then, narrowly missing the wheels of a cart, she stepped back into the road and stared up at the windows. A terrible thought occurred to her. Suppose they *all* had the plague – if that is what it was? Suppose the good doctor and his sister were lying unconscious in *their* beds? In that case she might well be the one who saved *all* their lives and the entire family would be indebted to her forever!

'Doctor Meridith!' she shouted. 'Mistress! 'Tis I, Fanny, come with important news!'

She jumped up and down, trying to peer into the downstairs window but the ground fell away into deep ruts made by the wheels of passing vehicles and she lost her balance and fell sprawling in the road. Blushing furiously, she scrambled up and, as she did so, caught a sudden glimpse of the black cat as it jumped over a nearby fence and disappeared from view. Feeling distinctly uneasy she shouted again at the house and then, remembering her mistress's instructions, abandoned the house and went in search of help.

'A physician, you say?' The old woman pursed her lips and frowned. 'There's old Doctor Martin in the next street but he's not to my taste. Too much bleeding and purging to my way of thinking. But some folks set great store by him, none the less. Give me a chart man any day. My old doctor, God rest his soul, could ferret out a disease in no time, just by consulting his celestial charts.'

'Which house?' cried Fanny.

The old woman was not going to be hurried. 'But now Doctor Martin, he might not be in. Times like these the physicians are nowhere to be – Well!' She tutted angrily as Fanny darted away. 'There's a thing!' she grumbled, and raising her voice, shouted, 'Saucy young baggage!'

But Fanny had gone. In the next street she had better luck.

'Doctor Martin? That's his house.'

Fanny ran to the door and, finding no knocker,

jangled the door bell. To her intense relief it was opened by a woman who turned out to be the physician's wife and she went to fetch him. Breathlessly Fanny recounted her story and at the mention of Doctor Meridith's name the physician's interest sharpened.

'His son, you say? How unfortunate. I'll come at once.'

Fanny led him back to the house, told Sophie that she had received no answer from the Merdiths and was promptly sent back to try again.

She was soon back at the Merdiths' house only to discover that there was still no answer to her knockings. She sat down to take stock of the situation and after some thought decided that perhaps she had panicked unnecessarily. The doctor might well be visiting patients and Lois might be visiting friends. She would wait for one or the other to return.

Time passed and the church clock struck the hour, the quarter and the half. Fanny got to her feet. If she went home without news of the Merdiths she would be sent back for a third time. She decided to go in search of Jem, to tell him the arrangements about the house and the dog and to find out if he had news of Charlie. She would return to the Merdiths in an hour.

As luck would have it Jem was nowhere to be found and she wondered how to while away another hour. She baulked at the idea of visiting Charlie again and finally idled her time away, looking at the

few wares which remained on sale in the little shops
and chatting at the Holborn conduit. At the end of
the hour there was still no reply at the Meridiths'
and she decided to go home and inform her mistress.

To her surprise she found a very young man
standing on the step, whistling. He was very tall and
thin with a long nose and small mouth. His hair was
very pale and flopped over his eyes. She was reminded of a long-legged bird she had seen in one of
the children's books.

'Well?' Fanny asked him sharply. 'Are you going
in or coming out?'

He regarded her loftily. 'Neither,' he said. 'And
what business is it of yours?'

'Because I live here,' she told him, 'and you're
blocking my way'.

'Not any more you don't!'

Taken aback by his assured manner, she asked,
'Don't what?'

'You don't live here any more,' he repeated and
then taking pity on her confusion, added, 'There's
plague in the house. I'm waiting for the carpenter to
fix the lock. No one goes in and no one comes out.
The physician's orders.'

Fanny's mouth fell open in shocked disbelief.
'Not even to – but I *must* go in. The mistress'll have
need of me!' Her thoughts spun. 'Who's in there,
then?' She thought that perhaps she had missed
Doctor Meridith and his sister and that they had
somehow ended up here without her intervention.

'Just her and him. The physician left some time ago.' He sat down on the step and wrapped his hands round his knees.

Thoughtfully, Fanny sat down beside him. So it was the plague. And the house would be shut up for forty days. It sounded remarkably like a prison sentence, she thought grimly. Perhaps Fate had been kind to her. Perhaps it was not such a bad thing that she was excluded from the house. But poor Antony. And poor Mistress Devine. How on earth would they manage? She felt immediately ashamed of her selfishness. And poor Ollie and Lizbeth. They would be so disappointed when their mother failed to return. And suppose her mistress caught the plague from Master Antony!

For a long moment she and the watchman sat in silence and then he asked, 'Who are you then?'

'The cook-maid. My name's Fanny.'

'My name's Jon. I'm the watchman.'

'You don't look like one to me!' Fanny told him, recalling Will Stookey. 'The last one I saw was a useless article if ever I saw one! He was a lot older than you, too.'

'I was a prentice. Worked for a master weaver by the name of Edwin Coates. See, you can't forget it.' He grinned. 'He *weaves* cloth and then they make it into *coats*!'

Fanny gave him a withering look.

Jon went on hurriedly, 'When the plague worsened he upped and left, took his family up to Chester to live with an elderly aunt. He had to leave me behind – had no choice. I had no job and no money so when they said they wanted watchmen I went along. First they said I was too young but I lied about my age. Said I was older than I look.'

'You look about twelve!' said Fanny, crushingly.

'Twelve! I'm nearly twenty! But I said I was twenty-six. They couldn't be bothered to argue and here I am.' He looked at her with an earnest expression in his eyes. Nice brown eyes, thought Fanny, if a bit on the small side. ''Tis a responsible job, this. I had to swear an oath! And here I am, sitting on your mistress's doorstep. Funny old world!'

'Very funny! I'll die laughing!'

She turned to give him a long, appraising look. He wasn't as handsome as Antony (He wasn't as handsome as anybody!), or as charming as Charlie – and probably not as reliable as Jem but there was something about him which touched her. Perhaps it was his eagerness to impress . . . or the fact that he had not been rude to her.

She smiled at him suddenly and, startled, he smiled back. A shy but genuine smile.

'I dare say, Jon, you're courting,' she said casually, staring with apparent interest at a sparrow that was pecking among the garbage.

'Not exactly,' he said but added hurriedly, 'Not for want of chances, though!'

Slowly she turned to look at him again. 'Same with me, Jon, to tell the truth!' she said. 'Lots of admirers but I'm choosy where men are concerned.'

They regarded each other uncertainly until Fanny broke the spell by jumping to her feet with a cry of dismay.

'What am I about!' she cried. 'I must tell the mistress I'm here!' and she raised the knocker in preparation for a major assault but thought better of it. Poor Antony might be sleeping.

*

Sophie appeared at once but before she could open the window Jon jumped to his feet and said awkwardly, 'Forgive me, mistress, but you mustn't open any window at street level. They were very strict about that.' He looked apologetically towards Fanny. ''Tis more than my job's worth to allow it.'

Sophie tutted with exasperation. 'You are right. I quite forgot. Wait there, Fanny.' She disappeared and shortly after reopened the upstairs window instead.

She looked flustered and Fanny said, 'I'm sorry about poor Master Antony. Him of all people!'

Sophie nodded. 'Yes, poor lamb. But he has come out of his deep sleep which the doctor thinks is a good sign. He is very restless with pains in his limbs. All we can do is pray, Fanny.'

'Oh I am, mistress!' Fanny told her. 'I'm praying that hard He can't help but hear me.'

'Good girl!' said Sophie. 'Now, listen. I shall throw down two letters but you must not touch them. Take off your apron and wrap them up and take them to Lois Meredith. She will treat them with hot stones. One letter is for them, the other is to be sent to Woolwich to tell Giles what has happened. He will need to know of my changed plans.'

'The children!' cried Fanny. 'They will be so disappointed.'

As soon as the words were out she regretted them for suddenly her mistress looked near to tears. 'I cannot tell you how wretched I am not to be seeing them again but what can I do? I couldn't desert Antony even if I wanted to.' She shook her head helplessly.

Fanny said, 'I wish I was in there with you, mistress. I'm sure you'll need me.'

'You'll be more use to me outside,' Sophie assured her. 'I shall need someone to fetch and carry.'

Jon jumped to his feet and looking up at Sophie said quickly, 'That be my job, mistress, and I'm more than willing.'

Fanny gave him a quick look. 'We'll manage it together,' she suggested, not willing to relinquish her own role. Vaguely she was beginning to see that the situation offered her a great deal more freedom than she was used to – not that she wanted it at poor Antony's expense, but she might as well make the best of it. She saw also that Sophie might well come to rely on her more; to appreciate her true worth. She might even earn a few pence more – not that she wanted to profit by Antony's misfortune but if Sophie insisted she would accept the money gracefully. She heard herself at some future date saying to Jem and Charlie, 'I don't know how they would have fared without me.' Perhaps she would word it a little more modestly but they would take her meaning.

'Fanny! You useless girl, you're not listening!'

She realized with a start that Sophie was telling her something and was now glaring down at her.

'Do pay attention, girl! This is no time for day-dreaming.'

Embarrassed by Jon's presence, Fanny stared up crossly.

'I have told Doctor Martin that Doctor Meridith will want to take over his son's treatment. *If* he is still able to do so. God knows how we shall fare if he, too, is stricken.' She put a hand to her head with a gesture of despair and Fanny knew suddenly that her mistress must be near to breaking point. She promptly forgave her for her recent sharp remarks and listened attentively.

'I shall also drop a purse of money to you,' said Sophie, 'and a prescription. They also must be dealt with. When you have delivered the letters you must give the prescription to the apothecary who will give you what Doctor Martin has recommended. Then you must fetch food. The physician tells me that nursing Antony will demand all my strength and I mustn't neglect my own health. Since you can no longer eat with me you must either buy pies or else food which you can cook at your father's.'

'What of the leftovers? Last night's supper party?' Fanny had been looking forward to a veritable feast.

'The leftovers? Oh, you can scarcely eat those now. They may carry the infection although I don't see how but better not to risk it. I shall have to throw it all out.'

'Banna might like it,' Fanny began but then added hastily, 'Can dogs catch the plague?'

'Fanny! I don't know and I don't care!'

Her mistress's tone was sharpening once more and Fanny cursed her runaway tongue and pressed her lips together to prevent the escape of any more careless remarks.

'The dog is the least of our worries. I am sorry this makes life difficult for you, Fanny, but at least you are free of the plague and will not have to be cooped up here for forty days.'

Jon, seeing that none of this applied to him, sat down again on the step. Fanny began to listen carefully.

'I suspect that if Doctor Meridith or Lois are in when you deliver the letter, they will come straight round.'

She paused, distractedly, and Fanny said, 'Should I go now, mistress?'

'Yes, and when you come back rap at the window again as you did before.'

Another thought occurred to Fanny. 'So you won't be visiting the pesthouse to ask after the master.'

'I cannot visit anyone!' cried Sophie. 'Don't you understand? I am trapped here!' She thought for a moment and then said, 'But you can go to the pesthouse for me and make inquiry. Do that after you have finished the rest of your errands. Now, wait a moment.'

'Yes, mistress.' Fanny caught Jon's eye and raised her eyebrows. She took off her apron as directed and gathered up the purse and letters which Sophie threw down to her. When they were well wrapped up, she said, 'I'll be off then,' before Sophie could think of any more errands.

'God speed!' said Sophie and closed the window. As Fanny set off towards the Meridiths' house once again she began to wonder if this new situation was to prove to her advantage after all or whether she would live to regret it.

*

Jem, meanwhile, had had a reasonable day with a total of five fares, one of them a good one. He had come to terms with the idea that his days were numbered and was awaiting the onset of his sickness with something akin to curiosity. His acceptance of his fate removed all his anxieties about the future and in a strange way he felt almost happy as he pulled in and tied up at Temple Stairs. It was the not knowing that scared folk, he told himself. Now that he knew, his worries were over and he could die with an easy conscience for there was none to mourn him but Fanny and Charlie and who could say but they might be next to go. The entire Rice family might be wiped from the face of the earth. So be it! He shrugged. Jem could do nothing to save them. He was resigned to the worst.

He looked around him as he nosed the boat into the bank. He had the river steps to himself which was another stroke of luck. If a fare came along he was first in line. He shipped the oars and sat back, easing his muscles. He wondered how many more days he would spend in this boat, rowing up and down the Thames. Three? Five? A dozen, even? He felt his wrist in search of a pulse and then felt his forehead for fever. So far, nothing. His heart was still beating and his mind was clear. He began to whistle. The sun shone on the water and gulls wheeled overhead but the scene was spoiled by the smell of mud and rotting garbage.

Jem stared idly at a three-masted schooner that had moored on the far side of the river opposite Arundel House. It was a Norwegian vessel, Jem recognized the flag, and its cargo was pine – he could smell the warm resin as he sniffed appreciatively. He watched the crew unloading it, scurrying from ship to shore, balancing the long planks on their shoulders, their backs bowed under the weight. No doubt they had grumbled at being moored so close to the infected city but the ship's owners would have little compunction about their crew's safety. Jem thanked God that he was not a sailor. It was a dog's life, if what he heard was true. Small wonder that press-gangs were required to force men to serve in the King's Navy. He smiled contentedly. The Thames was good enough for him. He had no urge to see the open sea. No time now to see it even if he wanted to!

'You know a man by the name of Rice?'

The question startled him and he looked round cautiously. 'Who's asking?' he said. If this was a Revenue man or an irate husband in search of Charlie then Jem would know nothing. Charlie might be a fool but he was family.

A man stood at the top of the steps and Jem had the feeling he had seen him somewhere before.

'I'm asking.' The man was about fifty, well dressed. 'I'm looking for a James Rice and you seem to fit the description I have of him.'

'That's me,' Jem admitted warily, 'but I've done nothing wrong. I swear it!'

'Ah!' To Jem's surprise the man hurried eagerly down the steps towards him.

'If you're James Rice then I'll ask you to step ashore, young man. I've good news for you and I'd also deem it an honour to shake you by the hand.'

Encouraged by these words which were followed by a broad smile, Jem stepped ashore.

'I'm Nathan Gould and my brother's a physician at St Thomas's Hospital.'

Light dawned. Jem said, 'The physician! That was your brother? The man stricken with the plague!'

'The plague? No, no, Master Rice, 'twas no such thing.'

The man grasped him by the hand and shook it vigorously. Jem stared at him in confusion. It was *not* the plague? If the man had been free of the infection then he, Jem, could not have taken it from him, and might live after all. For a moment he felt bereft, cheated but then hope flared and he began to smile.

The man went on, 'My brother feared you would suspect the worst and was insistent that I put your mind at rest on the matter.'

Jem's smile broadened but he said nothing.

Nathan Gould was regarding him warmly. 'My brother suffers from time to time with severe apoplexy. It was that which brought about his disorder and he was greatly impressed by your generosity of spirit. He is partly recovered, I am glad to say, and sends his thanks.'

Jem said, 'So he didn't die?'

'Certainly not! Fit as a fiddle! And will live as long as the next man. Thanks to you.'

Jem began to protest that he had done very little.

'Ah, but you did!' Nathan Gould smiled again. 'Most men would have deserted him. Some would have robbed him. Oh yes! Not all watermen are as upright as you, young man.' He pulled something from his pocket and gave it to Jem. 'With my brother's heartfelt thanks.'

Wordlessly Jem took the small object which was

wrapped in velvet. Wonderingly he unwrapped it and discovered a gold sovereign. Unable to speak he stared at it. A sovereign! He had never had so much money in his whole life nor even expected such a windfall.

At last he found his voice and stammered, 'A sovereign! I can scarce believe it. Oh thank your brother for me, sir! He will never know how much this means to me.'

The man's hand rested briefly on Jem's shoulder. ''Tis my brother who thanks you for his life. 'Tis heartening to meet an honest man, Master Rice.'

He turned to go. 'And take good care of yourself,' he warned. 'These are evil times.'

Jem watched him go, still dazed by his good fortune. Reverently he lifted the sovereign to his lips. He was about to kiss it when all the warnings flooded into his mind about the possibility of coins carrying the contagion. Now that he was back among the living it was better to be on the safe side. Carefully he wrapped it up and thrust it deep into his pocket. He climbed back into his boat and sat down to think. If he wasn't going to die he would not be joining Maggie and his son. For a while this saddened him but then suddenly his eyes gleamed with satisfaction. He knew exactly how he would spend his sovereign.

*

It was difficult to distinguish night from day in the

twilight world which the inmates inhabited. The windows of the pesthouse let in very little light even on the brightest day and during the hours of darkness a few lanterns served merely to brighten the gloom. Their wavering light cast flickering shadows over the rows of beds and gave the vast room a sinister appearance which was exacerbated by the cries and groans of the unfortunate patients. Natural sleep was almost impossible and nights were haunted by the delirious babblings of the seriously ill. Many patients fell exhausted into a drugged sleep and woke each morning to the sight of shrouded bodies being carried past them to a place unseen where they would await the next visit by the plague cart.

Matthew woke slowly on the morning of the eighteenth to the familiar confusion of pain and grief and, without opening his eyes, he knew his world was shrinking. He was aware of the smell of juniper and frankincense which burned day and night in the large chafing dishes in the middle of the room. This was overlaid with the sharp and unmistakable smell of death. He was aware, too, that his besieged body was surrendering to the invading sickness and that he no longer had the will or energy to fight. His skin burned, his limbs ached, his mouth was parched. His mind was a mass of disjointed fragments of information which sometimes merged to make sense but more often slipped away. Names floated like driftwood in a sea of confusion. He tried to grasp at them, desperate to remember something of the life he had once known beyond the walls of this strange and terrible place. He could still hear. His ears detected the sound of urgent voices, muffled footsteps, coughs, groans, the clatter of unseen instruments, metal on earthenware. Faintly from outside he heard a bird singing and recognized the rattle of wheels and the clop of hooves. There was another world outside these walls but now he could recall little of it. He felt light-headed as though his mind was emptying. With dreadful inevitability he imagined the sands of time running out and a lifetime's knowledge escaping with it. This knowledge was what made him who he was. Once that was gone he would be nothing. Nobody. He made a last attempt to recall what he knew.

Matthew. He knew that was his own name and he clung to that. He could not remember what he used to do every day or where he lived and sometimes that frightened him. But he knew he was Matthew.

Elena. That was a name he knew. Her face was familiar to him and caused him no anxiety. Elena would wash him and pray for him. He saw her every day and sometimes she came to him at night and held his hand and whispered words of comfort.

Lois was a name to him, nothing more. But he heard the name every day and when they spoke it they gave him calves' foot jelly and light custards which he swallowed obediently but she was a stranger to him.

Meridith. Was that another name? It meant nothing to him. After a moment, too tired to care, he let it slip away.

Sophie was his wife. Her name was like a dull reproach. Had he betrayed her? Sophie was the mother of his children but she had abandoned him to his fate. He tried unsuccessfully to summon her image – but he loved her still.

And Anne. Who was Anne?

His wandering thoughts were interrupted by a fearful scream and somehow Matthew managed to open his eyes. He glimpsed a woman in the next bed who was sitting bolt upright, staring ahead with terrified eyes as though she had seen a frightful vision. As he closed his eyes once more he heard familiar footsteps approaching, hurrying towards him. Matthew drew a long, shuddering breath. He was so weary and so full of pain that he longed for oblivion.

Suddenly he felt a cool hand on his own.

'God sees your pain, Master Devine.'

Matthew recognized the soft, caring voice of Elena. He opened his mouth to speak to her but his brief venture into consciousness had exhausted him and his thoughts slid away. He found himself falling back into that harrowing darkness which passed for sleep.

When he next became aware of his surroundings he heard whispered voices and felt gentle hands examining his body. Words floated by him and he sensed, rather than heard, that they concerned him.

He wanted to open his eyes but they remained firmly closed. He wanted to move his hand but it lay limply on the blanket and would not obey him. Strangely he felt no pain. Was this death, he wondered curiously. No. He was still breathing.

A phrase registered in his baffled brain.

'. . . losing him . . .'

Is that what they were doing? Losing him? He felt lost already . . . adrift . . . a speck on the ocean. Someone was holding his hand, rubbing it. He knew they were rubbing his hands and yet he felt nothing at all. If only he could open his eyes! They were losing him and he wanted to see for the last time; he longed for one more glimpse of humanity before he was no longer part of it.

'Sophie!'

The word startled him. Had he spoken? Was that hoarse, tortured voice his own? Was that Matthew's voice?

Fingers fluttered over his eyelids. He heard Elena say, 'Poor man!'

And with a faint sigh of relief he knew it was time to go.

*

On the other side of the ward a young, blond man watched the drama unfold. He was sitting up in the narrow truckle-bed, taking an interest in all that went on around him. He particularly noticed the nurse they called Elena. She was young with a sweet serious face. Her calm manner was greatly at odds with the frenzied activity which appeared to be normal in this place. He called out, 'Snuffed it, has he?'

The physician turned to frown on him and Elena looked at him reproachfully and put a finger to her lips.

Unabashed, he grinned and went on in a loud voice, 'How many's that, then? Two yesterday and one today. Not a very good score!'

Elena came towards him quickly saying, 'Poor Master Devine is dead and I must ask you not to talk so disrespectfully. There is no excuse for bad manners – and you will make Doctor Lymme angry.'

'I'm only trying to work out my chances. I rather enjoy a gamble.'

Her lips twitched but she kept her face straight. 'We do all we can.'

'Devine,' he said thoughtfully. 'I knew a man by that name.'

She sighed. 'Poor Master Devine. For a while we thought we could save him but – we are all in God's hands. Even you!' She smiled briefly

The doctor had by now left the room and Charlie decided to change the subject 'Elena! That's a beautiful name. I have fallen in love with your name. I think on it all the time.'

'Then more fool you!' she chided. 'You should spend every moment in repentance and prayer.'

He rolled his eyes. 'Elena! Elena!'

He reached for her hand but she withdrew it.

'You must think about your position, Master Rice,' she told him. 'You may well be called to account for your misdeeds and should be asking forgiveness –'

Charlie ignored this homily. 'This man on my right – is he dying? Or is he dead? He hasn't moved since I was brought in yesterday.'

She glanced solicitously at the huddled figure. 'Master Levitt is unconscious, poor man. You should not mock the afflicted for fear you are soon in the same predicament.'

'Aren't you fearful?' he asked, genuinely concerned that she was exposing herself to such a risk.

She smiled. 'I have already had the plague,' she told him. 'God saw fit to save my life and, in gratitude, I am devoting it to others.' She gave a wry smile. 'My parents begged me to rejoin them in Honiton but I cannot do that.'

'And your husband?' he suggested.

Her smile faded. 'I came up to London to be wed but my intended died shortly before I arrived.'

'Of the plague?'

'Oh no. He was operated on for the stone and did not survive. He was much older than I am but I was fond of him.' She shrugged. 'Then I fell sick with plague and now I find myself here.'

'You should go home!' he urged.

She shook her head. 'I shall work here until the outbreak is at an end.'

He shook his head, reluctantly impressed by her humility and dedication. Suddenly he frowned. 'But they say a man may catch the plague a second time!'

'If God wills it. I am content to put myself in his hands.'

'Will I die?' He was annoyed to hear the tremor in his voice that gave the lie to his bravado.

'I trust not. We will do our best for you. If you make your peace with God, He will succour you.' And with a final smile she moved away in answer to a plaintive cry from someone further down the room.

He waited until she had gone and then surreptitiously and with great care, slid the fingers of his right hand under his left armpit where the swelling had been covered with a poultice, long since grown cold. Was it going to break, as the physician hoped? They would tell him so little, afraid to commit themselves. He had never had much time for medical men, believing them all to be rogues and charlatans. Now he hoped this Doctor Lymme knew what he was about. Apart from the swelling he felt well enough. He felt a throbbing in his temple and a certain lassitude but nothing to alarm him. If this was the plague, he was almost disappointed. At least it had served to get him out of that hell-hole they called The Fleet. He wondered idly how many others had caught the disease from him before he was removed, then shrugged. He was out of there and that was all that mattered. Thrown out with indecent

347

haste, if the truth be told. His feet had scarcely touched the ground. He grinned at the recollection. Poxy jailers! But here he was a free man and he still had all the money he had made from his numerous 'marriages'! All he had to do now was live long enough to spend it!

He thought about Elena and what she would think of him if she could see into his murky past. For the first time in his life he felt vaguely ashamed of himself but promptly resisted the emotion. He may not have led a blameless life but he had never killed a man. Cheating, lying and robbing were hardly crimes, he argued. A man must live. It was dog eat dog out there in England's most wicked city and he was no worse than the next man and better than some. And if he had stolen a kiss or two here and there from another man's wife there was no real harm in it.

'Make your peace with God,' Elena had said. 'Confess your sins.' For a moment he considered the suggestion, but almost immediately decided against such a rash step. His sins were so numerous he would scarce know where to begin. If he were to start down that road, he thought ruefully, he would be dead and buried long before he had finished!

He watched Elena move swiftly to another patient who was now leaning over the edge of the bed to vomit. She looked too frail for the work, he thought irritably. Why did she have to be such a saint? Since no one would survive to sing her praises she might as well return to Honiton and look for another husband. Fortunate man!

She was holding the patient's head and soothing him, cleansing his mouth with a damp cloth. Ugh! Disgusting work for such a woman.

A sudden disturbance at the far end of the room attracted his attention and he saw that one of the patients, a woman, had thrown back the bedclothes and was climbing out of the bed. Many heads turned as the distraught woman, muttering deliriously, balanced on trembling legs and began to lurch unsteadily between the rows of beds. Some of the patients watched apathetically, a few shouted to her to return to her bed and one cheered her on as though she were competing in a race. Elena glanced up in agitation but she was unable to leave her own patient.

The cat-calls faltered, however, and her tormentors fell silent, appalled by the apparition. Her face was as grey as her wispy hair, her eyes wide with fear and pain; her body was skimpily covered in what remained of a once white gown which her agitated fingers had long since torn to shreds. Her arms were outstretched and she swayed from side to side in an effort to stay upright, shuffling slowly through the hushed ward like a phantom.

Before he realized what he was doing Charlie had left his bed and was hurrying to the woman's side. He reached her just as her strength finally failed and caught her as she fell. He looked down at the suffering women and was suddenly overwhelmed by compassion for the pathetic scrap of humanity he held in his arms. Fleetingly he was reminded of his mother who had died so recently and whose death, until now, had hardly touched him. Pierced by an unexpected sense of loss and half-blinded by tears he carried the woman back along the ward and deposited her gently on her bed where she lay exhausted. For a moment he stood looking down at her then, seeing that she began to shiver violently, he pulled up the blanket and tucked it gently round the bony shoulders.

She spoke suddenly. 'Is that you, Amos?'

He hesitated then said, 'Yes. Yes. 'Tis Amos. You sleep now.'

Her ravaged face relaxed into a faint smile and she drew a long, shuddering breath. Then she closed her eyes. He looked at her in alarm. She mustn't die! He leaned forward anxiously and was able to satisfy himself that below the blanket her chest still rose and fell.

Elena appeared beside him and laid her hand on his arm.

'Thank you, Master Rice.' There was something in her voice that he did not recognize, something unfamiliar that he could not place, but later that day it came to him. It was respect.

Chapter Twelve

SOPHIE SAT AT her bedroom window, her tears spent, sucking one of the lozenges which Luke had told her must always be in her mouth to block the infection. In the fireplace a pan contained a mixture of brimstone, hops and pepper and the fumes from this disinfected the room, although it did nothing to improve the stuffy atmosphere. Outside the day was hot, July was at an end and the longed-for rain had never materialized. Sophie's morning had been spent caring for her patient, polishing the cutlery and washing a few small items of clothing which now hung on a cord across the scullery. The small yard at the rear of the house would have been more suitable but Sophie now knew all the regulations and only broke them twice a day when she lowered Banna in a basket. She allowed him ten minutes' exercise and then had to coax him back into the basket. These were the moments when she almost wished she had not rescued him from the dog-catcher, but for most of the time she had no regrets and was properly grateful for his friendly company.

She had suffered so much in the past weeks, but now her emotions were numbed by weariness. Matthew was dead – she still could not totally believe it. It still seemed possible that some day, when the nightmare was at an end, he would walk in at the door at the end of a working day and kiss her. It seemed inconceivable that his body should be taken away in a cart with other bodies for a hasty burial without even the dignity of a proper service or a headstone. So very inconceivable, she thought, and yet in her heart she knew it was so.

Lois had brought the bad news but, locked out of the house, had been unable to offer her any real support. Rather than call the news up to the window she had written a letter full of condolences but Sophie had read the tragedy in her expression. Lois had waited while she read it and had then said simply, 'My dear Sophie, our prayers are with you.'

Sophie, stunned, had nodded and had then withdrawn without a word, closing the window, sealing herself in with her loss. She thought she had prepared herself for such an eventuality but when it came it had still been unbearable. She had cried for more than an hour, denied the feel of an arm around her shoulders or a word of comfort. Only the dog offered solace, laying his head sadly upon her lap, his large brown eyes fixed on her face, occasionally wagging his tail if she happened to glance in his direction.

Now she sat drained and exhausted at the upstairs window, with Banna, like a faithful slave, lying at her feet. She stared with unseeing eyes at the scene below while Antony slept in the back bedroom, his breathing stertorous, his movements restless, his chances of recovery thin despite Sophie's devoted care and his father's efforts. But Sophie's thoughts were not with the living but the dead as she remembered her husband in happier days. She recalled his excitement when told she was with child for the first time and the way he had fussed over her health, insisting that she have extra help in the house during the final months. His delight at the birth of a boy had gladdened her heart and he had whispered, 'Now my mother will love you. You have given her a grandchild!'

Very quickly she had conceived again and Lizbeth's birth had been difficult but mother and child had survived. For a while, Matthew had eyed his daughter with a certain amount of unspoken resentment as though the child was somehow to blame but gradually he had accepted her. He had been a loving father, she thought, and her eyes filled once more with tears at the realization that he would never see them again. Nor they him. The children would have to be told that their beloved father was dead. And Ruth! She would be devastated. Poor Henrietta would be burdened with the sad task of telling them of Matthew's death since Sophie still had weeks to go before she would be allowed to leave the house again. If she ever did. It was quite possible that she herself would take the disease from Antony and might not survive.

'Dear God!' She bent her head and prayed, her voice sharp with anguish. 'Spare the children their mother, I beg you. They have lost their father. I will do anything if you will spare my life for their sakes!'

If she died, Henrietta and Giles would no doubt care for Ollie and Lizbeth and Sophie knew they would not starve – but there was Ruth also. How could Giles and Henrietta be expected to shoulder another burden?

'I must live!' she told Him. Not for herself although she did not want to die, but for those who depended on her.

She thought, not for the first time, and with increasing bitterness, that this chain of disasters had started with the Redditch woman. If Matthew had never met her, or at least had not pursued her, he would most probably be alive today and she, Sophie, would still be safe in the country with the children.

'Damn you, Anne Redditch!' she cried. 'I hope you roast in Hell for the trouble you have brought upon this family!'

Yet, in fairness, she knew that Matthew was equally to blame. But he was her husband – *had been* her husband – and he was dead and she did not want to lay blame at his door. She would never see him again and she wanted so much to think kindly of him. All she could do for him now was remember him with love and to cherish joyful memories but sadly she felt that the Redditch woman had stolen even that from her. The truth, which Sophie could not bear, was that even before the plague took him, he had been lost to her. Sophie could not foresee a time when she would not feel bitter. Sitting in an almost trance-like stillness, she lost track of time and was surprised by a sudden knocking on the front door. Banna leaped to his feet, barking wildly.

'Hush, Banna! You'll wake Antony!'

Opening the window, she looked down and saw that it was Luke Meridith. At least she assumed it was. The tall figure garbed in leather was unrecognizable. A monk-like stranger. Was it really time for his call, she wondered. Had the morning passed already?

'Is that you, Luke?' she called.

Jon shouted, ''Tis Doctor Meridith, mistress. Shall I let him in?'

'Yes please.' She was astonished that her voice sounded so normal after all she had been through. She went out on to the landing and watched with dull eyes as Luke came up the stairs towards her and she braced herself for his commiserations. She thought she could bear them, for she surely had no more tears to shed for the man who had once meant all the world to her.

He said, 'Dear Sophie, what can I say?' His voice was muffled.

'Matthew was a good man at heart,' she told him. 'I do believe that.'

'Most certainly he was.'

'He bought me this locket.' She fingered the small silver locket which she always wore. 'For my birthday, when I was twenty-five. He said it was a milestone. He said –' She swallowed. Why was she talking to Luke in this way, she thought. What did he care? What did anyone care? It was just a locket and Matthew was dead.

'I wish I could say something helpful,' he said and dimly she recognized the longing behind the words. He did want to comfort her, she knew, but she also knew that no one could help her through the lonely weeks and months that lay ahead. It was a solitary path and one she must tread alone.

'Such a deep sigh!' he said.

'Did I sigh?' She had not been aware of it.

He took her hands in his. 'Sophie –'

'Don't!' she warned quickly. 'If you are too kind I shall weep again.'

'Tears are meant to be shed,' he reminded her.

To distract her mind from her own trouble she forced herself to think of Antony. 'Your son is no better,' she said, 'but no worse.'

Perhaps soon Luke, too, would be bereft, she thought. He had already lost his wife; if he lost Antony, how would anyone comfort him? She could not bear to think about it.

'I'll look at him,' said Luke.

Together they walked through into the back bedroom where Antony tossed deliriously in his bed. For a while Luke became the professional man, making clumsy notes with his gloved hands. Luke's treatment had so far followed the accepted method which was to sweat out the initial fever. The fever had broken which was the first hurdle. There was however no sign of a swelling and this made the next stage of the treatment much less certain. Patients reacted to the disease in different ways and treatment that helped one might weaken another. Sophie realized that Luke was relying on his intuition to a large extent. Her own dilemma was a difficult one. For Luke's sake she wanted to nurse Antony as well as she could, yet he constantly urged her to spend as little time as possible in Antony's room for fear of catching the contagion herself.

'Did he sleep at all last night?' he asked.

'I believe so. For an hour or two, maybe. I came in to him after midnight and he was thirsty. I gave him the draught you prescribed.'

He nodded and she searched for something encouraging to tell him. 'I think he has a better colour,' she suggested.

'The fever seems to be abating,' he agreed, straightening up. 'I don't want to bleed him just yet. It can be so weakening. He has so much natural resistance, I want to give nature a chance first.'

'And you and Lois?' she asked. 'Are you both continuing well?'

Luke nodded. 'The numbers are still rising. The King and his Court have gone to Isleworth and the Admiralty is moving to Winchester for the duration of the epidemic.'

Sophie nodded.

Luke said, 'July the twelfth was a day of fasting and humiliation! What a mockery! People are already starving and we are humble enough in the face of this scourge.'

She said, 'Will you take a mug of small beer? Have you eaten – Oh! How foolish of me!' Offering food from an infected house was dangerous.

He shook his head. 'Lois has fed me well. Poor woman. She does so envy you. She would give her soul to be nursing Antony.'

'Please tell her that my grief for Matthew will not render me less attentive to her beloved nephew. I love him like my own brother.'

'Sophie –' he began but then fell silent.

His eyes were hardly visible through the eye-pieces in his helmet and she could not read his expression but she could and did discern something different in his voice.

She waited.

'No matter,' he said abruptly. He became once more the professional. 'I'm not changing Antony's treatment, at least for one more day.' He handed her a paper. 'This is for you. A colleague of mine speaks very highly of it.'

She read it with growing dismay. 'Peel and mince

three cloves of garlic. Stir into new milk and sip slowly. Fast for an hour before and after.'

'Must I?' she said, with a hint of a smile.

'Do it for me!' he said.

He took one more look at his son who lay tousled and uneasy.

Sophie said, 'I shall sponge him down again with warm water as soon as you have gone.'

He nodded. 'Do you have enough money?'

She was embarrassed. 'Oh yes! Giles, my brother, sends me enough. He is concerned for my well-being.'

'I will call again tomorrow. Unless he takes a turn for the worse.'

'If he does, I shall send Fanny or Jon to fetch you.'

She closed the door behind him and heard Jon turn the key in the padlock.

The house, without Luke, was suddenly empty.

*

The letter was dated July 25th and had taken a week to travel between Woolwich and London, proof, if any were needed, of the difficulties faced by the postal system at such a time. As Sophie unsealed the letter she was grateful that people still dared to handle the letters, many of which, if penned by the hand of a sick man or woman, might carry the contagion.

My dear Sophie, [Giles had written.]

The news of Matthew's death came as a great blow to all of us and emphasized what we already knew, that the plague has no respect of persons. Henrietta shed a few tears for him but so far his mother has shown a most unnatural composure. No tears, no lamentations, but a reiteration of God's purpose for the world and not a few references to sinners and their punishment. The doctor believes her composure will break eventually and has recommended a restorative for her when that should happen.

For myself, I shall miss him. We did not meet as frequently as we might but I always found him civil and until recently, believed him to be an honourable man. No matter. For charity's sake I will say no more.

We had intended to keep the knowledge of Matthew's death from the children until you could be reunited with them. Unfortunately his mother spoke of it to them before we could alert her to our intention. Lizbeth is puzzled by the notion of death and I doubt she has fully understood that she will never see her father again. Oliver is very tearful and cannot sleep at night but Henrietta has given him a kitten to care for as a distraction to his grief.

My main concern is for your future now that you are a widow with no financial support. You will be making plans and we have discussed the matter. We cannot offer you all a permanent home with us but should the Lord see fit to take you, we would take the two little ones into our family.

Naturally I will continue to help you financially to a small extent but I urge you to look for an occupation as soon as possible. The best solution would be to marry again and you must consider that in the fullness of time. You are still a young woman and handsome.

Forgive me for these blunt words but I would do you no good service were I to prevaricate at a time when you need firm guidance.

We hope to hear that young Antony Meridith has recovered and we all pray for him daily. When at last you are free of the house and wish to return to us, do remember *to apply for a certificate of health. It must be printed by your parish and signed by a magistrate or else it will carry no weight and you will be turned back along the way, so great is the fear here of the pestilence. A certificate written by your doctor will not suffice. I tell you this not to frighten but to prepare you for the fear the villagers have of Londoners. I have myself seen three people dead of the plague who carried simple certificates and were prudently refused passage. Their bodies still lie by the hedgerow since no one will bury them. I never thought to live through such fearful times. As your mother-in-law so frequently reminds us, the hand of God lies heavy upon us! I shall pray for your deliverance.*

I enclose a letter from Oliver.

Your sorrowful brother, Giles.

Sophie was hurt by the speed with which Giles had pointed out her straitened circumstances and urged her to find work. His words brought home to her the delicacy of her position and the difficulties which she must eventually face. She was no longer the wife of a well-paid senior clerk but a penniless widow who must somehow pay the rent and feed and clothe herself and two children. And Ruth.

'Oh Matthew!' she murmured. 'What have you done!' Panic sapped her ability to think and for a moment she surrendered to the despair which had always threatened. Yet Giles had promised a home for the children should she succumb to the disease and for that she was grateful. Leaving them alone in the world was her greatest dread.

Slowly she opened Oliver's crumpled epistle. His writing was awkwardly formed, the ink had splattered and yet the words still leaped bravely from the page.

Dear Mama now that poor Papa is dead and buried I shall care for you and lizbeth as soon as I am a man your loving son Oliver.

Oliver's letter brought fresh tears to her eyes but she wiped them away and forced herself to reread Giles's uncompromising letter. He was right, she told herself. There was no time for the luxury of mourning.

She must begin to think positively about the future. What *could* she do to earn money? She could cook and sew but was that all? She sat appalled by her apparent lack of skills. Was a second marriage the only alternative? She shuddered at the prospect, familiar with the notion of step-fathers who, try as they might, could not love another man's children. Perhaps she could find work as a housekeeper. Or write letters for people like Fanny. Could she become a children's tutor? She could write well enough and knew a little arithmetic. Addition and subtraction and a little multiplication; also how to deal with money and measure cloth. Or she could teach the virginal? Her expres sion softened with hope and a little of her panic left her. She was not as ill-equipped as she had first thought. Somehow she could and would support her family if only God would spare her. So far her health remained good and Luke was confident that she showed no signs of the disease but they both knew there was still time for it to develop. She put her hands together, bent her head and began once more to pray.

*

The following evening, Fanny hurried through the streets feeling distinctly nervous. She was going to have 'a light supper' at the Meridiths' and was not exactly looking forward to it. Indeed, she had tried to wriggle out of it but Lois had insisted that she looked half-starved and was probably neglecting to eat properly. In fact, Fanny had been sharing what food she could afford to pay for with her father and brother who were finding it impossible to earn a living on the water. Pride, however, prevented

Fanny from explaining this and she had agreed to present herself at the Merediths' house soon after eight.

She carried a small pomander which Sophie had given to her. It was stuffed with rosemary and thyme and this she held to her nose as she negotiated the filthy thoroughfares, stepping around the piles of decaying rubbish that the few remaining street scavengers had neglected to remove. Soon, she thought, there would be no one left to do any of these jobs. The summer heat was intensifying and the street smell was disgusting. The sight of three black rats scurrying together among the shadows did nothing to reassure Fanny that the authorities could continue to provide the normal public services which its inhabitants had for so long taken for granted.

She passed an old woman who quickly drew a deep breath and, throwing her apron over her face, brushed past Fanny as quickly as she could. A young man, no older than Jon, was propped against one of the wooden stanchions that served to separate pedestrians from the worst of the horse-drawn traffic. His face was flushed and his mouth hung open. Feeling miserably callous, Fanny ignored him and left him to his fate. She had strict orders to speak and touch no one. From an upstairs window there came the fretful wail of a baby and, in spite of herself, Fanny hesitated anxiously until she heard the mother's voice pacifying it. All around her the city bells were tolling mournfully for the day's dead and their clamour seemed to echo and re-echo among the narrow streets so that the din became oppressive, even threatening.

Would it one day toll for her, Fanny wondered. Or for Jon? At the thought of the young watchman her mood lightened a little. She liked the earnest way he talked and the shy way he smiled. He no longer struck her as unattractive; she thought of him as plain but honest. She was doing her best to make him like her and she thought she was making some headway. Yesterday he had said she was 'pert as a sparrow' and she thought it was meant as a compliment although, in her view, sparrows were drab birds at the best of times and definitely ten a penny.

And Jon was cleverer than he looked, she reminded herself proudly. When she had remarked on the brightness of the day, he had pointed out that, since many of the soap boilers had closed down, the sky was probably clearer than it used to be and let the sunshine in more easily. She never would have thought of that in a hundred years! Oh yes, Jon was not stupid and one day he would be a weaver and might be looking for a wife.

Thinking of wives put her in mind of poor Jem and his dead wife and child and that made her think of poor Charlie who was now in the pesthouse where Master Devine had just died. Fanny was sorry that Charlie was ill but she knew he wouldn't die. Not Charlie! And Jem had been given a gold sovereign! If ever a man deserved a bit of good luck it was Jem. *He* deserved it.

With a sigh she thought of her father. He was growing weary of the long, unrewarding days on the river and was talking about 'backing up stream' to sit out the plague. Some of the other watermen had done this and the idea had a certain merit. They had made their boats into temporary homes, tied up alongside Lambeth Palace and beyond. Her father had asked her advice but she of course had none to give. Her mind was already full with other people's problems and she had plenty of her own. Her father must make up his own mind, with God's help.

Deep in thought, she was surprised to find herself at the Merediths' door and realized how hungry she was. Resolutely shelving all her worries, she prepared for the coming ordeal, praying that she wouldn't say or do the wrong thing. Hastily she smoothed her skirt and tidied her hair and then she took a deep breath, lifted the brass lion's head and knocked. At the very worst she could be embarrassed, she reminded herself, but she would eat as much as she could. Times were hard and there was no telling where her next decent meal would come from – or even when it would come.

*

Soon after six the next morning, Jem made his way to St Sepulchre's churchyard where his wife and child were buried. The fingers of his left hand were closed around the sovereign and in his right hand he carried a small bunch of violets. His eyes, for so long dulled with grief, gleamed with excitement. He had decided how best to use his windfall and the idea gave him enormous pleasure. His first sight of the churchyard, however, brought him to an amazed halt. There were so many new graves! He stared in amazement and dismay at the rows of mounds, some large, some pitifully small. And now there was no more room. He understood for the first time the need for the mass graves that had been dug around the outskirts of the city. Presumably all the grave-yards were as full as this one.

A sudden anxiety seized him. Would he now be able to find Maggie's grave where she lay with her arms around her little son? Quickening his footsteps he made his way along the path towards the cypress tree near which they had been buried. From the corner of his eye he saw a shabbily dressed man approaching and Jem instinctively hurried on to avoid contact. The man, however, raised his voice.

'Good morrow, master!'

Jem nodded briefly in his direction and moved on. He found the tree and was relieved to recognize the grave by the simple wooden cross which marked it. He had been at pains to memorize the exact shape and size of the rough wood, and knew there were two small knots on its horizontal bar. As he stood looking down at the rough mound he was annoyed to see the man shuffling over the grass towards him.

He was small, of an indeterminate age, and his weatherbeaten face bore several days' growth of beard.

'You remember me, master? I'm the gravedigger.'

Jem regarded him with narrowed eyes. He did not look familiar but then, wrapped up in his private misery, he had been in no state to notice the gravedigger.

'Someone dear to you, was it?' the man persisted. Jem ignored the question, hoping to deter him from further conversation. He was in no mood for idle gossip, especially with strangers. He dropped to one knee and laid the violets on the grave.

'A loved one?' the man repeated. 'A fine resting place, master. You couldn't have chosen better, though I say it meself and I should know. Gravedigger to this church – man and boy and my father before me, God rest his soul. Buried thataway, he is.' He jerked his thumb towards another corner of the churchyard.

Jem felt obliged to nod.

'Lost my Pa ten years ago,' the grave-digger told him, 'but it seems like yesterday. Not that I grieve for him, master. Oh no! I don't grieve for him because we all gotta go some time and 'e went peaceful. Plague was it, your'n?'

Exasperated by the man's insensitivity, Jem closed his eyes as though in prayer. It made no difference.

The man went on, undeterred, 'Mine drowned.

Fell in the Thames. They fished him out and up-
ended him but he was gone. Nice way to go, I
thought. In his cups after a night's roistering in The
Saracen's Head, if you see what I mean. Dare say he
went without knowing anything about it. Sobered
up and found he was dead! Too late then for fretting
and fuming.' He threw up his hands at the futility of
regret. 'You could go worse ways.'

Jem hardened his heart and said nothing. He bent
his head and moved his lips. Surely the prattling
fool would take the hint! But no.

'Lovely church this, master,' the man continued
cheerfully. 'St Sepulchre's. The name has a fine ring
to it, I always think. And a fine peal of bells, too.
The bells of Old Bailey. That's what folks call 'em.
Built hundreds of years ago, the church, I mean, not
the bells. What they calls a historical church. At
least, so I'm told and who am I to doubt learned
men. Built as a church for the monks at St Bartholomew's by a court jester many years ago. Ah! I
see that surprised you, master!'

The man laughed, wheezed and began to cough.
When he recovered he continued, 'Yes indeed. A
court jester by the name of Rahere. A heathenish
name, if you ask me, but I'm told it on the best
authority, master. But he gave up jestering and
became a monk. Went to Rome on a pilgrimage and
met a vision, so I'm told. "Get back to London and
build St Sepulchre's church," said the vision. They
were his exact words. Oh 'tis a fine story, master –'

His tone changed slightly as he added, 'And a *long* one!'

For Jem light dawned suddenly and a smile lit his tired face. Despite his irritation with the man he felt a sneaking admiration for him. What was a grave-digger to do to earn a crust when there was no space to dig more graves? Beg on the streets? No doubt the authorities would offer him a pittance by way of relief, for the King was very firm about such matters, but this man had shown surprising initiative. He would encroach on the grief of the bereaved until paid not to do so! A few groats here and there; there was no shortage of mourners. Jem stood up and took a handful of small coins from his pocket; the stream of information stopped in mid-flow and an outstretched hand was offered. Jem selected two coins and held them out.

Without a moment's hesitation the man took them, slipped them into his pocket and touched his forehead. 'And a good day to you, master,' he said and turned promptly to seek out further victims. Jem watched as he picked his way towards a man and woman who stood beside another grave. Jem grinned as he listened to the familiar introduction.

'Good morrow to you both. 'Tis a fine place you have chosen to bury your beloved . . .'

Alone at last, Jem knelt once more to speak to his wife.

'Maggie? Dearest Maggie? Can you hear me? 'Tis Jem as loved you so very much – and still do and always will.' He smiled down at the grave. 'I've been given a sovereign, Maggie, by a man I was able to help. 'Twas nothing but he was grateful. Listen Maggie. I'm going to buy you and Alfie a tombstone! Yes! A fine stone tombstone. The finest I can get, for you deserve the best. With proper writing on it. I shall tell them your name and Alfie's – they'll know how to spell, don't you worry. It shall be done properly, I promise you.' He waited a moment to allow her time to appreciate the news. 'It might even be one of those statues. I can't rightly say yet, not 'til I inquire of the stone-mason. But a little statue! Think on it. You'd like that, wouldn't you?' He nodded for her. 'So you'll tell Alfie, won't you, love. About the tombstone and –'

His ears caught the sound of weeping and he glanced up, annoyed by this new interruption. Turning his head he saw a young woman crouching beside one of the newest graves. Her hands covered her face; her shoulders shook with the anguish of her tears. He sighed deeply. Let her weep, poor soul. 'Twas the best way. He returned to his own affairs and tried to continue his conversation with Maggie but the sobbing tore at his heart. Finally he said, 'Pardon me, Maggie. There's a poor wretched woman –' and stood up stiffly, brushing soil and grass from the knees of his breeches. Tentatively he approached the weeping woman who appeared unaware of his presence. He coughed loudly and she scrambled, startled, to her feet. He saw then that she was young and with child, maybe five or six months into her time.

'Leave me be!' she cried. 'I'm doing no harm.' Her face was streaked with tears, her eyes red and swollen. She had fine dark hair and grey eyes but in her worn, faded clothes and shoddy shoes she reminded Jem of a scarecrow. For a moment they stared at each other warily. Jem recognized the desperation in her eyes, the feeling that the world would never have more to offer than heartbreak and woe; the longing to be with the dead loved one, at peace.

He said, 'My wife died and my little son.'

She hiccupped and her sobs faltered.

Jem shook his head. 'These are sad times.'

'Was it plague?' she asked.

'No. A child-bed fever.' He indicated the new grave and she answered the unspoken question.

'The baby's Pa,' she said simply. 'Died in Newgate a week since. Fighting, he was, with another prisoner. Fell and cracked his skull. But they'd have hanged him anyway. Stole half a sheep from the market.' She looked at him defiantly. 'Folks have to eat!' she added bitterly.

Jem said, 'My brother was in The Fleet. Now he's in the pesthouse. 'Tis hard to know which way to turn these days.'

She nodded. Lifting her apron, she wiped her eyes and, lacking a handkerchief, sniffed hard.

They talked for a few minutes and then Jem heard the church clock strike.

'I must get down to the river,' he told her. 'There just might be a fare!'

She nodded as he began to walk away. Suddenly she called after him, 'Will you be here tomorrow?'

Jem turned. 'About the same time,' he said and left her to her grief.

He walked by way of Shoe Lane and Fleet Street and his thoughts were with the unfortunate girl he had just left. A child on the way and no father, he mused. He was a father with no child! The world was a cruel place.

As he reached the boat he realized suddenly that he had forgotten to ask her name.

*

Sophie was writing a letter to the children when it happened. One moment she was tired, sad and lonely; the next moment she was all those things and something more. That something was an awareness that within her, at that precise moment, a shift was taking place; a subtle shift from health to sickness. It was not a pain, not even a twinge, but she recognized it with an icy feeling of finality. Alien elements had entered her body and she knew it for what it was – the onset of plague. A moment of deep and paralysing dread seized her and the quill fell from her fingers. Her first thought was for the children; the second for Antony, so perilously ill. Her third thought was for herself. She did not want to die. Nor did she want to suffer as Antony had suffered.

She knew only too well how the sickness ravaged and weakened a body so that the most skilful and devoted physician could not be sure of saving it.

'Oh God!' she whispered. All other words failed her as she sat in a cold sweat of fear which robbed her also of movement. Looking at the lines she had written to the children, she saw only a blur and yet her eyes were empty of tears. A fresh fear took hold of her as she realized that her eyes were no longer focusing. Was the sickness taking hold already? She had heard it said that the disease could come slowly or like lightning. Suppose she were to fall dead *now*! Anything was possible.

With an effort she tried to think. She gripped the table edge with both hands and willed herself not to faint. She must somehow master the terror which held her powerless for if she surrendered to it she was lost.

'Please God!' she cried again but her voice trembled. She thought about her condition and what she could do for herself before Luke's next visit. She reached for the lozenges at the back of the table and with shaking fingers thrust three into her mouth at once. When she felt strong enough to walk she would add more herbs to the chafing pan. A shawl would stop the shivering but, for the moment, she could not attempt the few yards to the chest where it lay.

'I mustn't die!' she said aloud. 'I *won't* die!'

She waited for further signs of the attack but

there were none. Her head did not ache. Her stomach was steady enough. Certainly she had no fever as yet. But it was there! The seeds of the disease had taken root and were flourishing within her; even as she waited, small malignant changes were occurring inside her which she was helpless to prevent. It was the uncertainty. Did she have years to live, weeks, hours or only minutes? Perhaps she should finish the letter to the children. It might be the last one she would write to them; the last contact she would have with them. If only she could see them once more before she –

She pulled herself up sharply. She would *not* think of death but would fight every inch of the way. Despair would be her enemy. From the back bedroom she heard Antony call out, his voice weak with delirium. Normally she would hurry to his side but now she hesitated. She would need all her energy to survive and she must ration it carefully. She would go to Antony later. For the present she would sit here, composing herself and marshalling her fragile courage.

Time passed and there were still no symptoms. She began to feel calmer. Her courage was returning and with it the beginnings of hope. She decided to finish the letter but when she reached for the quill she found to her horror that her arm moved stiffly and her fingers would not bend. She was again seized by a terrible panic. Antony called again and she tried to stand. At once her legs buckled under her and she was pitched forward on to the floor. She felt herself falling . . . falling . . .

Chapter Thirteen

LOIS LAID DOWN her stitching and frowned uneasily, alarmed that Luke was so late. It was two days since he had discovered Sophie unconscious on the floor; two days since Lois and her brother had almost come to blows over the question of who should nurse both Sophie and Antony. Lois had insisted that with Sophie sick there was no one else but her left and, regardless of the risk involved, she desperately wanted to nurse the two invalids. Luke had reminded her that officially the Devines' house was shut up and no one was allowed in or out except the doctor. 'And a nurse!' Lois had protested but to no avail. She had protested that it was not proper or seemly for a man to undress, bathe and attend a woman, but he had snapped at her. 'To me she is no longer Sophie Devine, merely a female patient.' Frustrated beyond bearing, Lois had called him 'a stubborn fool'

(among other things even less complimentary) but nothing had moved him. Luke refused to allow her to enter the house under any pretext and had undertaken to nurse Sophie and Antony as well as he could himself.

It was far from satisfactory but, apart from employing one of the unscrupulous nursewomen, who enjoyed such a bad reputation, there seemed to be no alternative. Luke's frequent calls at the Devines' house, on top of his normal round, gave him a very long day but today he was later than usual and Lois was growing anxious.

'Where are you, Luke?' she demanded. 'Come home and tell me all is well. Or as well as can be expected.'

With a sigh she picked up her sewing but the candle light made the fine work difficult. She was quilting a sleeveless bodice for herself, to wear with her Sunday dress but, of late, she had lost interest in it and sewed simply to occupy her mind. She dared not think about Antony, so she turned her attention instead to Sophie and her possible fate. It was the children whom Lois fretted about. If Sophie died they would be orphaned and Lois hugged to herself a possible plan for that event. Why shouldn't she and Luke care for them? She would suggest it. Two more mouths to feed were not an intolerable burden and it would be fun to have young people in the house again. She knew, of course, that she would have to prepare the ground very carefully before she made such a suggestion to Luke but surely it was a sound idea. *If* Sophie died.

She might recover but Luke was seriously concerned about her. The suddenness with which she had fallen prey to the disease had surprised him. Lois knew that what made the plague so difficult to treat was the variety of guises in which it appeared and the apparently haphazard way it developed, varying enormously from one patient to the next. He had told her only yesterday of a young prentice who appeared to be in robust health. In the middle of a conversation, literally in mid-sentence, he had clutched his heart, rolled up his eyes and died. It had seen him off in less than ten seconds!

Suddenly she heard a key in the lock. Luke was home. Throwing down her sewing, she ran to greet him. As she went she cried, 'Oh Luke! You are home at last!' but he was already on his way upstairs to the room where he fumigated his protective clothing and he waved her back. She called after him, 'How are they?'

He paused and without turning said something that sounded like, 'Forgive me, Lois, Antony is dead,' but she knew she must have been mistaken. He went slowly up the last few stairs and turned on to the landing. For a moment she was frozen with horror but then she told herself it was impossible. She gathered up her skirts and ran up after him.

'You didn't say – Luke! Wait! Did you – is –' She could not find the right words. She *must* have been mistaken. That wretched leather hood did muffle Luke's voice so.

He went into the room and slammed the door behind him. She stared at the closed door. Luke never slammed doors. He was a quiet man.

'Not Antony!' said Lois. She tried to swallow but her throat was dry. She said, 'It can't be true!' She called, 'Luke?' Her voice quavered and she stood half-way up the stairs, clutching the banister. She bit back further questions. If she did not ask again then Luke need not answer and she need not know. Antony, her bright-haired Antony, could not be dead. Luke would never allow it. Lois drew in a long shuddering breath and sat down on the stairs. 'Not Luke's beloved son! Not Antony!' she whispered and tears fell on to her hands as they twisted unhappily in her lap. She looked at the tears with loathing for tears meant sorrow and sorrow meant that she would never see her nephew again and all the plans for his future were meaningless. He would have no future. There was nothing left but the memories of what he had once been. Oh God! It was unbearable.

But even as she waited for Luke to come out, the certainty was growing. She had no thought now for Sophie or the fate of her children. Antony filled her thoughts, crowding out everything else. She had loved him more than anyone else in the whole world; more than her beloved brother, although she had tried never to let Luke know that. Antony had been the child she could never have, making her life complete.

The door opened at last and one frightened glance at Luke's face confirmed her worst fears. He had been crying; his face was ravaged by pain and loss. He stood on the landing shaking his head and he reminded her of nothing more than a sick, dumb animal. In that moment, she loved him more fiercely than at any time in her whole life and she clambered to her feet and ran frantically up the remaining stairs to throw her arms around him.

*

Two days later Jem found himself in the yard of a stone-mason who had been highly recommended by the friend of a friend. There seemed to be no one around and he coughed once or twice without bringing anyone from the nearby shed. He went to the door of the shed and knocked. There was no answer. He went to the house next door and knocked and a woman opened the door. She said that her husband was in the Pig and Flute having a pint of ale and he had been in there since before noon and he was the laziest man she had ever had the misfortune to wed and she would go and shake some sense into him and he would be back in two minutes! She told Jem he could wait in the yard.

'Right, then,' said Jem. He fingered the coin in his pocket and felt very strange to be in such a place on such an errand. People in his walk of life did not have tombstones to commemorate their passing; they had wooden crosses. His wife and child, however, were going to have a monument made of stone. Possibly a statue. He returned to the mason's yard and began to look around, taking stock of the various half-finished memorials to the dead. In one corner there was a huge pile of stone slabs, some gleaming and new, others darkening with the inevitable soot thrown out each day from London's chimneys. One large slab was of a bluish-grey stone which Jem imagined as granite. The lettering had been started but he could not read. He did know numbers however and he saw 1660–1665. Five years! Such a short life. He sighed and moved on. In one corner, a statue of an angel lay propped against the wall at a rakish angle. The right arm was missing but the left hand, thrust out in a dramatic gesture, now supported a scuffed leather bucket full of rusting chisels and a mallet. He was embarrassed for the angel's undignified use and hurriedly looked away, wondering how much the mason would charge to carve such a statue. A good deal, probably. He warned himself against raising his hopes too high. A stone-mason was a skilled craftsman and such people did not work for a pittance. He discovered a further pile of slabs, this time of marble, and his thoughts changed direction slightly. Perhaps he would abandon the idea of a statue in favour of a *marble* tombstone! He ran his fingers over the dusty surface of the top slab, liking the smooth feel and the way the warm pink and brown colours swooped and blended across it. He had spent an hour the previous day examining the large variety of tombstones in St Sepulchre's churchyard, approving some, rejecting others, and he now felt himself to be something of a connoisseur. The large box-shaped tombs were too clumsy; the flat ones did not inspire him. He liked the upright ones which he thought were more striking and could be seen from a distance. Also they were easier to read. He felt that Maggie and Alfie would prefer the latter.

Two headstones were propped against the wall and Jem moved towards them for a closer inspection. The first had a fancy fluted design around the upper edge and Jem rather liked that. Would a chiselled edge cost extra? Most likely, but he had a whole sovereign. The second, partly hidden by the first, appeared to have a more intricate design cut into it. To Jem's untrained eye they were leaves and flowers. Leaves and flowers would be bonny, he thought. Maybe the mason could do violets. Maggie had always liked violets. He made up his mind to ask him.

The clock struck half past three. The mason was certainly taking a long time over his ale. Maybe his wife was right about him and he was lazy. A man who could misuse the statue of an angel might well have other faults. Jem decided to take a closer look at the design of flowers and leaves and to do this he began to lever up the slab that was obscuring it. It was much heavier than he expected and suddenly, as it swung away from its fellow, it reached the point of no return and before Jem could stop it, had crashed heavily to the ground. For a few shocked moments Jew stared at it, mesmerized. One corner had broken off and seemed to stare up at him accusingly. Jem felt weak with fright as a terrible thought struck him. The stone-mason would probably expect him to pay for the damaged slab! It might take all of his money! Briefly his conscience fought with his instincts. He knew he should offer to pay for the damage but if he did he would end up with nothing.

He glanced round furtively, feeling the sweat break out on his body. Surely the lazy wretch would choose this very moment to return from the Pig and Flute – or else his wife would come out to investigate the noise. He waited, hardly daring to breathe.

Nothing happened. Jem drew a deep breath but time was precious. He must make a decision and quickly. His eye alighted on the fallen angel and it came to him that this particular stone-mason did not deserve the work; would, in fact, be the very last person whom Jem would wish to employ. Perhaps the broken slab was a just punishment for his laziness. Without further ado, Jem strolled as nonchalantly as possible from the yard. Once past the mason's house, he ran as fast as he could for the corner of the street and hurtled round it to safety.

*

Ruth read and re-read Lois's letter telling them of Antony's death and Sophie's sickness. It would seem Sophie had been stricken very suddenly and without warning of any kind and in Ruth's opinion that was the most dangerous form of the plague. Lois had said that Sophie was being properly cared for and they must pray for her. It was a short letter but Ruth could imagine the heartbreak behind it. Ruth understood grief although she did not give way to it herself, considering it something of a luxury if not a sign of weakness. Matthew's death had shaken her faith severely, but he had sinned and the Lord sought out sinners for retribution. She could not blame Him for that. It was all in the Bible for anyone who cared to look. She had brought Matthew up to be a God-fearing man but he had rejected her teachings and had paid the price. She had loved him dearly and missed him very much but no man could offend against the scriptures and expect to escape punishment. No doubt Antony, too, had failed the Lord in some way; Ruth found it impossible to believe, as some did, that death was a random affair, a mere whim of the Lord. If she leaned towards that view, her faith would crumble and her life be meaningless.

She now puzzled over Sophie's affliction for, to her knowledge, Sophie was comparatively blameless. She might, however, have a few secret sins of which only God would be aware. Time would tell, she told herself. If Sophie died then she was guilty of *some-*

thing; if she lived she was innocent. Ruth hoped she would live for the sake of Matthew's two children. Oliver and Lizbeth were a source of great anxiety to her because if both parents died she, Ruth, would be their next of kin. In fact she would be their only surviving kin, with the exception of Sophie's brother, Giles, whom Ruth had already weighed and found wanting. No. If Sophie died she, Ruth, would be responsible for Oliver and Lizbeth. True, Henrietta had hinted that if the worst happened she and Giles would feel it their duty to care for Sophie's children but Ruth had sensed their unwillingness. They had a family of their own and limited resources. Ruth was nevertheless offended by their reluctance and felt a deep resentment that they did not appreciate the value of Matthew Devine's children who, in Ruth's eyes, were so obviously superior to Henrietta's own unruly brood. She put their lack of enthusiasm down to jealousy.

It had also dawned on her that presumably Giles would not wish to 'adopt' an elderly bedridden lady and Ruth's own position was giving her serious pause for thought. If Sophie should die, and it seemed very probable, life would have to change drastically and she suddenly knew exactly what had to be done.

Carefully she folded the letter and pushed it under her pillow. Then she threw back the bedclothes and turned herself on the bed so that her feet were hanging over the side. It was an odd feeling but not uncomfortable. To herself she said, 'Now take things slowly, Ruth!' She must not fall and break a bone or knock herself senseless. That would be the height of folly and would achieve nothing. She reached out to clasp the back of the bedside chair and then slowly allowed all her weight to transfer to her legs. Still no ill effects, she thought triumphantly, but it was too early to claim victory. When, after a moment or two of elation, she released the back of the chair and stood unaided, she almost cheered but satisfied herself instead with a small 'Hurrah!'

Her legs felt ridiculously weak but they had not let her down. For the first time in more than four years she was standing upright on her own two feet. She imagined that inside her the various organs of her body were warily settling into long-forgotten positions and grumbling about it. Well, let them! Her body had had it easy for far too long. Times were changing and she would change with them. She felt a rush of confidence. She could walk. She *would* walk. Slowly, keeping close to the bed, she edged her way round to the far side.

'Thank you, God,' she said and lowered herself carefully on to the edge of the bed. She found that she was smiling, flushed with success and eager to attempt more. Her achievement thrilled her and at once she began to plan further expeditions. When she had recovered her breath she would walk to the window and back. Then she would climb back into the bed and no one would be any the wiser. The idea of keeping her 'little walks' a secret appealed to her. She would practise daily, doing more and more, and then suddenly, when the time was ripe, she would go downstairs! Her smile broadened at the thought of all their faces when she suddenly appeared in the doorway. No doubt they had considered her of no account. A liability, even. She would astonish everyone!

Her imagination soared. As soon as the plague was at an end, she would travel to London and investigate Matthew's affairs. Hopefully he had made *some* provision for his family in case of an untimely death, and she herself had a small income of her own. If necessary she would talk to Henry Bolsover! If Sophie died she would take the children from this unappreciative pair and make a home for them in London. In her mind's eye she saw amazement and admiration on everyone's face and heard their incredulous comments. 'She's wonderful!' ''Tis a miracle!' and best of all, 'God looks after His own!'

She smiled. She would bring Matthew's children up in her own image – No, no, in *God's* image! she amended hastily. She would be strict – none of Matthew's indulgences or Sophie's leniency. The children would be brought up to walk the straight and narrow path to Godliness and would live to thank her for it. She levered herself upright once again and set off towards the window.

*

Sophie opened her eyes and drew in a long breath. Her mind was suddenly as clear as a bell after a long period of confusion. She knew that she had been ill – was *still* ill. The left side of her neck throbbed painfully but she was too frightened to explore further, knowing she would discover the tell-tale swelling. She knew it was plague and with a frightened gasp glanced at her hands for any tokens but saw none. Her hands, however, shocked her. The knuckles appeared inordinately large and the skin was pale, almost transparent. So, how long had she been ill, she wondered, and, how was Antony? And who had nursed them both thus far? And how had poor Fanny managed alone? She listened for sounds of movement from Antony's room but heard none. Doubtless he was sleeping. She recalled that Luke was a great believer in the healing power of sleep.

Questions crowded in on her, followed by vague memories of Luke Meridith bending over her, holding her wrist, combing her hair, sponging her burning skin. Luke? She was startled at the thought of such intimacies but felt too fragile to let it worry her unduly. She wondered which day of the week it was and what time of day. She felt desperately hungry and guessed that for some time she had probably eaten nothing. Gradually she became aware of a restlessness in her limbs and cautiously began to move her arms and legs, flexing the muscles gently. She felt cool and strangely relaxed but perhaps Luke had fed her a sleeping draught. If so she was enormously grateful, hoping that she had slept through the worst of the sickness. She did not for one moment consider that she would die. Luke would save her; he would save them both. Her faith in him was absolute.

Eventually she drifted into a light sleep, dimly aware that time was passing, and woke abruptly to the sound of a key turning in the street door. Luke was here. She wanted to sit up and surprise him with her recovery but, as soon as she moved, a fierce pain shot from her neck into the base of her spine and she fell back on to the pillows with a gasp of disappointment. The footsteps on the stairs were slow and she could imagine how exhausted he must be.

At last the door opened and the familiar hooded figure came in.

'Luke! Is that you?' She hardly recognized her own voice.

'Yes.' She waited for him to speak further but he merely put down his bag and reached for her wrist to check the pulse.

'Luke?' He gave a slight nod and something about his manner and lack of words frightened her. Her euphoria faded suddenly and a sharp suspicion thrust its way into her mind. She hardly dared put the question to him but she had to be certain. 'How is Antony?' Her throat was dry and her spirits sank under the realization that all was not well. She put a hand to her throbbing head. Still he did not speak; dare not, she thought shrewdly, for fear his composure would crack under the strain.

Seeing that he could not answer she asked, 'Is he —' She could not utter the dread word so substituted, '— still with us?'

Luke shook his head briefly.

'Luke! Dearest Luke!' He made no sign that he had heard her anguished words and turned back the covers to listen to her heart, then gently examined the swelling on her neck.

'I shall open the swelling in a day or two,' he said finally and remained for a while looking down at her. Then, to her horror, he pulled off the protective hood, threw it on to a chair and crossed to the window.

'Luke!' she stammered. 'Your hood! You must take care! Oh please, Luke! 'Tis such a risk.'

''Tis of no matter now,' he said and his tone was dull. She had caught a glimpse of his face, flushed from the heat, and his eyes, dark with defeat. His hair was tousled and his mouth vulnerable in a way that caught at her heart. He reminded her, unbearably, of Antony. She watched him helplessly, unable to offer comfort, afraid to express her compassion for fear of causing him further distress.

'I call myself a physician,' he said at last, 'and I let my son die! My only child!'

'You didn't let him die.' With an effort, she

rallied her failing energy. 'You did all that was humanly possible. And it won't help for you to die also. Oh! do please –' As he half turned towards her she indicated the hood although she knew he would take no notice of her. His grief was such that he considered his own life was worthless.

'Antony would want you to live,' she told him but he gave her a look of such despair that she relapsed into silence. He was his own master, she reminded herself. He must make his own decisions; take his own risks. But he looked desperately tired; there were dark circles under his eyes and his face was haggard. His shoulders sagged with weariness and his eyes seemed devoid of hope.

'My dearest Luke!' she whispered. If only she were well, she could comfort him, hold his hands perhaps, but now she had nothing but empty words to offer. Even now her presence was a physical threat to him.

As though reluctant for her to see the depths of his misery he turned again to stare down into the street.

'I buried him myself,' he said, with a heavy sigh. 'I could not let him go into that terrible cart. Not Antony! Never!'

Sophie could not answer. In her weakened state it required an immense effort of will even to stay awake.

'I've heard such rumours,' he went on. 'They treat the dead with such disrespect. Not all of them, but some. They are ignorant loutish brutes with no feelings. I bribed the sexton to open up my wife's grave. She would have wished it. I tell myself they are together now. Reunited.' There was another long silence. 'I dared not wrap him in his shroud to carry him through the streets so I sent Fanny to buy a large blanket and to wait for me with it in the church porch. I carried him in my arms through the streets with his head against my shoulder so that he seemed to be sleeping. No one stopped me. No one cared.'

Sophie's heart ached as she imagined it.

'As I neared the church I called out to Fanny to put down the blanket and leave, which she did.' He turned briefly. 'She was in no danger.'

Sophie nodded.

'I wrapped him in the blanket and – and kissed him. I could not let him go without a kiss. Then I lowered him gently into the grave and said a short prayer. I filled in the grave myself.'

Sophie said, 'You did all you could for him, Luke. You mustn't blame yourself for anything.'

He shook his head and turned towards her, an agonized expression on his face. 'But I *do* blame myself. I should have saved him. I should have known how. I'm a physician! I saved others. Not many, but a few. So why not Antony? All my skill and years of experience. I go over his treatment in my mind and wonder where I went wrong.'

Sophie opened her mouth to remonstrate but he

rushed on. 'If only he had been in Padua! I should have convinced him two years ago but I was too weak. He should have been far removed from this damned pestilence but I gave in to him. I believed that he had no vocation for the work but all the time it was there, within him, this longing to heal. You heard him. He wanted to be a physician. I should have known. I should have insisted.'

As he fell silent she searched her tired mind for further words of comfort.

'You could not *force* him to it,' she said at last. 'He had to come to it in his own time – as he did!'

'But too late, Sophie! Too late!'

To distract him Sophie said, 'And Lois?'

'It has broken her heart.' He gave a short, harsh laugh. 'We are a sad pair.'

'Then I, too, am to blame for Antony's death,' she told him. 'I was his nurse but I let him slip away. I did all I could but –'

'Oh no! Sophie, you must not think like that!' he exclaimed, startled out of his apathy. 'You were a devoted nurse. You nursed him as though he were your own flesh and blood! You cannot blame yourself.'

'Yet you do, Luke,' she said softly. 'You did all you could but you find ways to blame yourself.'

He stared at her, forced to consider the logic of her argument.

'Dear Luke, please listen to me,' she begged. 'Antony loved you, you know that. He knew you did everything you could to save him. He was bright enough to know that. What do you think he would say if he could speak to you now?' Luke was silent. 'He would say what I say, that you did all you could! He wouldn't want you to live with this terrible burden of guilt. He may be gone from *us* but he is still somewhere. Maybe he is watching us now. Maybe he is wanting to help you through this terrible time. Put yourself in his shoes, Luke. Pretend you are ill and Antony is your physician and tries to save you – and fails. You are dead, Luke, and he is full of remorse and blame. Would you want to see that, Luke?'

He was silent.

She went on softly, 'I may die, Luke. You are doing all you can but I may die. If I do, I will never hold you responsible. How could I? I shouldn't want to think that if I die you will add me to your burden of guilt!'

'I wish I could see it that way,' he said.

'Do you really think Antony wants you to do penance for the rest of your life? Oh Luke!' she cried passionately. 'Give him credit for a generous spirit!'

He smiled faintly. 'You have a very persuasive tongue, Sophie!'

'I want to help you, Luke.'

'I know. You are very kind.' He shrugged. 'You have suffered also. First your husband is unfaithful to you and then he dies. I am ashamed. I behave as though no one else grieves but me.'

Sophie was feeling emotionally drained. In her present weakened state, she wanted to do nothing more than sleep and yet she could not desert Luke when he needed her most. She was afraid to let him leave in this mood; men had hanged themselves for less. Somehow she found the strength to continue her argument. 'Don't give up, Luke,' she urged. 'The living still need you. *I* still need you. And poor Lois!'

'Oh Sophie! My sweet, kind Sophie!'

Was it her imagination or did he stand a little straighter? Was there the beginning of hope in his voice? She could not be sure; in spite of her good intentions her eyes were closing. Soon sleep would claim her once more. Neither spoke for a long time and then abruptly Luke crossed to a table in the corner of the room and poured some medicine into a small glass.

'Drink this,' he said.

She drank dutifully.

He handed her two small round pills and a little water.

'Swallow these,' he said.

She obeyed.

'I must go,' he told her, reaching for his hood. 'I'll call in about eight with some broth which Lois is making. She sends you her love and good wishes.'

'Give her mine,' Sophie said drowsily, keeping her eyes open with an effort.

He opened the door and she heard her own voice

say, 'Luke! I love you!' but the door had closed behind him and she slipped gratefully into a deep and restorative sleep.

*

Charlie held a spoonful of gruel to the sick man's mouth.

'Just one spoonful,' he said coaxingly. 'One spoonful. 'Tis good, nourishing stuff. You want to recover, don't you?'

The old man nodded feebly.

'Then take down this gruel before it gets cold.'

The mouth opened, the spoon slipped in, but the old man spluttered so that half of it ended up on the sheet. Charlie shook his head with exasperation.

'One more spoonful,' he said. ''Tis for your own good.'

In the middle of August, the pesthouse presented a very different picture from the one Charlie had seen when he first arrived. Now every bed contained two patients instead of one and many more lay on straw pallets on the floor. The noise was greater, the smell worse and the air of desperation markedly increased. Charlie had made a complete recovery and was expecting at any moment to be sent back to The Fleet. With hindsight he kicked himself for recovering so quickly and unequivocally. If he had had any sense, he would have prolonged his invalid state. But Charlie, not being blessed with the best brain in the world, he had bounced back from death's door in an effort to impress Elena. He was up and about, helping with the other patients, earning a word of praise from her now and again. Such words were music to his ears and he could not pretend otherwise.

Charlie Rice was in love with Elena and, although he knew his chances were slight, he could not resist hoping that she might return the feelings, although common sense warned him against such folly. Elena came from a good family; he was from humble stock. She could not possibly take his declarations of love seriously although that did not prevent him from making them at every opportunity. She laughed, not displeased, and bade him, 'Get along, Master Rice!' She would not call him Charlie even though he had once gone down on his knee to her. She found him amusing and was flattered but never for one moment did Charlie think she took him seriously.

As he spooned gruel into the man's unresponsive mouth, he wondered if there was any way he might convince her of his true and abiding love. Probably not. She did not seem interested in affairs of the heart; certainly not in *his* heart! She teased him good-naturedly but then went about her work as though he had ceased to exist. But then Elena *was* an angel, he reminded himself, and the minds of angels were on a higher plane altogether. They mingled with the purest minds and were on speaking terms with God.

He looked up now as she approached the bed, aware of the familiar tug at his heartstrings but with a humorous remark on his lips. Her expression, however, rendered it unsuitable. He waited with trepidation. This was it! His summons from The Fleet.

'Master Rice, may I speak with you?' she said.

He stood up.

'The Fleet authorities have asked for your return,' she told him. 'I have delayed matters as long as I could but they are now very insistent.'

He could only nod. He would never see her again.

'I have, however, a suggestion,' she said, a trifle hesitantly. 'I have told them you are very useful and that, pressed as we are on all sides, we would like to employ you here until the emergency is at an end.'

He felt a surge of hope. Was this a miracle, he asked himself. Did he deserve that?

She continued, 'It depends on you, Master Rice. You would have to understand that if you remained here, among so many sick and dying, you might well contract the disease again. We could give you no guarantee on that. None whatsoever. I live with that knowledge every day.'

He said blithely, 'I would risk anything to be near you, Elena!'

'This is no laughing matter, Master Rice.'

Was she blind or stupid? Could she not see how much he loved her? 'I do not jest, madam!' he said, with a mocking attempt at dignity, but she merely smiled at him as though at a precocious child.

'Please be sensible!' she urged. 'Your life is at stake, Master Rice, and you must not gamble with it lightly.'

'My heart is at stake!' he corrected her gravely. 'I would do anything to stay with you.' He spoke sincerely and yet even to his own ears the words had a hollow ring. Little wonder that she would not take him seriously.

'Think on what I have said,' she suggested. 'I will ask you later for a –'

'I have thought,' he said. 'I will stay here with you.'

He tried to read the expression in her eyes. Amusement? Pity? Tolerance, perhaps? Did she know he was in earnest, he wondered. What else could he say? He was at a loss. For most of his life he had played with women, paying them absurd compliments, amused by their frailties and often exasperated by their little vanities. He did not know how to speak to someone like Elena.

'You are certain?' she asked.

He searched her eyes for a sign that she was pleased, that she wanted him to stay, but saw nothing to encourage him.

He nodded. 'I want to be near you,' he said humbly, astonished at himself.

She smiled. 'Then I'll tell them. You are ours for the duration of the plague. After that –' She hesitated.

He grinned. 'After that, it's back to the leg irons!'

'Oh dear! Poor Master Rice. I hope not!'

Master Rice! If only she would call him Charlie.

To his surprise, she moved a little nearer and lowered her voice. 'When the time comes –' she began. Obviously finding what she had to say difficult, she took a deep breath. 'When the time comes for you to go back if we should wake one morning and find you gone –'

He stared at her face which was suddenly flushed with guilt and saw that her eyes were suspiciously bright. She was suggesting that he might abscond – with her connivance! Charlie was astonished.

'Do you see what I mean?' she whispered urgently.

'Yes,' he said. 'I see.'

She swallowed hard and turned to his patient. 'Drink your gruel, Master Bennow,' she said briskly and moved quickly away, leaving Charlie in a state of utter confusion. If she wanted to help him then surely she must feel something for him, rogue that he was. His spirits soared to dizzying heights. She did not want him to return to The Fleet. She *cared*! Absent-mindedly he held out a spoonful of gruel but, missing Master Bennow's dutifully opened mouth, tipped it neatly down the front of his night-shirt instead.

Chapter Fourteen

THERE WAS SOMETHING eerie about the churchyard in the half light but Jem walked boldly along the path, noticing for the first time the air of accumulated neglect. In spite of the lack of rain, stinging nettles flourished in dark clumps, climbing weeds clung tenaciously to the tombstones and the yellowing grass was ankle high. On the graves themselves, a few flowers had withered and the sun had dried and cracked the newly turned earth. Presumably there was no one left to care for the place or no one who thought it of sufficient importance at such a time. The noonday heat had passed but the oppressive air was scented with the now familiar smell of woodsmoke and herbs. It was the hottest August Jem could remember and humid with it. He longed to be out on the water where a slight breeze was sometimes present but the river was almost deserted, with traffic severely depleted, and Jem thought it a waste of time to take the boat out for the few fares he would carry.

He made his way to Maggie's grave with a heavy heart, aware that he must tell her of his defeat at the stone-mason's. She would understand, he knew, but he would have preferred to bring better news. The coin was still safe in his pocket but every day brought risks that someone would steal it or that he might lose it. As he neared the grave he saw the young woman he had spoken to previously and noted with pleasure that she recognized him and raised her hand in a greeting.

'So you're here again,' he said.

'I came before,' she told him. 'In the morning but you weren't here. I thought you'd –' She shrugged.

Taking her meaning Jem said, 'No. I'm well enough. And you?'

'Seemingly.'

'I forgot to ask your name. Mine's Jem. James Rice but people call me Jem.'

'I'm Bess. Bess Tanner – and they call me Bess.' A faint smile curled her lips.

She looked very dirty, thought Jem. She was standing beside the grave of her child's father, her hands on her hips.

'I was just telling him what I thought of him,' she confessed. 'Leaving me and the littl'un without a roof over our heads and not a penny to bless ourselves with! Not that he meant to go. He wasn't a bad man. Just stupid. Fancy breaking his skull!'

'Where do you live then?' asked Jem curiously. He was wondering how he could introduce the matter of the tombstone. She'd be impressed with that.

She shrugged. 'Under arches – in doorways. This weather 'tis easy enough. Better out of doors than in.'

She said this defiantly but Jem saw her lips tremble and was at once reminded of Maggie's friend who had died from exposure in similar circumstances.

'But the baby,' he said.

She shrugged again. 'We'll survive. I'm tougher than I look and when the plague's over I'll work. I used to work in the tavern at the end of King's Street. D'you know it? Now 'tis mostly deserted and I'm not needed. Not that I care. Too many sick folks about for my liking, and all think they can drink their troubles away. Sots! I hated them! I was glad to leave.'

Jem said casually, 'I'm thinking of buying a tombstone.' He was pleased with the way the words rolled off his tongue. 'I went to a stone-mason's to have a look at some stone but –' He pursed his lips to show his dissatisfaction with the quality.

She was staring at him. 'A tombstone!' she exclaimed. '*A tombstone*! Whatever for?'

'For them,' said Jem, a little puzzled by her reaction. 'For Maggie and little Alf.'

Bess was staring at him incredulously. 'A tombstone! For them? What good will a tombstone do *them*? They're dead!'

'So?' Taken aback by her challenge, it was all Jem could think of to say. He felt hurt by her attack. She was saying the wrong things; pouring scorn on his grand design.

She went on, 'Tombstones cost money! A lot of money.'

'I've got money,' he told her, his tone as lofty as he could manage.

There was a strange gleam in Bess's eyes. 'Enough for a tombstone?'

'I've got a sovereign,' he told her and, seeing her expression change, added, 'And I didn't pinch it! I did someone a good turn and he sent it me by his brother.'

She was looking at him as though he was a backward child. 'You've got a *sovereign* and you're going to throw it away on a *tombstone*! God Almighty, Jem Rice! You must be a bit short up here!' She pointed an accusing finger at her temple. 'Times are hard and things'll get worse before this damned summer's out. They say there'll be a hundred thousand dead.' She laughed harshly. 'A hundred thousand dead and the rest of us out of work. Strewth, Jem! We'll all be starving, like as not, and you're going to buy a tombstone!'

She spoke so passionately and looked at him with such scorn that, reluctantly, Jem began to wonder whether or not she was right. If the plague lasted all summer he would be hard pressed to feed himself and there was part of the rent to pay on the room he shared with his father. He might even find himself like Bess, reduced to sleeping on the streets. But he was doing it for Maggie and his son. Surely she understood that.

He said hoarsely, ''Tis my money! I'll do what I choose with it.'

'Then more fool you!' Bess tossed her head, turned on her heel and walked away in the direction of the gate. The tilt of her head signalled defiance yet she moved with that awkward gait with which pregnant women are affected, leaning back a little to balance the weight of her child. He thought at once of Maggie when she was expecting Alfie. "I'll be glad when I can see my feet again!" she said and they had both laughed. Jem watched Bess Tanner with a mixture of resentment and regret. She had spirit, he'd say that for her. Not afraid to speak her mind. On the other hand, she'd no right to scoff at his plan. It was *his* money and he'd spend it as and when he chose and be damned to her! Cheeky little pipsqueak! And grubby with it! A good wash would do her no harm but he supposed she had no money for luxuries such as soap. Well, a good riddance to her and her sort! He swallowed miserably because now the tombstone did seem a foolish idea and all the joy had gone from it.

She reached the church gate and he thought she might turn back and give him one last glance but she walked on, her head held high. He sighed unhappily. Probably thinking of all she would do with the money if it were hers. A sovereign would transform her wretched existence. To her he was probably a prince among paupers!

He opened his mouth to call her back but then was glad to see that she had gone. Yes, good riddance! He could not abide women that knew everything. Maggie had been just the opposite; soft, helpless, clinging almost, but in a nice way. She had depended on him. He stared down at Maggie's grave.

'Trouble, that one!' he told her. 'You can always tell.' He thought of Bess's unborn child whose father had just died in Newgate. 'Times are hard,' he said and by way of apology for Bess's remarks added, 'She's in the family way. You remember how it is.'

To change the subject he said, 'Pa's going up river. Living on the boat. He'll be fine, this weather. Wants me to join him but I said not just yet. Too much to do . . .'

He began to wish he had given Bess a few pence to buy a pie. If he wasn't going to buy a tombstone he could spare them and he could have told her to get to a conduit and wash her face. Most likely she was getting very low in spirits. Being with child played tricks on women. It was all too easy when you were alone to stop caring about your appearance. Suddenly he began to run towards the gate but by the time he reached the road there was no sign of Bess. He tossed up in his mind which way he should go – left or right – and chose left.

It was the wrong way.

*

A week passed and Lois still struggled to break free from the black misery which threatened to overwhelm her. She watched her brother with growing anxiety, aware that he had aged dramatically since Antony's death, and the contrast with his earlier buoyancy was very marked. He had no appetite and was losing weight; she could see it in the contours of his face. He carried on with his work but only with a tremendous effort of will, and she sensed with alarm that he was near to breaking point. She tried to talk to him but he was short-tempered. He no longer discussed his patients or showed any interest in the progress of the epidemic. The few mealtimes they shared together were silent affairs, haunted by the memory of Antony's bright young face. The empty chair had saddened her so much that she had removed it, thinking that Luke, too, would find it poignant but without a word he had restored it to its place at the table, as though determined to punish himself with a constant reminder of his failure.

Her brother seemed unaware of her own desperation and made few attempts to comfort her; it was as though he was locked into his own suffering and could no longer see the outside world. Her unhappiness was not lessening but the sharpness of pain had been replaced by a dull ache and somehow she forced herself to concentrate her mind on Luke's deterioration. As she searched for a way to reach him, she became convinced that she must confide in Sophie and enlist her help. With this in mind she took up her pen and settled down to write.

Dear Sophie

Luke tells me that you are all but recovered and I am relieved that your children will soon be reunited with their mother again. You must miss them terribly but at least you know they are safe.

I thank God every day that He gave Luke the power to save you. I will not speak of my sweet Antony whom He saw fit to take except where it touches the reason for this letter. I am writing to you in strictest confidence and trust you will never divulge the contents of this letter to Luke. He would resent my frankness and I could not bear his displeasure – he is all the family I have left in the world.

You have surely seen how low in spirits he has become and you will understand that I am anxious about him. I almost fear for his sanity. He is so changed of late I hardly know him. I cannot think of a way to save him except to ask for your co-operation. 'Tis simply this. Before Antony died Luke was in love with you and that love, undeclared though it had to be, was sustaining him through these dark days to a wondrous degree. He would not speak because your husband was sick but I think after Matthew's death, after a suitable time, he would have confided his feelings to you.

Now he is cast down to the depths of his soul and I fear he may do something rash and make away with himself. There. Now 'tis out. You see how fearful I am and why I dare to write to you in this way.

My dear Sophie, you are left with two children to support and Luke loves you. Could you ever love him in return? Would you ever see fit to wed him? If so, then I beg you to forget your pride and speak to him of your hopes on the matter. He might yet drag himself back from the edge of despair if he felt you needed him.

It has been difficult for me to write this way, but you are my only hope. I will send this by Fanny's hand in utmost secrecy.

In deepest distress, your friend, Lois.

When she had folded and sealed the letter she tried to imagine a new way of life with a new sister-in-law and two small children in the house and at this cheerful prospect her sad heart was warmed by a small flicker of hope.

*

Fanny arrived at the house the next day beaming with importance at being entrusted with 'an important mission'. She waved the letter at Jon who had sprung to his feet at her arrival.

'This is most secret!' she told him, 'Doctor Meridith must never know I have brought it.'

'What's it about, then?' he asked.

'What's it about?' Fanny tossed her head

derisively. 'How should I know? I told you 'tis most secret!' She glanced up but saw no one at the window. 'Is the mistress still on the mend?'

He nodded, pleased to have something equally important to impart. 'The physician said she is well but weak in body and I've been to and fro searching out nourishing things for her to eat, though 'tis not easy with so few provisions reaching the city. I wonder how many are dying of hunger, let alone the sickness, with so many street sellers gone to meet their maker?' He jerked his head skywards. 'There's a rumour that the house confinement is to be short-ened, too, so that twenty days after a sick person is recovered he might venture abroad again. If that be true, then your mistress might well be free to go to Woolwich within a week or so. And my job here will be over.' He looked at her, hoping for a sign that this news was unwelcome to her.

'Where will you be?' she asked.

He shrugged. 'Don't rightly know – except 'twill certainly be another doorstep job! The physician says he can't see an end to it all while the weather's hot and he reckons September will be the worst so –' He waved his hands. 'But I dare say I could seek you out here and let you know. You could visit me if you'd a mind.'

'I'll miss you,' she told him, sobered by the realiza-tion that this camaraderie would soon be at an end.

He grinned suddenly. 'I was thinking that when your mistress goes away and the house has been aired and fumigated you'll be in and out all on your own. Looking after the dog and what not. You might get lonely. You might want a bit of company – nights!'

Her mouth fell open with shock. '*Nights*!' she stammered. '*Nights*! Jon Lummett! What are you suggesting?'

His grin broadened. 'I mean you might decide to stay on here one night rather than risk being robbed in the streets and then you'd find it a creaky old place all on your own. But, with me there to keep you safe, and all those empty beds – after they're aired, of course,' he added hastily. 'We could have a bit of fun. A few kisses and a cuddle and, well, who knows what else!' He was warming to his theme and Fanny was trying not to find it irresistible. ''Twould be like living in our own house and who'd be any the wiser? You might make me a bit of breakfast of a morning and I'd be willing if you was?'

'Jon Lummett!' she repeated but she said it thoughtfully and knew she did not sound as shocked as she should have done. She had never exchanged more than a kiss with a young man; had never expected to. Yet here was a young man who seemed to find the prospect an exciting one and she did not want to frighten him away. Suppose there was another servant girl on his next doorstep who was prettier than her! On the other hand, the physician thought the plague would still be raging for weeks to come so there would be plenty of time for her and Jon to become properly acquainted. He might even look at her in that certain way, as though she was the most desirable woman in London! Fanny had watched lovers arm in arm in the street and had envied the women for the expression in the men's eyes. She would like Jon to look at her that way. True, she might be plain as a pikestaff but so was Jon!

He nudged her gently with his elbow, waiting for her answer. Fanny thought desperately. If the mistress were to hear about such goings on, she would probably box her ears but how could she hear anything, tucked away in Woolwich and frightened to come back into town.

She said, 'I might.' She found herself wondering if he had ever lain with a girl, but she dare not ask him. He would undoubtedly lie and say 'yes' – and might ask her about her conquests and then she would have to lie also.

'You see, I wouldn't work nights,' he said, as though that would swing the decision in his favour.

Fanny considered her shoes in their clumsy wooden pattens, avoiding his eye. She mustn't seem too eager nor too reluctant. Tentatively she said, 'Pa would kill me if he knew.'

'I won't tell him!' He snorted at the mere idea. 'Will you?'

'I dare say there wouldn't be no harm in it –' she began but, just then, the window opened above them and Sophie called down.

'Is that Fanny I hear?'

Fanny sprang away from Jon and tried to look as though she had just arrived. Panting slightly she said, 'I've run round with this letter from Mistress Meridith. 'Tis most secret and –'

'Most secret? Then don't shout it all over the street, girl!'

Jon winked at Fanny who struggled to keep a straight face as the basket was lowered. Standing well back she tossed the letter in and watched it being hauled up again.

Jon lowered his voice. 'So what d'you think, Fanny?'

After a long and hopefully decent interval, she whispered, 'I don't see why not!' and began to wonder how long it would be before her mistress would be able to leave for Woolwich.

*

By the end of that same day Jem had seen his father installed in his new home on the river in company with a few dozen other watermen. They too had finally given up the trade – it was getting too sparse and riskier by the hour. The wherry was tied up alongside another craft which was, in turn, tied up to the river bank by way of a twenty-foot rope. Above his father's seat they had constructed a make-shift roof to protect him from any rain which might fall on the beleaguered city and its river before too long. Four stout poles had been bound in place to form four corners and three flour sacks had been opened up and roughly joined together to form a roof and one wall. Hay, begged from a stable, covered the floor of the boat and blankets completed its furnishings.

The arrangement was that Jem would bring whatever food and drink he could to the river bank each day and would alert his father. He would then withdraw and leave his father to collect them when he considered them safely 'aired'. The same plan had been adopted by other watermen with considerable success and they were confident that by this means they would survive.

Already developing among the inhabitants of the floating community was a feeling of goodwill and a sense of optimism. In one boat, there was an entire family, father, mother and five small children. Further along, a sailing barge had been hired by two families who had combined resources. Each boat was separated from its neighbour by a distance of eight or nine feet, which was considered adequate. The occupants were within easy hailing distance of each other and when Jem had left his father that morning, the old man was striking up a cheerful conversation with three men who shared an abandoned tug.

As soon as Jem was back on terra firma, however, he quickly forgot all about his father for he had other more pressing matters to attend to. He had thought over what Bess had said about the sovereign and had abandoned his decision to buy a tombstone. The more he thought about his abortive attempt to buy a stone, the more he felt that God had intended the damaged slab as an omen. The Almighty intended Jem to use the money more wisely and he knew what he must do. His first task was to track down Bess and that was proving difficult. He had waited around in the churchyard every day for the past week, without success, and was beginning to wonder if some harm had come to her. They had parted on less than friendly terms and he was already regretting the angry exchange. Bess was right. Money should be spent on the living, not the dead, and he wanted to spend it on her and the child. He wanted to be a family man again and the thought of the baby inspired him. Would Bess consider marrying him? Not that either of them would ever replace Maggie or Alfie in his affections. Oh no! That was understood. Maggie and Alfie were his first and dearest family but he had convinced himself that if Maggie could look down and see how lonely he was and how empty his life was, she would surely approve of his plan. Nor would she want to deprive Bess and her child of a few home comforts and the protection of a husband and father.

As to love, Jem paid it scant attention. It was a luxury which he could ill afford; if it flowered between them it would be wonderful but if not he would settle for a mutual respect. But where *was* Bess? He was trying to be disciplined in his search and had spent the previous day prowling the back streets around Covent Garden and along St Martin's Lane. Before that he had searched along Drury Lane, mingling with the depleted crowd in Clare market at great risk to himself. Today he would explore Holborn and Chancery Lane. The problem was that he had no idea where he might expect to find her. Had she found work? It seemed most unlikely for someone in her condition. Paid work was hard to come by and hundreds went in search of the few jobs that were available. Was she begging in a doorway?

As he walked along Chancery Lane, it was growing dark and his hopes were fading fast. He heard nine o'clock strike and knew that before long the streets would empty and shortly after that they would resound with the sombre cries of 'Bring out your dead!' Nobody cared to hear those dread words or to witness the lowering of limp bodies from upper windows; few could bear the sight of the bereaved crying out in protest as the loved one was tossed with very little ceremony on to the growing pile of corpses in the dead-cart.

The air was stiflingly hot but a sudden rumble of thunder in the sky made Jem and others glance up hopefully. The sky was overcast but the longed-for rain would not fall. Grass sprouting between the cobbles had been bleached to a dull yellow by the fierce sun. A solitary dog, its ribs visible, slunk guiltily towards Jem as though aware it was living on borrowed time.

'Don't fret!' Jem told it, with an attempt at humour. 'The dog-catcher's probably dead!' But at the sound of his voice the animal turned away with its tail between its legs and disappeared into a convenient alley.

A man with a small but suspiciously clinking sack on his back hurried past, his face averted and Jem wondered idly what he carried. Cutlery, pewter plate? There were so many abandoned houses that offered easy pickings for the unscrupulous. With a houseful of people dead, it was tempting for poor folk to disregard the risk of infection and help themselves to furniture and fittings which could make their own lives more comfortable. The penalties for looting were harsh but Jem knew it still flourished. Like most people he turned a blind eye, concerned only with his own safety and with no time to waste on others.

As he turned left into Fleet Street he met a swarthy man pushing a wheelbarrow which contained a small, fat man whose short arms and legs hung limply over the sides. Quickly Jem inhaled on the handful of herbs he carried.

'Sixpence!' said the swarthy man, setting down the barrow and wiping his sweating face on his bare arm.

'What's that?' asked Jem, keeping his distance.

'Sixpence. To get this lump of lard into the next parish and save our money!'

Jem looked at the fat man nervously. 'Is he dead?' he asked.

'Lord no, but soon will be.' He laughed cheerfully. 'Still, why should I care? This is the fourth sixpence I've earned today. That's good money! I find 'em in the street, struck down all of a sudden, then I wheel them into the next parish so they're *their* responsibility.'

He reached for the handles of the wheelbarrow and went on with his burden. As Jem watched him go he saw three women approaching arm in arm, staggering from side to side. He drew back into a doorway and they passed without noticing him, leaving the unmistakable smell of brandy on the air. He shrugged. It took folks in different ways, he thought charitably.

The rubbish had not been raked up for days and the street smell was worse than he had ever known it but, at least, there was less horse dung in the streets. Few gentlemen now chose to ride through the tainted air and many carters and waggoners were either sick or dead. Jem stepped over a pile of rotting cabbages; he was getting used to the neglected, unlovely city and found it hard to imagine a time when it would return to some kind of normality.

The area round the Fleet River was notorious for cutthroats and rogues of every sort and Jem felt distinctly uneasy as he moved through the narrow street, peering into every shadowy corner and jumping nervously at every sound. He sincerely hoped that Bess was not sleeping rough in such an area but if she were then he hoped to find her before she fell victim to a crime. From every doorway, haggard faces peered up from slumped bodies, pale blurs in the failing light, and Jem bent to each one in case it was Bess.

By ten o'clock he had given up for the night and was returning home by way of Shoe Lane and Holborn. He was tired and hungry but he knew that at home he had a large dish of jellied eels waiting for him and a loaf of bread, for he had taken Bess's advice and broken into his precious sovereign. He had hoped Bess would be sharing the little feast with him but that was not to be. Poor Bess, most likely, had nothing, but tomorrow he would look again. He would concentrate his search on the area alongside the Thames, Knightrider Street, Carter Lane and Old Fish Street. He told himself sternly that he would never give up until he found her.

*

A few days later, Henrietta made her way wearily up the stairs, reflecting sourly that she might as well be running a hostelry; up and down the stairs, twenty times a day! She was feeling very frayed after an argument with her husband before he had gone out to milk the cows. She had only suggested that they take on an extra pair of hands to help cope with all the extra work! His argument had been that because of all the extra mouths he now had to feed there was less money than ever to spare for extra help.

Mornings only, she had offered. He had refused point blank. She had told him angrily that she had never known him so intractable. He said he had never felt so crowded and harassed in his life. They had finished their breakfast in a bad-tempered silence and Henrietta now felt disgruntled and thoroughly hard done by. The rest of the morning had been full of problems; the children had squabbled incessantly and one of the cats had messed in the airing cupboard. It was the sort of day when she wished with all her heart that she had remained a spinster. Family life, seen through today's eyes, was sadly overrated!

Now, just after midday, a sullen calm had descended over the household. Giles was in the stables dosing a sick horse, Oliver and Lizbeth had been banished to their grandmother's room, and her own brood, scowling and resentful, were laboriously copying out lines from the Bible by way of punishment for their rowdy behaviour earlier in the day. Feeling somewhere between an ogre and a martyr, Henrietta reached the top of the stairs, her arms full of clean linen for Ruth's bed. There was so much extra cooking to be done for such an extended household and so much extra washing! It was not that she begrudged giving kith and kin board in times of trouble but, when all was said and done, they were *his* family, not *hers*, and at the very least she had a right to expect sympathy and understanding from her husband. Giles truly was a most insensitive, intolerable man, she told herself as she knocked briefly and pushed open the door to Ruth's room.

Inside she stopped abruptly. The bed was empty. For a moment her heart seemed to stop beating but almost immediately she saw that Ruth was standing by the window, smiling at her. She was flanked by Oliver and Lizbeth who had their hands clamped over their mouths to hold in their excitement.

'Great heavens!' she stammered, weak with relief but still confused by the sight of the old lady on her feet and apparently suffering no ill effects.

'Well, Henrietta?' said Ruth, and at once the two children broke into loud squeals of delight and triumph at the complete success of the surprise.

Henrietta gasped, 'Oh but – Should you? –'

Oliver shouted, 'She can walk! She can walk!' and began to skip around the room, unable to express himself adequately in any other way.

'*She* is the cat's mother!' Ruth reproved him but she was still smiling at Henrietta.

Lizbeth said, 'Grandmother wanted it to be a surprise. Do you like it? Do you like the surprise?'

As though in a trance Henrietta watched as Ruth walked confidently towards her and took the linen from her hands. 'I'll change the sheets for you,' she said and Oliver gave another whoop of excitement. Lizbeth began to giggle at the astonishment on Henrietta's face who now began to play up to her part.

She sank on to a chair and fanned herself and cried, 'Mercy on us! Am I seeing things?' and looked from Lizbeth to Oliver for an answer.

'No!' Oliver told her. 'The Lord has seen fit to grant Grandmother –'

Lizbeth said earnestly, ''Tis a miracle because Grandmother has led a godly and righteous life.'

Henrietta said, 'I see! So that's it!' But she was truly surprised and touched by Ruth's achievement. All her earlier gloom had vanished.

Ruth said, 'I really felt I must help you in some way. You and Giles have been so generous to us.'

'I'm astonished!' said Henrietta. 'And so happy for you!' And then, perversely, she felt like crying and had to blink rapidly, afraid that tears would spoil the children's fun.

'I shall need some clothes,' Ruth said.

Oliver stopped capering round the room and said, 'She can't – I mean, *Grandmother* can't come downstairs in her nightgown, can she!'

Lizbeth cried, 'In her nightgown! Ooh! No, she can't!' and then hid her face in her hands at the very thought of such impropriety.

Oliver looked at Henrietta soberly. 'Grandmother is going to take us all for walks when God makes her legs strong enough which will be quite soon and then you can have some peace and quiet and she will iron the clothes and bake us all a pie –'

Ruth said hastily, 'With your permission, Henrietta, and only when you wish for a rest from the cooking –' With a flash of pride she said, 'You need not fear, Henrietta. I don't intend to get in your way.'

Impulsively Henrietta sprang to her feet and kissed Ruth's pale cheek. 'I shall be most grateful,' she said, 'and I shall thank God in my prayers that you have found your strength again after all this time. 'Tis truly a miracle.'

Oliver said, 'Won't Mama be surprised!'

Henrietta said, 'Shall I look out a skirt and bodice and – things for you? Do you want to get dressed today?'

Ruth smiled. 'I want to come downstairs, if I may. I think I have been an invalid for too long.'

Henrietta smiled broadly, her day quite transformed by the unexpected event. 'I shall look forward to you joining us,' she said. 'Giles will be delighted and I shall make a special syllabub for supper by way of celebration!'

*

Two days later Luke, minus his hood, pronounced Sophie quite recovered and advised her to eat plenty of good food to build up her strength.

'Today is the thirtieth of August –' he began.

'The thirtieth!' cried Sophie, genuinely surprised. 'I can hardly believe it! Where have all the days gone?'

He merely nodded. 'Ten days from now you could be reunited with your children,' he told her. 'I will give you a letter to take to the magistrate so that they can issue you with a certificate. By that date, by my calculations, you will have been recovered from the disease for the requisite time and may rest easy that you are no longer a threat to anyone else. But you must prepare yourself for possible trouble. Travel out of the city is not encouraged, so don't expect it to be easy. I hear the road to Woolwich is manned by a constable and several other men. The surrounding villages are most unwilling to allow strangers in. Without the certificate they will certainly turn you away.'

Sophie nodded but she was not really listening. She had read Lois's letter with some surprise and had given it a great deal of serious thought. The last thing she wanted was to rush into a second marriage which might prove a mistake but, on reflection, she had to confess that she did find Luke attractive. In other circumstances she might well have considered him a very desirable partner but the idea of forcing the issue troubled her. Surely they both needed time. And yet, Lois thought that, for Luke, time was running out. If anything happened to him she would never forgive herself. She had finally decided therefore to 'sound out his feelings', delicately, and then, perhaps, she could make a more subjective judgement.

She took a deep breath and said, 'I can't thank you enough for all you have done, Luke. I owe you my life and I don't know how I can repay you.'

He was closing his bag, reaching for the hood, preparing to leave. 'There is no need for thanks. I am simply doing my job. Sometimes I am successful, at other times –' His mouth tightened into a hard line and she knew he was thinking of Antony.

'I shall miss you' she cried. 'Oh Luke! Don't go just yet. Won't you stay a few moments longer?' Something in her voice made him glance at her face. She rushed on. 'Luke, I – Oh Luke, what will you do when I'm gone? Back to Woolwich, I mean?'

She cursed her clumsiness. She was doing this very badly.

He said, 'Why, carry on with my work. What else is there?'

She dared not mention Lois or he might suspect their collaboration. 'Will you ever –?' She could not get the words out.

He was looking at her, puzzled by her obvious confusion.

'Luke, will you ever think of remarrying?'

He shook his head at once.

'I wish you would,' she told him. 'I think you should, Luke. I don't care to think of you alone and grieving.

'Alone? I am not alone. I still have Lois.'

'Lois? Oh yes, but –' She swallowed hard and glanced down at her hands. 'A man needs a wife, Luke. I know Lois loves you but a sister is not what I meant. A man needs – why, he needs love, Luke. A little love in his life.'

He shook his head. 'I have all I need.' He lowered his voice. 'All I deserve.'

She stared at him, appalled by his words. 'All you

deserve? Oh Luke, you must not speak this way. Nor think it. You deserve no more and no less than the next man!'

'I have my work,' he said flatly.

'But a man cannot work all the time. There must be something else in life.'

'I have been content all these years without a wife,' he said, but he sighed as he said it.

'But then you had Antony!' she cried. If only she could find the right words, she thought desperately. Her chance was slipping away.

He looked at her with an expression she could not read. 'I did think once that perhaps I would remarry but –'

'But what?' she demanded eagerly.

He hesitated. 'But it was not to be. And in the circumstances –' He shook his head. 'I am not fit company for any woman now,' he said. 'Losing Antony – I can't explain. I was a different person then. I was Antony's father. We had plans. We talked about the future and it was bright. I had someone to live for. Now –' He turned away hastily but not before Sophie had glimpsed his unshed tears. 'Now I am a lost soul. A physician. Nothing more.'

'You are still a man!' cried Sophie but he went on as though she had not spoken, his eyes averted.

'The future is grey and it reaches ahead for ever and ever. Amen.' He gave a short, humourless laugh. 'Can you understand any of that?'

'Yes – and no!'

'I would not inflict myself on anyone,' he told her. 'Lois is my sister and she knows me as well as anyone. We can jog along together.'

Sophie longed to put her arms round him but the gulf between them now was too wide and it seemed to be growing. Nothing she said had the desired result. She could not reach him. In desperation she decided to try another line of argument.

'I have been thinking of my own plight,' she said quietly. 'As you say, life goes on and I must plan for the future. I shall have to wed again.' She waited but it seemed he was unable, or unwilling, to make the connection between his plight and hers. At last she said, 'My children need a father to love them as well as a mother.'

'Ah, the children!' he said. 'How I envy you. I would give my soul if I could bring Antony back.' He looked at her with anguished eyes. 'There are so many things I want to tell him. That I loved him. That he meant all the world to me. That I'm sorry I let him die!'

'Luke!' Her tone was harsher than she intended. 'That's not fair. You did not let him die. He died in spite of all you could do. Why do you persist in –' She stopped abruptly. He brushed a hand across his eyes.

'I must go!' he said. 'This doesn't help me!'

The words were a reproach and she was immediately angry with herself. By her stupidity she had added to his grief.

'Let me help you, Luke!'

She had uttered the words before she knew it but already he was gathering up his things. He went to the window and looked down. 'I see Fanny is below. I shall tell her what you need. Now I must leave you, Sophie. Forgive me.' He was all efficiency, impersonal, the physician had taken over from the man.

She said, 'Please don't go like this, Luke. I want to help you. I want to love you if you will let me. Couldn't we help each other?'

'I must go,' he repeated and turned away without another word.

'Luke!' she cried, but he had already left the room.

His footsteps sounded on the stairs and she leaned back against the pillows, exhausted by the encounter and shocked by the extent of her disappointment. Did she mind so much that he had rejected her? It was ridiculous, she told herself. She hardly knew him except as a friend. She had never thought of him as a lover until Lois's letter.

Downstairs the street door opened and closed again.

'Goodbye, Luke!' she said.

So that was that! If she wanted a father for her children she must look elsewhere. If Luke had once loved her, as Lois had suggested, he obviously felt nothing for her now.

Humiliated, she slid down between the sheets and

tried to convince herself that she did not care in the least, but in her heart she knew she did. In her eagerness she had totally mismanaged the scene, had been too precipitous altogether. A forward woman! How men loathed them. 'Sophie, you are such a fool!' she told herself angrily and found herself blaming Lois for her rejection. And yet Lois knew him better than anyone and she had genuinely believed that he might take his own life. So there had been cause for haste. Not that it had achieved anything. 'Forgive me, Lois. I tried but failed,' she said and thought uneasily of Lois's letter. Would Luke, whose vocation was to save life, really choose to die by his own hand? She did not want to believe it but it was just possible. Any man in such despair might consider his life worthless.

'Don't do it, Luke!' she whispered. 'Please don't!' With a deep sigh she turned over on her side. The matter was out of her hands. She must put the incident from her mind. Soon she would be with Ollie and Lizbeth again. That thought brought her a little comfort and she finally fell into a refreshing sleep with a smile on her face.

Chapter Fifteen

❧

CHARLIE DIPPED THE head of the mop into the bucket, shook it round in the none too clean water and began to wash the floor, pushing it under each bed and working it from side to side with a practised flick of the wrist. He was wondering what he should do about Elena who had so far resisted all his amorous overtures with the air of a tolerant adult dealing with a precocious child. For the first time in his life he was at a complete loss to know how to deal with a woman. He began to fret for fear she had found a husband but his subtle inquiries on the subject had set his mind at ease. She was alone but seemed happy with the situation and gave no sign that she secretly longed for a home and children. Charlie's problem was that even if he could persuade her that she would be happier as a wife and mother he could see no way to give her the security of a settled home. No legitimate way, that is. He could continue to steal and trick money from what he called 'the undeserving rich', but he did not think she would approve of that. Her wealthy family *might* be prepared to finance their union but he did not think it very likely. As far as Charlie could see, his only chance was to find work but that idea filled him with dread. The thought of paid employment was anathema to him and always had been. He considered that those who were shrewd enough to relieve others of their money deserved to do so and he had no sympathy for the careless or gullible.

Apart from this philosophy, he admitted to a definite resistance to the state of respectability. It had such a dull ring to it, unlike the excitement and romance of living on your wits and never knowing where the next crown would come from or whether it might be two crowns. He could not envisage a life without the thrill of the chase, the roll of a pair of dice or the turn of a card. These things would certainly not merit Elena's approval. He sensed already that his stay in The Fleet and the activities that had put him there in the first place had caused her some distress. For her peace of mind he should have wished them undone but in his heart he could not do this. He had been caught and punished but that was one of the risks he was prepared to take. Or had been until now. Thoughtfully he pushed the mop under the fourth bed and one of its two occupants reached out and caught him by the sleeve.

'Master Rice! A word in your ear!' The agitated

fingers that clutched at his arm were burning hot and the eyes that looked into his were red-rimmed and bright with fever. Master Seckett was not yet delirious, however, and his voice was shaky but otherwise normal.

'What is it?' Charlie asked, detaching the clutching fingers gently but firmly. Master Seckett had been admitted the previous day and was still dazed with the horror of those newly aware of the nature of their affliction.

'My bedfellow! Master Flint. He's very quiet. Too quiet.'

Charlie looked across the bed at its second occupant who lay with his eyes closed and mouth wide open. 'He's sleeping,' he said.

'No, no! He snores in his sleep.'

'So do you,' Charlie grinned.

'No, no. He snores but he is not snoring *now*. He's – he's finished. I'm certain of it. He was snoring and then he stopped. He doesn't answer me. I can't be expected to share a bed with a corpse!' His pale blue eyes were wide with indignation. 'He must be removed at once. You must fetch Elena.'

Charlie was all in favour of this but he knew from experience that she would reproach him if he disturbed her without good reason. He walked round the bed, took hold of the withered arm and shook it gently.

'Wake up, Master Flint!'

There was no reply and the arm felt suspiciously cold.

'I'll fetch her,' said Charlie.

Master Seckett's eyes widened. 'Then he is — gone?'

'I think so.'

Abandoning his mop Charlie walked along towards the small room which served as a dispensary. Here Elena was often to be found mixing medicines or rolling pills which had been prescribed by the physician. She was sitting with her back to him and her narrow shoulders drooped with tiredness. Charlie tutted to himself. If only he could somehow acquire great riches. He would take her away from all this wretchedness and set her up in a fine house with a serving boy and a blue-eyed cat and a silver-backed brush for her hair. He allowed his imagination to run riot. He would buy her a cage full of singing birds and would hire the finest dancing teacher to guide her dainty feet. She would sleep in silken sheets and drink nothing but the finest French brandy! Charlie's imagination could stretch no further.

Hearing his step she turned and smiled. 'Master Rice?'

If only she would call him Charlie he would be the happiest man alive! For a moment he was silent, forgetful of his mission, watching with fascination as her slim fingers rolled the tiny pills and dropped them into a wooden pill box. He envied them her gentle touch.

He said, ''Tis Master Flint. I think he's dead.'

'Oh no!' Her eyes darkened with regret. 'Not Master Flint!'

Charlie marvelled anew at her continuing compassion. After all these weeks she still grieved over each patient they lost to the plague.

'He has a wife and two daughters!' She stood up, distressed by the news and Charlie stepped back to let her pass. She was so close he was tempted to put out his hand and touch her but instead he followed her silently to the bedside where a brief examination convinced her that Master Flint was indeed dead. This done, she was immediately at pains to reassure Master Sickett.

'We'll move him at once,' she told him. 'Meanwhile, you must try to sleep.'

But Master Sickett, unconvinced, twisted his fingers distractedly. 'I'm going to die too, aren't I!' he cried, his voice thin with fear. ''Tis just a matter of time. You do your best but the plague is too strong for you. No one leaves this place alive!'

Charlie said quickly, 'You are wrong, Master Sickett. You see before you one of Elena's successes.' With an expansive gesture, more suited to the playhouse than a pesthouse, he threw wide his arms and twirled neatly on his toes so that the patient should see him from all angles. 'Do you see a jot of plague remaining?' he demanded. 'They dragged me back from the very jaws of death!'

Master Sickett said, '*You* were sick with the plague?'

He turned to Elena for his answer.

She nodded. 'Indeed he was,' she told him.

Master Seckett smiled, albeit a trifle unhappily.

Charlie told him, 'St Peter was opening the gate for me when –' He snapped his fingers dramatically. 'They dragged me back to life! Your case is much less serious. I heard the physician call it a mild attack.'

The man looked up at him with sudden hope. 'A mild attack? He said that?'

'Most certainly he did,' Charlie assured him. 'Less fibrication than normal and no sign of secondary halosis. They were his exact words!'

'Secondary halosis?'

'A medical term,' said Charlie airily.

'Ah! And fibricosis?'

Fibri*cation*!' Charlie corrected him as he tucked the sheet around the thin shoulders. As the patient looked up eagerly, Charlie saw that a little of the terror had left the man's eyes.

'And that's a good sign?' he asked Charlie, eager for reassurance.

'Most hopeful!' Charlie told him.

'Well, well!' Master Sickett let out a long sigh and smiled at Elena who was hiding her face behind a handkerchief, apparently smothering a sudden and somewhat explosive cough. 'I do find that most encouraging. Yes indeed.' His smile broadened. 'When my wife calls by will you tell her that, Master Rice? Will you put her mind at ease?'

'Most certainly,' said Charlie.

'I think I shall sleep now.' He turned on his side, facing away from his unfortunate bedfellow and closed his eyes.

Charlie hurried to fetch the wooden trestle top which served as a stretcher and he and Elena manoeuvred the body on to it and carried it away to an anteroom.

'Fibrication?' Elena repeated, her mouth twitching 'And secondary halosis! What nonsense! You are quite incorrigible, Master Rice. The lies slip so easily off your tongue!'

Charlie shrugged humorously. 'Better to die hopeful!' he suggested and for a moment he fancied that in her eyes he read more than amusement. He was suddenly struck with a wild hope. Could such a woman ever love a rogue? For such a woman, could he ever stop *being* a rogue?

'Charlie Rice!' she whispered. 'You truly are such a —' She drew in a sharp sigh and in her eyes he thought he glimpsed a sudden wistful longing. In that moment Charlie wished only that he could die for her.

She went on breathlessly, 'Such a charming, wondrous, reckless fellow! Oh Master Rice!' Her voice softened again. 'A woman could warm her hands around your heart!' She swallowed and to his horror two tears ran down her face. Slowly Charlie put out a finger and wiped them away.

'Charlie!' he whispered. 'Call me Charlie! Just once!'

After a brief hesitation she whispered the word. A fierce and loving desperation held Charlie silent but as he stared into her eyes he prayed, Please let her love me!

She rested a hand gently on his sleeve but her next words broke the spell. 'But you know it won't do for us. You know that, don't you?'

He nodded, unable to speak for the terrible sense of loss that seemed to fill his whole being. Elena reached up, brushed his lips lightly with her own and then walked quickly away.

*

5th September 1665
My dear little sparrows,

This letter is to tell you I am quite recovered from that horrid plague and the physician says I may soon be with you again. I shall leave London on the eleventh of September and should be in Woolwich by the evening. I shall most likely hire a horse to ride since the carriages are considered unsafe. When you hear 'clip clop' along the road it will be your Mama!

Aunt Henrietta tells me you have been good children. I knew you would. Also that Grandmother has found her feet again. How exciting . . .

She wanted to mention their father but could not decide what to say. She did not want them to feel that he had disappeared from their lives without trace but in fact it would not even be possible for them to visit his grave since he was buried with so many others. After a little thought she wrote:

> *I miss poor Papa very much. I expect you do, too, but you and I and Grandmother will soon be together and happy once more . . .*

The prospect of seeing her son and daughter again had cheered her tremendously and she was counting the days until she could escape from the horrors of London to the comparative serenity of the country. Her only regret was that she would be leaving Luke, particularly as she knew that she could have loved him. In her present situation, newly widowed with two children, she faced an uncertain future but second and third marriages were commonplace. She was hardly in a romantic frame of mind but she knew intuitively that she could have made Luke Meridith happy. She admired his intelligence, appreciated his gentle manner and respected and shared his values. He was probably fifteen years older than Matthew had been but that was no barrier to a relationship. She knew from Luke's devotion to Antony that he would have made a good father to her own two children and was certain they would have learned to love him in return. Perhaps, in time, she consoled herself. When the plague was at an end and they all returned to London she could renew her friendship with the Meridiths – if he and Lois were still alive! The plague was still raging and their chances of survival were slim.

She was still considering the future when she heard Luke's voice in the street outside and then Jon unfastening the padlock on the front door. He had brought her the vital paper which confirmed that she was recovered from the plague.

He read it aloud.

This is to confirm that Mistress Sophie Devine of Watling Street having succumbed to the plague is now quite recovered from the contagion and cannot pose a threat to any other person or persons. I declare that the treatment of the said Sophie Devine has proved entirely efficacious and ask that this certificate of true health being granted her will allow her unhindered passage to the village of Woolwich where she wishes to rejoin her children. This authorization to take effect from 10th September 1665.
Signed Luke Meridith
Physician

He said, 'That should suffice. They should not refuse you a certificate with this guarantee of your health.'

'I'm most grateful to you,' said Sophie, clutching the precious document to her chest. 'I can scarce believe I am going from this place.'

Luke nodded. 'I came past the Old Bailey this morning on my way here and there were hundreds waiting. I suggest you send Fanny to queue with this letter. You would find the long wait too much in your present weakened state.'

'But don't I have to apply in person?'

'I think they will give it to Fanny. If not then you will have to go yourself, but wait and see. Fanny must tell them that you are not fit enough to stand for hours in this punishing heat. And 'twill give Fanny something to do.' He hesitated. ''Tis scarcely my business but she is spending a great deal of time with your watchman. Did you know?'

Sophie frowned. 'I suspected it,' she confessed. 'I simply had no energy to deal with the problem. Is he an unsuitable person, would you say?'

'No, no! I can speak no ill of the youth but servant girls can have their heads turned very easily and I'm sure you do not want her to –' He gave a slight shrug. 'I do not intend to malign Fanny, but a great many wenches are surprisingly gullible and sadly they end up with child.'

Sophie's expression changed. 'Oh, I see!' She paused uncertainly, considering the ramifications of Luke's words. 'We always thought her a sensible girl but –' She looked at him anxiously. 'I was going to leave her in London when I go to Woolwich, to mind the house and feed Banna. Oh dear!'

He went on, 'Lois has suggested that, if you wished, we might employ her for a few hours each day until you return. That way she would be kept occupied and could still keep an eye on your house and see to the dog twice a day. At least she wouldn't be roaming the streets as free as air.'

As Luke spoke, she studied him surreptitiously. He looked slightly dazed and his voice was flat, devoid of expression. There was no sign of the eager, humorous man she remembered from their last shared supper. Her heart ached for him but he was still speaking and she attended once more to what he was saying.

'. . . she could sleep in our kitchen on a straw pallet.'

Sophie nodded. 'That may be the solution,' she admitted, 'and once again I am in your debt. You and Lois are so kind, Luke. I wish so desperately that I could do something for you in return. If it weren't for Ollie and Lizbeth I could wish I were staying in London – just to be near you.'

He gave a short, almost harsh laugh. 'I am past all help, I fear.' To avoid meeting Sophie's eyes he stared fixedly at the letter he still held in his hand, then he went on, 'I have almost forgotten what it is to be happy. I tell myself that this pain will pass, that the wound will heal – but I don't believe it. I have spoken so many trite words of comfort to others in the past but now they have a hollow ring to them. I do believe . . .' His voice broke suddenly. 'I do believe I shall carry this anguish to my grave!' He covered his face suddenly.

'Oh Luke! I wish to God –' She bit back the words but the intensity in her voice made him look up.

After a long pause he asked, 'What do you wish, Sophie?'

'I can't tell you,' she said awkwardly, 'for fear you misunderstand me.'

'Tell me,' he insisted.

Sophie drew a deep breath. 'I wish I could comfort you; put my arms around you and hold you close. But I can't. I am nothing to you and never shall be.'

'You have such a generous heart,' he said. 'But I should be a poor husband for any woman; a miserable companion. You deserve happiness and I could not give you that. But you will marry again. You will make a new life for yourself.' He took hold of her hand and his look was kindly but Sophie, seeing nothing else in his expression, was overcome with regret.

Luke looked at her earnestly. 'I will envy your husband with all my heart, Sophie.'

'Oh Luke!' She searched for words with which to convince him but they eluded her and she remained silent.

'You must not spend the rest of your life alone,' he told her. 'You will make someone very happy.'

Desperately she insisted, 'I would make *you* happy, Luke, if you would let me!' But as soon as the words were out she felt her cheeks burn and wished them unsaid. Her outburst was unforgivable. She was practically proposing to him and yet he had made it clear that he was not interested. Now he would think her forward and she would go down in his estimation, probably for ever. 'I'm sorry. I spoke out of turn.' She tried to laugh lightly. 'I think the plague has affected my judgement! I don't usually speak so boldly. I hope you will forget what I said.'

'No,' he said. 'I shall always remember, and when I am old and grey I shall no doubt curse my stupidity for allowing you to slip through my fingers. The truth is that if I thought I could make any woman happy it would be you. Before Antony – before I lost Antony – I was very much in love with you, Sophie, but could not speak because your husband was still alive. By the time Matthew was dead Antony was sick and then you were stricken. Now I am so confused and wretched and cannot see further than the end of each day. I fear Fate has conspired against us, Sophie.'

'Don't say so!' she cried. 'Isn't time on our side, Luke? We have both lost someone we loved. You have lost your son and I–' Her face hardened momentarily. 'I had lost my husband long before he died.' She put the thought of Matthew to the back of her mind and suddenly threw caution aside. Passionately she cried, 'You need someone to love, Luke, and so do I. And my two little ones need a father. We could comfort each other, Luke. We could be a *family*! The future will be what we make it!'

Abruptly he turned away and moved to the window to stare down into the street. After a long silence he spoke with a calm finality that shattered Sophie's hopes. 'I envy you your plans for the future, Sophie, but I seem to be trapped in the past with nothing but memories. I might see clearly again. I might not.' He sighed. 'I don't seem to care about myself let alone anyone else. Poor Lois needs more affection and support than I can give.'

'Poor Lois!' Sophie could think of nothing more to say and regretted that she had already said too much. If there had once been a spark between them, she felt now that her stupid persistence had effectively snuffed it out. She had only herself to blame, she thought wretchedly, and vowed to put Luke out of her mind for ever. She would think only about removing herself to Woolwich and being reunited with her children.

It appeared that Luke, too, thought the subject at an end. He put the letter he had written into her hand and, for a brief moment, Sophie felt his fingers touch hers. In spite of her resolution she was aware of a fleeting excitement. Then it was gone. Had Luke's sad heart been touched, she wondered. If so, he gave no sign and she hoped her own feelings were well hidden.

He said, 'Tell Fanny to take the letter to the Old Bailey and say it must be countersigned by a magistrate and two sheriffs. Now I have other calls to make and I must leave you. You must forgive me.' He looked at her directly and she saw that he was indeed lost to her. She swallowed hard and could not speak as he turned to go. Without moving, she listened to his footsteps descending the stairs and heard him bang on the door to attract Jon's attention.

To hide her mortification she said angrily, 'Go then!'

She wanted to run to the window as she usually did to watch him to the end of the street but she resisted the urge. Instead, she hid her face in her hands and repeated, 'Go then! I don't need you. Be lonely!'

She sat down on a nearby chair and said, 'Yes, Luke Meridith. I *will* meet someone else and I *will* marry again!' But her words lacked conviction. 'Because life must go on!' she added fiercely. 'By the time you realize that 'twill be too late!'

For some time she sat on the bed, struggling to come to terms with her disappointment. Slowly, one by one, her present troubles reasserted themselves and a little of her composure returned. Finally she went to the window to call Fanny and send her on her errand to the Old Bailey.

*

Jem was nearly in despair. Bess seemed to have vanished from the face of the earth and he became increasingly worried about her. Had she thrown herself in the Thames? Or taken up with a criminal? Or succumbed to the plague? He knew that pregnant women were less able to resist the infection than their sisters. Or perhaps she had committed a crime and been arrested. He asked at all the jails but no one of that name had been admitted. He asked at the pesthouses without success. Finally he decided he would go to Maggie for advice. Perhaps she would inspire him.

He had almost reached the grave when he noticed something different about it. He ran the last few yards and stared down at the familiar mound. The soil had been disturbed! He fell on his knees and began to feel around in the earth.

A familiar voice said defiantly, ' 'Tis only a few bulbs.'

Relief swept through him and he turned to see Bess standing beneath a nearby tree. She looked as ungainly as ever and her face was set in a scowl.

'Bess!'

'A few bluebells. They'll bloom next spring.'

'Bluebells?' He could not think of anything else to say. His joy at finding her unharmed was so great.

'I got some for him, too.' She jerked her head in the direction of her dead husband. 'Walked to the woods just this side of Dorking and dug a few up.'

'Dorking!' he cried incredulously. 'But that's miles away!'

'So what? I've got legs. And I've nothing else to do!'

'But how did you eat?'

' 'Tis called begging!' She looked at him defiantly. 'You hold your hand out and folks put food into it!' She was ready to argue the rights and wrongs of it with him if need be. Jem, however, said nothing and she went on. 'I got a few rides along the way. Not that they ever knew. I just hopped on the back of each cart when the driver's back was turned and took my chance!' She laughed 'I dare say the horse noticed it, though, for me and the little one together is no light weight, but the poor nag could hardly tell.'

'So that's where you were.' Jem could not hide his exasperation. 'I've been tramping the streets, looking for you and thinking you must be taken or sick or dead and all the time you were digging up bluebells in Dorking!'

'As like as not. Bluebells grow wild there, under the trees. Hundreds of them. They won't miss a few. We went there once, him and me. He couldn't get over it. There was this fair on and he won a shilling wrestling. He could look after himself, that one. That's why it was so stupid, to die the way he did.' For a moment her expression darkened. 'He was fighting for a wager, stupid devil! He could never resist a wager. They said he slipped on an apple core and that's probably the only way he'd go down. An apple core! God Almighty!' She shrugged. 'I thought he'd like a few bluebells and then I thought most likely yours would, too. I reckon a few flowers make you feel cheerful even if you're dead.'

'You're very kind,' he said and suddenly he was grinning ecstatically. 'I'm glad I've found you. Thought you'd copped it, one way or the other.'

'Copped it? Not me!' She looked pointedly at

Maggie's unaltered grave. 'When you getting your tombstone then?'

He shrugged. 'I'm not. Changed my mind. Thought about what you said and you were right.'

'You don't want to take no notice of me,' she said in an offhand way that did not deceive him. 'I say lots of things. Talk through the back of my head sometimes.'

'But, you were right – about the dead not needing money,' said Jem. 'So I thought I'd spend it on us. Me, you and him.' He pointed.

'Or her!' she said.

She seemed to be taking it very calmly, he thought. 'So what do you think, Bess? I've got a few things and we could stay in my Pa's place. He's gone on the river 'til the plague's over. There's a bit of a crib and some clothes. We'd get by.'

'Yes,' she said.

'Yes?' He was stunned by the speed with which things were happening. 'You mean yes, you will?'

'Yes.'

'Oh!'

She laughed at the look on his face. 'Well, come on then, Jem!' she chivvied. 'I haven't eaten for two days.'

He was at once contrite, concerned to the point of fussiness. He took her hand and they began to walk away from the graves. Suddenly Jem halted.

'I ought to say a few words to Maggie –' he began, embarrassed.

'No need,' said Bess. 'I've already told her about us. And him. They understood. You can talk to her tomorrow.'

'But how —? I mean, you didn't know —' he stammered.

'Yes I did,' she assured him. 'First time I set eyes on you. Jem Rice is one of the world's gentlemen, I said to myself. An honest-to-God gentleman. And I was right, wasn't I?'

Jem could only shake his head in astonishment.

'So can we go now?' she asked. 'I tell you, Jem, I'm ravenous. I could murder a mutton pie!'

And as they walked together along the path Jem felt a crazy desire to break into song and caper about. With Bess's grimy hand in his, he could feel the spring of happiness bubbling inside him.

*

Meanwhile Jem's sister Fanny, holding one of Sophie's pomanders to her nose, made her way to the Old Bailey with a face like thunder. She was smarting under the news that during Sophie's enforced stay in Woolwich, she, Fanny, would be sleeping at the Meridiths. Jon had been none too pleased at the ruin of his plans and had made his displeasure known in no uncertain way. In fact he had sulked! Fanny, herself an expert in the art of sulking, had sympathized with him but had insisted that it was not *her* fault and had told him loftily to 'be a man, for Lord's sake!' which had only made him worse. So all the excitement to which she had been looking forward had been snatched away and she was full of resentment. Worse still was the knowledge that Jon would shortly be posted to another doorstep where he might meet someone else and be tempted to transfer his affections. Fanny's hopes of a possible husband had been dealt a crushing blow and she blamed Sophie.

'Serve her right if, while I'm at the Meridiths, thieves break in and steal everything!' she muttered. 'And kill Banna!' She stepped round a smouldering fire in the middle of the street and averted her face from the thick grey smoke which climbed lazily into the still air. 'And leave his poor, dead body for the rats!' she added. This gruesome image cheered her for a moment and she raised her head and looked about her. Since the fifth day of the month, the new regulations had come into force. Fires must be maintained in the streets, one outside every twelfth house, and the cost for these was to be shared by the unfortunate householders. Nobody really believed that the smell would cleanse the air but the authorities, frightened by the spiralling number of deaths, had grown desperate. Eager to be seen to do *something*, however ineffective, they had ordered the fires as a last hope and these were fuelled by coal, faggots or even empty tar barrels.

Fanny suddenly became aware of how quiet and deserted the streets had become. The phrase, 'the silence of death', came into her head and her spirits plunged again. All this scurrying through the plague-ridden streets was enough to kill anyone, she thought angrily. Little they cared whether she died a maid or lived to wed and produce a family.

'Go there!', 'Fetch this!', all the blooming day! The wise stayed at home, avoiding the risks which people like her must take. Neatly she avoided a pile of dry, rotted refuse and wondered why no one had thought of using the refuse to fuel the fires instead of putting the burden on poor afflicted citizens who had enough to worry about. Or was that too simple?

Serve them all right if I ran away! she thought, returning to her main theme. But where could she run to? Sophie would be sorry if she was attacked by one of the desperate people who still wandered the empty streets, delirious with pain or dazed with hunger.

'Little do *they* care about the likes of us!' she told herself, bracketing her employer with authority in general. In her heart she knew this was rather unfair because there was a poor relief being distributed wherever people in need could be located but it was a pitifully small sum and Fanny was in no mood to split hairs.

As she turned into Old Bailey and came in sight of the Courthouse, she was shocked to see a disorderly group of people, all clutching the letters or certificates which, appropriately signed, would make their escape from the city possible. A harassed official was trying in vain to persuade them to wait patiently for their turn. Fanny, eager for some excitement, joined the crowd and waved her own letter. A middle-aged woman with a balding head turned to her furiously.

'This place is a disgrace. I was here all day yesterday and here I am again today. They are so slow! Talk about snails! And when you get there and 'tis your turn they query every last thing. Is this signature true or false? Is this date correct? Who will you live with? Where are you going? Do you have any money?' She snorted in disgust. 'Anyone would think they were determined to keep us here. Perhaps they *want* us to die!'

Fanny said, 'My mistress wants to go to Woolwich. I have a letter from her physician.'

'Huh! Much good may it do her!' She tossed her head scornfully. 'Have you seen the Bills this week? Seven thousand dead! In one week! No wonder the streets are empty. Will they ever be full again? Will there be anyone left when this plague is over?'

Fanny regarded her nervously. 'My mistress is leaving me behind –' she began.

'Oh, she would! 'Tis the way they think!' The woman shook her head, her face red with anger. 'They leave us servants to die! We can fend for ourselves. My master is off to Colchester to his sister but there is no room for me. I can perish for all he cares!'

Fanny wondered whether to tell the woman about her own plans involving Jon which had been so neatly nipped in the bud, but on reflection thought better of it. She was recovering a little of her good nature and did not wish to malign Sophie unjustly. In her heart she knew that Sophie would take her to Woolwich if it were possible.

A man came out of the door and rushed past them, triumphantly waving the precious certificate. 'At last! I can go!' he exulted.

'Bastard!' said Fanny's new-found friend, but she spoke without any real hostility. 'No doubt he has bribed someone.'

Inspired by his success, the crowd pressed forward once again and the small official screamed at them, urging them to behave in an orderly fashion.

Fanny's friend said, 'Little turd!' and sighed loudly. 'Mind you, the time to leave London was weeks ago. Now 'tis a chancy business to travel anywhere. I think I would rather stay here than take my chances on the highways,' she told Fanny. 'You hear such tales! One man yesterday spoke of his master's brother who had started out for Kensington. Set upon, he was, by a band of four men who stole his certificate and then demanded money or valuables. He parted with both and was forced to return to London. He says 'tis a jungle outside London where a man takes his life in his hands. If your mistress wants to go to Woolwich, good luck to her say I, for I'd not risk it. Travelling alone, is she?'

'As far as I know.' Fanny was beginning to feel

distinctly uneasy. If anything happened to Sophie she, Fanny, would be in desperate straits.

'She'll not get there,' said the woman. 'You can be sure on it.'

Fanny said, 'Some people must get through.'

'Oh, some do,' the woman agreed. 'Some have money to burn. They get through. The likes of us are lucky if they don't set the dogs on us! A woman I know was travelling with her master and mistress to Oxford. They reckoned if 'twas good enough for the King 'twas good enough for them! But no! They got as far as Tyburn and was turned back. Papers not in order. Certificate not signed properly, or so they said. Any trumped-up excuse will do. Threatened to throw them into jail! And what can you do? They have fierce dogs and even muskets, some of them, and will kill you as soon as look at you. You'll be lucky if you ever see your mistress again!'

Fanny had already forgotten her ill-humour as her mood switched, instead, to one of anxiety. There was nothing she could do to help Sophie but she began to see that, depending on her mistress's fate, her own future might be darkening ominously.

'Let's hope you're wrong,' she said with an attempt at indifference.

Dimly Fanny was beginning to realize that she was one of the powerless ones with little choice but to play out her allotted part in the wider drama that was unfolding. She was nothing more than a puppet and she presumed that God was holding the strings.

It took her four and a half hours to collect the vital signatures and when she finally hurried home, the precious document was folded tightly in her left hand and the hand itself was thrust deep into her apron pocket.

*

On the evening of the tenth, when Sophie's incarceration came to an end, she went round to the Meridiths who had invited her to supper. Fanny waited on them with scant grace for Jon was now officially removed from Sophie's house and she did not yet know his new posting. To all effects and purposes, therefore, Fanny had lost track of him and this she blamed on her employer. She did not relish her forthcoming part-time employment because she would have less freedom than of late. Instead of looking upon free time as a luxury, she now considered it her right. Having to cook and clean for the Meridiths felt to her like a great burden unfairly imposed by unfeeling superiors.

The evening was not a success, partly because Fanny was sulking and partly because Sophie was embarrassed by her recollection of the advances she had made to Luke. Lois was annoyed with her brother for what she considered his 'pig-headedness' and she was grieved by the fact that her plans had misfired. Luke was courteous but withdrawn, still deeply depressed by his recent bereavement. Towards the end of the evening however he rallied a

little and tried to inject a hopeful note into the proceedings.

Raising his glass he said, 'I propose a toast to our
continuing good health!' and they drank to that.
Lois, not to be outdone, said, 'To Luke's skill which
has saved Sophie's life!' They drank to that also.

Sophie suggested, 'To absent friends', and they
drank in a sad silence and then, after a few more
moments of desultory conversation, Sophie made
her excuses and left with Fanny to find a linkman
and make their way home.

*

Next day, just before dawn, with her bag packed,
Sophie made her way to the stables from which she
had hired what she hoped would be a good-natured
hack. Fanny accompanied her and together they
inspected the small piebald which bore an ancient
side-saddle and frayed bridle. This, she thought with
a sinking heart, was to carry her to Woolwich. It
had dull eyes and a listless manner but Sophie assumed it to be acceptable. With so many people
leaving London and so few returning she had been
lucky to find a horse at all. If she rejected it, she
might never find another.

'It looks docile enough,' Fanny said encourag-
ingly. 'You don't want a frisky mount.'

Sophie said, 'True enough. I dare say 'tis an
elderly animal and –'

The groom, overhearing this comment, interrupted her with a short laugh. 'That nag never was frisky!' he told them. 'Nor ever will be.'

'But 'tis in good health?' Sophie said hopefully.

'Good health?' He laughed again. 'That nag doesn't know the meaning of the word!' He shook his head, apparently amazed by their optimistic ignorance, then reached up and slapped the horse's rump. Apart from a slight tremor it did not move. The groom turned to Sophie. 'This animal will get you to Woolwich, mistress,' he promised. 'If it drops dead thereafter 'tis hardly your concern.'

Sophie decided not to rise to his obvious bait and said instead, 'And I am to leave it at the stables to the rear of the Dog and Bottle?'

'Exactly.'

'Does it have a name?' Fanny asked. 'I mean, what does it answer to?'

She was rewarded with a withering look. 'A nag's a nag,' he said. 'If your luck's in, it answers to a whack on the rump. There again, a whip might come in handy.'

Sophie and Fanny regarded each other unhappily.

'I must be off then, Fanny,' said Sophie, before the surly groom could create any more doubts in her mind.

'I suppose so but –' Fanny's face crumpled. 'Oh! do take very good care, mistress. Trust nobody. And come back soon – when 'tis all over.'

Sophie nodded. ''Twill not be for long, Fanny,' she said.

'And give the children a kiss from me.'

'I will.'

They embraced hurriedly under the scornful gaze of the groom and then Sophie handed over the money. The groom cupped his hands and tossed her into the saddle where she clung in sudden panic. The ground appeared to be a long way away and she saw her own fear reflected in Fanny's face but, she told herself, she must take heart. By the evening she would be with her children again and no price was too high to pay for that pleasure. While the groom tied her bag to the rear of the saddle Sophie settled her legs comfortably and Fanny darted forward to arrange her mistress's skirts so as to hide her ankles. Then Sophie drew in a long breath, gathered up the reins and with a final wave to Fanny, dug her heels into the horse's sides. The long awaited journey had begun.

*

Sophie was not alone. Accompanying her was a motley collection of travellers, almost without exception the poorer people, for the rich in their carriages had passed this way many weeks earlier. Today some of them were mounted like herself, others rode in carts of every description and many more were on foot. A few carried sacks on their backs or balanced bundles on their heads, others pushed barrows. The older men and women walked for the most part in silence, reserving their energies, but the children (of whom there were pitifully few) ran and shouted and laughed, determined to make the most of their adventure. In spite of the certificates of health which most people carried, the fear of the plague still lingered and there was little fraternizing among strangers. Officially, none of the travellers should be carrying the disease or have recently been in contact with any persons stricken by the disease, but no one quite trusted this to be the case. Whenever someone sat by the roadside to rest, passers-by gave them a wide berth. No one stopped to inquire, 'Are you sick?' or 'Do you need help?' No one could afford to be generous or sympathetic when there was so much at stake; so much to lose. Sophie understood this and her own instincts were no more generous. She had done her part, she told herself. She had nursed Antony and she had put herself at risk. Now God had granted her another chance and for the children's sakes she would be as selfish as the rest of them.

She dared not stop at an inn on the way for fear of contagion but instead stopped to dismount. She stretched her stiff legs, ate from the cold chicken and fresh bread that Lois had given her the previous evening and then made her way into the bushes to relieve herself. Before remounting, she drank a few mouthfuls of wine, also a gift from Lois, and after a little initial difficulty, clambered back on to her lacklustre horse and rode on.

By late in the afternoon, she was becoming used to the motion of the horse and had resigned herself to her slow progress. She tried not to notice the plight of those less fortunate than herself. A great many now hobbled along, suffering from painful blisters; a few weary children rode in the wheelbarrows which their parents pushed. The atmosphere was one of dogged determination, one grand pilgrimage, as all faces were turned away from London towards their one hope of salvation. There was still relatively little conversation and this situation pleased Sophie very well for she had a great many problems to which she wished to turn her attention and once she was riding more confidently, she was able to apply her mind.

Suddenly she became aware of a commotion up ahead. It had halted some of the travellers in their tracks and as others began to arrive, a crowd was forming. She reined in the horse and, keeping well back, waited nervously. A low murmur went up from the crowd ahead of her and they began to retreat.

'What has happened?' she asked a young lad.

'A man fallen sick,' he told her fearfully. 'Fell from the seat of his waggon and was run over by the wheel.'

'Is he dead?'

He shrugged. 'Who knows? No one will venture near enough to find out! I know I won't!'

'Poor man!' Sophie protested. 'Maybe he simply fell asleep and doesn't have the plague.'

Another man gave her a wintry look and wagged

a finger at her. 'You want to catch the plague, mistress, *you* attend 'im! I've a wife and children in Dartford and I want to live to see 'em. I don't want to take 'em the gift of plague, neither!'

Sophie was silenced and shamed by his logic. She had children in Woolwich. Was it fair to them to stop and offer help to a stranger who might be infected with the plague and, possibly, would kill them all? As the panic subsided, people moved forward again and Sophie, ignoring the young man who lay writhing on the ground, urged her mount forward with a heavy heart. He appeared to have been travelling alone. Would he lie there unattended until he died of his injuries? It seemed very likely and Sophie felt a shiver of self disgust as she left him to his fate.

About a mile further on, a waggon stood at the side of the road containing a weeping woman and three small children. Everyone passed them unflinchingly, staring straight ahead, and Sophie, to her shame, did likewise. It made her realize, with a shudder of fear, that if she fell sick or had an accident, the same treatment would be meted out to her. She could not expect even the coldest charity.

Six o'clock came and went and Sophie reckoned that she still had another four or five hours' travelling ahead, more than she had bargained for. The journey had taken much longer than she had anticipated and she was already desperately tired. Her body ached with a mixture of fatigue and discomfort.

She learned that even if she reached Woolwich before midnight she would be unable to enter. A constable and his fellow guards would refuse entry unless properly sanctioned. There would be no one to sanction entry between eight o'clock at night and six the next morning. Although she knew that Henrietta and Giles were expecting her that evening and would be alarmed by her non-appearance, Sophie knew she would not reach Woolwich in time. She came to the reluctant conclusion that she would have to spend the night in the open. It was obvious that others had come prepared for an overnight camp, with small, makeshift tents. Others were preparing to sleep in or under their waggons, wrapped in blankets.

Sophie slid thankfully from her horse and considered how best to pass the night. Her travelling bag could be pressed into service as a pillow to keep her head from the ground; by way of a blanket she had nothing more substantial than a thick shawl but that would have to do. Fortunately, at least in this respect, September was proving a sultry month and the night was mild. Choosing a spot under a young oak tree, she tethered the horse to a branch where the poor creature immediately began to crop the grass and pull down the leaves from the lower branches. Sophie curled up on the ground at the foot of a tree and made herself as comfortable as she could. She covered herself with her shawl and tried not to think about ants, spiders and snakes. Her purse she kept in the pocket of her skirt where it was unlikely to be found. She did not expect to sleep but, if she did doze, she hoped the horse would neigh if anyone approached them. She told herself that if someone should actually touch her she would wake instantly.

All around her people were settling themselves for the night and there were one or two small fires which scented the air with woodsmoke. The light was fading fast as Sophie closed her eyes. All her senses remained alert and yet she was desperately tired. She longed for sleep yet feared to render herself more vulnerable than she was already. Around her voices murmured in the deepening gloom. She would have paid handsomely for a mug of small beer or a mouthful of dry bread for her own few provisions had long since been exhausted. She resigned herself to the fact that she would not eat again until the morning when she would be safe in Woolwich. Stiff, hungry and thoroughly ill at ease, she lay awake for hours but the rigours of the journey had taken their toll and finally, in the small hours of the morning, she slipped into a troubled sleep.

Chapter Sixteen

WHILE SOPHIE WAS sleeping, Charlie, not so many miles away, was also in bed but he was wide awake and fully dressed except for his shoes. In his coat pocket he had a hunk of bread and a slice of salt pork which he had charmed from the cook earlier in the day. He stared at the moonlit ceiling, waiting for the church clock to strike one. In the days since his talk with Elena, he had formulated a plan for his escape from the pesthouse. This would not be easy because the pesthouse, full as it was of plague patients, was guarded as strictly as any private dwelling. True, the door was not padlocked but an officer sat outside twenty-four hours a day and no one went in or out without his approval. Charlie had decided to attempt it. His original plan had been to leave when the crisis was at an end but his recent talk with Elena had brought about a disenchantment with the pesthouse. The satisfaction he had once derived from his 'good works' had also largely evaporated. His feeling for Elena was as strong as ever but now common sense prevailed and he accepted the fact that she would never consider him seriously. That being so, he found her presence disconcerting and had convinced himself that, for his own peace of mind, he must put a distance between them. He nourished a subconscious hope that when he had disappeared from her life, without the luxury of a farewell, she would be heartbroken. He hoped she might even shed a few tears. Possibly (although it was a forlorn hope!) she might realize that she could not live without him and come in search of him. He enjoyed this last scenario and played it through in his mind as he waited for the striking of the clock.

Charlie understood the risk he was taking by absconding. He knew that the pesthouse master would have to be informed of his escape and, in turn, would have to alert The Fleet. Not only was Charlie a felon whose proper place was behind bars, he was also the inhabitant of a pesthouse and had not completed a proper quarantine period which made him an even greater threat to the general public. That meant that every constable in the city (assuming there were any left alive!) would be on the lookout for him. Charlie needed a disguise and, to this end, he had begun to grow a beard. He was pleased to discover that it grew quite quickly and surprised that it was darker than the hair on his head and with a reddish tinge to it. A moustache was also making its appearance and he hoped to wear it in the style of Lord Craven with a slight upward twist at each end. If Elena had suspected his motives, she had said nothing. In the darkened ward he had taken a pair of shears to his distinctive blond curls and they now lay on the floor beneath his bed, a sad sight, he thought, and one which he hoped would strike deep into Elena's soul when discovered.

Without the curls and with the new beard and moustache, Charlie hoped to go unchallenged in the streets. He might even buy a hat. Or, better still, steal one! He certainly would lie low somewhere for a time but he had no intention of leaving London. Already his heart warmed a little at the thought of the excitements that awaited him in the weeks ahead. He might even make his way to the young farmer's wife and discover how she fared. With any luck the husband might have succumbed to the plague, leaving a lonely widow with no man to comfort her. He recalled that she had had a roguish eye; no doubt about that one! He might even move in with her and become a farmer! Stranger things had happened.

He thought about the idea for a few moments, wondering uneasily about the amount of work that farming might entail but, before he had come to any conclusion, the church clock struck one and he jumped up from the bed, eager to be gone. After weeks of being locked up with the sick and dying, he was suddenly longing to be out and about once more where hopefully life had a few pleasures still to offer. He picked up his shoes and tip-toed to the door at the far end of the room. It had a squeaky hinge but he had oiled it earlier in the day with an application of goose grease purloined from the dispensary. Outside, the passage was in darkness except for a small gleam of candlelight from a doorway half-way along. It came, Charlie knew, from the desk where Elena sat on duty in the main ward. At the thought of her, his determination wavered for a moment. Should he bid her farewell? Should he give her the chance to flee with him? No, that she would never do. She had the morals of a saint! Would she allow him one kiss? Dare he chance it? He hesitated.

'No!' he whispered. 'Go, Charlie, while you have the chance!'

A fond farewell was altogether too great a risk. She might try to detain him, to persuade him to stay on, appealing to his better nature. Aware of her duty to the unsuspecting Londoners outside the pest-house, she might even feel obliged to raise the alarm! His stomach turned at the prospect of another ignominious arrest. No. He could not afford to blunder now. He turned in the opposite direction and padded softly along the passage towards the dispensary. There, earlier in the day, he had left a chair conveniently placed below the small, high window. He would have to go out head first but he had also ascertained that a small bush below the window would break his fall. He was soon inside the dispensary and standing on the chair reaching to open it when a voice made him freeze.

'I see you, you rogue! I see you!'

The voice was faint and husky, mercifully almost inaudible but Charlie swung round with a muttered curse. Master Sickett, barefooted and in an advanced stage of delirium, clung unsteadily to the door of the dispensary and stared up at Charlie fearfully. His pale face was flushed with fever and his eyes glittered with wild imaginings.

In a loud whisper Charlie cried, ''Tis I! Master Rice! Hush your noise, you foolish old prattler!'

But Master Sickett obviously did not recognize him. He raised a quivering hand and pointed accusingly. 'Thieves! Murderers!' he muttered hoarsely.

Charlie glared at him. 'I'm climbing *out* not *in*, you poxy old fool!' he hissed. 'How can I be a robber? And who'd want to murder you?' He hesitated, wondering whether to shut the old fool outside in the passage or keep him in the dispensary where his plaintive cries might not be heard. Above him the vacant window beckoned but he needed time to make his escape and had reckoned on at least an hour or two in which to go to ground before his absence was detected. If he locked the old man inside the dispensary, Elena might see his empty bed. Perhaps if he shut him out of the dispensary anyone finding him would simply believe he had wandered and would dismiss his ramblings about thieves and murderers as delirium. It was also possible that when Master Sickett could no longer *see* him he would forget all about him. With this aim in mind, Charlie climbed down from the chair and crossed the room in three long strides. To his dismay the man cowered back from him, one arm raised defensively across his face and yelled, 'Don't touch me, you rogue!' His voice was unexpectedly strident. 'Get away from me!' he cried again.

Somewhere further along the passage, Charlie heard a small commotion and knew that someone had been alerted, probably Elena. His heart began to thump. It was absurd that he should be so near to freedom and ironic that he be threatened by a man to whom he had shown all manner of small kindnesses. Charlie held up his two hands as though in surrender. 'No musket!' he said quietly. 'No knife. No pistol. See? I have no weapons. You are quite safe.'

Master Sickett regarded him dazedly and Charlie knew that he could probably see very little due to the intense fever that burned him.

''Tis I, your good friend, Master Rice,' he said calmly but the man began to back away through the doorway into the passage. He opened his mouth and shouted suddenly at the top of his voice. 'Thief! Robber! He's going to kill me!'

Charlie could wait no longer. He rushed for the window and was half-way out when he heard Elena's voice.

'Don't, Charlie! I beg you!'

She had used his Christian name again! Women! he thought angrily. They could tear at your very heartstrings if you let them! Without a word he forced himself through the small opening, closed his eyes and muttered a quick prayer to the patron saint of rogues. Then he dropped head-first into the bush. Although he did his best to protect his face he felt the fierce scrape and thrust of the thorned branches as he passed through them but they undoubtedly slowed his fall. But not enough. He hit the ground and a cry of pain was forced from him by the impact of the sun-baked earth and shrivelled grass. For a few seconds he lay there, dazed and winded, but then cautiously he sat up to inspect his limbs and assess the damage. He could deal with a broken head, he told himself, but broken legs would be his undoing. Mercifully he discovered that his legs were intact but when he staggered to his feet he felt the warmth of blood running down his face and his right arm had been badly twisted and ached abominably.

But he was alive and free. He waited a few seconds more to catch his breath and glancing up saw above him the pale oval of Elena's face framed in the window. From behind her, however, he heard an insistent wail denouncing thieves and murderers and knew he dared wait no longer.

'Charlie! Please don't go this way!'

He hardened his heart. If he listened to her entreaties he would no doubt find himself back behind bars. Elena would do her duty by the pesthouse; her first loyalty was to the patients and the pesthouse master. Well, to Hell with all of them! He threw her a kiss in the darkness and began to run, keeping low, supporting his throbbing arm and ignoring the blood that still trickled down the left side of his face into his eye. Behind him voices were raised and when he glanced back he saw lanterns appearing at the windows. They would come after him but they must never find him. He knew London like the back of his hand and would hide out in her many alleys and back streets until the hue and cry had died down. He would wear a wig, change his name, avoid old cronies.

Ten minutes later he had shaken off his pursuers and was grinning to himself as he crouched in a shadowy doorway. He had survived The Fleet and he had survived the plague.

'I'm a survivor!' he muttered and his grin broadened. Tomorrow he would wash himself and steal some decent clothes. From his pocket he drew the bread and pork and as he bit into the salty meat his spirits soared. To Hell with Elena! To Hell with all women! Who needed them? Charlie Rice was a survivor. He would live to see better days.

*

When Sophie awoke the next morning she was immediately thrown into a state of panic, and it took some moments before she remembered where she was and what was happening. Stiffly she sat up, feeling as though every muscle in her body was protesting at the uncomfortable hours they had spent on the hard ground in the cool of the night. In contrast to the heat of the day, a dew had formed overnight and Sophie found her clothes clammy and tight. Without opening her eyes she knew that her fellow travellers were already up and on the move. Horses neighed, wheels creaked, adult voices spoke irritably and children laughed at the adventure of waking under the sky. Slowly, almost reluctantly Sophie opened her eyes and prepared to meet the new day.

The first thing she noticed was that the travelling bag no longer served her as a pillow. With a start of alarm she looked about her and received the second shock of the day. The horse was nowhere to be seen. She thrust her hand into her pocket. Her purse was gone also!

'Dear God!' she whispered and was at once catapulted into the full horror of her situation. She had been robbed while she slept and everything had been stolen along with her only means of transport. She was immediately fully aware of the gravity of her position for, without the certificate of health, she would never be allowed into Woolwich. She would almost certainly have to return to London and without the horse it would take days. A deep moan of despair forced its way out of her throat as she scrambled unhappily to her feet.

But what good would her health certificate be to a man? It bore her name, Sophie Devine. But a man might sell it to a desperate woman who would make good use of it. Helplessly she looked around her, hoping to see someone who might help her but in her heart she knew there was nothing anyone could do for her. She would have to retrace her steps, ask Luke for another letter and reapply for the necessary signatures. But how long would it take her to walk back? It had taken the best part of a day to ride this far. Hatred welled up within her as she imagined the person who had crept up to her in the darkness and skilfully removed both bag and purse. She was astonished that she had not woken for she had always prided herself on sleeping lightly, alert to the children's needs. Last night she must have slept like the proverbial log. She swore under her breath. She was hungry, thirsty and very frightened.

From the corner of her eye she became aware of a young man watching her and turned to look at him. He was probably no more than eighteen years old, tall and thin with an open, boyish face and dark, curly hair. He was travelling alone. Was he the thief, she wondered. Was he watching to see the effect his theft had had on his victim? For a moment, she was unable to return his friendly smile. Trust no one! she warned herself but almost at once common sense argued that she desperately needed help and would have to trust someone.

He called across to her. 'Hardly the most comfortable bed!' He was rolling up a blanket and Sophie saw that his horse, a gleaming black cob, was tethered nearby. For a wild moment she was tempted to try and steal it. Why not? Someone had stolen hers. Her innate honesty prevailed, however, and she dismissed the idea as quickly as it had come. She also realized that since he already had a horse of his own he would not have needed hers so he could not be the thief.

Cautiously she returned his smile and said, 'I slept too heavily and was robbed.' She was annoyed to hear her voice shake. He tied the blanket to the saddle, untethered his horse and slowly walked towards her. He had a small scar down one side of his face but his blue eyes were friendly enough.

At his insistence, she explained briefly what had happened and the background to her predicament and he listened intently.

When she had finished he said, 'I am going further than you, to my uncle who has a house on the outskirts of Rainham Marsh, but I do know someone in authority in Woolwich and could make a brief detour. Simon Laconte is an old friend of my father's and was once a magistrate. I haven't heard from him for months but he will be pleased to know I have escaped the plague. If we could contact him he might be able to vouch for you. I fear your own brother's word would carry little weight, but someone who has once been recognized as an important member of the town –' With a light shrug he left the sentence unfinished and looked at Sophie for her reaction. 'Is it worth a try? You could share my horse.'

Sophie considered the offer doubtfully. 'Why should you help me?' she asked. 'I am nothing to you, just another stranger.'

He smiled, 'But a comely stranger – I never could resist a pretty face. No doubt one day 'twill be my undoing.'

Sophie was loath to trust herself to a stranger and yet he offered a possible way out of her difficulties. If his father's friend was able to help, she might be reunited with her children sooner. On the other hand, if he could not be found or could not help her, she would have even further to walk back to London. She was still undecided when he swung himself into the saddle and held out his hand.

'Are you coming?' he asked. 'I'm sorry I cannot guarantee success to the plan but I will do my best for you. We could keep a lookout for your nag and maybe overtake the wretch who has your letter.' He smiled suddenly. 'Do come with me. 'Tis rare that I have the opportunity to play St George to a damsel in distress!'

As she still struggled to make up her mind, he laid his hand across his chest. 'I swear you will be safe with me, Mistress Devine.'

She said hastily, ''Tis not that I don't trust you.' She thought of Oliver and Lizbeth waiting for her arrival; already she was later than expected. Henrietta and Giles would be growing anxious on her behalf. Impulsively she held out her own hand. 'I'll come!' she told him. 'I'll take my chances on your father's friend!'

They talked companionably as they rode and Sophie learned that his name was Thomas Gant and that he had been a tutor to the three children of a wealthy man in Fenchurch Street. The entire family had contracted the plague and all but the father and himself had perished. As soon as the house had been opened up, his erstwhile employer, having no further need of a tutor, had departed for Oxford where his sister had offered him a home for the duration of the plague. He had given Thomas enough money to buy a horse and provisions for the journey to his uncle in Rainham.

Sophie told him a little of her own background, omitting any mention of Anne Redditch, saying only that her husband had sent her and the children to safety and contracted the disease before he could follow them. The conversation passed the time amiably enough although the journey itself was less than pleasant, punctuated by the sights and sounds of people in various stages of distress. An elderly woman lay dead by the roadside. A waggon lay with three wheels in the air, having overturned and thrown its unfortunate occupants on to the verge. A hundred yards or so further on the missing wheel had come to rest against a tree. Again, no one had offered assistance and Sophie sighed unhappily as they rode by, leaving the unfortunate family to their uncertain fate.

'It goes against the grain not to help them!' she exclaimed. 'You have helped me.'

'Would your children thank you if you brought them the plague?' Thomas asked.

'But surely we all carry certificates of health? Without them there would be no point in travelling all this way – just to be refused entry.'

He laughed shortly. 'Do you carry papers? Where is your certificate?'

'Ah, but I am an exception. I have –' She stopped as he shook his head.

'You are too naive,' he told her. 'Too trusting. Anyone can pretend to have lost their papers. Some may be carrying forged papers. The trade is flourishing in London and forgers are lining their pockets. Any of these people might be carrying the contagion. I might!'

'Oh don't!' she cried.

'I doubt it, but who can say? The sad truth is that at such a time we cannot afford to be charitable. And as for helping you, I am hoping to but may not succeed. I may be unsuccessful and then I will merely have made your problem worse. You may rue the day you accepted my offer.'

'Indeed I won't!' said Sophie but an hour later she was beginning to wonder.

About a mile outside Woolwich a barrier had

been erected across the highway; a cordon which extended far beyond the roadway and into the bushes on either side of it. It consisted of a fallen tree trunk which had been dragged across the track, leaving a gap on one side just wide enough for a waggon to pass through. This was guarded by two men with fierce looking dogs and between them a red-faced constable sat at a rickety table, writing in a huge ledger. Further along on either side of the tree trunk, stakes had been driven in at intervals of a yard and these were connected by thick ropes backed by piles of impenetrable brushwood and manned by more men with an assortment of blunderbusses, picks and staves. The men were all grim-faced and Sophie's heart sank. Only the most foolhardy would attempt to enter Woolwich without permission and even though she knew herself to be entirely eligible she would not dare to try. The consequences of such folly would almost certainly be imprisonment and might even be death!

Against this barrier about fifty people pressed, waving papers and trying to attract the attention of the constables. On the far side, a crowd of friends and relatives from Woolwich were desperately trying to recognize the friends they were expecting so they could be on hand if any difficulties arose. There were also a few prentices who, having nothing better to do, watched the proceedings with interest.

The constable stood several yards back from the road block and called to the travellers to toss forward their documents for scrutiny one at a time.

Thomas Gant reined in his horse. 'Let's wait a while before dismounting and see how 'tis done.'

As he and Sophie watched, the constable pointed to a thickset man wearing a large brimmed hat.

'You with the brown hat! Let's see what you have?'

One of the constable's assistants held out a long pole to which a basket had been affixed and the man in the wide hat dropped his paper into it. It was withdrawn and the papers gingerly removed from the basket to be held for a few moments over a pan of vinegar and then dried off over a small fire. When the constable was satisfied that he had done all he could to render the paper harmless, he held it at arm's reach and began to read it. When he had finished, he looked carefully at the owner of the papers.

'And you are Donald Petterson?'

'I am.'

'And this signature here –' He stabbed the letter with a forefinger. ''Tis unreadable.'

The man leaned across the barrier to peer at the offending signature. ''Tis my physician, one Edward Bryde – see the E and the curling stroke of the B. B-r-y –'

'Yes, yes! I see it now.' He looked disappointed, thought Sophie.

'Master Bryde of Long Acre,' the man went on with a note of desperation creeping into his voice. 'A most respected physician ... And see! There's my father behind you!' He pointed eagerly to a small white haired man who was waiting on the Woolwich side of the barrier with his hands clasped in front of his chest. 'I shall lodge with him.'

The constable did not bother to turn his head. 'Anyone could claim to be your father,' he said suspiciously. 'You could have arranged it by letter a week since.' He held the letter up to the light as though suspecting a forgery. The men and women in the watching crowds held their breaths.

The constable puckered his lips and Sophie wondered how much of his caution was justified and how much was the enjoyment of power. In times like these, small men held sway and this particular constable appeared more than a little puffed by his own importance. Her own hopes began to fade. If they made all these objections to a man with a signed letter, what chance did she herself have of obtaining entry? She tried to imagine how lame her story of the robbery would sound and had to admit that her chances were slim.

The constable said, 'And you swear you have not knowingly been near any contaminated person or other persons who may have been near contaminated persons?'

How Sophie, wondered, could anyone swear to the latter, but the man claiming to be Donald Petterson was willing to swear to anything that might hasten his acceptance into the village. He nodded eagerly and said, 'I swear it on my mother's grave!'

'Hmm!' The constable conferred with one of his colleagues who, after a longish pause, nodded with obvious reluctance. The constable then spoke to the men standing guard over the only way in and they and the dogs moved aside.

'Come along then!' said the constable sharply and, as he wrote laboriously in his ledger, a beaming Donald Petterson was allowed through the gap, watched by the rest of the refugees who hoped to be as fortunate when their turn came.

Sophie said, ''Twill be hours before I am called forward. Will you wait that long?'

'Most certainly. In fact I have an idea.' He called to one of the prentices who came forward cautiously.

Thomas said, 'Will you fetch a man called Laconte? Master Simon Laconte. He lodges next to the Star and Garter. Tell him Edmund Gant's son wishes to speak with him urgently.'

'What's in it for me?' the lad asked.

'Here!' Thomas tossed a couple of coins into his outstretched hand and Sophie breathed a sigh of relief as the young man trotted off.

Thomas, however, looked a trifle doubtful. 'I wonder!' he said. 'He could easily lose himself and my money with him!'

'Oh surely not!' cried Sophie.

Thomas smiled. 'I told you, Mistress Devine, you are too trusting by far. Much too gullible for this wicked world! But we shall see.'

To his surprise, the young man reappeared about half an hour later but brought with him the disconcerting news that Thomas's contact had been dead for five weeks – of palsy. Thomas's face fell. 'We'll try none the less. But I think you should approach them, Mistress Devine. A pretty face will often work miracles!'

They dismounted and joined the growing throng round the barrier. It seemed to Sophie that the constable was turning back more people than he allowed in and her hopes began to fade.

When at last it was her turn she stepped forward and began to stammer an explanation of her situation. The constable listened impatiently.

'No certificate, no entry!' he said, before she had finished.

'But don't you see?' she begged. 'Someone, a woman, who may not be sound in health has tricked you into allowing her into Woolwich! She has given my name and handed in my papers! Don't you have a list of people who have been admitted to the village? Is there a Sophie Devine amongst them? If so, then I swear to you on my husband's grave that she is using my name.'

The constable hesitated. Sophie realized with a jolt of dismay that her logic would have no appeal for him. He would be reluctant to believe he had been the victim of a fraud, and even more unwilling to admit in front of his fellow villagers that he had allowed a possibly hazardous female into the village.

Sophie knew at once that even if he believed her, he was unlikely to admit such an error for fear he was held responsible for any possible future outbreak caused by the bogus Sophie Devine.

'I know nothing of any Sophie Devine!' he said abruptly.

Thomas moved to stand beside her. 'Won't you even consult your list?' he asked. 'If you see the name there you will know this lady speaks truthfully.'

'I'll know nothing of the kind!' he blustered. 'For all I know you have met up with the woman on the road from London and learned her name.' He scowled at Sophie. ''Tis *you* who might be false. Now let's hear no more from you. I've other folks to attend to. If you've no certificate you can get back to London – and the sooner the better.'

He waved her away and she and Thomas exchanged desperate looks. 'But my brother will vouch for me!' Sophie cried. 'He has lived in Woolwich for years. You may know of him. His name is Giles Benworthy and he farms on –'

'Never heard of him!' the constable said rudely. He regarded the waiting crowd with hostile eyes. 'You!' he called. 'Woman in the grey shawl with the baby!'

A woman pushed forward eagerly and dutifully handed over her papers. While Sophie and Thomas were discussing the failure of their hopes the woman in the shawl was refused admission also.

'Those signatures are unreadable!' the constable told her. 'Could have been written by anyone. Come back when you have something I can read.'

The woman began to sob that she had no money and could not possibly return to London. The constable waved a hand airily. 'Then camp out under the stars!' he advised roughly. 'A bit of fresh air won't harm you. Next!'

Sophie said dully, 'I shall have to make my way back to London. I mustn't detain you any longer, Master Gant, but I cannot thank you enough for your kindness to me.'

But he was not prepared to give up so easily. He sent the young prentice off again, this time to fetch Giles but after a wait of nearly an hour they had to accept that for whatever reason, neither the prentice nor Sophie's brother were coming.

'Even if he did come, I doubt his word would carry any weight,' Thomas told her. 'I blame myself for bringing you this far.'

'But you made the suggestion in good faith,' she reminded him, 'and the decision was mine. I must thank you most heartily, Master Gant, for your very great kindness and I would like to help you in return. I do have an idea. I dare say when this terrible plague is at an end, you will be seeking re-employment. My brother has spoken several times of his intention to find a tutor for his children. If you write to him explaining how we met I feel sure he would consider you.'

He brightened visibly at the suggestion. 'I may well take you up on that,' he said. He took her hand and put it lightly to his lips. 'I have enjoyed your company and wish you God's speed. I would like to give you some money but I gave my last groat to that wretched prentice.'

''Tis of no matter,' Sophie told him. 'I shall get there eventually and I am already in your debt.'

'As for the matter of tutor I dare say I shall do as you suggest. That way we might yet meet again.' He looked at her intently. 'I would like that very much, Mistress Devine.'

He seemed to be waiting for some kind of reaction to the compliment but Sophie was already considering her return to London and the safest way she might accomplish it.

He said suddenly, 'Forgive me but – may I remember you as *Sophie* instead of Mistress Devine? It would please me greatly.'

She looked at him, startled by the request. 'I – Yes, I dare say –'

He was looking at her with what she now realized was undisguised admiration and, despite the extent of her difficulties, she found his expression flattering.

He went on, 'Now that the time has come to go our separate ways, I am strangely reluctant to relinquish your company,' he confessed. 'I am almost tempted to return to London with you.'

She was horrified. 'Return to *London*! Oh no! I

wouldn't allow such a thing! No, no, Master Gant! I –'

'Please call me Thomas. I think you may need an escort on the return journey. Do please say I may accompany you.'

'No! I won't hear of it! Returning to London is too risky. You must ride on to Rainham. I insist.' She felt confused by his unexpected interest but touched by his concern. He was so very young, she thought, and so vulnerable. After her recent rejection by Luke Meridith, his compliments were not entirely unwelcome but she was not prepared to encourage him further. He had been kind but she knew very little about him. A chance encounter had thrown them together and he saw that as romantic but she must be sensible for both of them.

He smiled suddenly and said, 'Forgive me. I see I have been much too forward. I am an impulsive wretch. This is not the time or place, Sophie, but I hope I may see you again one day, in happier circumstances.'

'Perhaps –' she stammered.

'If I am to apply as tutor to your brother's children, we might well find time to get to know each other in more cheerful times.'

'That would be better,' she said. 'I don't mean to discourage you but at present my first thoughts are for my children and how to be reunited with them as soon as possible.'

'I understand.'

But he still made no move to leave and she knew

she would have to take the initiative. Now that she knew she could no longer hope to enter Woolwich, she was anxious to be gone. Yet there was a vulnerability about him that reminded her of Anthony and she did not want to hurt his pride.

'I shall think of you very kindly,' she said, 'and look forward to a future meeting.' She held out her hand and he held it within his own.

'Until we meet again,' he said and, releasing her hand, made a little bow, a gesture which she found infinitely moving. He swung himself back into the saddle and after wishing her God's speed, urged his horse into a trot. After about fifty yards he turned in the saddle and waved his hand. Sophie raised her own and watched him ride away with mixed feelings. When he was out of sight she sighed deeply. At least Thomas Gant had his whole life before him while Anthony's had come to an untimely end.

But there was no time to brood on the vagaries of fate. She had miles to go and another night in the open before she could hope to reach London once more. There was no time to waste. She straightened her shoulders, turned her back on Woolwich and set off on the long walk back to London. She was nervous, weary and very hungry but the realization that an attractive young man had found her desirable occasionally brought a faint smile to her lips and the future, once so dark, seemed marginally brighter.

*

Lois toyed with her supper and Luke pretended to eat his. Neither spoke. At last Lois burst out, 'I don't know why I waste time and money. Why don't we just starve to death? Who would care? Who would miss us?'

Luke said quietly, 'My patients, perhaps?'

'Your patients! I don't care a fig for your patients!'

'Lois!' There was so much suppressed anger in her voice that even Luke could not ignore it and looked up at her. She did not immediately meet his eyes but stared angrily at the remains of her meal. 'Look at it!' she cried accusingly. 'Good food, all of it, and neither of us can touch it. We both know 'twill end up on Banna's plate!'

'Then it won't be wasted,' he said unwisely.

In one quick movement Lois jumped to her feet, picked up her plate and hurled it against the panelled wall of the dining room. It struck the wall and fell, leaving an unsightly mess of food slithering down the wall.

'There are times when I hate you, Luke!' she cried, white-faced and furious. 'You sit there, picking at your food as though 'tis poisoned and – Oh, God help me! You are such a fool!' She burst into tears and sank down on to her chair. Luke allowed her to cry and made no attempt to comfort her.

'You always fussed with your food!' she said accusingly, between sobs. 'Always! Mama used to coax and bully you in turn – and Papa would threaten you, but, Oh no! You must pick and fiddle with the food. And you still do! You will never change. You were such a stubborn child and full of tantrums. Well, I'm tired of slaving in the kitchen –'

'Lois, please!' Luke pushed his own plate away. 'We both know this outburst has nothing to do with food.'

'I don't know what you mean,' she said but a splash of red burned in her cheeks as she stared back at him.

'Yes, you do.' He drew in a long breath. 'Something else is troubling you and has been for some days now. You slam doors; you march about the house with a back like a ramrod. I have asked you what is the matter and you won't answer.' There was a long silence. 'Are you going to tell me now?' he asked at last.

'If your conscience doesn't tell you –' she began.

''Tis about Sophie Devine, isn't it?'

Lois dabbed at her tear-stained face with a handkerchief. 'And if it is? What do you care – about her or anybody else? You are so wrapped up in your own self-pity!'

'I prefer to call it grief,' he said.

'Call it what you will! 'Tis still a fact that you now neglect the living in favour of the dead! Oh Luke! I never thought to rate you so low and that's the truth. Oh yes! Antony is dead! Poor, darling Antony

who I loved like my own son! He's taken from us
but nothing we can do can help him now. We did all
we could while he lived and I don't think we have
anything for which we should reproach ourselves.
But Sophie is still alive and she nursed Antony
devotedly and now you do not care a jot what is
become of her.'

'I did what I could for her,' he protested angrily.
'How can you say I care nothing for her. I saved her
life! Or is that of no importance?'

'You saved her life as a doctor, Luke, but you
broke her heart as a man!'

Brother and sister glared at each other across the
table as this barb sank in.

'How did you know that I – that she –' He
stopped suddenly and his eyes narrowed. 'How did
you know what passed between us?'

Lois made no answer.

'Sophie *told* you?'

Lois nodded and, as she did so, all her anger
seemed to drain away. 'I persuaded her to talk to me
before she went away. I wanted it for both of you,'
she said simply. 'You need each other.'

''Tis not your concern, Lois.'

'Well, I think differently. I love you both and I
see how happy you could have been – what a
comfort to each other. And you have thrown it all
away. You closed your heart to her when she almost
begged you to wed her! How could you, Luke?
How could you be such a fool? Can't you see how

happy we could all be together? Even Fanny could stay on with us. Another pair of hands –'

'She had no right to confide in you –' he began but his tone lacked conviction and she looked at him indignantly.

'She had every right, Luke. You broke her heart and she needed a word of comfort. She has suffered a great deal in these last months, not to mention that errant husband. Would you even refuse her a little comfort?' She dabbed at her eyes. 'And now we sit here and every mouthful chokes us because we both know how hazardous that journey will be for her and yet you let her go alone. You have told me yourself of the dangers that exist and she is a defenceless woman!'

'Her paper is in order. They will let her in.'

'If she gets that far!' Lois leaned towards him. 'She might be lying in a ditch, half dead, for all we know. Why did you bother to save her life if you thought so little of it?'

Abruptly Luke pushed back his chair and stood up. 'I loved her. You know I did.'

'*Loved?* You *still* love her, Luke! I know you better than you know yourself. You love her and yet you turn her away because Antony is dead. Where's the logic in that? Would Antony begrudge you a little happiness? Would your first wife want you to be alone in the world?'

'I'm not alone. I have you –' he began.

'I am much older than you and I shan't live for

ever, Luke.' She drew in an exasperated breath. 'I cannot understand you. You have always been so –' She waved her hands helplessly, lost for words.

'I *have* regretted letting her travel alone.' After a moment he said heavily, ''Tis true what you say and I won't pretend. I have fretted about her from the moment she left. I should have travelled with her. Seen her safely to her brother's farm.'

Lois shook her head. 'You should have asked her to wed you, Luke. She would make you a good wife and she needs someone to be a father to her children.' Her hopes were rising suddenly. 'She might give you another child. Oh yes! I know what you are going to say.'

'No other child –'

'Could ever take Antony's place! Certainly not. There will never be another Antony. But why shouldn't there be room in your heart for another child? Maybe a daughter – who knows? Sophie needs a man to love her, Luke, and she is a handsome woman. I can assure you of this. If *you* do not speak for her, someone else will! And then you will have to stand by and watch her with another man. You will regret it most fearfully, Luke, but 'twill be too late.'

Luke moved to the mantelpiece and leaned against it, one hand raised to his head. His gaze rested on the food which still dripped from the wall and he smiled faintly.

'I shall sponge it down,' she said quickly, seeing his look. 'There's no harm done.'

His smile broadened. 'I have never seen you do anything like that before!' he marvelled. 'You have always been so – so controlled. Is this a new Lois?'

'The same one, but very angry!'

'Perhaps, after all these years, 'twas your turn to throw a tantrum!' They both laughed shakily and then Lois waited. 'Well,' she said 'are *you* going in search of her or am I? I shan't rest easy until I know she is safe.'

He frowned. 'I could ask Doctor Harkley to care for my patients while I'm away,' he muttered. 'I'll see that she is safely delivered to her brother. Forgive me, Lois. I have been at fault and I knew it. You've brought me to my senses. If I can't hire a horse I'll go on foot. But I won't rest until I know she's safe.'

'And will you –?' Lois hesitated.

'Will I ask her to marry me?' He shrugged. 'That is another matter entirely.'

'Oh Luke!'

'I haven't said I won't!'

'Then you will think on what I've said, Luke?'

He took hold of her hand briefly and smiled. 'You always did try to bully me!' he said. 'Yes, I will think on it.'

*

The September sun continued to blaze down. There was no breeze to render the heat more tolerable nor was there a cloud in the sky which might promise the longed for rain. Sophie made very slow progress, partly because she was so weary but also because her day was frequently interrupted by small, time-consuming crises. She had decided that, to avoid contact with any possible plague carriers, she would walk to one side of the highway, but here the dry summer had baked the ground into deep and treacherous ruts. She stumbled many times and occasionally fell. Once she was accosted by two ruffians who appeared from behind a hedge and asked for food. Seeing that she had none to offer they decided to have some sport with her and pretended that they would not allow her to return to London. They barred her way, dodging to and fro, enjoying her obvious terror, until she was finally rescued by the appearance of a family in a waggon. While her tormentors were repeating their request for food to them, she made her escape, heart thumping, and very close to tears.

An hour later she found herself facing another unexpected problem in the shape of three fierce dogs who ran at her from the gate of a field and snapped at her angrily. One was a bull mastiff, the other two were lurchers but it was the mastiff that frightened her most. Fortunately, after her previous encounter, she had wisely armed herself with a stout stick and with this she tried to defend herself. She was still fighting a losing battle when a large man appeared carrying a gun. He was brawny with a matted beard and long, wild hair. One word from him sent the dogs scurrying away but by then Sophie's hand had been bitten twice and her right ankle was bleeding.

'Those dogs are vicious!' she cried shakily. 'You should keep them chained up. Had I been a child they might have killed me!'

'That's the idea!' he told her bluntly. 'I'm sick of you Londoners threatening my family.'

'I threatened no one!'

'You threaten us just by passing the farm,' he told her bluntly. 'With plague germs clinging to your clothes and hair! You think just because we're country folk that we're fools? Well, we're not. And there's a man thataway who learnt the same to his cost!' He jerked the gun towards the middle of the field and Sophie saw a crumpled figure on the ground.

'What's the matter with him?' she asked.

'Nothing now!' He laughed harshly. 'Because he's dead! He got on the wrong end of this!' He waved the gun.

'You shot him?' cried Sophie, horrified. 'But why?'

'Because he had the plague, that's why. And that's why no one's going to bury him. He can lie there and rot for all I care. Poxy villain!'

'How could you tell he had plague?' she asked.

'He staggered.'

'He might have been weary. He might have been as fit as you or I!'

'How do I know you're fit?' Seeing her fearful expression deepen he went on, 'I'm not letting any of you near my family and if I have to kill a few, so be it.'

In an attempt to hide her fear of the man, Sophie busied herself trying to staunch the blood from her wounds but he made no further move against her and eventually she straightened up warily. In her heart she could understand the man's fear but she was in no mood to be generous. Nor, she thought, could she afford to let him know how frightened she was. After her previous experience she knew that a woman alone was particularly vulnerable. Summoning all her courage she retrieved her stick and faced him.

'Those dogs should be locked up!' she told him. 'They're a menace!' To prove it she held out her leg, pulling her skirt up a little to show her bleeding ankle but he merely laughed.

'A scratch! Nothing more! You city folk are all the same – weak-kneed and lily-livered.' He waved the gun. 'You get on your way, mistress, before I set the dogs on you again – and don't come back! And tell everyone you meet that this farm's not a charity. I've no water to spare and no food to sell; no one's going to sleep in my barn and no one's going to put up a tent in my field. And that's how it's going to stay until the pestilence is at an end. And when it is, me and my family are still going to be alive! Now get out of my sight while you still can!'

Sophie gave him a look of pure loathing but he glanced in the direction of the dogs who were waiting a few yards away and she stumbled away resentfully.

When at last dusk fell, she was still a long way from London and she prepared for another night under the stars. Now she was glad that it had not rained. Carefully avoiding other sleeping forms she found herself a spot against a hedge where the long grass had turned into hay and offered some protection from the hard ground. Now she had no fear of being robbed for she had nothing worth stealing; nothing with which to make herself a pillow, but she was so tired and faint with hunger that simply to stop walking was a luxury. She made herself as comfortable as she could but sleep eluded her for many hours. She was conscious always of the whereabouts of others and fearful that someone, unwittingly carrying the disease, might pass it on to her. She had no idea of the passage of time but at last fell into an uneasy sleep.

She awoke with a gasp of fear to the realization that someone was shaking her by the arm.

'No!' she screamed, snatching back her arm, forcing herself awake – and found herself staring into the face of Luke Meridith!

'Sophie! My dear! Oh God! Look at you!'

She could see the concern in his eyes and wanted to weep with relief at the sight of a familiar face. Instead she heard herself say, 'Luke! What brings you here?'

It was so patently absurd that for a moment he stared at her in disbelief. She returned his stare with a stony expression, mindful only of the recent humiliation she had suffered at his hands.

He knelt beside her and in his face she saw regret and tenderness but pride held her silent and she hardened her heart.

He said, 'I had to know that you were safe, Sophie; that you had reached your brother's house. I have been out of my mind with anxiety, dreading to find that some ill had befallen you and aware that I am to blame. The last twenty-four hours have been a nightmare for me. Staring into the face of every unfortunate wretch that lay abandoned by the roadside, fearing it might be you. Asking for news of you from everyone I met and yet dreading what they might tell me.' He swallowed but she said nothing to help him. 'I tormented myself by imagining you dead. Oh Sophie! It has been such agony and yet I deserved nothing less. I should never have allowed you to travel alone at such a time. I shall never forgive myself.'

'I suppose 'twas Lois who sent you after me,' she said, hoping that he would deny it.

He hesitated. 'We both felt it was wrong —' he admitted and Sophie's mouth tightened.

'You need not have concerned yourselves,' she told him. 'As you see I have come to no real harm.'

'But you have travelled so short a distance!'

'On the contrary,' she said. 'I have been there and back!'

'To Woolwich?' He made no attempt to hide his surprise.

'Aye, Woolwich, but I was robbed of my papers and refused entry. You find me now on my way

498

back to London. I am hungry but otherwise quite well. You need not fret about me.' She spoke defiantly but her throat ached with pent-up misery and her eyes were filling with unwanted tears. She became aware of hunger cramps in her stomach and that her ankle was painful.

As though reading her thoughts, Luke touched her ankle lightly. 'This needs attention,' he said. ''Tis very inflamed.'

She winced at his touch. 'A farmer's dog,' she said bitterly and wondered if he had brought any food or water with him.

'I have an ox cart of sorts,' he said. ''Tis rickety but it has come this far without losing a wheel. Will you ride back with me?'

He spoke so humbly that she wanted to hug him but his kindness was undermining her resolve.

'I am perfectly able to walk,' she said.

'Not on that ankle.' He held out his hands and helped her to her feet. To her annoyance her swollen ankle began to throb angrily and she was forced to concede that walking on it would be difficult if not impossible. Suddenly she swayed on her feet.

'Sophie? Are you fit?' he asked, concerned.

''Tis only hunger.'

He shook his head. ''Tis hunger and exhaustion and pain and I shall take you home with me. You will not return to Woolwich until you are yourself again. Lois will care for you and I shall attend to that ankle. Pray God 'tis not infected.'

'But the children?' she protested.

'I will send word to your brother. The main thing is that you recover your strength.'

She could not argue. He had come in search of her and for that she was deeply grateful. Was it simply his conscience that troubled him or something more? Had he, perhaps, had a change of heart? For a moment neither of them spoke but the expression in his eyes puzzled her. She heard herself say, 'A young man made advances to me!' and regretted the words as soon as they were uttered. 'No!' she stammered. 'I didn't mean that. That is —' She stopped in confusion.

'A young man? Which young man?' Luke's voice was suddenly harsh. 'If he so much as laid a finger on you —'

'No, no!' she protested. ''Twas nothing. He was very kind.' She wanted to say that the young man found her attractive; that he had restored her self-confidence. She wanted Luke to know that someone appreciated her and yet she could not find it in her heart to reproach him. He had suffered enough these last few weeks and she must make allowances for him.

'If you will allow me, I shall lift you into the cart,' he began but the rest of his words were lost to her as she became aware of a roaring in her ears and a sudden blackness seized her. She tried to cry out but instead felt her legs crumple.

When she recovered she realized that Luke was

carrying her in his arms and her head rested against his shoulder. 'Luke!' she whispered. 'Oh my dear!'

'You fainted.' He swung her into the cart which contained a layer of straw. ''Tis hardly fit for a hog,' he remarked grimly, 'but 'twas the best that was to be had. 'Twill be a rough ride but I will get you home as soon as I can.' He tucked a rug around her, making her as comfortable as possible, avoiding her eyes.

'You are so good to me,' she said and, reaching out, touched his face lightly with her hand.

He caught it immediately and pressed it suddenly to his lips. 'My sweet, dear, Sophie!' he said. 'You must forgive me. This is all my fault. Lois was right. I have been very selfish. And so foolish.' Sophie shook her head weakly but he rushed on. 'I have been so blind. So arrogant! Believing that my own loss was greater than those of others. So wrapped up in my own grief. Wallowing in self-pity so that –'

'Luke, stop! You have lost your son. You are allowed to grieve.'

''Tis no excuse.' His expression was anguished. 'I was punishing you for my own guilt. I hurt you and I shall never forgive myself.'

'But *I* forgive you, Luke!' At his words all Sophie's resentments had vanished and Luke's rejection of her no longer rankled for she saw it in its true context. She knew that after all she could love this man.

'Please, Sophie, let me take care of you and the children. Sophie! Say you will marry me!'

'Oh Luke! I will!' Sophie was aware that Luke was smiling broadly now, his eyes bright.

He said, ' "Tis hardly the most romantic proposal but I do love you.'

'And I, you.' She was overwhelmed with relief and joy and yet she longed for sleep.

'Sophie!' He was shaking her gently.

'I hear you,' she murmured.

'I will make you happy!'

She nodded and smiled. 'I know it!' she said and then sleep claimed her.

The journey back to London was a merciful blur but, within two days, Lois's nursing and Luke's love had restored her to a semblance of her former self. She was aware only of a deep peace. Luke loved her and in the fullness of time she knew she would be his wife.

Chapter 17

IT WAS MARCH 1666. As Sophie leaned over to kiss Oliver goodnight he twined his arms around her neck, imprisoning her. Into her ear he whispered, 'Is our new Papa home yet?'

'Not yet, but soon.'

'Will he come to say goodnight to us?'

'Yes. You know he will.'

'But not last night!' He allowed her to withdraw her head so that he could look intently into her face.

Sophie smiled. 'Papa was late home last night. He came to kiss you but you were both asleep.' She tucked him in warmly for the winter had, mercifully, been a severe one. The low temperatures had routed the last of the plague and London was returning to something like normality.

Lizbeth had already snuggled down under the bedclothes but she uncovered her face for her mother's kiss.

'Fanny has forgotten my brick,' she said, 'and my feet are cold.'

'Forgotten it? Surely not!' Sophie reached into the bed and found the offending brick. It had been heated over the fire and was well wrapped in a piece of old blanket.

'Fanny never forgets your brick!' she said. 'She had pushed it down too far, that is all, and you could not reach it.'

'I can reach mine,' said Oliver, 'because my legs are longer than Lizbeth's.' To Lizbeth he said kindly, 'When you are as old as me your legs will reach the brick.'

'They do now!'

'Only because Mama has moved it!'

'Mama —?' began Lizbeth crossly, but Sophie put a finger to her daughter's small rosy lips.

'Hush now, Lizbeth! 'Tis time to sleep.'

Oliver said, 'I shall be a physician when I am a man.'

Sophie smiled. 'So you keep telling us, Ollie, and you will make a fine physician.

'So will I!' said Lizbeth sleepily.

'No you won't!' cried Oliver but Sophie said, 'Hush now, Ollie. Lizbeth is nearly asleep.'

'Aunt Lois hasn't kissed us yet.'

'She will be in presently.'

He smiled up at her gleefully. 'Then Lizbeth will miss her if she is asleep!'

Sophie tweaked his nose gently and blew out the candle.

'Sleep well,' she said.

As she entered the dining room, she saw that Luke had just arrived home and from Lois's expression she guessed that he had told her their news. Lois ran towards Sophie and hugged her.

'A baby!' she said. 'I can't tell you how pleased I am. When will you tell the children?'

'Not for a few months yet,' said Sophie. 'The time will go so slowly for them and they will become impatient.'

'Does your mother-in-law know yet?'

Sophie shook her head. 'Luke thought she was still a little frail after her fall for such excitement.'

'Too frail? What nonsense!' said Lois, forthright as ever. ''Tis the very thing she needs to bring her to her feet again. Do please let me tell her.'

Sophie had been looking forward to telling Ruth herself but as she looked into Lois's eager face she realized that to be the bearer of such news would be a great thrill for her. And perhaps she was right and it would prove to be the fillip the old lady needed to recover her spirits for only days after the wedding she had slipped in the icy yard. Being temporarily bedridden once more had depressed her and the news about the coming baby would undoubtedly cheer her.

'Yes. Do tell her,' she told Lois and watched her hurry out of the room, positively brimming with joy.

Sophie looked up at Luke as he slipped his arm

around her and saw what pleased her most – that the haunted look had left his face, hopefully for ever.

Outside the dining room, Lois almost fell over Fanny who, dressed in her outdoor clothes, had been listening at the door. Fanny, overcome with excitement, blurted out, 'A baby!'

Lois nodded, 'The master will tell you,' and hurried upstairs.

Fanny rushed into the room with Banna at her heels and two smiling faces turned towards her.

'A baby,' cried Fanny. ''Tis the best news in the whole world! Perhaps 'twill be another boy!'

'We'll keep our fingers crossed!' said Sophie. 'Are you off now?'

It was Fanny's free evening and they all knew she was being courted by Jon who, despite his somewhat perilous job, had also escaped the long hand of the plague and was now continuing his weaver's apprenticeship.

Fanny nodded. 'Can I tell Jon?'

Sophie smiled. 'I don't see why not. And remember. Back here sharp at nine. You were late last time.'

Fanny departed and the quick patter of her feet on the cobbles died away. While Luke went upstairs to change his clothes Sophie moved to the front door and looked out into the street, thankful that at last normal life was returning to the city. A few fine carriages were to be seen, the cheerful rattle of wheels and the clatter of hooves were again familiar sounds. Shops had reopened and those street sellers who had survived were once again calling their wares. Sophie thought of the tragedies of the previous year and whispered Matthew's name. So many loved ones lost, she reflected; so many voices that would never be heard again. But life must go on for those that remained. She thought of Antony.

'There's going to be a baby,' she told him. 'A sister or a brother for you!'

No one answered but in her mind's eye his bright image rose as sharply as ever and she saw that he was smiling and knew that he approved.